TALES OF SOMETHING DIFFERENT

A C STOCK

A C STOCK

Copyright © 2023 A C STOCK

Copyright © 2023 A C Stock

A C STOCK has asserted his right to be identified as the author of this work in accordance with sections 77 and 78 of the Copyright, Designs and Patents Act 1988.

All rights reserved. No part of this publication may be reproduced, stored in a retrieval system, or transmitted in any form or by means, electronically, mechanical, photocopying, recording or otherwise, without the prior permission of the copyright owner.

My Lovely

I am nothing without you

CONTENTS

Title Page
Copyright
Dedication
Epigraph
Preface
Afterword 582
Acknowledgements 584
About The Author 586

"Everyone has the ability to tell a story. So why not tell yours?"

MISS BAILEY (FERRARS SCHOOL)

PREFACE

As a child of 8 years old I sat behind a school desk and listened to my teacher Miss Bailey talk of famous writers. I remember sitting transfixed as she explained the power of the written word and how it could, inform, transport, educate and entertain. I recall the feeling of excitement as she faced us in that small classroom and said, "Everyone has the ability to tell a story, so why not tell yours?" In that moment as a wide eyed schoolboy I thought to myself, 'I will write a book one day!'

What follows is my first attempt to keep that promise to the young boy who always believed he could tell a story.

Gideon's Invention

Gideon had invented something. It seemed to him that it was nothing out of the ordinary, he was always inventing things. The object, for this was how he thought of it (I don't know what to call it) was, when studied, almost round, weighed as much as a bag of sugar and could have extra pieces added to it via the protruding rod that exited the slightly thinner end. He had imagined the idea as he stood wrapped in his great coat (I bought it from the army surplice shop) and was trying to force some warmth into his fingers from the old paraffin heater he used to heat the lock up garage that doubled as his workshop and an escape when life seemed too noisy. He had tinkered on his invention for approximately three weeks using parts from an old washing machine dumped on the children's play park, a rusty bicycle, springs from an old mattress and a canteen sized baked beans can. At the end of the three weeks he nodded with nothing more than gentle acceptance that his invention was working, before placing it in an empty shoe box and storing it high up on a shelf that contained curios he found on his frequent walks through the woods situated behind the industrial units on the south of the town.

Gideon's invention would have remained where it was, forgotten and gathering dust if it had it not been for a chance encounter with an old school friend (friend?) during one of his long rambling walks through the woods.

"Gideon. Is that really you?" The friend (acquaintance) had stepped closer holding a large Staffordshire bull terrier dog on a tight leash as it tried to mount Gideon's leg in a more than familiar way. "Wow, yes I thought it was. 'Ow are you Good God?" Good God had been a childhood taunt during Gideon's traumatic school years, 'Good God its Gideon!' An echoed call whenever he had moved closer to any respective group (clique) daring to become inquisitive over a half heard conversation or tit bit of information. "So 'ow are you then, still a scruffy bleeder I see." Gideon had merely shrugged unsure if he could even remember the dog owners name, (difficult to make introductions on the end of a swinging fist or boot.) "You still live round 'ere then?" Again Gideon shrugged (Tim something or other. Dog owner was Tim something or other.) "Of course you do. Where else would you live?" Tim something or other pointed in the general direction of the town, "I moved out of this shit hole as soon as I could. Full of nothing but thugs, scum and tramps. Suppose it suits you though." Tim something or other pulled at the dog which had taken to pushing its snout hard into Gideon's backside without so much as an excuse me. "I've only come back to put flowers on me mum's grave. She died a year ago. Suppose you heard?" (uh, no) "Went quick in the end, cancer got her. I sat with her outside the hospital last time I visited her and watched her drag that drip she was connected to over to the nearest cigarette bin. As ill as she was she managed to steer that pole on wheels all the way round the pot holes without that bag of fluid coming loose once, how she managed that I shall never know. Proper fighter she was. Anyway we sat having a fag together and she said to me, Tony.(Tony, not Tim.) Tony," she said, "You know what caused this cancer in me? Cars! That's right Good God, cars. My old mum had her finger on the pulse, she knew what had done for her, pollution from cars, petrol fumes." Tony not Tim paused and sniffed at the air, "Christ you can almost taste it, the pollution." He pointed towards the sky "A great big black cloud of death hanging over us and all from cars. I tell you Good God, pollution is killing us all. Someone needs to clean this up, sort it out. Fumes will kill us all in the end." Tony not Tim had pulled at the dog again (it won't stop jumping up me) "That's why I moved to London, live in one of those clean air zones don't I?" (Do you?) "Much better for me. I tell ya Good God, its expensive for me to drive the Range Rover but at least I know the air is cleaner there. I'm doing my bit for the environment ain't I?" Without waiting for an answer, he pulled again on the dogs lead, "Get down Tyson, stop jumping up at Good God you'll get yerself filthy." He pulled the dog to him and pushed passed Gideon forcing him from the narrow track, "Surprising to see you Good God." He called, "Thought you would have been long dead in the gutter by now. Come on Tyson, let's get out of 'ere before we get what mum got eh?" With that Tony not Tim marched away lighting a cigarette and blowing the smoke high into the air.

It was as he walked from the woods with the conversation still fresh in his mind that his latest invention made an appearance in his thought process. His latest invention high on the shelf, his latest invention tucked neatly in the shoe box, his latest invention that could possibly, save the world.

Gideon did not understand television (this is amazing) but research at the local library (only open Monday afternoon, Wednesday morning and all day Saturday due to cut backs) showed that to reach the largest audience, television was the greatest medium. Carrying a small wooden box (to sit on) to the town centre Gideon had settled himself in front of the large display of televisions reflecting brightly from the local 'Television and Electrical Superstore.' and watched as countless programmes flicked before his eyes, (research is painful) Eventually and just after someone had walked up to him thrusting a cheese sandwich wrapped in a cardboard container and a steaming cup of coffee in a paper cup into his hands with a,

"There you go mate, you look like you could do with this." And a cheery "God bless." Gideon saw pictures on one of the silent televisions amongst the banks of sets on display, that showed in bright (why is everything so bright on televisions) gold lettering announcing 'As Tight as Our Souls.' The show where inventors of new ideas try to rip cash from entrepreneurs.' Gideon watched as a finely chiselled man pointed from the screen and the subtitles scrolled beneath his image matching the white of his teeth, 'Do you have an idea that can tear the wads from the wealthy, does your idea impress the un-impressable, does you brilliance need air time? Then contact us on astightastv@local.com or #astightas. See if your idea can reach the masses. Who knows you could be the next Elon Musk (who is that?) Gideon wrote the words into the old school exercise book he kept for such occasions, ignoring the words 'Good God is a knob', scrawled in faded ink and stuffed it into the pocket of his great coat next to the cheese sandwich. Sipping the quickly cooling coffee (not nice) he made his way back to the library to see what this code was that enabled him to contact this helpful man who promised to take his invention to the masses.

As the television viewers sat in their respective homes glued to the flickering screens that dominated spaces large and small, eating high sugar, high fat content ready meals and snacks, Gideon was pushed onto a cross marked on the studio floor and glared at by a bespectacled girl in a flowery dress, large hooped earrings and a headset and microphone combination,
"You, stand there. Don't move or the camera angles will be all wrong." She wrinkled her nose as though suddenly prevailed of an uncomfortable odour, "Answer the questions but only look down camera 3 ok?" she pointed towards a large moving object that seemed to have a mind of its own, moving without any obvious assistance or human touch, "Have you got everything ready to show the panel, cos they don't like time wasters." The girl did not wait for an answer instead concentrating on her clipboard, ticking something off as she moved, "Yes Max," She said into the microphone connected to the headset "Yes, that

seems to be what he's wearing. Makeup said he refused. Good God no!" (perhaps she had gone to my school.) "No Max, no display stand just his carrier bag." She disappeared behind the moving cameras and was lost behind the blinding lights which darkened the blackness beyond. Somewhere in the distance a voice could be heard calling,

"Entrepreneurs to the set please, entrepreneurs please." Within moments four people entered the ring of brightness and sat in the once empty chairs that faced Gideon. One woman brightly dressed in oranges and greens spoke loudly into a mobile phone,

"Yes Larry darling. Once I've finished with this shit I will be straight over and we can get on with some real business." She laughed loudly, "Looking at what is standing in front of me I think we shall be done super quick today so keep yourself ready my darling." She laughed again only this time with a throatiness that growled deep from her chest. The man sat to her left glanced up from his laptop and shook his head, a sneer etched on his face,

"Dirty bitch." The woman spared him only enough interest to raise her middle finger in his general direction,

"Oh and Larry," She continued making eye contact with the man to her left, "perhaps this time we will use the ropes." (Perhaps she is in construction) she laughed again, loud and guttural folding her phone in half and placing it in the bag by her chair. The two other occupants of the chairs, a casually dressed man with a large ring through his left ear and a woman with large flowing folds of material as a dress, brightly coloured feathers as a hat, lipstick that glowed as brightly as the lights of this television studio and a beard that would grace the front of any barber shop window (Huh) ignored each other whilst scribbling on electronic pads with wand like sticks. The voice behind the blackness called again,

"Ok entrepreneurs, ready, and five, four, three..." The voice fell silent (unable to count backwards) "And cue Simon." A burst of applause filled the studio (but there is no-one else here) and the man from the television that played silently in the Television and Electrical Superstore, moved into the centre of the ring of light waving at no-one in particular, (there is no-one else here) and calling loudly,

"Ok, ok please, no please, settle down now, please no, you are too kind," (who was?) "Ok shall we begin tonights show?" A cheer rose loudly with more rapturous applause, (where were these people?) "And so, here we are in our usual surroundings at our mystery location. (Television Studios) Such is the amount of money carried by our entrepreneurs that we have to keep our location secret, (Television Studios) known to only our very small production crew, myself and the select audience, yes you, you lucky people." More laughter, (Who?) "The lucky audience who are brought here in darkened coaches and sworn to secrecy. Now I've spoken of money, I've spoken of the secrecy but I have not spoken of those behind the power of this secrecy and the money." Simon, the man with the brightest of smiles raised an arm towards the four figures in the chairs "Our entrepreneurs." Again the applause became deafening as the figures waved and smiled, "For anyone living under a rock let me introduce them. Firstly we have our married multi millionaires Tabitha and Lincoln Carmichael." The woman with the folding phone and the man to her left reached across the gap between them and held hands smiling brightly, "Yes folks Tabitha and Lincoln made their millions in water pumps used extensively in 'fracking' far from their humble beginnings selling tropical fish foods on Portobello market in London. Then we have Britain's most eligible bachelor Akeem. Akeem has more money than any beautiful woman could wish to spend, (why are people laughing?) but be aware ladies, Akeem is the hardest working young man I have ever met, growing his cement empire into the largest construction supplies chain across the world. If it's built with cement Akeem has a hand in it. And finally but never lastly, Chastity." The resplendent figure raised her hand in a circular motion (just like the Queen),

"Hi everyone."

"Hi yourself, you gorgeous person. Yes Chastity began their journey into billionaire status selling exotic toys and lingerie from a van around the Bedfordshire area. They soon raised their stakes and now own the largest adult entertainment empire in Europe if not the world. Chastity is the fourth richest person in the world and they (who is they?) are happy to service the needs of every person in search of happiness. As they once said, Porn was King, but now I say, Porn is Them." Again a round of applause followed by a cacophony of laughter from the audience. Simon waiting with the skill of circus ringmaster allowed the noise to settle smiling broadly and waiting for the optimum moment. Feeling the applause beginning to die away and touching the small earpiece discretely worn, he finally gestured expansively towards the four seated figures. "So my viewers there you have it, our entrepreneurs." More cheering and applause filled the studio until Simon waved his arms in submission. "And now you gorgeous people, shall we meet the first of tonight's hopefuls?" Simon turned and looked towards Gideon who until now had been cast in darkness, a solid mass of black amongst the shadows. As the beam of light gleamed with a brightness that illuminated with a brutal starkness, time seemed to stop and a small piece of television history was made as for the first time anyone could recall Simon's beaming smile faltered. It was just the essence of a flicker, a tightening of the skin around his stretched and sculpted cheeks, a narrowing, if that was possible of the perfectly taut skin around the eyes and for the briefest of moments a look of surprise that managed to wrinkle the flatness of his brow. This was barely a second in time but a moment that was perfectly recovered by the ultimate professional. This briefest of moments would be spoken of around the country via text and social media platforms alike. These would be messages that would send the shows ratings skyrocketing to a new level. Nano seconds that would guarantee a bigger pay bonus that would dwarf that of any of the other television presenters around the country. Simon thought of this as he gathered his composure, he thought of this as he pointed with a rock steady finger towards Gideon. "Entrepreneurs, audience, all of you lovely people at home we have before us..." Simon gave his well practised pause before opening his arms replicating the open embrace of a parent welcoming a child to them, "We have before us Gideon. Gideon is sixty two (fifty two) and brings an invention for our entrepreneurs to judge, an invention that could change his life"

The viewers around the country, ensconced within their homes, captivated by what had just unfolded, looked up from their phone screens, messages flashing beneath their fingers and saw the camera fully focus on Gideon's sweating face and gasped again in unison. Open mouthed they listened, hunched forward towards the screen which held their attentions from the corner of their rooms and listened as Simon spoke with a reassuring smoothness that belayed the horror they saw before them, "Yes this is Gideon amateur inventor who comes from…."

"A dustbin?…"

"A skip?"

"Oh Dad you are awful. Funny but awful."

"Look at the state of him…"

"Put me off my curry that has, shouldn't be allowed."

"Shh let me listen."

In the studio Simon continued brightly, his professionalism unwavering and buoyed by the viewing ratings that were being dripped into his ear from the director as he spoke,

"And Gideon is here tonight with an invention that he believes will make him his fortune, (save the world) oh yes Gideon here feels so strongly in his invention that in our little chat before this evening's show (what chat?) he said to me (no) that he had opened up a new bank account…. (bank account?) in readiness for separating our entrepreneurs away from their money, (huh) so Gideon," Simon, happy that once again his features were again exactly where he had paid for them to be, turned to face Gideon, "Why don't you show us what it is you have brought us here tonight." With a smile that threatened to blind the viewers, Simon pointed towards Gideon and gave a small nod of encouragement. Gideon was uncertain just how television worked but assumed that you had to smile. Gideon did not like to smile but gave it his best effort for what would be only the second time in his life, (what the hell Good God! Are you trying to smile, you freak?)

"Look at the state of him, is he pulling faces at Simon?…"

"What a mess, looks demented…"

"Good God. Hey Mandy, it's Good God on Tele. Jesus what a mess. Tony told me he had seen him a couple of months back. Christ what a freak. Mandy, come 'ere, look its Good God, 'ere on the tele. Quick Mand' come and have a look, freak looks worse than when we were at school. 'Ang on I will rewind it so you can see it from the start. Jesus what's the world coming to, Good God on the tele?"

Gideon opened his carrier bag and pulled out the shoe box.

"Well Gideon it looks as though you have taken some care packaging that for us." Tabitha grinned broadly as the laughter responded, "What is it? A pair of size nines?" Simon laughed along with the audience (my thing to save the world.)

"Now give him a chance Tabitha. Put those claws away until you have had a chance to see what it is that Gideon has with him.

"I'm beginning to think I've already seen enough." Akeem hid a yawn behind his hand and rolled his eyes dramatically.

"Now, now Akeem, why don't you give them a chance, they may have something of interest." (they, who else is coming in?)

"Yes exactly Chastity, thank you for that. I can certainly see you entrepreneurs are up for the fight tonight. I bet our clever audience at home can see that."

"Bloody right we can..."

"Sure can..."

"They will tear him apart..."

"Honestly Tony on tele now, yes mate, 'As Tight as Our Souls,' it's on now. Me and Mandy are watching it. Bloody hilarious. Watch it on catch up when you get 'ome. Old Good God is making a right tit of himself."

Lincoln Carmichael leaned forward a

look of confusion on his face.

"What is it. What does it do?" Gideon shrugged holding the invention in one hand and allowing the shoe box fall to the floor,

"Is it homemade, is that part of a baked beans can?" Next to him Akeem sighed loudly and crossed one leg over the other twiddling the large ring on his finger.

"Well I don't care what it is, I'm not parting with money for that. This is more like show and tell than an invention." With a disdain only achievable by a man who has the money to back his intolerance he reached to the small table at his side and picked up a large black, board on which was embossed a perfectly formed red 'X' and placed it upright for all to see. A camera moved swiftly towards him but out of shot of the other watching lenses that focused solidly on the faces of Simon and Gideon. From deep in the darkness the audience gasped their generated intake of breath shocked by what they were seeing. The audience from their homes understood what they were about to bear witness to,

"Wow, that's the quickest I've ever seen Akeem pull out..."

"What did he expect, comes in dressed like a tramp and shows them a baked bean can..."

"Melvin, text your Dad, see if he's watching this?..."

"Oh my, Good God deserves all he gets, tosser."

Simon saw the red 'X' and smiled wickedly, this was going really well, lamb to the slaughter. The viewing figures were soaring beyond belief.

"Ok Gideon, you can see that Akeem has placed his red cross. You know what that means? (Rubbish Gideon. Hardly legible, not good enough. A waste of my time) lets not panic though. Although Akeem is out, and he is a bad one to lose so early, why don't we carry on." Simon willed the viewers to follow him on this journey, an easy request. "But why not try your hardest to keep the other entrepreneur's on board eh?" His mocking tone carried just the right amount of sincerity, the ridicule of a friendly Uncle playing to the gathered family at a young nephew's expense. "So Gideon take a breath, calm yourself and tell us what this er...." Perfectly placed pause allowing the viewers to hold their breath for just a second longer, "What this er, thing does, (can't) come on Gideon give the entrepreneurs a clue eh?" Gideon reached into the pocket of his great coat feeling past the empty wrapper of the cheese sandwich that lay flattened against the fabric (a gift, for him) Closing his fingers around the creased page that lay scrunched beneath the wrapper, a ball of string, a pretty stone and the library card held in a small battered plastic wallet, (keep this safe Gideon, it's yours) he pulled it from his pocket knowing it contained the very neat handwriting of the friendly (what have you got there Gideon) and helpful librarian (Helen, her name was Helen) He thrust the paper towards Simon making sure he continued to look at the front of the camera marked '3' (stand there and only look down the camera marked three). For a few moments nothing happened until Simon ever the ultimate professional stepped forward smoothly reaching for the paper with the Balletic grace of a Prima Ballerina whilst ensuring the distance between himself and Gideon never moved closer than arms length. Pirouetting he moved back to his spot without so much as glancing for the mark. With mock humility he faced the entrepreneurs and gave a little bow. "It seems that Gideon here is ever the shy one. He has asked, (never asked) that I read this for him." Simon turned slightly allowing camera 2 to focus on the crumpled page he waved towards it. "And you all know just how much I hate being centre of attention eh?" The laughter erupted (but you enjoy television) "And so it says." Simon cleared his throat holding the page as though it were a soiled bedsheet up for inspection,

"This invention is something that can change the world. Gideon made it in his lock up garage with pieces he found whilst out walking. When he made it he wasn't sure what exactly it would be used for, but now is sure it will be something very important. Gideon has tried this invention on a small moped that had once been his fathers (daddy has gone away Gideon, he doesn't want to live with us anymore) and it works perfectly well. He believes that this can be used on any vehicle that has an engine. I do not fully understand what it does as I am only a librarian, (Helen, her name is Helen) who is writing this for him. From what I can understand this small invention can be fitted to any engine and charges two batteries. The first battery is the one driving the car for example, the second battery is the one in reserve that switches over to be the main battery when the first battery runs out. This little machine then charges the empty battery so that it is ready to use as soon as the other battery runs out of power. This seems to be achieved by simply using the power of generated air passing through it whilst travelling. It sounds as though this invention replaces the need for any petrol or fuel, as it makes the car totally electric and totally self charging. The power of the charging comes from a small fan blade fitted to the stick thing protruding from the front of the invention. The fan is driven by air passing through the front grill of the car as it moves along. I think that if I understand correctly (you do) this invention can be scaled up or down to fit any vehicle including aeroplanes so the need for any petrol, diesel or fuel of any kind is no longer required. I hope I have explained this correctly. I also hope that I have relayed everything Gideon wants me to say. (you have) On a personal note, I ask that you are patient with Gideon as he finds communication extremely difficult and I am working from no more than a series of drawings laid out in front of me sketched by Gideon on an old pizza box. (five cheese special, thick crust) I thank you for listening and taking the time to understand what it is Gideon is trying to show you. Helen, Head Librarian." (thank you Helen) Simon drops his arm as though the paper was suddenly immensely heavy and the effort to read it had drained him to exhaustion,

"I think you will agree that there is much to take in entrepreneurs. So much, erm, detail. Do you need to take a moment or have we all understood this. How about you viewers at home. Does this sound viable to you?"

"Viable? The man is as mad as he looks…"

"A baked bean can that totally does away with petrol? He's lost the plot…"

"I'm not getting on a plane that relies on a wind turbine made out of old junk, I mean what happens if the wind doesn't blow the same in the clouds as it does down here. No give me good old

petrol and sod the expense..."

"Save the planet? Jesus we heard on the tele only last week that for every flight made they plant a tree. Now if that's not saving the planet I don't know what is? While you are on your feet Sarah, bung another log on the fire, it's freezing in here..."

"Bloody hell, Good God has definitely gone proper mad, worse than I remember him. Who does he think he is eh, Barns Wallace? Messing around with planes, he'll have us falling out of the sky."

"Ooh that reminds me, Jennie and Pete can come with us to Torremolinos."

"Brilliant! Beer, barbecues and a jet ski. Mandy book us in for those sun beds in town, need to start building my tan up."

Simon grins into camera 2 and waves his hand towards the four, seated occupants in the halo of light,

"Akeem as we know you are out of this process. Have you any regrets now that you have heard what Gideon's invention does?" Akeem wipes a hand through his glistening black hair and blows a long loud whistle.

"Simon, I need to ask two question before you move on to my esteemed colleagues here beside me." Akeem pauses understanding fully the art of drawing viewers in and tightening not only his power over the screen but his social network profile, frowns deeply into camera one. "Firstly are we to be treated to no more than you reading a note from mum?" (Helen, Helen the Librarian) "What are we, school teachers accepting get out of P.E. notes?" A slight giggle wafts over the studio from the audience and Akeem seizes his chance waving away the question, "No don't bother answering that Simon but do answer me this,(you said two questions, three, that's three questions) we have worked together for what, three years now?" Simon glows brightly, elder statesman to upcoming understudy,

"Yes indeed Akeem, thanks to our dedicated and loyal followers, we have graced the screens for three wonderful years, twice a week, Tuesday and Saturday also available on all good catch up services." He switches his gaze from Akeem and stares into the lens of camera 1 which pans in tightly capturing the beatific features that graces many a screen and billboard "I mean this most sincerely and from the bottom of my heart when I say, without the support from all of you out there, this show would not be what it is today." A small tear forms in the corner of his eye and it takes just a fraction of a second for him to wipe it clear, a fraction of a second that brings lumps to the throats of all who watch from their homes, young and old alike. As though shaking himself from a place of pure, heartfelt reflection Simon turns his attention back to Akeem who waits patiently for the performance to end, "Yes Akeem." He says purring the words to perfection, "We have worked together for three glorious and respectful years now." Akeem nods in slow acceptance before continuing, his voice soft and dangerous

"Simon in all of that time, have you ever known me to change my mind?"

"No Akeem, I have not." Simon takes a step towards his left focusing on a point behind the nearest camera, "I have never known that and I am certain you the audience would say the same." As he finishes speaking, applause fills the studio, Akeem leans forward in his seat causing camera 2 to lower itself dramatically

"Well my friend." Akeem glares hard into the camera, his lips thin more scar than mouth, "This will not change tonight, but…"

"Dad turn the tele up. Akeem is going to do it!"

"He can't be?"

"Akeem is going to do it, I'm certain of it…"

"Oh my. Quickly Denise get in here. Akeem has that look about him…"

"Shit Mandy. Bloody hell. Old Good God has done it now. Mandy leave that sandwich, you can make it for me after this has finished. Akeem is going to do it!"

Simon throws his hands in the air with the command of an orchestra conductor,

"Now steady on there Akeem, you have the look of the executioner about you, (executioner?) What is it you are trying to say?" Simon looks nervously down the lens into the homes of each and every viewer, "What... are... you... up... to?" From his position in the third seat Akeem, cement magnate shakes his head slowly,

"Simon I do not do this lightly." With the effort of a man three times his age and the weight of the world on his shoulders Akeem rises to his feet and splays his hands towards the nearest camera. "Tonight Simon, I am afraid that I must play the double 'X' card." The audience erupt with shock. Simon with mock horror takes a backwards step a look of terror twisting the perfect symmetry of his face.

"But Akeem not since show seven has the double 'X' card been played." He pauses pulling the handkerchief from his breast pocket and begins wiping his brow, the practiced movements of an eighteenth century dandy played out in perfect digital imagery. "Akeem think carefully now." He says pushing the handkerchief back into his pocket, "Your actions tonight could finish Gideon's invention almost immediately. A double 'X' now could end any chance of him making money (saving the world) for ever. Akeem are you certain?" The audience gasp again as Akeem steps from his chair moving without a word and strolls in front of the other seated figures as though inspecting soldiers on parade, pausing dramatically at the end of the line before retracing his steps. As though garnered in courage the multi millionaire playboy cement tycoon glances quickly over his shoulder before raising his voice in triumph,

"Yes Simon I am." With a flourish Akeem shoots out a hand and snatches the red 'X' card laying on the table beside Tabitha Carmichael and throws it onto the floor with a flourish. "I reduce the chances of this ridiculous idea." He points an accusing finger towards Gideon "And, may I add, I reduce the chances of this ridiculous man to receive any funding without being able to fully answer the five perfect questions." With the step of a roman emperor he stalks quickly to his seat and lounges comfortably, certain that his every wish will be granted. Assured that his place in television history has been cemented. Simon allowed himself a moment, allowed the television audience a moment. Once the shock of what had unfolded was sure to be hitting the internet at a frightening pace he allowed himself a well rehearsed heavy sigh.

"My word Akeem, you have certainly shocked us here tonight." He gestured to the audience, "I can only assume the shock they feel is echoed in the homes of the thousands who tune into us so regularly."

"Bloody right…"
"Wow, just wow…"

"I must just ask though, how are you feeling at this moment Tabitha, what is it that's going on in that magnificent brain of yours?" Tabitha Carmichael with the practised ease of a true performer, raises an arm in a tired gesture towards Gideon her eyes alive with a maliciousness that casts sparks across the studio.

"Well." She begins, "That person over there." She allows her arm to flick a gesture towards Gideon almost dismissively. "That person over there has achieved something I have never seen before, something I scarcely believed would be possible." She heaves herself from her chair and heads towards Charity who with statuesque precision has managed to remain aloof throughout the entire interaction between Akeem and Simon. Stopping in front of her, Tabitha gently reaches out a puffy hand and pats Charity's bearded cheek, "You my dear were the last person to offer up a double red 'X' all those years ago. At the time I was horrified that you, lovely you, could enact such a thing especially as the poor woman had only suggested the tablet she had spent many years perfecting could be used for gender reassignment."

"Connie Fitzwarren, yes, show number seven. Unable to answer the five perfect questions." Simon recalled the facts seamlessly, speaking the words fed to him through his headset as though they were his own.

"Mmm, yes, possibly." Tabitha waved her hand as though distracted by a bothersome fly. "At the time we all wondered what would become of her, what did her future offer, how would she cope with the public shame?"

"Found dead in a hotel somewhere off the M25 (dead, like Mother) overdose of her own tablets." Tabitha Carmichael barely acknowledged the statement instead twisted her body so that camera 5 could capture her features completely.

"Yes I wondered, we all did, whether we had gone too far." Simon dropped quickly into sombre mode and spoke from his entertainers heart,

"Our wonderful sponsor paid in its entirety for the so simple funeral she would have wanted, and offered a years free television licence to her family, alongside a free six months subscription to 'As tight as our souls'. I am sure you can agree a generous and worthy offer." The studio audience clapped furiously.

"Yes generous indeed, generous to a fault." Tabitha leaned heavily on the arms of the chair forcing Charity back into her seat. "It is only now dear Charity that I, being on the receiving end of the snatch of my red 'X' truly understands what it is like, what drives one of us entrepreneurs to behave like that." With a sudden movement that for the briefest of moments catches camera 5 off guard she snatches the black card from Charity's table and holds it aloft triumphantly. "Well this creature before us has made a mockery of all we stand for. A machine that completely makes irrelevant any form of fuel? Balderdash I say. Impossible. The man is a dreamer, a fraud, unable even to tell us of what it is he has supposedly invented. Librarian indeed, (Helen, her name is Helen) I have no feelings towards being snatched of my 'X' in fact I triple red 'X' him." In full view of cameras 3 and 4 she hurls the card to the floor and stomps heavily back to her seat her masterstroke of upstaging complete.

"Oh my God…"

"Three red 'X's' shit man!…"

"Honestly Tony you must get home and watch this. Good God totally screwed up…"

"Poor man, how's he going to deal with this?"

*"Poor man. Are you serious mum? Look at

the state of him."

"No not that scruffy sod he deserves all he gets, Simon, I mean how's Simon going to cope?..."

Simon is ecstatic. The numbers coming from the control room for viewing figures and social media coverage have gone through the roof. His team have played this situation superbly well. Of course Akeem has used this time to hike his own falling social media figures. Of course Tabitha has trumped Akeem with her own fantastic display of barely controlled but perfectly managed fury. Lincoln Carmichael will do what he always does and sit mute allowing his wife to create the waves that carries him along to his next fortune, and then there is Charity poor old billionaire Charity who will be unable to rip into this scruffy creature caught like a rabbit in headlights because she, sorry they, has or is it have? To be seen, and heard to totally respect everyone. Oh yes this had gone fantastically well. He had to admit that when the light had first come onto this Gideon character he was taken aback, shocked even, this had car crash written all over it, but how brilliantly this had all unfolded. As always Simon's sense of professionalism rose to the fore, now it was his time to shine, his time to bring this to a fitting end. Ignoring the voices in his earpiece demanding he sticks to the script for emergency situations such as this, he turns slowly and faces camera 1 his face etched with pain, a mask of hurt.

"Ladies and Gentlemen, They and Them's, viewers sitting there in the comfort of your own homes. You tonight have been witness to something that is truly quite remarkable, truly unique. Our entrepreneurs have for the first time in the long history of this wonderful show been forced, and I do not use this word lightly, forced to act in a way that has never been seen before. We have stood in front of us a man of such low moral standing that he believed he could force our dear, dear entrepreneurs to part with money (no) to line his pockets for no good reason, (to save the world) he came with nothing more than a pretence to deceive and a so called note from a friend, (Helen, Librarian Helen) he by deception wanted to fool not only you the viewer but our wonderful audience here tonight, all of whom will be offered free counselling so as to fully recover from the trauma of what they have so shockingly, so bravely witnessed. Now; What hurts me the most in all of this is the fact that he, Gideon," Simon shoots out an arm, ramrod straight, Michelangelo's creation of Adam, and points an accusing finger at Gideon, "Yes he, wanted to fool you our wonderful audience at home. Any reprobate (just ignore them Gideon, just ignore them) who thinks himself clever enough or important enough (you will always be thick Gideon, scum, now remember your place) to try and take money by deception will be found out." Simon bows his head slightly and takes a moment to recover his composure,

> *"Oh look, poor man is nearly in tears..."*
> *"Proper moving this is..."*
> *"That tramp should be ashamed of himself..."*
> *"Didn't fool me for a second..."*

"Our magnificent viewers." Simon reaches to them through their screens, "You have been protected from these falsehoods and deception by our wonderful, magnificent and sharply intelligent entrepreneurs. If it had not been for their diligence this, and again I do not speak lightly, this fool of a man would have conned his way into our lives without so much as a thought of what he was doing, (saving the planet) he would have fed from the breasts of angels with milk freely given."

> *"Is that from the bible?"*
> *"What a man."*

" I cannot speak on, such is the rage that burns within me, but what I can say is that there will be no five perfect questions segment of the show as I think you will all agree," Simon paused as though waiting for answers to float towards him through the camera lens, "A fraud such as this deserves no second chance." With the look of a disappointed parent Simon allows his words to settle, allows the audience at home to feel the gravity of what he was saying knowing that television history was even now being carved in digital mega bit stone. Finally in the voice that attracted viewers by the millions, the voice that dripped sincerity and love, he continued "I will close for this evening by saying thank you again to our brilliant entrepreneurs who stood up for us all by seeing through fraud and doing the right thing. Most of all I once again thank you our formidable viewers for your continued support, for being there with us through all of the trials and tribulations our little show brings." The beaming smile drops away as smoothly as it had arrived and is replaced with the flat sincerity of a priest as the lowered voice almost whispered in reverence speaks, "I will end this evening with just this thought. When a person approaches with gifts wrapped in golden paper, check the contents before gushing with praise. For the Devil wears rags as often as he wears a cloak. (the Devil is here) I thank you all for your support and ask that you keep subscribing to our show as your subscription is what makes all of this good work possible. My thanks will never be enough to truly relay my gratitude to you all, but know my thoughts are with each and every one of you, always." With a switch of stance and the returning smile Simon raises his voice with the cheery bonhomie of a lifetime friend "So until next Saturday evening at 7.30pm I wish you all a good night and a peaceful week. Remember it could be you who has an invention that could change the world, (I have) it could be you who finally prizes the money from one or all of our entrepreneurs. So until we meet in person or via you welcoming me into your homes, I am Simon Andrews and this has been 'As tight as our souls.' Goodnight." The four figures in the chairs waved enthusiastically as Simon Andrews held his hand over his heart nodding his head as though answering questions that no one could hear.

Brilliant, bloody brilliant..."

"Have we renewed our subscription?..."

"Yes Tony. What a tosser Good God is. As you say, once a prick always a prick...."

"I've searched that tramp Gideon up on all the sites he doesn't seem to appear anywhere..."

"We know what town he lives in, Simon said at the start. Just write a letter marked for Gideon in that town. Can't be many Gideon's can there? Post

it off. It will reach him. He needs telling. What a disgrace he is...."

"And that, is a wrap." The girl with the headphones who had told Gideon to stand where he was emerged from the blackness her smile as bright as the lights that had now blasted into life revealing the empty studio (where are the audience?) Simon, brilliant just brilliant. Max is over the moon. He panicked for a moment there, thought you had gone too far but good God (yes) what an ending." She faced the entrepreneurs who were all bowed over their mobile phones tapping away and no doubt viewing their likes on different platforms, "Entrepreneurs, well done, well done indeed."

"Thank you yourself, you darling thing." For the first time since the show had began Lincoln Carmichael oozed words with the smoothness of warm honey. "I am sure sweet thing that you were very much involved up there in the gantry, the little woman behind the power." To his left Charity snorted in derision. Undeterred Lincoln continued rising from his chair and moving towards the bespectacled girl "It's Amy isn't it?" He said pulling at the name badge which dangled from a lanyard between her breasts, "I was wondering Amy if perhaps you would like to share dinner with me this evening, for I fear I shall be eating alone." He glanced over his shoulder towards his wife who turned her back on him speaking loudly into her phone,

"Larry darling, finished early. Run that bubble bath nice and deep, oh I shall want more than my back scrubbed this evening. "Turning his attention back to the young woman in front of him Lincoln almost crooned with seduction, "So.."He paused for a moment straightening his tie, "Perhaps we could discuss you being the little woman behind my power?" He tugged playfully on the lanyard before placing it gently on her chest. With barely a hint of reaction Amy glanced at the clipboard she still carried

"No thank you Mr Carmichael. I will be eating with my girlfriend, she's waiting for me in the restaurant." Nodding Lincoln Carmichael smiled smoothly, picking at some non existent fluff on his waistcoat.

"Bring her along why don't you? I am sure we can make it work just as well with three." Before she could answer a voice echoed around the studio.

"Ok everyone if I could just have a moment of all of your time in the green room. I have some amazing news to share. Oh and Amy, get rid of the tramp." As though shocked by the use of her own name Amy turned and glanced at Gideon who stood alone placing his invention back into the carrier bag.

"Right Gideon, thanks for coming. If you could go through that door there and follow the arrows on the floor you will come to the exit." Without pausing to wait for any answer she turned and called in a voice which carried an authority that could not be ignored "Right, you heard Max, all of you to the green room." Waving her arms as though she was herding cattle she walked to the far end of the studio ushering out the four entrepreneurs and the figure of Simon who seemed to have taken on the glow of an ancient holy saint.

Gideon stood where he was, alone and still. With barely a sound he moved towards the four empty chairs and picked up the three pieces of black card embellished with their bright red 'X's' and placed them on the table (pick up your litter) he turned around and moved through the door marked exit and followed the arrows.

Gideon's invention would have been heard of no more. It would have languished where it sat, back on the shelf, nestled against the wall and covered by an old table cloth which long ago had been used as a floor covering when his father had been decorating. It would have remained there if it had not been for a certain Mr J. D. Rockwood the III. Gideon knew of America, of course he did, but he had never visited it nor in fact had he ever thought about visiting it. But what Gideon did not realise as he stood contemplating the best use for an old inner tube, a small broken tricycle and some dirty plastic sheeting he had discovered on his latest walk through the woodland was that the fact that he had never visited America did not matter, did not matter at all because, America was abaout to visit him.

"So this is it eh?" J.D. Rockwood. Owner and head of the board of one of the largest, if not the largest car manufacturers and developers in the world sat back in his cow hide covered executive chair and puffed noisily on the cigar, a permanent fixture to his wardrobe. "You have called me from my meeting to watch some television show from England?"

"Yes J.D. but I think they refer to it as Britain."

"What?"

"I think they refer to it as Britain not England."

"I don't give a rats arse what they call it Chester. All I know is this had better have been worth my while." Chester Armstrong Head of Development blanched under the weight of the voice hurled towards him from the large man ensconced in the chair at the head of the table. If this proved to be a mistake it would be a costly mistake, J.D. took no prisoners and suffered fools all the less. "Well J.D." He hesitated trying to find the right words.

"Come on man, God dam, can no one say what it is they want to say around here? Spit it out, I've got things to be doing." The fact that he had received this so called urgent call just as the girl he was spending a small fortune on to visit him had arrived had soured his mood. He needed to have finished and sent her on her way by 6.30pm so he could attend his wife's birthday dinner promptly. J.D shivered in anticipation recalling the dark high heels and the tight fitting dress which left little to the imagination, "Come on Chester get a move on, start the damn film!" Chester breathed a small sigh of relief or was it resignation? Quickly he reached for the remote control and pointed it to the large screen that filled one wall of the penthouse office.

"This is a programme that came to my attention only two hours ago."

"I know, now get on with it!" J.D. tossed the cigar butt into a marble ashtray and began the noisy work of lighting another, filling the room with clouds of sickly smoke.

"Well it's from a British show called 'As tight as our souls."

"As tight as what?"

"Our souls, J.D."

"What kind of freakin name is that?"

"I don't know J.D. it's just what it is called."

"Ok get on with it man."

"Right, yes J.D. Now this show introduces new inventors to the public and a group of so called wealthy British business people…"

"Wealthy my arse, the Brits don't know what wealthy is."

"No, erm yes J.D. well anyway these British millionaires decide weather to back the project or to toss it aside…"

"God damn Chester you are boring me to death. Get on with it!" Chester took another large breath hoping to stop his heart from pumping so noisily.

"Well J.D I need you to ignore the state of the man who's brought his invention in and just…."

"God damn you Chester, show me the film before I personally throw you from the window!" Hurriedly pointing the remote control at the screen Chester waited as the opening credits to 'As Tight as our Souls' sprang to life. The figure of Simon Andrews emerged from the darkness and the patter so familiar to audiences across Britain filled the room.

"Skip this on Chester, show me the freakin invention." Chester pressed the button and the scene moved forward until the sight of Gideon removing the invention from his plastic bag sprang into life.

"What in the name of Jesus H Christ are you showing me? Who is this bum?"

"That J.D. is the inventor. Please Sir listen to what's said." J.D Rockwood III settled back placated by the use of the word Sir and happy to let this play out so that he could fire Chester's arse the moment this mess had come to an end. Forty minutes had passed in total silence except for the sucking emanating from J.D.'s Chair on a cigar which had thankfully extinguished itself,

"And that J.D. is why I thought you must see this immediately." Chester closed off the large screen with a click of the remote and turned to face his boss unsure if the next few moments would see him without a job or flying through the air from the penthouse window. J.D. Rockwood III leaned forward and slowly took the gold lighter from his desk. He sucked greedily on it as the flame caught the end of the cigar. Satisfied that the cigar was alight he leaned back in his chair and studied the plume of smoke as it billowed away towards the yellowing ceiling of his multi million dollar office.

"This could be ground breaking." Chester remained silent, he knew the rules, could sense the thought process working through the great man's brain, "Jesus." J.D. sucked again on the cigar his large lips smothering the end as though he were about to devour it whole. "Jesus." He said again wiping a large hand over his face heightening the redness that constantly coloured his cheeks. Reaching again towards his desk he plucked his mobile phone towards him and scanned the screen finding the number quickly. The person on the other end answered immediately no doubt aware of who was calling. J.D. flicked the cigar to one side of his mouth in a practised move and barked into the phone.

"Hey Brad, listen up. There is a girl in my regular suite at the Empire. I won't be needing her now. What, no? There is nothing wrong with her, fine piece of arse, its just that something has come up. Look get yourself to the Empire and shift her ass out of there. Hey Brad I tell you what, as a gift from me help yourself to her, just tell her J.D. sent you. Yeah of course buddy, knock yourself out she's all paid for. Hey Brad no problem. What? Hell yeah see you at the dinner party, Patty's looking forward to having you and Vee there wouldn't be a birthday celebration without you two now would it. Ok Brad, oh and Brad if the girl has helped herself to the mini bar tell her its coming out of her fee." He pressed a button and tossed the phone carelessly onto the desk and turned his attention back to Chester as though he had only just entered the room. "Ok Chester, this invention, will it work?" Chester felt the bead of cold sweat run under his armpit and studied the page of writing which lay on the desk in front of him,

"Well J.D."

"Yes or no Chester goddam it! Will this thing work?" Chester Armstrong swallowed thickly and contemplated the freedom of falling forty floors to the ground.

"Well J.D. We do not have much to go on but the boys in the lab zoomed in as much as possible on the invention and taking into account what the host of the show read out, it seems as though although the information is shaky…"

"Jesus H Christ Chester, will this goddam thing work or not!" Chester Armstrong laid the sheet of paper back on the desk and sat heavily in the uncomfortable low to the ground chair feeling as though he had already hit the sidewalk below.

"Honestly J.D. It looks as though this man has invented something that will quite literally revolutionise travel. A God honest, totally self charging system that can be moved from vehicle to vehicle and quite possibly has the life of, well, just say, forever."

"You have got to be shittin' me? Goddam freakin hobo piece of shit." J.D. Rockwood III lurched from his chair and threw the cigar to the far end of the board room, an impressive arm, hangover from his quarter back days at university. "Do you know what he's done Chester, do you know what this low down bum has done?"

"Beat us to the punch J.D.?"

"Beat us to the punch? Yes he's beat us to the punch but do you know what else he has done? Well do you?" Spittle flew from the large man's lips and his face reddened darker than Chester had ever seen it. "Well do you?"

"No J.D."

"I will tell you what he's done, he's ruined us. The whole car and oil empire will crash and burn because some freak in England found how to make engines run without the need for any fuel. What kind of an idiot would do that. What kind of no hope, low down, shit kicking, wino deadbeat would invent something that could be the end for millions of people around the world?" Panting for breath J.D. flopped into his chair which creaked in agony replicating the noise emanating from the large man who wheezed submission to his recent efforts. "Christ Chester get me a drink."

"Whisky J.D.?"

"Whisky! What the hell are you talking about whisky. I won't drink that foreign stuff get me a bourbon straight up, and make it a large one, I need to think." He pulled another cigar from the endless supply in his desk drawer and spat the end noisily onto the floor before snatching the glass and taking a large swallow of the bourbon offered to him. "This is a hell of a mess Chester, a hell of a mess." He took another gulp, swirling the contents around the inside of his mouth before swallowing. "Chester we need to get ahead of this before it sends us all off the rails, do you understand?"

"Yes J.D."

"We need to get ahead of this before some do-gooding, save the planet, hippy freak finds out it's out there. Do you understand?"

"Yes J.D."

"We need to get ahead of this before our competitors find a way of buying into this shit and sending us down. We need to be first. Understand?"

"Yes J.D. Of course J.D. But how, how do we get ahead?" J.D. Rockwood III swallowed the last of the bourbon and blew a long hard breath staring hard out of the window across the city skyline smiling wetly to himself.

"You know what Chester?" He said eventually "That is why I and people like me will always be the head of our multi billon dollar companies and people like you will always be those destined to wipe the shit from our arses and thank us for the privilege. Do you know why Chester?" He didn't wait for a response, it was rhetorical, purely the chance to take a breath, "I will tell you why," He pointed the cigar at Chester as though it were a sword ready to pierce his heart, "Because, I have the answers. I have the answers that make the solutions. These solutions need money to make them work and I Chester have that money, more money than you can dream of. My money makes things work, whereas you?" He clamped the cigar back between his teeth and spoke around it as though his words could only be shouted around the edges "All you can do is ask "how?" Point made, he leaned forward grunting at the effort and reached for the phone he had moments before tossed onto the desk. Chester watched as the fat finger scrolled for another number and his brow furrowed in frustration as the answer did not come immediately. Hearing the click and the tired voice on the other end J.D. spoke gruffly giving no room for comment. "Hey Dick you gonna do something for me." Again another statement, "Ever heard of the show 'Tight as something or other?"

"As our Souls J.D." Chester watched the big man carefully, hoping against hope that any moment now the large vein that throbbed on the side of his bulbous head which had been caused no doubt from a life of excess, would explode leaving him slumped over the desk to be mourned by many but missed by few.

"Yes that's the one, some Brit show. What you are going to do, is get in touch with that oily bastard who fronts it, what's his name?" J.D. clicked his fingers in a hurry up motion towards Chester who scrabbled for the piece of paper scanning the notes quickly,

"Simon Andrews sir. He's under contract with…"

"Simon Andrews, looks like a Commie bastard if ever I saw one. Well you are going to offer him a vast sum of money to come to our good old country and front a show especially designed for him." J.D. without warning yelled into the phone squeezing it as though he wanted to crush the life out of the man on the other end, "I don't give a goddam flying rats arse, I don't care if you need him or not at your station. I want him there before his plastic face has time to produce a frown of mock surprise, you got that?" He listened for barely a second before blasting with even more vigour fresh instructions down the phone, "Offer him a contract tighter than the skin on his cheeks, a contract that locks him in to you for ever, don't you let him find any wriggle room. He must never again be seen in England, you hear me? Once the dum schmuck realises he is on the arse end of some god forsaken hick town network watched by half witted inbreds, who would sooner sleep with their own mothers than watch his shite it will all be too late." He listened again, frowning with annoyance "Listen Dick don't worry about the money, give it three years and he will be found with his trousers down in some freeway service station paying a rent boy to service his needs. I don't know if that's his thing!" He bellowed to the man on the other end of the call "But I can sure as hell arrange it." Slowly J.D. settled back into his chair and smiled, a look that told anyone who cared to look that this was a man totally in control "Oh and Dick I suggest this is all done by the end of the week. I want that show disbanded and forgotten by the fall, you get me?" He took the cigar from his mouth and spat a small flake of leaf onto the floor before ramming the brown cylinder of tobacco back into his mouth, "Now Dick lets speak as friends." The words were purred, almost hypnotic in tone, "I am sure that you will make this all happen for me, won't you Dick old boy." He swapped the phone to his other ear nestling it tight against his jowl. "I mean after all Dick, I would hate for your bosses over there in that T.V. land to suddenly hear how you 'were' actually in that motel room with the dead girl and not here with me." He laughed without any humour, a wet phlegmy sound. He nodded slowly the smile stretching wider across the puffiness of his face, "No I thought not." With the speed of a twister changing track his voice took on a more business like edge, hard, demanding and straight to the point. "Ok Dick good talking. I look forward to hearing from you soon oh and Dick, if while you are chasing down this Commie bastard host you manage to find out who that bearded dame is on the show, I would love to meet her. Always fancied a go on one of those." Without waiting he pressed the button cutting off the call and again turned his attention towards Chester who tried to hide the annoyance in his face that the large vein had actually stopped throbbing. "Ok Chester. Now that has taken care of the man who could be called on to say that this invention thing was actually viable. Give it two weeks and he will be forgotten quicker than you can say Ron Forbes."

"Who?" Chester tried to recall the name but was certain he had never heard it before.

"Ron Forbes was your predecessor, stood right where you are standing. Thought he had more power than he actually possessed." Chester grew clammy knowing he was going to ask and yet not wanting to.

"What happened to him?" J.D. nodded slowly, remembering,

"Once to often, well, once, he decided that it was his place to undermine me. It seems, if I remember it correctly a lucky police stop saw his boot full of class 'A' narcotics. A reliable witness came forward who informed on him, told the court he was selling the drugs to school children." J.D. laughed for the second time that day his face full of schoolboy mischief. "Turned out to be the end of him ended up doing some years in the state Pen' not a good place for a pretty boy like him. Didn't last long I recall." J.D. re-lit the cigar and puffed contentedly for a few moments enjoying the power that his money acquired. J.D. wafted a hand as though dispersing smoke only to change his line of thought, "And now for this hobo." He needs to dealt with in a more personal way."

"A hit, do you mean a hit J.D?" Chester blanched, unable to comprehend what he was hearing.

"Jesus Chester. If ever a statement proves my point that you will always be the ranch hand and never the ranch owner this is it. Of course not a hit. England may have people with money who cannot see a great business opportunity when they have it presented to them on live TV but they do have one of the best law enforcement agencies second only to the FBI. If I was to order a hit over there christ, they would be onto me in days. No there will be no hit." Chester felt the tightness in his chest loosen and thanked God that the quick prayer had worked.

"No Chester, what is going to happen is that you are going to go to England and buy that goddam invention from the bum. Offer him a million dollars or whatever it is they use over there these days but buy it from him and get his word that it will never be mentioned again, ever. You can threaten him, do what you need to do, but buy his silence. Do you understand me?"

"Yes J.D., whatever it takes." J.D. Rockwood settled back in his chair satisfied that all would be right with the world. That damned presenter would be taken care of. The millionaires would keep their mouths shut, of course they would, had they not publicly on television announced to the world that this god damn invention was a fraud and the hobo was no good. This Gideon creature? Well he would take the money and the warning and keep his dirty mouth shut. The invention? What invention? By this time in two days it would be safely travelling back to America in the arms of Chester never to be seen again. J.D. stared out of the window and wondered again what sort of idiot would try and take on the car and oil industry? "Goddam save the planet ass holes should be shot, all of them."

"Sir?" He looked around surprised, he hadn't realised Chester was still in the room.

"What you still doing here? Get your ass out of here and on the next plane. Get me that invention." He watched the young man scuttle through the large oak door as though his tail were on fire. J.D. tossed the cigar butt into the ashtray and reached for another settling back into his chair to at last smoke in peace. He blew smoke towards the ceiling and thanked his lucky stars that he had been able to sort this mess out, and pronto. He had just single handedly saved the world from an economic catastrophe. Because of his actions today the world would be a better and safer place. Watching the city below move about its business oblivious to what had just been averted J.D. couldn't help but wonder what perfectly delivered and disgustingly deviant sexual act Brad would have managed to acquire from the girl? He would have to get a blow by blow account tonight. Laughing at his own joke J.D. Rockwood III blew thick plumes of his favourite Cuban cigar high into his office, after all if Brad did not feel in the mood to share his stories, there would always be the video footage.

Gideon had only ever had one person visit his lock up garage before and that had been a man from the council who was checking that he didn't in fact live there (the house is yours Gideon, Mum left it) he didn't live there. Today a man (Chester from America) had called.

"Hi Gideon. I've come to visit you all the way from good old America (no one wants to be with you Good God) I've seen you on the television. I wanted to meet you (you're that tosser off the tele) good to finally meet up with the man that has, well become somewhat a legend state side." The man (Chester) stood inside the lock up holding a large heavy bag in his hand swinging it slowly backwards and forwards. Its like I say Gideon, J.D. (who?) would like to buy your invention (you are a fraud) yes we want to buy your invention, we think it has great potential (you tried to con people out of their money) we think we can do great things with it." Chester drops the bag onto the floor and nudges it towards Gideon with the toe of his dark tan leather shoe, "I think you will be more than happy with the offer J.D. has made, think you will be able to do a lot of good with it (save the world) who knows perhaps buy yourself a new coat, get a haircut and a shave (save the world) you can do what you want." Chester looked around the lockup seeing the detritus that seemed to fill every available space. Could this really be him, the man who could solve the worlds dependance on fossil fuels for ever? It hadn't taken long for him to find this Gideon, he was somewhat of a local talking point, a celebrity for all the wrong reasons.

"What Gideon, the oddball who tried to con those so wonderful entrepreneurs?"

"You will find him in the last cottage on

the left out of the village, the run down place that could do with demolishing if you ask me, or in that bloody lock up garage he uses."

"Gideon poor love. You're not here to hurt him are you? Knew his old mum. Lovely woman." He had been in the lock up surrounded by mess and an overpowering smell of what? Sweat and petrol? So far the conversation had been very one sided, Chester had introduced himself, explained why he was here, shared some details of J.D. and his honest to goodness interest in the invention. He had even offered him a million and a half in English money but so far Gideon had not spoken a word. "So what do you think Gideon (lots) would you like to sell me the invention so that I can take it to America, can you do this and promise not to speak a word about it ever again?" He pushed the bag again with his foot, "Well?" Gideon shrugged, a heavy almost tired shrug. Slowly Gideon reached to the shelf and pulled down a plastic carrier bag, the very bag Chester remembered from the television show and placed it on the floor next to the bag. Chester reached forward and opened the bag carefully seeing the shoebox inside, its top askew and revealing the invention. "Wow Gideon you sure are going to make J.D. a happy man, I can't thank you enough. You are an ok guy. Today you have made a real difference (Saved the world?) probably saved the world."

Without waiting for an answer, in fact certain there would be no answer, Chester walked from the lock up glad to be free of the smell and away from the odd creature who lurked within. He made the decision that he would walk back to the centre of the village instead of calling for an Uber. Did they even do Uber here in the UK? It was a pleasant enough day and the walk would do him good especially with such a long journey home in only a few hours. He looked at the gold Tag Heuer on his wrist and felt for the first time a tiredness creep over him perhaps the result of too much scheming and deception that and travelling at only a moments notice. Feeling buoyed by the thought of all the money sitting in his own account he decided that perhaps there would be enough time to stop off at one of those odd little public houses and partake in a warm English beer. As he walked, wishing he had worn something more suitable on his feet for the cobbled stones that seemed to cover much of his journey, Chester couldn't help but to stretch his grin into the widest of smiles. This whole trip had been an amazing success especially for him. Sure it had cost J.D. a million more than he had wanted to spend, half a million extra for Gideon and half a million for himself. His half a million neatly deposited into an account hidden from public sight and in his mothers maiden name. The momentary concern he had first felt over the deception soon faded as he realised that he had thought everything through to the minutest of details, he already had formulated, an explanation that was solid and could stand up to the full scrutiny of J.D. Chester's smile almost turned into a laugh as he pictured the conversation on his return to the board room. back home.

'The man bargained hard J.D. Said he had someone else that would be interested. I had no choice but to raise it to two million, I hope that was the right thing to do?" As the scene played out in his mind, Chester shifted the weight of the bag in his hand and for the briefest of moments his smile disappeared, "I wonder if there was a possibility this invention could really work?" As quickly as the smile disappeared it forced its way back onto his thin lips flashing a small woman with whoes shopping trolley crackled over the cobbles a bright unreturned grin. Shrugging, Chester turned and watched her go. Perhaps if she had just deposited half a million pounds of someone else's money into her own account she would have returned the smile without a thought. "Jesus Chester, you are good!" He said out loud as he thought of how easily he had been able to divert another vast sum of money from the giant of a man who thought himself untouchable and yet was so easily picked clean. Turning into the dark interior of something that called itself a local inn, not pub, Chester ordered himself a beer and something called a cheese ploughmans. As he watched the bartender disappear from sight he sipped the dark beer and thought to himself, "Why the hell not."

Gideon picked up the bag and glanced inside seeing the bundles of notes rolled into tight tubes held together with elastic bands (those bands will come in useful) he pulled the zip closed and placed the bag under his bench. Turning out the light he pulled open the door and closed it firmly behind himself and walked slowly along the lane to the road at the end. He stopped only once, sniffing the air (I cannot smell any of the pollution) He would head towards the centre of the village and visit the library (Helen would help him with the letter from the electricity company) it was a warm day, perhaps too warm for a great coat but he liked the feel of the material, it made him feel safe. Gideon moved along the street ignored by so many people, avoided by others. As he shuffled passed the overtly bright fronted 'Television and Electrical Superstore' his attention was caught by an image he recognised (Simon Andrews) the television presenter. Words scrolled along the

TALES OF SOMETHING DIFFERENT

bottom of the screen. Gideon paused by the window and read the words as the rolled before him, his features unchanging, (leaves his television show for ventures anew in America. Public devastated as top TV personality and a friend to all Simon Andrews sensationally quits his show after receiving a magnificent offer to front ....) Gideon walked on feeling the crumpled letter from the electricity company in his pocket (Helen will help) he wasn't sure what a final demand was but it sounded very important. As the large, peeling wooden door of the library came into sight Gideon stopped dead in his tracks much to the annoyance of a young woman pushing a pram who barely missed hitting him,

"Freak!" (knob Good God, you are a knob) Slowly he pulled the old school exercise book from his pocket and looked for a blank space amongst the copious notes and drawings contained within. Pulling the pencil stub that sat unnoticed behind his ear covered in the grey of his long dank hair, Gideon began to write in slow thick letters, (machine for making heat in houses for free) He sucked on the pencil and screwed up his eyes trying to think of a name for his latest invention but nothing came to his mind. Gideon often invented things that had no name.

Blackbird

He pushed open the small, wooden, slit window of the bird hide and stared out over the whiteness of the frost covered lake. There would be no real spotting today, nothing to focus on. As a matter of habit he raised the binoculars to his eyes and scanned the lake and the surrounding trees.

"Nothing." He muttered, a dull heaviness to each word. Certain he had fully covered the vista he lowered the glasses and leaned his arms heavily on the small sill blowing a cloud of quickly cooled breath through the glassless slit. A sudden movement in the trees to his left saw him swing his binoculars back to his eyes focusing as they moved, years of practice, years of solitary practice.

"Hello bird." He whispered "It must be cold out there." The blackbird hopped from the branch in which it was sat and dropped to the floor busily pecking and pulling at the white frost edged leaves as though sorting them into piles which only it would ever understand the pattern it was creating. "Anything good to eat under that lot?" He watched for a while as the bird 'Turdus merula' went about its busy routine stopping only briefly to flash the orange of its beak against the low hanging, clouded sun which fought to break through the crispness of the frost. He concentrated on the display playing out before him, fascinated more by the hardiness of the small creature than actions he had seen enacted so many times from so many hides. Feeling the coldness wrapping itself around him he shivered involuntarily and placed his binoculars on the shelf before reaching into the old green, canvas rucksack he always carried with him. The flask he pulled free was as battered as the rucksack and to look at and if he was totally honest, like the rucksack not quite up to the job anymore. It would as he came to expect serve him lukewarm coffee but he didn't care, could never quite bring himself to let it go in favour of a new one, too many good memories. The coffee was tepid at best but he drank it slowly savouring each mouthful as though it were the finest champagne.

"Champagne." The thought sent a shiver through him, just what had he been thinking? He could hear himself, feel the warmth of humiliation passing through himself again. He closed his eyes and groaned "What a fool. Stupid, just stupid!" He tipped the last of the coffee into his mouth hoping to wash away the feelings of abject sorrow that had suddenly dried out his tongue and tightened his throat. He screwed the cup onto the top of the flask and placed it onto the narrow wooden bench seat next to him picking up the binoculars and began studying the lake again. Nothing moved, everything was still.

"Even the birds have deserted me." He was about to lay the binoculars down when the blackbird hopped into view slightly closer this time. He could instantly recognise it as the same bird because of the flash of white that seemed to crown the top of its head. He frowned,

"Albino, birth mark?" He wasn't sure but it made it stand out, made it different enough to be easily recognised. The thought of standing out in a crowd seemed to crush at him, force him to deepen the frown that had etched itself across his face.

'I was wondering if…' He groaned again, just what had he been thinking? He had been perfectly happy. He had gone about his life contentedly for 50 years, considered himself comfortable and then? And then! Cathy. Cathy who had been transferred in from Head Office. He shook the thought away from himself and looked again for the blackbird sudden panic filling him, it had gone. No. There it was, closer, so close in fact he no longer needed the binoculars to see it clearly. He watched for a few moments as it hopped around picking at things which were too small for him to see. The bird was happy, just happy being itself, just as he had been. Just as he had been before Cathy arrived.

"Hello you must be Allan. I'm Cathy. From Stevenage." Her smile, it was her smile he first noticed. He remembered mumbling searching for something to say, her smile blinding him.

"Hi. I'm Allan." It had been a weak response, she, Cathy had known who he was, He remembered trying for something else, something more fitting, "I once had someone ask me where St Evenage was." God had he really said that? Was that the first thing he had said to her? He must have sounded more schoolboy than Head of Finance, but her smile, oh her smile.

The blackbird was in a bush close by, picking at itself, preening. He watched for a few moments recognising the need to suddenly take care, to 'smarten one's attire' as they would say in those black and white films he so loved watching. There had been nothing finer than sitting on a cold Sunday afternoon with a warm drink and perhaps two digestive biscuits watching the films, films that showed a time gone by, a time when the world had standards. He had bought himself new clothes. It seemed to be the right thing to do especially when in the office. Cathy had brought a sense of elan to the work day, carried herself with a poise that was almost balletic in action. Cathy, he realised was the light that had been missing from his life. Sitting in the cold of the hide he understood now how much of a fool he had been. He looked again at the blackbird which had stopped its preening and was now standing totally still except for the sudden jolting of its head as it no doubt surveyed the territory it considered his. Cathy had brought that sense of pride to him, that wish to show her what he had achieved both in work and with his home life. It had begun simply enough, the odd question about a certain set of figures or balance sheets. It had progressed to little chats in the small kitchen space shared with colleagues, she had actually said that,

"I love our little chats." Placing her hand on his arm and smiling up at him warmly, oh that smile. It had moved at pace when they were thrown together to work on the 'Shelley account.' A million pound deal that could bring prosperity to them all if successful. They would sit together shoulder to shoulder, faces close, discussing and planning. Together they worked the facts and figures until all that existed was the paper thin space that seemed so comfortable between them and the aroma of her perfume.

His stomach rumbled as he remembered the closeness he had been certain was there and he automatically reached for his rucksack opening the drawstring pulling out the green

Tupperware box that contained the homemade cheese and pickle sandwiches he so loved. He again unscrewed the flask and poured the coffee into the cup only to realise that he was not in fact hungry or thirsty and that the rumbling had been no more than the embarrassment of last night. He dropped the sandwich untouched back into the box and looked out into the whiteness that seemed to have grown in its thickness matching his own quickly growing mood. The blackbird had flown from the bush and was now only feet from the hide hopping in little jerky leaps that was not quite flying and not quite jumping. Without realising he was going to do so he reached for the sandwich and broke off a few small crumbs dropping them gently from the slit onto the ground in front of the hide. As though the sight of an arm suddenly extending from an invisible hide was the most natural of occurrances in its day the blackbird made two large leaps and greedily pecked at the crumbs snatching at one before dancing towards the next in a display of total satisfaction. He smiled for the first time today, in fact for the first time since last night. Breaking off a few more crumbs he tossed them towards the blackbird who seemed to take no fright in the sudden movement only to hop towards the base of the well hidden construction.

Cathy had enjoyed their first meal out after work, a pizza. Why wouldn't she? They were friends. It had taken all of his courage to ask her after all he didn't want to overstep the mark, cross a boundary that shouldn't be crossed. It had been a simple thing in the end. They had worked late, the account was going well, so well in fact that they were ahead of schedule. Cathy had mentioned that she would be having something simple for dinner tonight and asked what he would be having?

"I'm going to get a pizza. Perhaps you would like to come with me?" Not the most romantic of suggestions but one that was effective it seemed as Cathy accompanied him chattering brightly as they walked slowly to the rather sad looking pizza restaurant who's advertisement displayed pizzas that were never actually served. After that it had become routine, every Thursday evening after work became Pizza Evening although not at the same establishment.

The blackbird sat patiently waiting as though fully understanding that the mysterious arm would eventually drop more crumbs from the slit. He would not disappoint the bird, he could not disappoint the bird. His coffee was cold but he drank it anyway raising it in a toast towards the blackbird.

"New friends." He said "And missed

opportunities." He sipped the coffee grimacing at the coldness, perhaps a small punishment for getting it so badly wrong. The blackbird looked as though it had lost interest as the crumb supply now seemed to have dried up and it began the hopping action of earlier flicking at leaves on the ground turning its back on the mysterious supplier its tail twitching in what, a sign of disgust?

"Allan. I've been offered a new job. In the city. It's far too good to turn down. I haven't said anything sooner because I really didn't think I would get it." The words had cut through him. He could have cried aloud. How could this be?

"I should have said. Honestly I didn't think I would…" She had fallen silent the crystal champagne glass sparkling in a tapestry of diamonds the reflected light as she raised it to her lips. "I'm sorry." She said "I'm sorry." He hadn't known what to do. Sitting at the restaurant table he thought back, looking for the signs. Had he misread them, had he misunderstood what had passed between them over the past year? The answer was obvious, of course he had. Why would someone as bright and as wonderful as Cathy ever be interested in a loner like him? She had everything to offer, what did he have except an interest in old films, birdwatching and figures and yet he had hoped. He had moved carefully, slowly, it was his way. Pizza nights, cinema, walks, talks of plans, hopes and dreams as though they were teenagers and not moving quickly towards middle age. He sipped at his own champagne and thought of the velvet box in his jacket pocket, not a ring, no too soon for that. A necklace, silver with a small diamond a token of his…"

Swallowing the last of his coffee and feeling the cold seep into his bones he screwed the flask shut and placed it along with the Tupperware box into his rucksack taking a moment to look at the velvet box which lay forlornly in the side pocket unopened. He wasn't sure why he had brought it with him, self flagellation perhaps, a reminder that his old way was the best way.

"God what a fool I've been." His voice sounded hollow, flat. He wished he could have handled it better, wished he could have been the hero from one of his favourite black and white films who would have shrugged with a slow and steady nonchalance, smiled brightly, wished her all the luck before kissing her softly on the lips and walking away into the lamplight. He shrugged his rucksack onto his back and looked around to make sure he had left no mess shaking his head at the way he had behaved, the lack of decorum he had shown. He was no hero fit for a film instead he had risen from his chair quickly, perhaps too quickly and mumbled something about needing to go to the toilet before returning to finish the meal in total silence, too hurt to talk. Cathy had tried to engage him, remained upbeat, kept that smile on her face. Oh God, how he was going to miss that smile, but he couldn't hear her, couldn't focus on her words. Closing the slit window of the hide he moved towards the door a heaviness to his tread, a weariness to his soul. As his hand reached for the wooden latch the tinny theme tune of 'Gone with the Wind' vibrated from his mobile phone, a message. Flicking open the screen he frowned at the name which appeared on the screen, her name, Cathy, a feeling of intense sadness washed over him. He pressed the icon to read the message and sank heavily to the wooden bench as the words she had written, slowly became clear.

My darling, darling Allan. Last night was difficult for us both.
I cried myself to sleep thinking of the hurt look on your face, how typical of you to think that my good news is bad news
for us. I tried to explain that this is far from the end but just
the beginning. My new job means good things for us as a
couple. I love you and have done I think since

first we met.
Please come to mine as soon as you can. We have much
to discuss. No job shall part us but make us stronger
together. You are mine as I hope I am yours.
I love you X X X
P.S. bring some biscuits as Brief Encounter is on the television this evening.
X X X

Allan wiped the tears from his cheeks and blew his nose loudly into his handkerchief. He pulled himself to a standing position his legs moving as though the body they carried was as light as the air surrounding him. Pulling open the door he stepped out into the chill of the mist which now seemed to be tinged with the pinkness of the sun which was breaking through its shroud. As he moved through the woods towards the car park the sound of a blackbird singing in the distance accompanied his every step.

Headline News

The smell of sweat is strong in the confines of the motorcar. I open the door, just a crack, which I know is against all protocols but I can't stand the smell anymore. The large figure next to me (and the cause of the tepid odour filling my nostrils) slowly turns the page of his 'Chicago Tribune'.

"Hey Mack. You gotta keep that shut." His voice is slow, deep, tenor in quality I guess. It matches his frame, large, wide shoulders rolling to arms that are thicker than the average mans legs. His neck is a mass of sinew that forces its way from beneath the collar and tie threatening to burst the collar from its buttons at any moment, and a face that looks as though it has taken one too many painful punches. Inwardly I curse, but of course he's right, I know he is, but I'm not about to let him dictate to me, again.

"I need air." I silently curse myself for such a week retort, I sound like the whiny kid he obviously thinks I am, but hey, it's a start. I take a couple of deep exaggerated breaths instantly regretting my decision as the blast of rotting food from the two nearby dumpsters assails my senses and I close the door with a thunk and snatch my Fedora from the dash and begin fanning myself furiously.

"Mack, take it easy there, relax." Again the slow voice working in tandem with the rustle of paper as he turns over another page. "You keep moving about like that and you will be exhausted before anything happens." I feel him twist his torso towards me (the rocking of the car gives him away) and before I have seen it his hand snatches my hat from my grip and tosses it over his shoulder. This doesn't seem right, a man of his size should not be so fast. "Why don't you grab some shut eye? You look like you could do with it." He concentrates on his newspaper again closing the pages and folding it neatly in half. "I remember what it's like." His face does this funny thing that I realise is his attempt at a smile "New baby and all. A girl isn't it?" I'm shocked, I didn't think he was interested, in fact I was unsure if he even knew. He wasn't in the room when Mr Ness gave me the cigar, perhaps one of the others mentioned it to him. I move my hand to the outside of my jacket feeling the shape of the cylindrical tube that has sat untouched for the past three weeks.

"Yes." I hear myself croak (Damn the man, why does he affect me like this?) "Elizabeth Mary Montague Brown." I nearly shout the words determined not to be in this man's shadow for ever, especially where my new darling daughter is concerned. If I was expecting the fury of my words to affect him in any way I was immediately disappointed. In his usual slow manner (Where had that been a moment ago when he snatched my hat?) he purses his lips and lets out a long shrill whistle.

"Phewee! That certainly is a mouthful and no mistake." He waves his stubby finger in my face and shifts his body, to get a better look at me I suppose. Then with almost the closest thing to reverence I have heard from him he begins again, "My old ma said to me once, when I asked her why my name was Joe and not Joseph like the one from the bible? She got down on her knees and looked me straight in the eyes and said." He was doing that smile thing again "Well." She said, "Honey, me and your pa decided that when you were born it was best to give you a short name. We did this for your own good, mind, we did this in case you grew up to be a no brain child like us. What's the point of having some long fangled name that a no brain child can't spell eh? Now you be happy with Joe, cos Joe is a good solid name." His focus turns back on me and he winks, he actually winks at me, "Elizabeth Mary Montague Brown." He puts a heavy hand on my shoulder and crushes it beneath what I am sure is supposed to be an encouraging squeeze, "You are a smart guy, Mack, you really are, but perhaps you should start calling young Elizabeth, Bess, just in case eh?" He makes a sound that I now realise is a laugh despite the menace it somehow portrays and turns himself straight in his seat staring through the windscreen out into the gloom of the settling night. I follow his gaze and sigh deeply, I'm confused. Two weeks I have been partnered with Joe and he has been nothing but brusque, his manner is as hard as his demeanour. For days (or should I say nights now) we have been relocated from one location to another just as grim location, squashed together in the motorcar staring down one alley way or another waiting. In all of this time I don't think Joe has offered any more than the occasional grunted instruction or gruff put down at any of my suggestions. In truth, I have grown to dislike him more with every hour we spend together. I would have complained to Mr Ness, asked him to put me with someone else, but, ahh there it is, my problem. I am a bright guy, someone destined to move upwards quickly, (or so the agency report on me says.) I want to do well, I want to succeed, especially since Molly and me had little Elizabeth, (I will continue to call her Elizabeth) and because of this I know the pitfalls. Oh yes young, bright, Michael (yes Michael, not Mack) Brown knows the pitfalls. If I start to make a name for myself as a whiner, a man who wants to be moved when the going gets tough, he stays exactly where he is, stuck down an alley waiting for the latest tip off to bare nothing but lost hours, with a man who offers nothing but bulk, body odour and the personality of a stone wall. Oh yes, Michael Thomas Brown (my full name) knows how to play this game, sit tight, wait it out and let your brain come to the fore. As my mother says, 'cream always floats to the top.' and you should always listen to your mother. He starts flapping the pages of his newspaper again, studying it as though it were the bible itself. He is squinting at the print from the weak light which is offered to us by the nearby street lamp, his mouth sounding the words silently his hands gripping the pages as though frightened they may escape. He had cursed when he saw where we had to park, didn't like the light 'displaying us like a freaking Christmas tree.' He actually got out of the motorcar and walked around the street looking for a better position but returned heavily, the scowl set even more deeply on his face, his muscles bunching under his mac as though dancing to some unheard tune. That had been three hours ago. I steal a look at my watch twisting my wrist to share the light. Correction that was two and a half hours ago, I can't help but sigh.

"You bored already Mack?" Oh sweet Jesus it seems that for some reason my partner (ha, who am I kidding, partner?) is in a talkative mood.

"No, not bored. I just wish something would happen so I can get involved." That was impressive. I said that straight out. Spoke like the man I am, Michael Thomas Brown married to Molly, father of Elizabeth, future director of the FBI, future President of the USA? I smile to myself, hey why not, why not dream big?

"Hmm." There it is, Joe's standard response before the put down, his clearing of the throat before verbally slapping me down. I wait, but nothing comes, the silence stretches on interminably as Joe settles back to read his paper. See he's done it again, what did he mean by 'Hmm?' Was that a good hmm or a bad hmm? I realise I have let him get under my skin again. This monster of a man only has to mumble and I fall to pieces. Shit I must be tired. The warmth of the car begins to take a grip of me and although I know I should stay awake, stay alert I feel my eyelids droop together just once too often.

"Hey Mack, you with me?" I jolt awake confused and angry. Confused because I was in the arms of my naked Molly, her soft flesh warm against my skin (enough of that.) Angry because I realise I have slept deeply, I am asleep at my post. Joe is punching me? No prodding me.

"Come on Mack, rise and shine. You've been snoring away there for nearly an hour. Daren't leave you any longer. Need you fully alert." Inwardly I scream at my weakness, an hour? Surely not it felt like moments, no more than a blink. Beside me Joe wipes a heavy hand over his face and stares blankly through the screen, his focus half way between the hood and the alley entrance (or exit.) "You feel any better now? Looked like you needed that."

"I. No. I mean, yeah, thanks. Sorry." I don't know what else to say, I'm embarrassed. Joe does his laugh thing again.

"Hey Mack, relax. It's ok. You need it. That's what good partners are for." Did he just say partners? He laughs again (I wish he would stop doing that) "Don't look so shocked. We are on stake out together that makes us partners. I've got your back." He focuses on me again "You're a good kid I can see that, perhaps too much need to be liked. You need to harden up a little, but a good kid." He sighs, actually sighs, deep and loud "Look I've been doing this a long time, too long." He stretches his arms forward as far as he is able before his fingers meet the screen. "Since just after the war, so you could say I have some experience of men catching sleep whenever it comes. Don't feel bad, it happens to us all. Stress can do that to a man." He stops talking and for just a moment his eyes take on a far away sheen and his jaw normally so tight slackens. As quickly as it comes over him it passes and he is back with me in the motorcar. What do I say, how do I answer this?

"You were in the war?" It was all I could think of (Not all I was thinking of, some of me was still in the arms of Molly) but Joe nods unaware.

"Yes, joined as soon as we entered. I had to, had to do my bit." He waves it away with a look of what, embarrassment? "Anyway, let's just say, I know how men react in most pressure situations, what they need." I want to ask more especially as my own Father had been killed in that war, a war that seemed unreal despite the horrors it inflicted and how it left so many children fatherless, but Joe had focused on his newspaper again the conversation over, leaving me to ponder on Elizabeth and the violent world in which we were bringing our daughter up in. There is no doubt about it, nineteen twenties Chicago is brutal, mob rule holds the city in its grip. Al Capone rules with a ferocity that no-one seems to be able to curb and everywhere is held in a feeling of violence. I suppose ultimately this was why I had joined the service, pushed myself to pass the FBI entrance exam (Second in the class, I thank you.) to make a difference, to make the world a safer place. High ideals? I suppose so, but that is why I jumped at the chance to join Mr Elliot Ness in his what. Crusade? Yes crusade, and that is despite my age and my obvious lack of experience. He saw something in me, something he liked….

"Would you look at that." I snap to attention leaning forward focussing on the alleyway.

"What is it, has he arrived?" Involuntarily my hand reaches for my holster but stops as Joe pushes the newspaper towards me. I stare blankly at the paper my heart struggling to calm its thundering beat.

"**DEEP END ABLE TO HOLD OFF CHALLENGERS!**" He reads aloud pointing out the headline on the back page, "There are going to be a lot of very unhappy bookies out there. The odds were stacked against him ever running again let alone coming through to win." I look at where his finger is pointing and then slowly at him, his face alight.

"Horses, you are talking about horses?" What a night this is turning into. After weeks of nothing, I find my partner (Yes, but he said it first) not only served in the war but enjoys the horses. He flicks the paper with the back of his hand.

"I sure am. Look at that, a horse that was close to the slaughter house after a horror fall comes good and wins the Belmont Stakes. Phewee." (What's with the whistling all of a sudden?) It's the stuff of movies. Good old Deep End." He claps a hand around my wrist engulfing it and raises my arm in a winners salute, "Good old Deep End." He repeats.

"I take it you had money on this horse?" I am seriously interested now, why wouldn't I be? His excitement is tangible.

"You bet I did." He looks again at the headline holding it closer to the side window angling it to soak in all the available light, "Only a mug would have placed hard earned money on that horse, the odds were stacked against it. Well guess what?" He doesn't wait for an answer "I am that mug." He falls silent, his fingers moving in a counting motion "I have won enough, to clear my debts and to give Martha and the kids what I owe them, what they are long overdue." He grimaces that smile of his for the third time this evening and closes his eyes prayer like. "It feels good Mack, it feels really good." I want to reach out and touch his arm, (What has come over me?) to show some support. Instead I settle for a verbal bear hug.

"I bet it does. To win big must be fantastic." I'm not sure of the correct terminology never having been a gambling man but it feels right.

"Hmm." Oh no there it is again, wait for it. "Hmm, yes it does. Yes it does feel good to win big." I feel proud of myself, I have entered into an adult conversation with a man who up until a few hours ago I was frightened of I was…

"But." (I knew it was coming, deep down

I knew it.) "But." He says again "Do you know what feels better than winning big?" As usual he doesn't wait for an answer but ploughs on. "The chance to have people look at me and say 'he made good.' To have people who have grown to despise you to look you in the eye and say 'thank you' and mean it." He opens his own eyes and nods (as much as a neck like his will allow him to nod) and faces me. "Mack do you know what it is to have people hate you? No of course you don't, you are not old enough." One day I will answer one of his questions before he does or at least I will try. I allow him to continue (I allow him. Really?) "I have made mistakes Mack, I haven't been there for people who I should have held close. I have drunk too much, fought too hard and long neglected what was mine where I should have cherished them and all in the name of law and order." He laughs, a tired sound "Well now I can put that right, I really can." He waves the paper towards me again "I can put things right. At last I can put things right." He lays the paper in his lap and rests his head back staring at the roof of the motorcar, his breathing relaxed, a different man than that which climbed behind the wheel only hours before. I sit quietly allowing him this moment, hoping now that perhaps he is drifting off to a quiet sleep, a sleep full of dreams of money and of forgiveness.

"Have you ever wondered Mack?" He snaps back to full attention, not asleep, just thinking it seems. "Have you ever wondered what the headline would be for you?" Now it seems is the time, the time for me to actually answer a question of his as he's fallen silent. The only problem is that I do not understand what he is asking me, and so I say.

"Hmmm." And guess what? It works. He looks at me as though I have slapped him (Would he even feel that?) I frown as though I am considering his question, after all I have never been in this situation with him, I have never made him feel uneasy before. Just for effect I say "Hmmm." Again. For the briefest of moments I think I may have overplayed the Hmmm situation as he raises both shoulders in a massive shrug, but as slowly as they rose the shoulders drop and his hands splay open on his lap.

"Exactly." He says, although what he means by 'exactly' I am not sure. "Difficult isn't it?" And yes you've guessed it he doesn't wait for an answer, normal service has been resumed. "I mean if you had to write a headline about yourself what would you say, what would your wording be?" Now it's my turn to shrug.

"I don't know Joe, perhaps?" I was close to getting a whole answer out but he pushes on ignoring me.

"What would people say about you, what would they write. It makes you think doesn't it?" I don't try answering, he's on a roll. "I bet people would say about you." He points in my direction his fist as large as a boulder "People would write, intelligent, loving, caring, missed. Well that's what I think they would write about you." He turns in his seat again as best he can, facing me, attention fully focused, eyes more alive than I have ever seen them before. "But it's about what you think they would write about you. Do you see what I mean?" I curse myself, again a pause and I have no answer (is he doing this on purpose?) I shrug

"I'm not sure." I try a smile but he doesn't seem to notice.

"Look." He says "We can all guess what others would write about us, that's easy, we just pick anything we would like to hear said about us, but what would we say about ourselves? After all it is us who knows us better than anyone else right?" At last I can answer I'm on the same page as him.

"Yes, I suppose so." (how weak was that?) He wags his finger again.

"Yes, of course we do, we know ourselves better than anyone else. So if we had to write our own words about ourselves how would we stack up, what would we write?" He sits back forcing his legs back beneath the steering wheel. "What would we write?" He asks again more to himself than to me. A warm silence falls over us, I should be used to our silences by now and yet somehow, this is a different silence. It is the silence of two men, partners, law enforcement officers deep in thought, comfortable in each others company.

"Broken." The word breaks our new silence noisily. I face him unsure of how to respond

"Surely not. Broken? That doesn't seem right." He shrugs again.

"Sure it is. Broken marriage, broken relationships with my kids, broken noses and bones in fights, broken friendships, broken promises. Yes I think broken sums me up perfectly. He tries the smile thing again but this time fails producing more grimace than smile. I have to respond, the look on his face urges me on.

"But Joe you have always tried, you have always…" He interrupts my flow, cutting me short

"Hey Mack you haven't known me long, no disrespect but I think I know what word suits me best." He tries again with the smile but gives it up as a bad job "You are a good kid and I know you are just trying to be kind but believe me, broken is the word that suits me best. nothing else fits." I try again,

"But look how you are going to pay back the money, how you are going to support your wife and children."

"Ex wife, and children who will always have doubt in their hearts about me." He sighs "No Mack broken is what they should write." He physically shakes himself as though a large dog shedding water from its coat "Anyway enough about me, what's your word, what do you choose?" I have to stop trying to placate him realising that my attempts are proving nothing but futile and concentrate on the question. Obvious words spring to mind, happy, kind, considerate, loved, loving, father, husband. I shake them off realising that I am somehow not fully respecting his question, I am answering for others. I bite my lip thinking hard and then I come to it or should I say it, comes to me.

"Frightened." (you will not be as shocked as I am) "Yes frightened." I repeat managing to look at him. "I think that is what I would choose for myself." He nods once

"Ok, why frightened?" (The son of a bitch isn't even going to try and dissuade me.)

"Well in truth, I'm frightened of failure, frightened of failing my wife and my child, frightened of not reaching my potential, frightened of being a no-one an also ran. I can't find a way of being truly heard, I'm not the man everyone runs to. In short I am frightened to be the man I could and should be." (wow!) Joe frowns, he is good at frowning.

"See Mack, that's the real headline, that's what they should write about you, it's what they should write about me." He loosens his mac from around his body again twisting himself to face me again, "This is what we have to change about ourselves. We have a chance to alter our own headlines create a new story, change the word they write." He points to the headline on the newspaper "Old Deep End could have had a totally different write up when he had that fall. He could have given up, been led to the slaughter house and ended his life with a headline that no-one remembered, but no." He tosses the paper onto the dash "He put up a fight and got the headline he will always be remembered for. You and me have to fight for our own headline, no-one's going to write it for us." He stops talking. Twisting his head slightly to the left he glances quickly out of the screen, out into the night. Before I have chance to react to the look that crosses his face this giant of a man somehow manages to move his body (that speed again) across the tight space, covering me with his mass just before the windscreen shatters. The smell of gunpowder and blood is strong in the confines of the motorcar. Joe is heavy across my lap (a dead weight.) I sit frozen, unable to move if I wanted to, my legs pinned to my seat by the dead body of my partner. A partner who had my back, (and my front.) I am deafened by the noise, choked by the smell, wet from the urine that soaks my legs and terrified at what is to come next. It is then that I see the newspaper laying perfectly still in the heat of the night on the dashboard and I start to smile. The headlines have been splattered with the blood that seeps from the large hole in the back of Joe's head. Large droplets have stained the page in their redness marking the page altering the layout where the headline screamed **'DEEP END ABLE TO HOLD OFF CHALLENGERS'** blood has obliterated the second 'E' in deep, obscuring it from the word the rest of the words are hidden beneath the thick pool of blood that seeps into the paper. Now all that remains in bold, black letters for all to see is one solitary word **'DE P END ABLE**.' I gently pat my dead friends back speaking more noisily than I probably intended (still deaf from the gunshot.)

"Well Joe, it looks as though you managed to re-write your own headline. I smile noticing for the first time the thug (Capone's man) who had stepped close to the hood of the car bringing him only a few feet from my position. Joe, always vigilant had seen him exit the alleyway and had only some split seconds to decide on his course of action, he had chosen to protect me at the sacrifice of himself. The thug raises the gun and points it towards me holding it level, an experienced killer a man who knows his trade. I take a quick glance at Joe's new headline **'DEPENDABLE.'** I look back towards the thug and the word 'frightened' flashes before my eyes. My headline. My story.

"Ready to die flat foot?" I want to ask him if in fact anyone is really ready to die? But I stop myself, 'my headline?' With a calmness I didn't know I possessed and with little hope of any success in a loud clear voice I say

"Fuck you!" and I reach for my gun as the thug……..

The Walk

He walked slowly. He'd noticed that about himself recently but dismissed it out of hand. He ignored his own lumbering gait and the fact that he more meandered than strode these days. How walking with a purpose had became wandering at ease and why stopping for no real reason other than to enjoy the air had become the norm he simply did not know. The weather is crisp, not so cold that he could see his own breath in the air but cool enough that he kept his collar pulled around his neck just in case he caught a chill. Moving forward he breathed deeply enjoying the sharpness of the air in his lungs. God, he loved this walk! He stepped through the kissing gate and admired one more time the vista before him. The long unblemished view of the undulating landscape and the slow gentle rise and fall which bewitched him. He recognised again how the scene majestically altered with each step, painting for him a picture which lay across his eyes as permanently as tattooing them onto his skin. It had this effect on him, always had, held him in raptured silence, captivating him again just as it had from the very first time he had ever set foot through the wooden entrance gates.

Breathing deeply the freshness of these familiar surroundings he closed his eyes and felt that familiarity, he was this and this was him. He stepped forward with care continuing along his well trodden route. First the hills, gentle slopes that were not too hard on the knees but enough that if you rushed your breath would burn metallically in your throat.

"All aboard hold on tight. This snow is just right for sledging." Ancient calls echoed back to him as now he pushed not palms on the wood of the sledge but hands on knee which aided his ascent, a reminder that the loping run to the top to begin again was lost in the distant past. Cresting the hill, he stood catching his breath admiring the thin scar of trees that stretched away into the distance leading the eye towards the thickening darkness that changed from pathway to copse an area that seemed to take possession of the landscape, solid and dark, a fortress fit for kings.

"Find me Daddy, count to ten." He smiles at the voices which pull at him, so thin they drift away, lost amongst the breeze.

"We shall build a den and call it ours, picnic under the stars."

"Can we bring mummy, she must come?" Voices earnest and true. Robin Hood and his merry men living off the fat of the land.

"Build it Daddy, build it strong. Mummy

is Maid Marion and we must protect her from the Sheriff of Dottingham." Ahh Dottingham, the innocence of youth. Long gone now, the stick built dens, but the memories remain of rope swings and hiding places, palaces and prisons, a playground for Pans' lost boys.

Turning left from the copse he follows the contours of the hill avoiding hangman's tree, where old time Sheriff Stompy Stan defeated the naughty gang with nothing more than a finger gun that shouted bang and a tickling torture for surrender. He skirts the dry stone wall noticing sadly that the cows have moved on leaving nothing but churned ground and the remnants of a healthy diet. He loves the cows, gentle in their size, how they move with a stillness that belays their bulk and a silence that defies their presence. Most of all he realises yet again that its their eyes that hold him, take them to his heart, the wide open, long lashed look of innocence seducing him to the core. He leans against the wall fingering the moss that binds the stones just as the surroundings bind his heart. Trancelike he continues his step reaching the narrowest point. Opening the gate, the metal clasp screeching against his patient struggle he steps through, mourning the old wooden five bar gate that has long since passed into memory, the gate where she… He closes the clasp and leans against the gate now feeling the cold seep through his jacket, icy in touch and yet unable to freeze the memory.

"I'm pregnant." Even as the thought comes to his mind his chest swells with pride renewed in vigour and strength. Here, this very spot, her straddling the top of the gate, hand knitted woollen jumper, blue calf length trousers and the silk scarf he bought her their first Christmas wrapped around her neck, fastened tight with the gold hoop that glistened in the sun. His eyes water now, the wind bringing salty tears as her words had done so long before.

The call of the red kite circling lazily upon the breeze above him, brings him back to now. With neck craned and holding a hand to his brow, desperation drives his need to seek a glimpse of this mighty creature, a bird so familiar and yet only recently acquired. They are the permanent Gods of the air as he is the God of his past. Following for moments the flight of the bird he descends the path slowly, careful not to slip on the wet grass his wellington boots worn with age more familiarity than protection.

Below him the sound of the small stream pulls him to his newest destination. He catches a glimpse of the dark silver slash that cuts its way greedily through the landscape with a hunger to travel, determined in its task. It is swelled by the heavy downpours, it bubbles and spits, the familiarity so often the soundtrack to his memories.

"My boat will win."

"No mine will. Tell him Mum, tell him."

"On your marks, get set, go!" Paper sails, cardboard hulls bobbing and twisting, lurching and swirling, crayon designs flashing bright against the force.

"I won, I won." Hooray and three cheers. Sweets for the winner, sweets for second, sweeties for us all. He follows the stream wishing for the boats, remembering the reddened cheeks cold against his kiss, the mud on his hands as he prizes water filled boots from tiny feet, tipping the wetness back to its place, giggling at make believe naughtiness and the semi sternness of hollow rebuke. The fun of youth. The stream bends away to the left but he forks to the right into the avenue of trees, fallen leaves beneath his step.

"Kick the leaves high into the air." See them swirl on the breeze, a cloud of golds and browns." Crunching boots, sticks for swords.

"Find the conkers, beware the shells, balls of needles prick the skin. Tears of pain that scratch at his heart. Kiss it better Daddy. He thrusts his hands deep into his pockets a man lost in thought, a man solitary and yet not alone, when he is here how can he be?

His legs ache with the effort of the walk, weak where they were once strong, slow where they had once run. He climbs the style unwilling to use the gate, determined to show his strength, unwilling to accept his age. Certain of his footing he steps from the style listening to the wind in the trees, hearing the voices that call and screech in delight.

"Over here, I'm over here, find us if you can." He searches his pocket for the handkerchief he always carries and wipes the lens of his glasses wet with mist and memory. Now a downward path, a shallow dip towards the holly bush, the bush who's cuttings adorned the Christmas wreath and sat atop the pudding. The bush that holds the old dogs ashes protecting them with the sharpness of its own vicious bite.

"Come on boy, fetch the stick. Good dog, good dog." The first of four but the best of all. "Come on boy, walkies."

The mist is growing heavier now a pattering rain. He pulls the woollen hat from his pocket feeling the familiar warm comfort as it fits the contours of his head, a memory of its own. He ignores the brightness of the hat, the yellow harsh against the greens and browns and smiles at the warmth. The final stretch back towards the gate, back towards the road. Holding tightly to the top of the kissing gate he nestles his way through, conscious of the voices of the past calling to him, aware of the pain of walking away.

"We shall miss you here. You shall be missed." Daring no backwards glance he ambles along the pathway his step slow and sure, his heart heavy and sad.

When the Sun Dies

A balloon pops! Or is it a cork escaping the neck of a bottle? The celebration from the office next to ours is in full swing now. Whatever it was, the popping sound, neither myself nor Stan could draw ourselves away from the chart in front of us. Can this be true? Could this really be about to happen? Stan stares at me, the corner of his mouth giving that tell tale twitch, a nervous thing.

"Surely this must be wrong? We must check again!" I shake my head, abject fear causing beads of sweat to line my top lip even in the coolness of the air-conditioned room. We both know there is no mistake. Our calculations are correct. Every digit and symbol checked and checked again. Nothing has been left to chance. Everything has been verified. These results are one hundred percent accurate. We stare silently at each other across the metal topped work bench seeing our own terror mirrored in the face opposite. Two colleagues, friends, alone with their thoughts and yet joined together as no two people have ever been joined before. The charts spread before us, the portent of our terror displays the awful truth. At some point approximately mid day two weeks from now, the sun is going to explode and in doing so bring to an end all life for ever.

TALES OF SOMETHING DIFFERENT

Myself and Stan or should I say Stanislav Andropov have been tasked over these past two years with heading this, The International Research Body. This body consists of some of the worlds most powerful and intelligent brains in existence. In every corridor, canteen, exercise area, office space or rest room I rub shoulders with, astro physicists, mathematicians, fellows of highest academia, computer experts, astronomers and astrologers alike, you name them, they are here. The great and good from every aspect of the sciences, nothing has been ignored, everything has been included such is the magnitude of our task. In simple terms the object of this scientific bodies remit is to study a large black spot that has appeared in the centre of our sun. The blackness as it was called in the early days was captured in the first instance by the Nautilus space probe. It was a blurred image, it, not being the focus of the fly by, nor in fact the intended subject matter and so correctly, was ignored. The original point of observation was a small cloud or haze at the suns edge which had been observed on three different occasions over four years. This haze was both unusual in size and in its direction of travel. We were certain then that it was no more than a trick of the light but this theory was soon replaced by a strong belief that it was likely to be a solar flare reacting to certain conditions, perhaps the thinning of the ozone layer or solar winds whipping usual movement into unusual patterns. The Nautilus was realigned and for many months recorded any activity over the area at the edge of the sun from where the flare had emanated on the previous occasions. When, after a period of two years and thousands of images, no activity was seen Nautilus was then repositioned at great expense to continue on to its original destination, concentrating on a new planet discovered deep within the Milky Way. The mysterious haze cloud of the sun was written up as

'no more than an abnormality. After careful examination this flare is the natural reaction of gases which have now burned themselves out.' In short the Scientific community found this minor excitement to be no more than a noted but minor irrelevance. As with all discoveries it was by good luck or pure fluke that a junior member of the Keilder Observatory in Northumberland, Helen Farrow, whilst cataloguing the now defunct captured images for storage asked if there was

'something wrong with the lens on Nautilus?' It seemed that her interest had been piqued, noticing as she did that to the left of the intended area and close to the centre of the sun captured with digital clarity, the images all seemed to show a slight blur, a subtle distortion that repeated over many of the images. At first this distortion was dismissed as no more than heat haze or perhaps space dust on the lens. It was only once these images had been passed to me and I ran remote tests on the probes equipment that I discovered no issue with the lens could be found. This was not heat haze induced. The only and obvious conclusion was that this was something of great significance. It seemed that whilst our attention had been solely focused on the edge of our sun, there in the centre, growing in plain sight sat a blackness that had not been there months before. We as a race had been found wanting, neglectful in our duties. Whilst the millions of lenses pointed at our skies, focused further and further away and seeking life or threats from afar it was our closest star that indeed should have held our attention. This blurring was now perceived as a major threat, so much so that NASA decided to reroute its closest space capsule 'Voyager Twenty Seven' to fly closer to the sun than any space craft had ever dared fly before. Its mission was simple. To gather detailed images and to send probes towards the sun to collect space matter for testing and examination.

As many miles above us Voyager bravely set about its task we here on Earth began staring at images sent directly to us via live feed hoping that what we were seeing was no more than the sun gradually losing some of that immense power we had all taken for granted throughout our history. Hope grew with each image that perhaps what we were observing natural changes in temperature or elemental reaction. We were certain that this had probably happened many times before, perhaps it was just that this time we had opened our eyes and noticed it. Those of us involved at the time remained upbeat, buoyant even, that here we were witnessing something that would in the future be called 'a phenomenon' perhaps even be named after one of us. We were excited by the challenge, impressed with our cleverness and expertise, speaking loudly and with certainty that there was

"Absolutely nothing to worry about." For many months the site at the centre of the sun was studied. Helen Farrow the young scientist who had first noticed the smudge at the centre of the photos received a well deserved promotion and stood beside Professor De Angelo, leading professor of The ASI, the Italian space agency. In those early days we looked to Professor De Angelo as she measured and assessed the blackness in the centre of the sun, carefully calculating time and again each minute detail, leaving nothing to chance, taking no shortcut. Finally the scientific community began to relax as for the first year nothing altered. The blackness remained static, its measurements remaining fixed and in this normalisation hope grew anew that this minor change in the condition of the sun was part of the natural cycle of a star as of yet unobserved. The start of the second year proved just as promising and thoughts wandered from the strange phenomenon that had consumed so many waking hours and moved back to more familiar and comfortable research with hopes of new and dare I say exciting discoveries. It was in late November that these hopes were dashed and fear rose amongst us all as word came from the ever watchful and dedicated De Angelo that the blackness had grown and at an alarming rate. It was then that the world of science implored their governments to take action. We argued as a scientific community that there was a real and present danger to life if we did not come together with unlimited and open cooperation to research this phenomena immediately. Governments saw the urgency and understood the need for quick action. How could they ignore what was before them? The evidence was overpowering and alongside the passioned arguments of Professor De Angelo all barriers and resentments that existed between countries seemed to fall away as easily as tearing tissue paper. With unprecedented speed, a research team was funded and organised under the watchful leadership of De Angelo who began in earnest to find a solution to the worlds biggest problem. I was recruited at this time to work directly alongside this the greatest of physicists, my hero and my guiding light in the world of science. I admit I was in awe of her, prone to stumbling over my words like a star struck child in the presence of a rock goddess. My reaction may have seemed out of place or in fact surprising, for had I not only five years before been hailed as the greatest mind of British science and lauded with praise and accolades alike. Was I not gifted the honour of being the youngest winner of the Nobel prize for physics at only nineteen years of age? Now here I was standing in the shadow of greatness. The most enormous influence on my scientific dreams Professor De Angelo was referring to me as 'her second in command.' It was true, the man who was once a boy genius was now her sounding board, her go-to man. Where she went, I went, we were inseparable. The decision to place us together proved to be a sound choice we worked well as a partnership, we were a great team. We shared everything academic together. Our discussions became things of myth, whispered about over formulas and computer screen alike by scientists who I am sure wished they were there with us, as in the early hours accompanied by copious notes and charts with a warming glass of genuine single malt Scotch whisky we sat and discussed our latest findings. In these discussions nothing was dismissed, every prospective route was considered. We worked like this side by side, teacher and student, focused and certain. Our work continued in this way for three whole years, nothing stood in our way, everything was possible. Everything was possible that was until..... I did not go where she went. I chose to remain in the lab studying the latest figures as she boarded a sky shuttle from London to Washington. The hour long journey ended in a disaster that rocked not only that of the scientific and academic community, but destroyed who I was completely. The sky shuttle Professor De Angelo sat aboard crashed on landing killing all occupants along with their immense knowledge, instantly.

In a haze of mourning we had to reorganise, had to focus on continuing the work. I was tasked to take on the mantel of overall lead on the research. I was asked to find mankind the solution. Those first years were difficult for me, difficult for us all, as everywhere we looked, every crumb of information we touched, every piece of research we examined had the fingerprints of Professor

De Angelo firmly embedded on them. Helen Farrow finally requested that she be released from the team, unable to continue her role with any real conviction such was her own personal sense of loss.

The team around me grew slowly at first as we forced our way through unknowns and uncertainties but as we made progress each answer brought a new question. To answer each of these new questions we needed new expertise, new minds that could stand by us, working through their own specialist subject matter. Soon the research team had grown so large and expanded to such a point that the necessity for security grew beyond what could be maintained in our laboratories. We were moved to a newly developed secure and safe bunker, deep below Ben Nevis, Scotland. Our ever growing demands for the finest equipment were greeted with promises of unlimited assets and unrivalled support. Alas as with all things tagged as governmental those promises seemed short lived, or hard to achieve, as from the very moment of installation the newly installed computers proved to be incompatible for the job in hand. Technicians bemoaned the streams of gibberish, mystified by the unfathomable numbers and data that flashed across the screens in regular bursts, wiping the hard drives of recently added information and research.

With each new pulse of gibberish the program was pushed back to square one as often as a dozen times a day. All research activity had to be halted, everything paused as for just over a week our technical department had no option other than to wipe the memory banks and re-programme each computer individually. I wish this had been the only problem we encountered but the whole site seemed to be plagued with break downs and false starts. For many months after our arrival we battled our own fatigue alongside the ever persistent technical faults . As Scientists we are graced with it seems, the ability to be able to remain calm and patient with many problems we face, and so it was that after a long period of inactivity it was announced that the technicians had solved the problems and we were finally able to move forward at pace.

We had known from early on that the conclusion to our research would show only one result, the sun was losing power. This was something we laughingly agreed any low level schoolchild with a basic knowledge of science could work out without the need for billions of poundsworth of equipment. Our task however was not to find the answer as to why the Sun had began this catastrophic event but to strain our backs as horses to the plough to stop it from continuing. We became transfixed on bringing this to a stop, to cease the sun, our life bringing planet from depleting itself fully. At first this task was daunting. With any major problem or question placed before scientists the answer can be only one pencil mark scribbled in a notebook, one calculation scrawled on a napkin, one formula displayed on a floating screen away. In pure scientific terms what was daunting became a challenge, what was a challenge became the drive and what was the drive would become the success. Together we toiled, hidden away a mile below the rocky surface entombed in our unnatural, tomblike surroundings, all of us ensnared in the same task. We needed to find a way to plug the blackness in the sun. We needed to find a cure for the cancer that ate the sun to its end. We had to find the answer to this blight that threatened our end. Our best hope, soon became apparent to us all, we had to somehow fill the void that was growing at the sun's core, we had to plug the hole. Our calculations lead us to one jointly agreed decision, we would fill the hole with an artificial light. We were certain that this would be the only way to help the sun repair itself. I am not certain who thought of the mantra we developed as we worked but soon, scrawled notices and hand painted banners were seen around our rabbit hole home brightening the stark surroundings in their garishness. 'Fill the hole... Save the sun!' Gentle relief for work weary people.

Standing here now the two of us fixed in place across the work bench, bookends to the chart, I know our mantra was wasted. There will be no sun. Our efforts have been futile, our energies wasted. We have failed in our task, we have failed mankind. I rock forward and lean heavily on the table the weight of the defeat suddenly crashing upon my form forcing it to buckle under the strain. I have no power to defeat what is now certain to happen. I am now, despite my learning and knowledge, my awards and my intellect no more capable of changing, unable to alter what is to be. For all my so called prowess I have no more aptitude to save the world than any other person alive. For the first time I understand the true meaning of being powerless. I am no more significant than any other person on this planet.

The focus of our large illustrious team changed after our first attempt to plug the hole. A specially designed space ship known as Rhapsody, entered the hole in the sun and deployed a spray of gasses that would directly duplicate the gasses of the star itself. Once the finest of mists had been emitted all of our calculations showed that they would, in the intense volcanic heat, expand. The hope was that once expanded they would add to the suns own gasses working in exactly the same way, filling the void and burning with the same natural intensity as those ancient gasses formed millions of years before. As we waited with bated breath huddled over our monitors deep below the mountain, mankind moved about their lives certain from the scant news reports they received that all was very much under control. Why should they be concerned? After all were they not protected by the most amazing men and women on the planet? Were their lives not protected by the very people who had brought about nuclear powered travel, replication food units, waterless showers and pollution free oil. Who could blame them? Everything was running as normal, wages earned, taxes paid, births, marriage, death, life itself continued just as it should. We were masters of all we surveyed, we were the most powerful species on the planet.

For six months we studied the hole. At first the signs were promising. Rhapsody had entered the sun and released its cargo and the change was almost instantaneous. Stanislav who I considered at first to be no more to me than my patient second in command, quickly proved himself to be so much more. So close was our time spent working together that we soon seamlessly moved from colleagues. Stanislav became my closest friend and my most trusted confidant in all matters. I could trust Stan, he had my back as I had his. It was because of this trust that he became my natural choice to head the team who studied the gasses as they ignited and fired reducing the hole by barely millimetres a day. The results were little and slowly achieved but they were enough. The signs were promising, the hole was defiantly moving in the right direction.

Regular updates on our predicted successes were given not only to the scientific world but to the heads of states and countries alike, each gain celebrated as though the battle itself was nearing an end. It was at one of these regular meetings as I sat before a communications monitor moments away from sharing the latest data with the gathered representatives that Stanislav passed me a note, his face fixed as always with the mournful look that was hard to read. The note contained three simple words, 'De Angelo has grown.' We had named the hole De Angelo in honour and memory of our much missed and desperately needed friend, Francesca De Angelo a recognition she would have held in contempt such was her humility. My heart had grown heavy, I was certain that we were on the right path, we were winning the battle. I returned to the lab and checked through Stan's findings, not that there was any need to, I knew they would be exact.

Over the next months the black spot in the sun changed. Through the scopes its blackness was darker, the depth was growing at an alarming pace and the width slashing wider with every passing day. The darkness grew with such pace that soon it became obvious not just to the thousands of telescopes pointed in that direction but to the naked eye of anyone who dared to look towards it. Before long the press had called the blackness Sauron, named after Tolkien's dark force from the novel Lord of the Rings. A name that seemed to fit with a frightening similarity. Deep below Ben Nevis hidden in our warren of laboratories we too heard the name and shared a knowing nod at the perfection of it. There was something to be celebrated in the name for although the novel took many violent twists and turns of fortune, eventually Sauron Lord of Darkness, was defeated. It was still however in the silence of the night that fear pooled sweat around my pillow. In the crush of the silence I truly realised that although we were living in no more than a hole in the ground, unlike Tolkien's Frodo and Sam, we were no Hobbits. We had no ring to guide us, nor wizard to aid us. We were alone in our task and would remain so. I could foresee no eagles to carry us to safety once the power had been destroyed. Deep in my living tomb I curled up against the fear that tomorrow would be the end, and we would have failed in our quest.

I thrust myself away from the work bench and straighten my shoulders, forcing myself to step towards Stan who for the first time I think I can ever remember displays a readable look upon his face, a look of defeat. The stub of his pencil lays atop his dog eared folder abandoned on the bench top. His hands hang loosely at his side, eyes vacantly staring at the middle distance somewhere between his nose and the chart. I reach instinctively for him and squeeze his shoulder firmly.

"Come on my friend," I hear myself speak, the words thick in my throat. "There is a baby shower next door for Julie." As if on cue a cheer sounds from the room next to ours and the disjointed sound of drunken voices bellow 'for she's a jolly good mother' with gusto. I nod in the direction of the sound "We should go..." Stan shakes his head, slowly at first then more furiously

"To celebrate the coming birth of a baby that will never be born?" He points at the chart which lays on the work bench, aggressively mocking us "What is the point my friend?" His voice is low and flat. There is nothing unusual in this as his voice always maintains a dullness, it has no inflection, no lift or lilt, as though he is no more than an automated being inside the flesh of a man. Now, as he stands before me, his eyes flat pools of cloud which suck me bodily into his abject misery his voice takes on an unworldly tone. This is a tone that sends an involuntary shiver through me. It is the voice of one who is lost to life and shares its realm with the already dead. My friend Stanislav is a stranger to me. Where once resided the most powerful of brains now stands a creature that struggles with its own existence. A creature who is more shadow than man. Stanislav like me has learned the meaning of his own abject failure. We stand for many moments lost in the vagueness of who we are whilst in the room beyond, the sounds of singing begin again in earnest. Stan looks tiredly toward the sound of celebrating voices that crash jarringly against our own torn emotions and wipes a heavy hand across his tired eyes. "Ian, why? Why celebrate something that is wasted. Something that will be allowed no time to be born? A life extinguished before it has a chance to live." As always my friend only speaks in facts, only utters truths as he knows them. I want to agree with him. I want to scream into the space of the room, howl with anger, turn tables and sweep equipment to the floor in rage and write in large blood red letters across the floating airwave computer screens 'What is the point!!!' complete with three exclamation marks but ironically, what would be the point? Somehow, I manage a smile. Is it the absurdity of my thoughts or the cruelty of fate? I try to speak calmly, maintain a semblance of professionalism, but I am certain my face betrays me as Stan's betrays him

"As always my annoying Russian friend, you are correct." I reach out and hold his face between my hands, an action that in normal circumstances would have been as unthinkable for me as it would have been unbearable for Stan, an action that is far outside the bounds of our friendship. I want to laugh at my own stupidity. Why should I not show my friend some tenderness in these times for are these circumstances not as far from normal as they can be? "We can change nothing Stan. We, it appears, are now finally beaten." I drop my hands to my side where they swing loosely for a few moments as though embarrassed by the action they have taken, I stuff them forcibly into my lab coat pockets where they find comfort in the familiarity of the detritus accumulated over the many months. "We are the only two people in this whole facility who are currently aware of exactly how things are, how little time we have left. Let us not spoil what is occurring next door. Let these people have their moment of pleasure. Tomorrow will come soon enough but for now should we not allow ourselves one last evening of pretence, one last shot at celebration over life and all it brings, the hopes and dreams? Let us live as happy people amongst friends and colleagues for one more evening. Let us allow ourselves this much at least, for tomorrow will come quickly enough and then…" I sigh deeply allowing the expression to carry the weight of my unspoken words. " Come on Stan let us join them, let us live a little before.…" I pause again not wanting to finish my own train of thought. I smile more broadly than I believed would have been possible such was the moroseness that weighed against me crushing every grain of my positivity. As our boundaries were already broken I again rest a hand on Stanislav's shoulder and look into his eyes trying to force a spark of life back into the greyness I observed. "Come on my friend. At a time such as this do we not at least deserve the right to allow ourselves just the smallest glimmer of fun?" I nod at him encouraging him to follow suit. Stan responds with the briefest of shrugs, an action I realise I had never seen in him before. As though too shy to fully meet my gaze he shifts his weight to one side and steps quickly past me, speaking as he moves.

"I will come with you." He stops moving patting at the pocket of his lab coat, before turning back to the work bench reaching for the notebook and pencil stub pushing them into his pocket as though they were jewels to be hidden from sight. He faces me now, his features set back to the ones I know so well. "I say now, enjoyment will be the last thought I shall have on my mind Ian. I shall be no good company for you or for Julie." I nod with understanding.

"I shall feel the same Stan, but let us at least try eh?" Eventually he gives a small nod and moves a hand to begin the process of unbuttoning his lab coat. His hand pauses mid move and he frowns deeply as though a thought has caught him off guard, halting his action.

"But I worry Ian, that I shall be unable to keep the secret. I am concerned that the sadness on my face will, how do you say, give the game up?" " I smile, my previous effort now a genuine full faced gurn.

"Away. It is give the game away." I stare dramatically at him frowning with an exaggeration which a mime artist would be proud of. "I would not worry about giving the game away my silly friend, your face is always so miserable, no-one will be any the wiser." I shrug myself out of my lab coat and toss it casually onto the workbench stretching expansively as though freed from a straight jacket. I watch in amazement as Stan shuffles across our lab, ignoring my humour as expected. He reaches the coat hooks and carefully hangs his own coat onto his named peg, straightening the sleeves so that they hang in perfect symmetry. He stands for a few moments and I see the tell tale twitch of his lips as he works through some information or a sudden thought that has come to him but eventually his face returns to the slackness that has plagued him since our discovery.

"I just wondered if…" He begins before turning to face me but his posture tells me that his question is baseless and he has dismissed it before it has started.

"Enough now Stan. We have done all we can do." I raise my voice suddenly trying to force a cheerfulness that does not want to appear. "Let us go to this party. Let us enjoy ourselves whilst we can. I don't know about you but I am going to drink far too much. So much in fact that I wake up tomorrow lost in the depth of the fiercest hangover I have ever had. Come on my friend let us suffer the curse of the demon drink together." As I walk from the lab I know that this will not happen, neither of us really drink. Stan refrains because of his firm belief that drink kills brain cells, and me? I haven't touched alcohol since my last single malt with professor De Angelo.

I wake to the sound of the buzzer alarm

placed on the small cabinet by the side of my bed.

"Off." I mumble thickly, feeling the words echo around a head that I am not certain can be my own such is the numbness with which it is working. I try to open my eyes but a family of ravenous mice appear to have infiltrated my skull gnawing and biting my brain with sharp hungry teeth. I breath deeply begging them to be still, to stop their gnashing whilst I understand what has happened to me, why I am in such pain. My mouth is dry, my tongue stuck to the roof of my mouth, the need for water urges me to move. Gingerly I try to roll over and feel the room begin to spin outside of my closed eyes. I scrunch my eyelids harder together fighting hard to stop the nausea that battles the liquid contents of my stomach. "Oh God." I groan. Slowly I stretch my legs, moving myself from the foetal position that is clearly not working hoping to find more solace in laying completely prone. As I stretch, my foot makes contact with a foreign object. I stop moving, thoughts of my hangover thrust to the back of my drink sodden mind. I wriggle my foot next to the warmth of the object recognising a softness that can only be the skin in the shape of another persons foot.

"That tickles." The voice next to me is husky, somewhere between awake and asleep. I reach out beneath the thin cover and feel the solid shape of a body. "Hey easy there. Only when asked." I open my eyes forgetting the splitting headache that awaits their opening and fight hard to contain another groan that wants to escape my cracked lips. Instead I turn my head slowly half in fear of the pain that awaits the movement, half to avoid alerting the form next to me that I am studying them. The body of a woman lays barely covered beneath the sheet next to me. Too quickly I roll my head squarely back onto the pillow and witness the room spin and twist alarmingly. I grip the sheet covering me trying to control my breathing and to fight the nausea that accompanies my every move. I stare up at the assimilated star scene displayed on the ceiling of my pod breathing heavily. I lay completely still desperately trying to understand the missing hours that have quite clearly elapsed and just what has happened to me. Squeezing my eyes firmly closed again I feel some relief from the headache that is now growing in strength and fight for clarity. I clearly remember myself and Stan going to the baby shower party. I mingled, I spoke to Julie and her partner. I try to recall his name but with little success although his face comes to me easily. Bright eyes, wide toothy smile, a scar just below his left eye.

"Got it as a kid trying to create an

electrical collar for our dog that would buzz him every time he stepped from the path onto the road." Why could I remember this and not his name? Just how much had I drunk? I remember being offered a drink, a Mccallan 18 year old, of course it was. I only had one. I remember saying 'just the one.' That was all I had, wasn't it? I shudder, feeling a chill from the moving breeze of the thermo unit which pumps synthesised air around our tomblike complex and realise I am naked beneath the sheet. I steal a side eyed glance at the woman next to me, why the bloody hell can't I remember who she is? Just how much did I drink? I lay quietly picking through the vignettes of pictures that flash into my mind, grasping at them, desperately trying to force them into a semblance of order. I have made a fool of myself, of that much I am sure. I have been loud, boisterous even. I have been the life and soul of the party. Did I really dance to ABBA? Snatches of conversation come to me, all answered with the false humour that must so often be that which accompanies the condemned man and like that soon to be executed soul the need for comfort before the certain death becomes prevalent. My head swims with the affect of the alcohol prompting the schoolboy response of, 'never again' I am aware with solemnity of the certainty that for once this thought carries more weight and assurity than ever before. In the silence that lays beside me I realise that I will have to move, have to discover exactly who this is next to me. An embarrassment joins the growing thundering ache of the hangover as I realise I am unsure how to start. Do I say 'excuse me', do I say 'thank you for last night?' What if nothing happened, what if….. Before I have the chance to make any decision an insistent hammering on my pod door breaks the silence.

"Ian, come quickly, Ian, come!" Stan's voice muffled by the insulated door thuds into my ears "Ian be quick. It is me Stanislav. Ian I think I may have the answer!" The banging on the door intensifies and I groan, I hear the urgency, I want to spring from my bed and greet my friend, my friend who has just announced very loudly that he has the answer, and yet my intoxicated body will not allow me to move, keeps me stuck to my mattress.

"Door open." I manage to disengage my tongue from its position feeling the roughness inside my mouth. My pod door slides silently revealing the disheveled figure of my friend Stan who almost falls into the room waving his notebook in one hand and a sheaf of papers in the other tears streaming down his usually stoic face.

"Ian it could work. I have worked on this all night, I have experimented some scenarios.

It could be the answer." He slaps his hand against the pages the noise loud against my ears. "It needs work but you will have a way to help me Ian. I think possible is now, I think possible to survive." I have never seen Stan like this before. Stan does not show emotion, he does not express feeling. When feelings were given out Stan received granite." "We just need to build it bigger...." He stops talking and casually bends and picks my jumper from the floor and tosses it to the female form who has silently made her way from my bed and is making her way nakedly towards the bathroom. We both stare at her disappearing figure, me admiring her dark brown skin and slender hips, Stan I am sure is trying to work out a formula in his head as to how I could possibly have attracted such a fantastic looking woman to share my bed? Before I have a chance to make any comment Stan has already continued as though simply wiping away any image of what he has just seen.

"Light neutrinos." He pauses waiting for me to react, but laying prone on my mattress the effort is unbearable. Quickly he continues. "Professor Narwoo." He waves the loose papers towards me "Professor Narwoo wrote papers on them, on light neutrinos. Professor Narwoo proved that old knowledge was incorrect and that they do travel faster than light." He flicks through the pages finding the place and reads aloud. "Although previously believed to travel no faster than light my experiments prove without doubt that light neutrinos do in fact travel at least half as quickly again and burn with 5% more brightness than the sun itself when mixed with natural corresponding elements. It is possible that in the future, light neutrinos could be the answer to failing fuel levels and a safer energy source than nuclear energy itself. I believe that..." I raise my hand to stop him speaking, partly to allow my head to clear from his excitement, partly to take in all he is saying but mostly to acknowledge the lady who has just walked from my bathroom. She drops my jumper to the floor and reaches for her dress that is casually draped over the hoop backed chair in the corner of the pod. Her dress is a patterned piece of material which quite honestly looks no bigger than a scarf most women would wear on their head. Silently she pulls it on whilst simultaneously slipping on a pair of ankle length boots. Bending over she zips the boots straightening the small tassel on the front as she does so. My mind suddenly fires into action and I remember her now, how could I have forgotten? She is even in the midst of my hangover, quite simply, beautiful. Looking up she catches me staring at her, it is almost as though she has only just become aware of my presence. Rubbing her hands over the material of her dress to flatten it to her figure she smiles in my direction.

"It was," She pauses, frowning "Nice, Doctor Stone." She smiles warmly a 'fill your face' sort of a smile. Looking around the room as though searching for anything she may have left behind. She walks to the side of the bed, leans over me and places a small deft kiss on my forehead the heady scent of her perfume strong in my nostrils. Brushing again at her dress she walks towards the open door flashing that smile towards Stan who stands aside as though he were a doorman on duty. We both remain silent for many moments as the door hisses closed blocking the view of her retreating figure.

"She wears no underwear."

"What?" I manage to pull myself from the bed fighting the nausea that hits hard at the back of my throat.

"I said she wears no underwear." Stan points to the door frown on his face. I shut him off angrily.

"No. What did she mean nice. Is that it, nice?" The idiocy of the statement does not hit me until I have spoken it aloud. Here I am desperately hung over, naked with time flashing away to what will be the end of life for all here on earth and my ego has been pricked by the word 'nice' being directed at my sexual prowess. God men really are shallow. To cover the bright, burning embarrassment at my childlike display I begin storming around my room gathering the strewn articles of clothing that were hurriedly dropped at some stage late last night or was it early this morning? My head is on fire and my stomach feels ready to burst and yet as I snatch a pair of socks that had somehow found themselves on the side table and add them to the pile now snuggled in my arms my brain is working hard.

"Professor Narwoo also states that light neutrinos are also now more easily stabilised and controlled with a negative proton." I speak to cover more of my own embarrassment as I realise I am standing before my friend totally naked. If Stan realises this he he does not react other than to nod in acquiescence acknowledging my understanding of the facts. "As any school child would be able to tell you." I say sinking to my mattress as I now allow the thoughts to formulate fully, "Narwoo discovered that there are both positive and negative protons in the atmosphere in any given moment coexisting side by side, remaining compatible so long as there is no outward intrusion to the density of their mass. His discovery was a breakthrough of the greatest magnitude. It is still a fact without dispute that because of Narwoo's discovery, science and our understanding of Science was moved further forward than any time before and I include Ransome's discovery that Einstein had because of the misplacement of one decimal point miscalculated his theory of relativity." I felt more awake, more able to function. My head was spinning now, but not with alcohol but with the aid of information and calculations which spun like dancing girls whipping patterns across my minds eye. I rise from the bed and face Stan uncaring now of my own nakedness. "Give me ten minutes my friend, I need to shower." I head towards the bathroom "I shall meet you in the lab." I step into the bathroom calling "shower on" relishing the feel of the dust cascading over my now fully awake body from the overhead ceiling powder sprays. "Oh Stan, brilliant work." I call peering around the doorframe but Stan is not there. I picture him, that awkward gate legged lope of his surging him towards the lab his mind already deep in thought, already fully engaged. I rub the powder hard into my body feeling the tingle as it cleanses my skin. "Yes brilliant work indeed." I whisper into the hiss of the falling powder spray.

I stare at myself in the mirror. The spray has done its work. My skin glows with a freshness that tries its best to hide the puffiness under my eyes and the redness in my eyeballs. I am tired, no exhausted would be a more exact diagnosis and yet I feel for the first time in many months a sense of of what. Hope? Perhaps that is the sensation, hope, and yet it has been such a long time since I felt anything like it I am unsure. The scent of apple blossom sticks to my skin and I wrinkle my nose. It takes me a moment to realise that she must have chosen that when she entered my bathroom. In my haste to ready myself I forgot to change it to the natural scent of wood pile. I sigh loudly, there is no time to waste with a second shower I would just have to spend the rest of the day smelling of a flower garden,

"Ahh the dangers of drink," I say to myself as I press the button on the nourishment distributer, set into my wall and listen to the thunk of the dehydrated coffee bar which appears in the slot. Taking two quick bites I chew ravenously enjoying the instant hit of the caffine, relishing the impact it gives me. How anyone could start their day without a coffee I did not know, anyone that is apart from Stan who would chew nothing but a whole milk dehydrated bar. I punch the buttons again and wait as two thunks present me with two slabs of the milk bar, a gift for Stan. Pushing the last of my own coffee bar into my mouth I chew slowly.

It is time. Stopping once more in front of the mirror I give myself a last look over. I am I hope now fully presentable, everything seems to be in order. Before I leave I reach out and touch my reflected image promising myself that I will not return to this room until I have worked through every possible scenario to make this work. Turning away I head to the door and hear the bubble of activity along the corridor. The facility is waking to another day, going about their business. If only they knew what was in store for them all, how their day would truly begin. As I walked the short distance to my own lab where Stan would be waiting for me I composed the message I would be sending to all employees of our facility. How do you begin a message that foretells of a very last chance to save the world?

'Hi all. myself and Stanislav have a plan that if it does not work means the end of the world will be sometime in the next two weeks. Have a good day. Ian.'

I mentally wipe the message from my mind and begin again.

Entering the lab all thoughts of messages are forgotten, things are in a state of chaos. Stan is bending over his key board, fingers dancing across it with the finesse of a concert pianist. Without slowing his dancing fingers he accompanies his own silent music of the keyboard with shouts of

"Yes you. Place it there. You try with Ransomes theory. It is outdated yes, but do not forget the man disproved Einstein." I watch from the doorway as white lab coated technicians and scientists alike jump to his call adding and removing theories and mock up models of electrodes and atoms to chart and model alike. As though he has used some sixth sense he stops his typing and turns to face me speaking the moment we lock our gaze. "I do not understand. It is not working." he takes a step towards me hands splayed out as though beseeching for himself forgiveness. "It worked on paper, as you say it is a sure thing, no." He seemed to shrink before me, his large shoulders sagging, the look of defeat from yesterday now firmly fixed on his face. "I thought it was good. I thought it was a working plan, but now it is just." He leans back heavily against our work bench "But now it is just…" He shrugs.

"Nice?" I say an ironic smile on my face.

"What?" He shakes his head not understanding, "No Ian it is not nice. It is not working." Someone once said that 'a joke is only funny if both people understand it,' perhaps this was one of those times that the joke was misplaced. I sigh, my natural response these days, I am still smarting from the 'nice' comment but the look on my friends face cuts me deeply. I look past him concentrating fully on the display of the large airwaves computer screen floating in the middle of the room. Equations and numbers fill it. Two lab technicians who had been frantically swiping backwards and forwards moving the figures and data to the required places as fast as Stan could create them stand panting, hands on their hips their breathing coming in heavy gasps. Three scientists all of world worthy note, lean heavily on the constructed model board, the next set of atom models clutched in their hands awaiting further bellowed instruction as to the placement of each piece. A group of technicians marker pens in hand stand silently by banks of coloured charts hastily arranged on large a frame boards. Old style science. I nod at each group and smile warmly.

"Thank you all. Perhaps you should take a break whilst Professor Stanislav and myself confer." I see them look at each other before looking back towards me, as well as exhaustion I see fear on their faces. They are aware. They have been told. I smile again, the grinning executioner perhaps? "Please take a break, there is nothing more you can do for now. Take an hour then report back to your own heads of department. Report to them what you know from here. Work alongside them help us fix this issue." Still they seem unwilling to move but I usher them away with promises of call backs as soon as we know what we are heading towards. Once the room is clear of everyone except myself and Stan I turn to this great Russian brain and watch as he paces from work bench to chart, to airwave, to model and back again all the time muttering and mumbling to himself. "Stan, talk to me. Explain." He keeps moving as though unaware of my words. I try again, softly, "Stan. What is it? Tell me." He stops by the floating screen staring at the last set of displayed numbers which flicker in readiness as though themselves awaiting the next command. I walk to his side and point at a set of symbols highlighted in orange. "Tell me old friend. What are these? Let us see if we can make sense of them together eh?" He turns from my side and sits heavily on the stool by our workbench opening his leather bound notebook. I have often teased him for his love of this book when screens are available and so much more accessible but he has rebuked the jest.

"In days of old Ian, real science was completed on slate or on simple parchment with quill. I shall make my notes and calculations where possible in my own way as scientists did in the 20th century. I shall be a scientist of old." He opens his notebook and flicks to what I can see are hurriedly scrawled notes, drawings and annotations. He turns the book to face my direction as I sit across from him, our usual positions.

"I discovered during the baby bath party last night that perhaps we had been looking at this problem the wrong way." I ignored the mistake in his use of grammar and signalled for him to continue. "I was discussing the new baby to be born with the babies mother, Janet."

"Julie." I correct him unable to help myself but he shrugs and continues with a wave of his hand.

"Janet said that in such a difficult time she worried that the baby was being born into danger. I agreed with her how could I not? It was then I think that perhaps the idea was first growing in me, it was then that I said, 'perhaps it would be best if the baby was not born now'." I gasp at him unable to keep the shock from my face.

"Stan surely that is not what you said, at least, not like that?' Stan nods, his expression unreadable. "My God Stan what a thing to say to a mother-to-be." He frowns exasperated more by the interruption to his train of thought than the small rebuke for his actions. He forges on with his story, his voice as always robotic in delivery, his face set.

"I have said this thing to her and she

suddenly became angry." I nod,

"Unsurprising."

"She says that I am an uncaring man and that I am not pleased that her baby is being born." I can't help but laugh at the shocked look that creeps over him suddenly.

"Well it did sort of sound as though that is what you were saying." Stanislav looks back towards his book, eyes half closed in concentration.

"Mmm yes. I suppose that she may have thought that this was my intention." He says without the merest hint of regret or contrition. "But Ian it was then that I had the thought, it was then that I called her back to me. I shouted her to return, I shouted Janet…"

"Julie." I correct again

"Yes, Julie. I called to her Janet, you have misunderstood my meaning." He looks at me now with genuine puzzlement "She did not return." Before I can explain the many reasons why this may have been so, Stan continues hurriedly. "I could not explain to her but this did not make my thoughts wrong this was not the truth. My thoughts were certain, they were precise." He flicks again at his book, opening to a page covered in a series of small drawings, drawings that seem no more than hieroglyphs and totally undecipherable to me but which obviously hold some great and powerful meaning to him. I realise he is talking again, becoming unusually for Stan more expansive in his gestures. "I did not mean I wanted her baby not to be born, simply that it would be better if we could just go back and change the fact that it was being born. See?" He raises his hands to me in a 'you must understand now' sort of a gesture, but I do not, I do not understand, I am confused. Regardless of my silence Stan surges on, he is now determined to lay out his process.

"I realise that together we have tried everything, there is nothing we have not simulated or planned. There has been as you say no stone unturned, every thought has been exhausted. Together here in this laboratory we have melded our minds and we have come up with nothing. We have failed mankind and in less than two weeks time we will end because the sun will have exploded." Now it is my turn to shrug, how fragile life has become with that one simple statement. He is watching me and I feel the pressure to speak in some way

"No Stan, we cannot stop the sun from exploding." It is as though he has been waiting for me to answer this statement in such a way. As my words end he expells a large expulsion of air that for anyone else would have been considered a guffaw but for Stan was no more than a dismissive gesture.

"So we do not stop it from exploding

Ian. No we stop it from reaching the point where it is going to explode." My friend smiles at me. He is gripping the edge of the workbench so tightly that his knuckles are paler now than their usual hew. I can almost feel the electricity of excitement radiating from him, as he waits for me to answer "Well. Now Ian do you not see it. Surely this something that we must explore. Is this not something we have not looked at?" His excitement forces him to speak in a rush, confusing him, his English is slipping. "We must look now, it must not be not looked at, let us search this answer from my mind, No?" I know I am displaying my 'what on earth are you talking about' face as he thrusts the notebook across the table in my direction, calling to me.

"Look at my notes Ian, can you not see?" I shake my head wearily, the headache from earlier is returning hitting hard behind my eyes. I walk from my side of the work bench to the small sink in the corner of the room and grab a cup placing it under the cold stream of water that emerges from the tap on my command. I swallow deeply the coldness freezing my throat but seeming to help with the burning that has spread across my forehead. I allow the feeling to settle before facing Stan,

"I am sorry my friend, I do not understand. Please explain to me again, but slowly." I urge, walking towards him and heavily taking the seat next to him. He swipes his palm over the workbench and the keyboard lights up the space in front of him. With a few deft strokes he has his theory highlighted on the floating board. He points to the screen speaking slowly as though I was an inerrant child.

"You see now, you understand?" The bold heading flashes at me 'Light Neutrinos' I stare at it but nothing takes shape in my mind the workings out below the title make no sense.

"Stan." I say feeling more foolish than I had this morning on finding a naked woman in my bed "I am fully aware of light neutrinos, of course I am, any scientist worth his salt understands the theories both old and new, but…" I pause looking for the answer to hit me as hard as the headache had moments before. "What I do not understand is what have light neutrinos got to do with our problem here?" I'm sounding like a confused, petulant schoolboy but the sense of frustration is unbearable. Stan arrived with bluster shouting of his new theory, babbling of light neutrinos and how they would save the planet. I am unable to stop myself from inwardly cursing my friend, here I am in the last days of my life looking at nothing more than a board full of calculations that show how a science we understand can do no more than what we already know. I want to believe him I really do and yet I can make nothing of what he is saying except 'babies should not be born now' and that 'we have to stop the sun exploding', I want to shout at him 'elementary my dear Watson!' But as usual, Stan seems to be oblivious to normal human responses and plows on with that gleam in his eyes exited by the science despite my obvious frustration.

"As you know Ian, light neutrinos are now proven to be the smallest molecules known to human kind," He waits for me to acknowledge this fact, I nod, which reminds me again of the headache which seems to be stubbornly kneading at my brow despite the large quantity of coffee bars and warmed goats milk I have consumed which has proven itself over the past twenty years as the perfect defeat of all hangovers. "It is now known that light neutrinos bombard our planet from the sun all the time." He continues as though unaware of my inability to answer with any purpose. "We know yes that this proof is that light neutrinos being of so small pass through any object here on earth, they slip between the molecules of any object, yes." Again he waits for my ascent, "We now know that these light neutrinos are what causes the ageing process in all objects, it is a fact we know, a fact!" he pauses, I am sure it is for effect, it seems that it is now that my friend is becoming the master showman. He moves his arms in large, sweeping gesticulations, the once turgid speaker is taking me with him on his journey. "When I said to the baby mother that it would be better if the baby was not born now, I suddenly realised that what I was saying was that it would be better if the baby could be born in the past, and whack, there it was light neutrinos." He smiles at me and at last despite his total lack of the mastery of the English language I am with him, I have made what he has been seeking, I have made the connection. I leap from my seat and stare at the floating board.

"Stan if I understand this correctly." My words come in a whisper, "You are talking of doing something that has so far been only speculation and myth. You are talking my friend of reversing the light neutrinos." I rock back on my heels as though pulled from behind, wrenched from close proximity of a genius. "My God Stanislav, that is brilliant." I feel with a tingle the excitement growing within me, whilst frantically trying to ignore the small seeds of doubt that gnaw at me. If this works Stan will have saved mankind. I step closer to the floating screen and peer at it as an old man stares hard into the faces of those he does not quite remember "But can it be done?" He draws himself closer to my side and stares at the board for some moments. I feel his shoulders droop and his presence lose the fire that only moments before had lit up the room,

"I believed it could. When I called for you this morning I had it in my brain." He slaps his own head twice the sound hollow, painful, anger at his most useful asset failing him in the final moments. "I followed the process as far as Professor Narwoo had written them in his papers. He was truly making significant changes to theory and to agreed science. Professor Narwoo had discovered something that he was on the course to proving. His study with amoeba showed that by reversing the light neutrino that entered them directly you could with careful increments, significantly reverse their ageing process." Stan tugs a small thread of cotton that has come loose from his button wrapping it around his finger until eventually the button falls to the floor and rolls to freedom coming to rest beneath the coat hooks. For the briefest of moments I see Stan's face alter as he stares in the direction the button had taken as though envying its escape. The look soon disappears and is replaced by the stoic look I have known over so many years. "All evidence is that the amoeba under his experiments did in effect travel backwards through time. His observations showed that once the light neutrinos were reversed, where there was once an amoeba there was emptiness they had now disappeared altogether." He falls silent staring at the pages of his notebook, flipping the pages aimlessly.

"Yes Stan, I remember the research. At first it was said and believed that all Narwoo had achieved was to kill off the amoeba." Stan nods in agreement,

"Yes this is so, but as we now know, the slides were watched and where there was once space an amoeba came into existence."

"And he realised that what in fact had happened was that the amoeba had not disappeared but travelled back through time due to the reversing of the light neutrinos to the very point before they were born." I move to the bench and sit on the stool ruffling my fingers through my hair and desperately trying to force my thoughts into order. Eventually when the silence in the room has grown to a painful pitch I look towards Stan who remained standing, an obelisk in white. "Stan." At first I can find no clear words, my throat is dry and this time with emotion and not alcohol. "My friend." I try again, "You have given us a glimmer of hope. You are a genius for even thinking of this, it is so far beyond the realms of possibilities that…."

"No Ian." He speaks with an anger that I have never seen, this gentle giant is expressing emotions I have never before witnessed. "Your words hurt me for I am no genius. I have failed.

I have started a thought that offers hope only to have it taken from me as quickly as it arrived." I realise that tears are falling as quickly down my own cheeks as they are on the man before me. His tears are I am sure are for the loss of science, his inability to solve the problem. My tears are for the hurt of my closest friend. I sniff loudly, try to pull myself together I need to regain control of my emotions.

"But Stan." My voice cracks betraying my efforts of self control, "The science is good. The way you have follow the breadcrumbs left by Professor Narwoo is sound. You have shown scientific practice and process. Narwoo was correct. Why can we not enhance his discovery, why can we not take it to the next level?" Stan wipes his eyes on his sleeve and smiles sadly, an action that cuts me deeper than the tears that had fallen so freely before.

"Ian look at my figures. The maths cannot lie. Two plus two can never make five." I stare at the screen and work through his calculations in my head. "You see Ian all I am doing is to copy Professor Narwoo, I cannot extend what he has already achieved. I cannot extend his experiments past the amoeba stage. I am doing what has been done before and no more." I open my mouth to speak but his voice floats towards me spoken as though in a dream. "I have tried each and every conceivable theory.

I have moved numbers and calculations from positive to negative but only one calculation remains, we have nothing that generates the power we need. We posses neither the numbers of staff nor the equipment and definitely not the time to create anything that reaches half of the power we need. You can see Ian that we, us mere mortals have not the strength to move mankind back in time." He walked to the far side of the workbench and pulled the stool from beneath but instead of sitting where he was he dragged it next to me and sat by my side staring towards the floating chart. We sat like this, two fishermen watching their rods. "Ian. You see all of the figures. I am correct. I cannot find the answer. I have hit the blank wall." I smile despite the sadness that fills the room,

"Brick wall, my friend, the brick wall." Despite my very real desperation to find fault or to prove him wrong, I have to agree. Everything before me matches his dejection. Those floating findings he has produced are all sound, they reach the same conclusion. They do not lie, Orwellian in their simplicity 'four legs good, two legs bad' it is just in our case "amoeba yes, mankind, no."

"If only Professor Narwoo could have been here with us now. He would have, if not known the answer, been able to move our thinking forward, I am certain of it."

"Yes. It was a great loss." As always Stan is the master of understatement. Narwoo and six of the leading scientists were killed aboard a shuttle to Jupiters space station some twenty years before.

"Yes a great loss." I agree for want of a response. "A great loss indeed."

We spend the rest of our day bent over the screens and magnifiers trying to find a difference, trying to find a way to move the science forward or were we just wasting time the only way we knew how?

"There just has to be missing data." I say in exasperation, "Are you sure you have checked all of his papers?" It is in part no more than a hopeful question there can be no real chance or expectation of a sudden revelation that Stan or myself have missed something, shown a lack of detail. I am certain that I have considered everything and Stan? I allow myself a small smile, well Stan never lacks detail. I bend my head back to the task in hand and spend many hours re-working what is before me.

"I have checked everything. I have had my checks checked. There is nothing left on the data banks that has not been studied by at least two pairs of eyes. Every scientific paper of Professor Narwoo has been digested." Stan moves his gaze from the microscope and removes the slide he was keenly studying, writing across it in red marker pen, another sign of failure. I peer into my own microscope but cannot focus there is something nagging at me, forcing my concentration from my work.

"Stan." I say slowly, forming my question carefully "You say that all of Professor Narwoo's scientific papers have been studied. Does that mean that there are other papers of his? Papers that are not scientific?" My friend makes an 'mmm' sound as his attention is again focused on the next slide he has placed carefully under his microscope.

"Yes Ian but they are only personal diaries. I of course have run them through the computer but there is nothing that is wording around any scientific discoveries. There is no mentions of amoeba, nothing of light neutrons or anything about discoveries. There are no hidden messages. His diaries are of family matters and interests only." He turns now to the desk screen and watches his recently entered numbers collide and mix before turning a flashing red. Another formula has failed. I look at my own screen. My own last failure is still highlighted, another stain on my spirit, I wipe my hand over the display dissolving the figures. I try to study my next prepared slide and yet I am unable to concentrate, my mind keeping its focus on the diaries, ignoring the work that I am pretending will make any difference. I have trained my whole life to be a scientist, not just in the accumulation of facts and theories but in the way I think, how I reason. Every waking moment is spent in discovery, many sleeping moments spent dreaming of answers to questions that have not yet been asked and it is this way of being that keeps my mind focused elsewhere, unable to concentrate on the slide waiting patiently on my microscope. The diaries, there is something about the diaries. Quickly I type the words 'diaries of Professor Narwoo.' and instantaneously pages of script flash before me and I read greedily. I miss nothing. Voyeuristically I watch a dead man's innermost thoughts scroll before my eyes. I see births and deaths spoken of in both sadness and in jest. I see travels and illness spoken of with the same amount of wonder and awe. I read of love affairs, passionate sordid encounters and gentle giving relationships. Of parties and meals, through births and deaths, weekends and days all spread before me. I stop reading raising my head to stare at the wall far beyond me, my mind is working frantically. A daughter. Professor Narwoo speaks of a daughter from a brief but fiery affair. I flick my glance back to the screen and the text follows my retina movement stopping at the mention. Yes there it is, an entry, short words making an all too brief sentence.

'Amanda gave me the news. Baby girl. Name undecided. I cannot commit now. My work is of great an importance.' That was it. I tap into the search bar of the diary all of the words that may correspond, daughter, mother, girl, female and watch the results flash before me listing themselves. Many results are speaking of 'mother ship, or female joints and female sex. Girl is a word mentioned only twice, once as a matter of genome within an organism and then…. My heart skips.

'My girl works alongside me. Her brain is one of intellect. Proven so often in her aptitude for science. I thank God she inherits from me the need for discovery and investigation and not that idleness which manifests itself in the desperate need for popularity as with her mother.'

"Stan. He has a daughter!" I speak too loudly and the words shock Stan from his stooped posture. I make a small flicking gesture over my screen and the text shares itself to his screen. I watch as he reads his brow lined in concentration. I see a momentary pause before his wild eyes stare at me across our workstations.

"Ian. His daughter works in the sciences. Perhaps she will know of his studies. Perhaps she holds other information." He stands quickly moving to my side, pointing at the screen. "It says she has the need for discovery, she may have continued his work away from prying eyes. Her work may be the answer to our problem." He is gripping my arm some of the old spark returning to his face. "Where is she, where does she live now?" I am already ahead of his thoughts tapping into the screen, searching for Professor Narwoo's daughter. The results come back blank, there is no other Narwoo listed anywhere amongst scientists living or dead. I pause pinching my bottom lip in concentration, "No scientist." I say "No scientist." I nod before typing again. The genealogist site which holds the details of every person who is living or has ever lived quickly lists only one direct descendant of Professor Narwoo. I laugh at my own stupidity. "Of course Stan. For a Nobel winning scientist I am afraid that sometimes your friend is verging on the side of stupid." Stan reads over my shoulder ignoring the predeceased and distant relatives, concentrating on Professor Narwoo only and the single line that descended from him.

"Arjun Narwoo, deceased, living relative female Betty Brown." She is not Narwoo, she is Brown."

"Yes, she is Betty Brown."

"Betty Brown?" He moves to his side of the bench his words to me more mumbled than spoken as he types into his own screen. "It is her mothers name. Her mother named her." Before I can answer he gives a small grunt of shock reaching for his stool to sit slackly, shocked by what he has read. "She is a research scientist, but no longer in her father's field." He looks towards me a small smile parting his lips, "She is an astrophysicist and...." Now he laughs, a genuine and I believe never before heard by anyone save perhaps his own mother, exuberant laugh. 'Ian she works amongst us here." Now it is my turn to be shocked, I sit back on my stool and stare at my laughing Russian friend. He cannot be serious, our luck, if there is any such thing as luck, does not run like this. My screen flashes and I see the message Stan has already sent to Betty Brown's private message bank.

'Dr Brown. Your services are required immediately by Professor Ian Stone. Please attend with immediate effect for this meeting in the main science lab in hub number one. You are welcome thank you.' I smile at the words, typical Stan so formal in his not quite working English way.

"Thank you Stan." I say smiling "Another fine effort." He looks at me with a frown before glancing back at his screen understanding my meaning.

"Am I incorrect in my words Ian?" I shrug dismissing his fears

"It matters not my friend, it matters not." I search the astrophysics file on my screen and see that Dr Brown not only works for us but heads a small sub section which has been studying the potential effect of the moons activity on the sun. The results have shown little promise although the dedication to the task has been without question. I notice that a footnote suggests that if there had been more time available the team working on this had found definite suggestions that there is water deep beneath the surface of the moon. I sigh at yet another lost opportunity. My screen lights with the message symbol and I see that Dr Brown is on route, having obviously acted on the request immediately. I already have a respect for the daughter of Dr Narwoo. Her willingness to answer the call is without question. I calculate that her subterranean shuttle journey will take approximately twenty minutes as her station is far below ours in section 'D'. Suddenly twenty minutes feels as though it is a lifetime but it is twenty minutes I will spend with more hope than I have had all day. Perhaps Dr Brown will have the answer, perhaps she has knowledge or notes on her father's works, perhaps she will understand the missing links, perhaps, perhaps, perhaps.

I try to be professional but fail miserably. I

cannot find a new plan of attack on this latest problem. Stan has tried a new angle on the light neutrinos but again come up short watching his experiment fail before it began. I have scribbled notes and drawn diagrams but my heart is not in it, I need more information. I am just about to suggest to Stan that we have a break, perhaps a coffee or milk bar snack when the door to our lab whooshes open. My heart skips a beat at first but soon settles as I realise only ten minutes has passed, too soon for our expected guest. I see Stan's eyes widen in surprise as he looks over my shoulder towards the door. As he stares his face turns red and he looks quickly towards the floating screen over his own shoulder as though it is the most important thing in the room. I twist slowly on my stool to see what has caused such a reaction and find myself understanding why Stan reacted as he did. Standing in the doorway now dressed in a white lab coat was none other than the mystery woman from my bed this morning. Images spring into my memory and I cough as I stand straightening my own lab coat around my thighs.

"Hi." I say as brightly as I can, instantly regretting my choice of the word 'hi' recognising it as the immature welcome of a tongue tied schoolboy.

"Hi yourself Doc'." She smiles sweetly "Erm." She begins, her attitude one of embarrassment "We need to talk." Unsure how to answer I simply nod in affirmation

"Yes," I say eventually, "Yes I suppose we do." I try my own smile, it does not seem to have the required effect as I see the look of confusion cross her face. I try again summoning every effort, "Yes we definitely need to chat. I had a great time." I remember the word 'nice' she used and wonder if I have just overplayed what occurred? I push on regardless "We really do need to chat. I would like nothing more than that, but now is not a good time." I hear myself and change tac "No honestly I would like to give you quality time for a discussion, to see where we are, let us meet up when I have more of the 'said quality time' to offer eh." I realise I am sounding pompous but plough on stoically "How about later this evening for a drink, something to eat. Say seven thirty?" Again my words fall short of their intended mark, she steps closer towards me shaking her head.

"No Doc'."

"Professor, it's Professor."

"Yes I know but I love the look in your eyes every time I say that." She smiles "I think Doc'," Her smile broadens, God she has a great smile. I inwardly shake my head and try to focus on what she is saying. "No Doc', we need to talk now." She steps past me and holds out her hand to Stan "Hi there, good to meet you again. Professor Stanislav Andropov I believe?" I notice, a little irked that she has Stan's title correct. She shakes his hand warmly looking around the lab. Stan reddens again either by her presence or her touch I am not certain.

"So how does seven thirty sound?" I say looking at my watch conscious of the time ticking along. "My place, or shall we say the canteen." I add quickly not wanting to appear too forward although perhaps that horse has already bolted. Again she smiles and shakes her head.

"No Doc'. We need to talk now." My stomach churns as a sudden thought takes hold. I hope that she isn't one of those crazy people who stalk their new conquest relentlessly, never hesitating to post messages and photos of themselves throughout their victims private message supplier. I try again, keeping my attitude light and airy.

"Its not that I don't want to chat, it's just that I have an important meeting in...." Again I look at my watch, more for the theatre of it than necessity. "Five minutes now." She walks towards me and raises her hand to her breast pocket pulling the name badge on its extendable cord close to my face.

"Yes Doc' exactly." She puts her head to one side and holds out her hand. "Let me introduce myself I am Dr Betty Brown. I believe you were expecting me?"

We sit quietly around the workbench, I nibble at the coffee bar, Stan cuts his milk bar into bite sized pieces and Betty, sips at the old fashioned concoction of steaming hot water poured over a coffee bar creating a mix of brown liquid lightened with a small piece of milk bar. She blows at the thin tendril of steam that rises ominously towards the high ceiling of our cold laboratory. The initial embarrassment was I realise more for myself than Betty who it seems has quickly put the whole episode of this morning or was it late last night into context.

"Look Ian, we are two single people heading at a most frightening pace towards our own mortal end. We found a connection all be it through a stupor of alcohol. We took full advantage of each other, we had a good time, who's going to judge us? This is going on all over the world in every research facility and government department. People who are in the know will not sit back and use the last weeks or days of their lives like saints, why should they? Relax, enjoy every single moment left to us." She grabs my knee and leans close her mouth almost touching my ear, "Who knows, the mood may take us again and this time we can enjoy it sober." She pulls away laughing and sips at her drink, "By the way I love your aroma, what is it apple blossom?"

"Yes it is." I say knowing full well her understanding of what has occurred.

"So as I understand it." Her tone changes in an instant and she takes another sip of her drink, "You asked me here as the daughter of Professor Narwoo." Stan pops another nougat of his milk bar into his mouth and talks around the morsel

"Yes, you are her no?" Betty nods affirmation. "You worked close by his side, on his work." It was a statement but Betty nods again a small frown wrinkling her oh so smooth complexion. "You have knowledge of his thoughts, how he moved his experiments. You have pages we have not seen his notes perhaps?" Stan begins firing questions towards her barely breaking for breath. "He tell you how he planned to move forward, he had you in his confidence?" Betty places her mug on the workbench and faces us both evenly.

"I am sorry to disappoint you but this is not the case. My father was an arrogant man, he barely spoke to me about his work instead leaving me the menial observations and low level note writing as my tasks. Unlike the fiction that has become my fathers legacy he was hard to work with, an egotist who shielded his work from others as though he was protecting his very life itself. No-one had eyes on his work until the day it was published as a paper and even then protective clauses were written into it maintaining future development for himself only. I am afraid that if you are looking for answers within my fathers discoveries everything you have is everything there is." She sits back on her stool and drains the last of the liquid from the mug. "I am sorry. I really am." Stan shares a momentary glance of disbelief with me before staring down hopelessly at the screen before him. We had banked on this, we had believed that yet again here was the final glimpse of hope, the final crack into surviving our destruction.

"But you followed him into science. He says in his diaries that you had a thirst for knowledge and learning." Betty gives a bark of disgust.

"Yes I read that too." She picks up the mug and realising it is empty places it heavily back to the bench "I advanced my keenness for science despite my father not because of him. I wanted to learn, that much is true but I did not want to be like him. I wanted to be liked for not being him. If my works were going to change the lives of people I wanted people to come on the journey with me. I wanted to make a difference in the world for the good of all and not at the expense of anyone." She stops talking anger, flaring in her eyes and breaths heavily to bring herself back under control.

"It seems you are as much your mother as you are your father after all." I say sadly but genuinely. No-one answers. Stan pushes his stool back noisily and approaches the floating screen studying again the flashing symbols.

"So again we are at the point where all is dead in the sea." Betty looks at me with a shrug of her shoulders,

"Dead in the water. He means dead in the water." We both smile sadly finding no real humour in what at any other time would have been comedic gold.

"Do you know what I would really like?" She speaks slowly as though only just realising her thoughts herself

"No." I'm not sure she wants an answer but I need to say something, I need to feel alive in this moment.

"I would like to take an evening off, have an evening to myself, wrap myself in nothing but a blanket and go up into the fresh air of outside. I want to open the blanket and stand naked against the elements, feel the wind on my skin and to celebrate being alive as our ancestors celebrated their lives." I choke over the mouthful of coffee bar picturing her naked to the elements or in truth, just naked.

"Seriously! You would stand naked outside. Who does that?" Her look is pure, full of an angelic quality.

"I would." I am aghast, this is an alien thought to me, nakedness is to be done in the privacy of your own room, shared with only those who you wish to see it.

"You would do that?" I sound more prudish than I had intended "Without clothes?"

"She wears no knickers." Stan does not turn from the floating board but I can tell he has been listening as the redness around his cheeks is embarrassment not heat. Betty laughs towards him.

"Ahh yes I see how you can think that Stanislav, but I can assure you I am in fact wearing knickers now." She crosses her arms over her chest as though hugging herself and stares up towards the ceiling of our laboratory and speaks again her voice wistful against the humming of the computers. "I don't know about you but honestly I have had enough of waiting here low in the ground waiting to die. I want to go out on my own terms, I want to be in control. Our ancestors were born, raised and died as naked as was natural, I want to do that. They worshipped the sun and the moon alike, not through telescopes live fed from high above our heads but there on the ground. They would stand, arms spread wide waiting for the sun to rise. Together they would live their days ruled by the warmth of the sun until it wained from their view only to be replaced by their second God, the moon. How many times have we heard of the pagan celebrations at the altar of Stonehenge before it was moved to the Museum of Ancient Man, in India. Grown men and women would dance naked in the reflected light of the moon worshiping as their forebears had from the earliest of times. I would like to offer my own dance to that goddess of the sky. I would forego the sun who brings us death and fill my soul with the love of the moon." She glares at me daring me to speak against her but I am transfixed. Her words have moved me, tugged at my heart but most importantly my brain. I am thinking, my pulse is flowing, lights zip and crack in my vision.

"Could it be that simple?" Although my words are not spoken to Betty directly she takes up the cue.

"Yes, nakedness is the chance to ground yourself, to be at one with nature and to centre your soul. What better way to do that than before the gods of old in our last days?" I ignore her and push away from the bench sending my stool crashing to the floor.

"Stan. Can it be that simple?" Stan looks towards me his face mirroring my own confusion from earlier as he laid out his own ideas and theories. "Do you not see? The answer has been here the whole time. We are as they say, reinventing the wheel." I dash towards the floating screen and wipe the last mocking figures from its surface talking to myself as I do so. "It was right there all the time. We need more power, something larger. It comes no bigger than the moon. It's about reversing the light neutrons." I begin to scribble notes in the air and they are replicated on the screen for the two other occupants of the room to see. "Stan, build the model to these specifications." I write and speak at the same time. Stan is soon joined by Betty although I am at first unaware of this. Together they move the molecule pieces into different formations adding some and subtracting others as I write. When I am lost in a fugue of concentration Stan knows not to disturb me. He understands that it is better not to ask questions or make suggestions. He knows that these can come later, for now he just follows my lead. We work in this way for many hours. I design theories and alter mathematical equations, Stan and Betty move the pieces to match. Hour after hour passes until eventually I fall silent spent of energy and idea alike. I face the two exhausted people and then look back towards the screen. I feel my legs buckle beneath me and I sink to the floor part in my own deep exhaustion, part in frustration. "I am so close Stan, so close." I look at my friend who nods agreement.

"I understand Ian. It is the closest we have been." We both look at the screen reworking in our minds the processes we have been through. Betty sits cross legged on the floor her eyes heavy lidded with fatigue watching us intently.

"I do not understand, well not all of it." She points at the first half of the board, "This section here is about the moon, I understand that, after all it is my area of expertise." She purses her lips before continuing, her face a picture of concentration. "The moon is a reflector, it has no light of its own, merely showing us the power of the sun. Again this is a simple basic understanding, the sun stops shining, the moon becomes a dark ball in space. Obvious. No it is this next part I do not understand." She looks at myself and Stan "I am sorry to say but your calculations on this next part are outside of my knowledge base." She waves her hand in a maybe gesture "Is it an attempt to retrace the suns beam, follow it in reverse?" Stan, who is the only one left standing points at a set of figures his hand trembling with effort.

"You are correct, in a simplified way. I understand where Ian found inspiration for his hypothesise. You mention the moon and standing in its reflected light, am I correct Ian?" I raise a hand to acknowledge his process. "Ian understood in that moment that we had no need to build a reflector that would carry the light neutrons back the way they came, back towards the sun. We had a purpose built reflector, built not by mankind but by nature herself." He waved his hand towards the ceiling of our laboratory to emphasise his point, "We have a reflector, the moon." Stanislav drops his voice to an almost reverential tone, the tone he used when he was working through his own thought pattern, pulling his words together making them into complete sentences. "If Ian's calculations are correct." He begins with a nod, "then we should be able to return the light neutrons back to the sun as they had originally began, newly formed and full of their own vitality full of their own youthfulness." He glances quickly towards us, probably aware that his words give the neutrinos an almost human quality, an identity that made them not what they were but perhaps small children fighting for our existence. I smile at my friend offering encouragement, there was something almost comforting in his analogy however unintentionally it had been made. Stan for his part accepted the humanisation of the neutrinos as perhaps no more than fatigue or his inability to sometimes find the correct words in English to keep up with the lightening speed of his own powerful brain. Closing his eyes to regain his thought patterns he continues again with his synopsis, "The neutrinos would return back along their original pathway, back to the sun, back to where they are." He punches one large fist into his open palm, "Back to waiting to be born." He opens his eyes and I see the familiar brightness of discovery firing his pupils, the prospect of invention setting aflame the beacon of science that is Stanislav. "To keep the neutrinos as they are in this way could... No!" He slows and corrects himself "Should, should reverse the ageing nature that is occurring." Leaning against the workbench Stan speaks more to himself than to us, using this time to reassert his own certainty in what he understands. "I am speaking simply, using small words to carry immense ideas. My language, why it belittles what is genius." He makes a small snorting sound but continues to speak through his thoughts. "In the basest of forms what has been discovered here today is that if, and here I again change my words and say 'when', the ageing nature of these neutrinos is reversed it will be as though they have not yet come into being, they are awaiting to be newly born, they are yet to be." His voice grows louder, not a shout or a roar, but a battle cry, a voice filled with the power of belief and certainty "And so if these neutrinos have not yet been in existence then they in simple terms, cannot be dying. They are waiting to be newly born, waiting to start agin, to bring new life to what is dying." Betty nods slowly trying to understand and yet I am certain she does not fully understand the magnitude of what she is hearing, how could she? This as she herself said is too far beyond her area of expertise. This is science in its newest form. This is greater than anything Stan and myself have ever witnessed or worked on before. What Stan is trying to explain with a simplicity that almost defeats him is perhaps to be the greatest potential discovery in science for generations. Caught in the moment and oblivious of Betty's obvious confusion Stan continues, "We, with enough light neutrons reversed, are turning back time, we will have the ability to travel backwards through our own timeline. We will become time travellers." He stops speaking as the words he has spoken settle over the room holding us in silence. "Just think Betty, if we can travel back through time just far enough we will have the ability to change our destiny, we will have the ability to make use of our own satellites, equip them to send us messages here in our future when the sun first loses its power. The messages will inform us of the breakthrough we have made using your fathers works. What we have learned here, now, will be sent back to us and we will hear a message from ourselves on our own computers. These messages will give us the answer we need. It will enable us to buy ourselves the time we need to fully build a reversing screen that will by design continuously takes a fraction of the suns own power and reverses it to fill the hole that starts to grow. What is our now will become our past, but in this past we will have the new information waiting for us to stop the sun dying as we watch. What is done here today, saves us all yesterday!" He steps towards us and spreads his hands wide, a prophet descending a mountain, "You see?" He stands back proudly, reminding me of a party magician I once saw as a child shouting 'Da da!' And awaiting his applause.

"No not quite." The three words although quietly spoken physically deflate Stan's spirit and he looks wide eyed towards me directly for assistance.

"What Stan is saying." I begin hearing the tiredness in my voice "is that we use the moon to reflect back some of the suns old energy to create new energy for itself. We do this by moving the whole planet back in time. Effectively we have just created time travel but not for an individual, no, what we have created is time travel for everything in existence."

"You my friend Ian!" Stan almost bellows the words, "It is you who has created time travel." He suddenly slumps before me and lays a large heavy hand on my shoulder and I am sure I see tears in his eyes before he speaks "Ahh, such a shame." He makes a sound as though kissing his teeth together "A shame that it is all to be wasted effort." He shrugs dejectedly "As you say it is all a pile of excrement no?" Despite his sadness I smile up at my faithful and dedicated friend.

"Close enough Stan, close enough."

"Why, why is it a wasted effort, what are we missing." Betty springs from the floor and rushes to the screen pointing wildly, "You said it yourself, we have the moon, you have the theory behind the neutrons, you can send them back. I do not fully understand your theories or for that matter your very long winded explanations Stan, but they sound solid. So why are they wasted?" There are tears in her eyes, I am not sure if they are tears anger or fear but she does not wipe them away. "If we are so close what's stopping you, us, from making this work. We could save the world, people will not have to die, I will not have to die. Ian I don't want to die!" I hear her plea, I recognise it in myself but understand yet again that I have failed.

"No-one wants to die Betty, especially me, but...." I try to make her understand, I try to keep it simple. "The plan is good except for one small issue." I pull myself wearily to standing and move to the workbench, igniting the screen on its surface "Here are the notes from your father's experiments. He found a way to reverse the light neutrons. We have achieved this with the use of the moon. He had to calculate exactly the amount of power needed to return the neutrons to enable the amoeba backwards through time. My calculations here on the floating screen achieve that. Your father had to build a conductor or conduit to carry the neutrons on a stable path back to where they originated. Now here is our problem. I have no chance of building the same equipment on such a massively large scale. I have no way to reproduce the system your father discovered." I lean against the worktop fighting weariness, fighting the want to scream. "I am sorry that yet again I have offered false hope. I should have reverse engineered my thoughts before leading you both on this false trail. I should have started where it ends not where it begins. If I had done so I would have seen the flaws, the impossibility of my idea, understood the errors. I feel such a fool" I hear Betty start to speak but her emotion is too heavy, her words can offer no comfort. Needing to be alone in the confines of the laboratory which now seems so small I turn from them and face the floating screen staring through the words into the furthest corner of the laboratory. With sudden dismay guiding my hand I write furiously towards the screen seeing the words appear as solid lines of script at the bottom of our calculations. **A conduit for guiding. impossible!'** Feeling nauseous I walk towards the small sink behind me and splash cold water on my face hoping to calm my thoughts, to gain control of myself.

"Ian I have a proposal." Stanislav stares solemnly at the screen. I cut him off not needing platitudes.

"I am sure your plan is good my friend but alas we have no more time." He faces me, a strange look upon his face.

"Oh there is much time for 'this' plan. I shall not be many moments." Without another word he walks silently from the laboratory accompanied by nothing but the hiss of the door. The room feels empty somehow with Stan's departure but we stand together unable to speak, scared of what we would say. Betty sighs once wiping the remnants of her wasted tears and lays her hand gently on mine squeezing my fingers in her own. We stand like this for many moments content with the human contact until the door opens again and Stanislav approaches carrying three glasses and a bottle of unopened Vodka.

"I was saving this for a wet day. Perhaps this is the day filled with rain, no?" With the reverence of a priest opening a holy book he unscrews the cap and I hear the satisfying crack as the seal breaks. He pours healthy measures into each glass and raises one glass for himself into the air "Na Zdrovie!" He chugs the drink down in one and slams the glass onto the table. I need no second invite. I grab my own glass and follow with the shout of 'cheers' and take a quick swallow of the clear liquid which burns my throat satisfyingly. I watch as beside me Betty raises her own glass and shouts 'Slainte Mhath!' and swallows the liquid with a gusto that puts me to shame. The look of satisfaction on her face is soon replaced with a look of disgust as she too experiences the caustic after burn. During the next half an hour we consume probably more vodka than is good for us but we do not care, we are alive and going to enjoy that feeling for as long as it lasts.

"I once went to a nightclub where bartenders used to set vodka on fire in your glass." Betty is sitting on the floor, legs outstretched back against the wall of the laboratory nestling the glass in her hand. The lab coat she had been wearing is now rolled up behind her head as a makeshift pillow.

"Really?" Stan seemed perplexed by the very thought of setting a match to his precious drink. "Why would they do that. What would be the purpose of this?" Betty shrugs,

"Oh I don't know. It did look pretty in the darkness of the club though, and once it had gone out the warming sensation seemed somewhat smoother. Perhaps the alcohol had burned off a little." She added with a tired smile.

"A waste." Stan pours another large measure into his glass and throws it roughly down his throat." I was surprised that a man who claimed to be against an alcoholic drink in any way managed to remain looking so sober. I looked at my own glass and sighed.

"I could do with something pretty right now." I held an apologetic hand up towards Betty who made a strangled squeaking sound from her position on the floor. "I'm sorry I didn't mean that you were not pretty I just meant…." The look of terror on my face started Betty laughing and was soon joined by Stan, who totally against character began chanting "Ian thinks Betty is not pretty." I could not help but to find the laughter infectious, aided I think by Stan's very shuffling dance that floated somewhere between drunken dad and an old film star from the black and white era. I laughed so hard that I soon found myself holding my stomach for relief. We all understood in that moment that we were laughing harder than perhaps the occasion warranted, perhaps fuelled by the alcohol, perhaps by our own impending doom which seemed to be rushing towards us, but we didn't care. As the laughter died away with a series of 'ahh's and 'oh dear oh dear's' I finally pushed myself away from the workbench

"I think that perhaps we should give it a try, the lighting thing." I said and moved to a large cupboard and pulling a very old Bunsen burner from its lonely position on the top shelf.

"You still have one of those? God I thought they went out of use before mobile phones." Betty stared at the ancient piece of equipment in my hand her eyes wide with excitement. I nodded proudly

"Yes. It's an antique circa 1980. I bought it at first as a decoration for my flat, but found it useful once some years ago in an experiment that needed live flame. I've adapted the tube." I waved the orange rubber tube in her direction keen to display the attachment I had added. "This here." I point almost lovingly at the small metal component. "Connects to the air heat pump and converts it to real flame. Clever eh?" Stan raises his glass and with a shout of

"Genius!" Takes another shot of Vodka. Without waiting Betty and myself join the salute and again begin giggling. I attach the rubber tube to the air heat pump and flick the switch. I love the sound of the flame as it burns bright and warm. There is something soothing, something ancient, something dangerous about it. Without waiting I reduce the flame and touch it gently to the top of my glass which Stan has filled again to the brim. I stand back awe struck as the liquid ignites and sends a flickering finger of blue light up from the rim. This blue vision dances seductively around the rim of the glass seeming to wave its intent with delightful allure.

"It, is… beautiful." Stan moves closer to my side and speaks in a whisper as though in the presence of a Goddess. "Lights out." He whispers never moving his gaze from the flame. The lights in the laboratory extinguish and the flame becomes brighter, almost painful to stare at, bewitching us. I am certain now that this, such a simple event is somehow being heightened by the effects of Stan's powerful vodka and yet even I hear my own voice crack with emotion as I speak,

"Just look at the beauty dance. It is like space itself, in a glass." I have not noticed but Betty has moved silently beside me. She rests her head lightly on my shoulder filling my nose with the sweet scent of her hair.

"It is better than I remember it to be." Without realising I am doing so I move to pick the glass up, unsure whether I want to just hold this magnificent being in my hands or to swallow it deep within me. Betty stops my movement, laying a gentle hand on my forearm.

"Don't." She says "You must extinguish the flame before you drink it." She takes the glass from my hand, placing it back on the workbench. Reaching for a petri dish she lays it over the glass waiting for the flame to extinguish. I feel an immediate sense of surging disappointment as the small flame disappears from sight but before I have time to dwell on this emotion Betty thrusts the glass into my hand and whispers seductively, "Drink it now." I raise the glass greedily to my lips and swallow the contents quickly. I stand for a few moments expecting... What? I am not certain.

"Erm." I begin "It doesn't really taste much different." My disappointment is palpable. "Perhaps a little warmer, but it's nothing.... spectacular." The disappointment must be written on my face for as the lights of the laboratory blast to life on Stan's command Betty begins to giggle.

"Mmm I know." She says brightly, "I did say it looked beautiful. I did not say that it tasted any better."

"You see. Just a waste yes?" There is something mocking in how Stan speaks, an almost childlike pleasure in seeing my disappointment. I want to ignore his remark, we are after all in the grip of alcohol just as we are overtired, stressed and only moments away it seems from our own impending doom, but I cannot.

"Perhaps if we had used a real spirit, something like whisky perhaps, the taste would have been enhanced?" I smile wickedly knowing that Stan has no taste for whisky calling it, 'burning smoke.' Stan reacts immediately as I know he will

"Vodka, my friend is a real spirit. I shall not sully my throat to the ravages of your burning smoke. Whisky should be used for no more than cleaning the toilets of the wealthy."

"And vodka should be used to clean the toilets of the poor." As I say this I raise my glass and take a large swallow of the vodka in a silent salute. Stan copies my movement and we both stand grinning at each other enjoying the schoolboy feel of the attack and riposte as we mock each other in friendly jest.

"Whisky is the water of life Stan just as it says in the name."

"As vodka is water itself." We both tilt our glasses in a salute towards each other and quickly fill them from the bottle before again swallowing deeply. I laugh through the warmth in my throat from drinking the clear liquid too quickly.

"And yet your water burns like fire itself. If I have too many more of these I shall definitely need more goats milk to calm the scalding to my throat." Stan smiles contentedly as he senses his victory close to hand.

"If my vodka burns like fire then your whisky warms only as gently as the tears of an old woman." He raises his glass again triumphantly "Vodka is the Tzar, whisky the peasant." I begin to protest but am stopped before I begin.

"Gentlemen. Please!" I am pulled away from our brief moment of lightness in what has been an otherwise gloomy day and realise that this is not the first time Betty has called to us. She has walked away from what I am sure she sees as overgrown children and is staring up at the floating screen a far away look on her face. She is with us in presence calling loudly to us as though she is a living breathing creature, whilst all the time she is nothing but a distant being far removed from our sphere. In unison and with an acknowledging nod that all which has been said in the last moments were words of fun with no intent to harm, we place our glasses on the workbench and move closer to her. I reach out a hand and place it softly on her arm as she had to me only moments before.

"Are you ok Betty, what is it?" Betty shrugs my hand away as though it is a distraction, an annoyance and points at the floating screen. As she points her manicured finger a quizzical look replaces the benign slackness that rested there before. I face the board but see nothing new, the equations remain the same, everything is as it was. I see Stan flicking between his notebook and the screen hoping to find a relevance at what Betty is pointing at but he too lacks any understanding. "I'm sorry, what is it that you are seeing?" She drops her hand to her side and turns slowly towards us a smile of pure brilliance crossing her face.

"Fire, Ian. Fire."

Three days have passed since Betty stood before that floating board. Her explanation had been so simple that both Stan and myself felt as though we should have kicked not only ourselves but each other for not seeing it earlier.

"Fire Ian. Fire." It had been so simple. Was it the flame dancing in the glass or the words Stan and I hurled at each other in our mock argument?

"If my vodka burns like fire then your whisky warms only as gently as the tears of an old woman." We were not sure what it had been but something in that moment had triggered her thoughts, filled her mind with a plan.

"You do not need to invent something as a guide for the neutrinos. We already have it. It already exists." When she pointed, she pointed it seemed not at our calculations on the board but at my words angrily scrawled at the bottom. Words which until now taunted me in their silence, words which cut me to the core. **'A conduit for guiding. Impossible!!!'** It took only moments for both Stan and myself to understand, what Betty had discovered. Fire could be our conduit, we could use fire to fight fire.

Hours pass quickly, food is consumed at our stations. Messages are sent and delivered to each department seeking answers. All focus is on the experimentation to make reality Betty's greatest discovery. Stan sends a message to me with his latest calculations and I nod in agreement, this is promising.

"Betty add these figures to the screen please and calculate the time difference between the need for the amount of light neutrinos in one hour raising the calculation by the power of five for each revolution." Stan those figures are great but just for certainty would you add a discrepancy of three to fully assimilate wind factors and potential solar flares." I bury my head over my desk screen and yawn tiredly. We are going to need answers within the next twenty four hours or we are going to have left it all far too late.

"Yes Madam president. We are as sure as we can be. Every number has been checked and everything leads to exactly the same findings. In all probability if the space shuttle can create our fire spiral directly from the surface of the moon to within five miles of the suns surface we can stimulate the neutrinos to flow backwards along the spiral. As the neutrinos engage with the sun the reversing should already have occurred. If our calculations are correct and I am certain they are, within forty minutes of beginning the process we should as a planet have been moved backwards through time approximately ten years." I look at the concerned face on my viewer and take a deep breath, "If all goes to plan, from where I am now we will be at least ten years in the past. My predecessor will through our efforts be receiving messages on her computer systems as will every known scientist around the world informing them all of the upcoming disaster. They will learn in our past of this situation from us here in their future. With our programme not only will they learn of what is about to unfold but also the answer to that exact problem." I expel the breath I have been unaware I was holding and look over my screen towards Stan and Betty who stand silently staring at me knowing there was now no other option.

"Is this our only answer Doctor Stone?" I stiffen slightly at the Presidents mistake over my title but decide that there are probably more pressing matters on her mind.

"Yes Madam President. It is the only answer we have." The sound of static buzzes from the screen as the silence fills precious minutes.

"Then this will have to be our plan of attack." Suravi Patel, President of the Allied Nations looks away from the screen and talks to someone who remains just out of sight. "Make everything clear to the crew of Voyager 27, shuttle. Yes." She pauses only momentarily considering a distorted and mumbled question from the offscreen figure. We must ask them to continue their work with haste. They must achieve all that is needed from them. The time has come to tell them everything. We can no longer keep them in the dark. Give them every detail as sent to us by Doctor Stone. Hold nothing back." She glances at an electronic screen in her hand before speaking again to the unseen figure, "Tell them that operation 'Stanbet Tunnel' must be achieved." I smile as the word 'Stanbet' enters her vocabulary but inwardly rejoice that at last my two loyal colleagues will receive some recognition. I avert my eyes from Stan and Betty as I am sure I will break into a very wide and truly unprofessional grin if we share a glance. "I must say this much Doctor, I am uncomfortable at the thought of messing with time in such a way but I see there is very little option." The President looks again at her small screen before facing me directly. "The crew of shuttle Voyager have been hard at work since first your plan was agreed. Now is the time however that these efforts must be doubled everything must be in complete readiness when the time comes." A figure of a man, the unseen conversationist I presume leans into the President and with little formality whispers close to her ear before stepping back into the shadows. "I have been informed that the President of America wishes to be updated on the progress of our plan. It appears he is only moments away from one of his rambling public announcements and wishes to be fully abreast of the fine work his countrymen are achieving aboard the shuttle." She briefly looks at the screen on her lap flicking idly at some information which no doubt continues to haunt her days as certainly as it terrifies our nights. "Doctor you have achieved so much for us all. Somehow a thank you seems to be so little a reward for all of your hard work." She stares hard into the lens as though willing me to feel her gaze more than just see it. "How odd it is that if this plan works we will never meet, never share these conversations. You will have no contact with many of the people who worked so well with you, shared, I am sure the most difficult and frustrating of times." She waves a hand towards the unseen figure as though dismissing an annoyance behind her. "If your plan works you will have provided future scientists or should that be past scientists the answers they need in the future." She blows a breath something that sounds like admiration. "I do not claim to fully understand how this happens and cannot reward you in any other way than to fully acknowledge your work and to thank you." She gives a wry smile "And of course if this plan does not work, well..." She tails off leaving the sentence unfinished. "I must depart now Doctor. I cannot in all good consciousness leave the President of America waiting, now can I?" She allows herself a small smile "Although in the briefness of time we will be back in the past and he will never know that I dared to make him wait." She laughs at her own humour and nods to the mysterious man beside her making ready to leave, "Oh Doctor." She sits herself back on the chair and leans towards the screen "Please pass on the worlds thanks to all of your dedicated team. Our gratitude can never be fully expressed but assure them the world truly recognises their diligence and sacrifice." She looks weary, more than her 53 years. Aged by responsibility or the knowledge that her decisions and quick action may have saved the world. "Doctor." Her voice shocks me from my musings "Will this truly work. Will we all survive?" I feel the lie form readily on my lips but I change my response before it is spoken.

"I hope so Madam President. I really hope so." The figure of the man reaches across the lens and extends an arm and the connection is broken. We stand in the silence feeling the terror that cracked our Presidents voice, a human like us after all.

"Stanbet. You called it Stanbet?" Betty is the first to speak bringing us back to our task. In answer I smile shyly

"Yes. It seemed fitting." Betty rushes towards me and smothers me in a tight embrace, kissing me warmly on the lips. Stan joins her grabbing my hand and pumping it in a shake that threatens to dislocate my arm from my shoulder.

"Thank you my friend, thank you. I do not deserve such honour as is what you have given me." We stand for a few moments comfortable in each others company, colleagues and friends, hopeful. A siren sounds over the internal speaker and lights flash across our screens showing a barrage of newly formed incoming messages. We read the message in earnest our faces mirroring the looks of fear that cross each of us.

"My God. No!" Betty recoils from her screen her hands clasped dramatically to her mouth.

"Ian, why now?" I look at the latest message sent to me from our furthest space station. 'Change in situation. All codes altered to critical. Sun imploding, repeat sun imploding.' I scan the repeated message looking for a time line, seeking out something positive. Stan as always seems to be one step ahead of me regaining his composure in his regimented way.

"Message A-7." He says flashing the message up on the floating screen. "It is from Station Alexi." I read the message quickly, making decisions as I read. 'Sun showing heightened activity. Potential to implode. Calculated advancement eight hours. Calculated outcome, devastation.' End message. I type quickly into my keyboard and wait for the message to flash crimson signifying a ready to receive signal. I press comms button on my screen and wait for the image to drift into focus.

"Hi there. Is that Professor Stone?" The voice so calm under what can only be extreme circumstances.

"Yes Professor Stone here. What is the situation?" From miles above us first pilot Chad Bowman grimaces a smile

"Well Prof' not good." His understatement is palpable as the picture shakes dramatically as the shuttle 'Voyager 27' rocks under some unseen barrage. "Things have gotten, well, a little hairy up here. I suppose you have seen the reports. It's not looking favourable." The picture rocks again but still this sturdy American remains calm, a first class leader. "Look we need to think again about your plan, what's it called Stanbet? A crazy name by the way." He shakes his head as though even now he has time to offer a choice over minute details.

"Think again?" I want to keep the fear I feel for him and the other five astronauts enclosed in the flimsiness of a space shuttle out of my voice. "There is no think again Chad. That was it. That was the plan." I calm my voice which I realise had raised itself over a few octaves, "Get out of there. Do your best to get home, perhaps see your families before it's too late. You have done all you can." I am shouting now, I know I am but I cannot help it my fear is at fever pitch.

"Hey relax there Prof', you are supposed to be the brains of the operation. If you go to pieces well then it really is all over." How in the name of Christ is this man staying so calm I ask myself, How can he be thinking so clearly? Stan waves a large hand towards me pointing to some figures on his screen, I read them quickly understanding the math.

"Sorry Chad, just had a bit of a wobble there." I try a half hearted grin feeling inferior to the astronaut in every way. "How far have you got with preparation for Stanbet?" I wait as Chad speaks to a female astronaut who floats silently into view clutching a clipboard.

"We are connected to the wires this end. Sue calculates another nine hours to fully extend and then two hours to fully ignite the spark, creating flame. How does that sit with what you know." Silence fills both ends of the communication, Chad's in patience, mine in regret.

"I'm sorry Chad." I manage to say "That will be about four hours too long. For the first time since we began our long distance conversation I see a flicker of emotion on the young man's face.

"Four hours? Jeees." He whistles softly "Are you sure Prof'?" I don't need to answer, he can see by my face that we are finished "Ok." He remains silent for a few moments his face locked in concentration, "That's if we follow the plan to the letter. What if we cut corners, what if we fly by the seat of our pants?" I am impressed, still planning still thinking. I look over towards Stan and Betty who are working side by side adding and deleting figures their faces frozen in concentration. "Well any thoughts Prof'?" Chad has been joined by another figure who passes a small screen to his Captain. Chad reads it thoughtfully then nods in acknowledgement.

"Don thinks we can cut half an hour if we do not fully extend the framework of wires towards the sun. Any good?" Stan immediately shakes his head and points towards my own screen. A pop up displays the maths.

"No. Sorry Chad. good idea but the distance from the sun is the one thing that cannot be altered.' Chad frowns calling quickly over his shoulder. "No Don that's a negative. Come on people keep thinking." He faces the camera and his figure sways as again the shuttle is buffeted. "Ok Prof'. we will keep thinking this end, you do your stuff your end, but make it quick eh?" His toothy smile fills the screen as his picture fades.

"It is the speed Ian, only the speed can change."

"I know Stan but how do we get the wires set and the fire to reach the end point any faster than we have calculated eh?" I stare at the messages which continually pop up on my screen each and every one of them harbingers of doom. I walk to the floating screen and close my eyes, not needing to read any of the calculations merely feeling their presence. It is all about speed. We somehow need to develop something that can deliver the wiring system at the very same time as initiating the spark that causes the flame in space. Each of these things needs to be done simultaneously, each event has to happen at the same time. I stop my thoughts where they sit and groan. 'Do not reinvent the wheel.' The words crash into me and I feel sick.

"Ian are you ok?" Betty watches me closely as I walk slowly back to my screen and allow my fingers to float over the keyboard autonomously. Within moments the calculations are set and the answer is revealed. I press the allow access to all notice and send the work to the floating screen unable to watch the reaction of Stan and Betty who turn and face me the horror obvious to any casual observer.

"Ok Prof'. We get it. Ma'am give me time to run this by the crew. We need to plot this correctly. Chad Bowman out." The picture fades leaving only the four remaining faces in view, my own, the President of the allied countries, the President of America and the representative of the dissolved nations.

"Well Dr Stone. Are we sure this is the only calculation?"

"It is a suicide mission."

"God grant them strength." The voices speak in unison a babble of noise. I stand mutely listening. There is no other way the three of us have manoeuvred the figures time and again, we checked and double checked hoping and praying that there may be some other answer, that another solution would make itself known to us.

"Professor Stone. We have run out of time, have we not?" At last she gets my title correct.

"Yes Ma'am."

"Then we are in the hands of those six brave people." Her voice is breathy, sad "We can do no more." Her statement hangs unanswered, heavy and dangerous. "I have matters to attend to, preparations to make, as I am sure we all have. I must impose on you for one final time Professor. I must ask you to confer with Captain Bowman. Inform him of the facts. Spare him no detail. Allow the Captain the time to make his choice." Without further discussion her picture fades quickly followed by the others ending their communications until only my face remains large on the screen. It seems that in times of trouble, power and position holds only one privilege, to roll the shit down hill and sit back. Reluctantly I call up Chad.

"Hey Prof', on your own?" I open the screen to 'all view' and the images of Stan and Betty join me "Hi there people." Chad is polite and yet now his face has taken on a heavy, thoughtful demeanour. "I assume you have been given the shitty end of the stick, been told to tell us what we already know?" When I do not answer Chad Bowman nods in simple acceptance. "Let me make this easy for you Doc.

We the crew have discussed it up here and like you, can see that there is no other option." He smiles, the teeth still shiny white but this time the eyes are flat with resignation. "You are the brains here, so why don't you talk us through exactly what it is we have to do."

"No." I say determined in my conviction. "I cannot ask you to do this." Stan and Betty nod in agreement our decision made.

"Hey Doc it's this or nothing. We know the score."

"But I am sending you to your certain death, you will all be killed…"

"Only this time Prof'." He stops me in my tracks "Only this time. Didn't you say that if this works we will be around in the past with ample time to set this thing up properly. Who else gets the chance to die twice and be a hero both times?" Now his smile feels genuine, now he feels alive across the vast distance. "Come on Prof' lay it out for us properly. Let's get this done."

All the world is watching, there is no going back. Our laboratory feels more like a film set than a place of work. In front of me is a camera operator, her long blond hair is tied back from her face revealing, round almost nordic features, her electric blue eyes burn into me. There is a frisson of quiet anxiety. A blue suited interviewer Harry Standon stands to one side of the camera operator speaking in hushed tones into a small microphone clipped to his chest.

"Now is zero hour. All that has been done to save the planet boils down to this moment. The great Doctor and his two trusted colleagues stand ready to press the button that will give us all chance of life. We are in their hands." I look at Stan who physically tries to shrink in size as the camera sweeps in his direction. Betty steps sharply sideways trying to avoid the cameras glare. "We wait with bated breath as high above us Captain Chad Bowman and his team no doubt ready themselves for a headlong dash towards death, a death that earns them the gratitude from all here on earth." In one swift action the news reporter clutches a microphone from the workbench between us and thrusts it hungrily towards me speaking as he does so. "Doctor Stone how does it feel to have calculated the formula that sends these brave souls directly to their death." I breath deeply trying hard to concentrate on every minutiae of what I am doing. "Come on Doctor Stone, a word or two for the watching people." Slowly I raise my eyes level to the intruding interviewer and blow out a long slow breath before I reply.

"If you don't mind it's Professor. Now Fuck off Harry!" As quickly as the microphone appeared it moves from my face and I can hear

Harry Standon making a hurried apology on my behalf. I look at Stan who raises two thumbs in a 'well done' gesture. With an explosion of noise from many miles above us the image of Chad Bowman comes into view on the floating screen.

"Wow Prof' quite the media circus down there." He is frowning and yet somehow managing to maintain a boyish charm. "We are all set this end. You give the word and we set off. The wires are spooled behind the shuttle. We reach our maximum velocity in nought point six seconds. As we strike the sun we press the button and 'boom' you have fire." He pauses. "Does that sound about right?" I can do no more than nod, how can I look this young man in the eye? I now know that if Harry Standon truly wants to know how this feels I can sum it up in one word, horrific. "Ok. Just give us the word Prof'." Before I can speak Harry Standon steps towards the screen followed by the camera operator.

"Hi Chad. Harry Standon here. Any last words for the viewing public?" I see Chad's eyes narrow but he is a military man, trained to perfection, he knows his role.

"Hi Mr Standon. Yes just a couple as I'm pretty pushed for time here. Jane I love you honey and see you back in high school ten years before now." He quickly turns his attention back to me his duty for reporters done. "Tell me when Prof'." I look at my small screen before nodding to Stan,

"Are you ready my friend?" Stan checks his notebook and nods once, his hands shaking violently.

"Yes I am ready." I look back to the image of the young man, the Captain of the Voyager. The dead man floating.

"Ok Chad. On my mark. Three, two, one. Go." I had not readied myself for this. A simple countdown and I was killing a man albeit for hopefully just under an hour. The picture on the screen shakes for a moment before the voice of Chad Bowman cuts through the idle chatter of Harry Standon who continues with his minute by minute description of events.

"We are go. Wires unravelling, all looks good. Speed is increasing to maximum, turbulence regulators on full, still as bumpy as hell. Direction on course, heat shields on half for next twenty minutes. Don check fuel levels after initial burst. All 'A' ok. Direction check again Simon, thank you. Monitors being switched off now folks no more peep show for you. See you when I was only just in my twenties. happy days." The screen goes blank. I have to concentrate, have to remain fully focused.

"Countdown Betty. Let Stan know

exactly when to send the message. We have to get this right." Betty starts her atomic clock timers, each set to specific points. Stan fiddles with his desk screen checking for the hundredth time his calculations. Time I have realised moves far quicker when something is about to end than when there is an excitement in somethings arrival. The intervals of time counted down by Betty come and go with frightening regularity, each count bringst a silence to the laboratory a silence that was thankfully respected by the irksome Harry Standon.

"Two to go Stan." Betty studies the two remaining timers intently, her eyes locked into position, all distractions ignored.

"Ready Stan?" I am superfluous at this point and yet I need to show them I am with them. A voice breaks the silence. "Professor Stone. If you can hear me, it's Angela Summers from moon observations." I looked quickly at Betty who gives a quick nod. It was one of her team. I press the intercom button and speak quietly.

"What is it Angela, We have asked for complete and total communication silence."

"The sun has sent a solar flare, the largest we have so far witnessed." I growl angrily.

"Of course it has, it's bloody dying up there. We expect as much...." When she speaks next her voice chills me to the core.

"Its heading to earth and its expected arrival is ten minutes from now, its impact point is definitely Scotland." I cut off her voice needing no more explanation.

"Stan?" I do not need to form the question, he is already answering.

"A solar flare strike here. We have no communication link to the satellite for perhaps twenty minutes. Our signal will not reach the satellite through the disturbance." I see Betty quickly calculate the remaining time needed.

"Fifteen minutes exactly Ian. The message must be sent in fifteen minutes." I work through the numbers certain that Stan is doing the very same thing.

"We must send early Stan, but how early?" For the first time I can ever remember the usually studious Russian shrugs.

"I cannot calculate that Ian. The time we need is the time we need. To send early, that is incalculable." He runs his fingers over the keyboard but pulls his hands away as though burned by heat. "The variables are too great for me to work with. Early is not perfect. Too early and the message arrives but could be distorted or wiped out entirely in our travel backwards through time. If we send it too late, well then, the message may not arrive at all." He stands solemnly at his work station a look of confusion his only companion. "I am afraid we will…" His face is a picture of confusion, he is about to make a statement that I am sure he has never uttered before. "Ian, we will have to guess."

"What is it you are guessing?" Unseen by the three of us the camera operator has moved nearer, her camera nowhere in sight. "I heard you say that you were going to guess. Does that mean your plan is not working. Are we all going to die?" Her smooth skin wrinkles in distress as large tears roll down her cheeks.

"The solar flare is going to cut communications to the satellite." Betty puts a consoling arm around the young woman shoulders. "But we will be ok. These two will work it out I'm certain of that." She gives an encouraging smile in our direction hoping to allay the woman's fears.

"What is this satellite, what is its job?" She is a better reporter than the man she follows around, her questions are direct and to the point. Betty takes a breath and points at the floating screen.

"Ian and Stan have created a stream of binary coding, this was coding used in computer language many years ago. This coded language will sit within this satellite. It was important to pick a satellite that was launched long before the date of the first discovery of the suns impending demise.

"Why?" The reporter shakes her head unable to fully understand, "Why can you just not pick any satellite or all of our satellites?" Betty points at some calculations on her screen "We had to pick a satellite that was already in place, we had to be sure that it was launched." The young woman shakes her head desperately trying to comprehend but unable to make sense of what she is hearing. Betty, who somehow seems frighteningly capable of remaining calm in this situation speaks reassuringly "We had to be certain that we picked a satellite that had been launched long enough ago that it would not be cancelled or altered and therefore not actually in our orbit when we needed it. Imagine if you can we chose a satellite that is launched only 5 years ago. What happens if in our past, decisions are made that change our present? Oh I don't know something like funding has to be pulled, well then, that satellite will never be launched and would be no use to us now, when we need it. By choosing a satellite that we know definitely launches because it pre-dates the time we are going back to, we will know it is set solidly in place because it is already there and working. The satellite we have chosen was launched over twenty years ago and fits perfectly our needs. The code Stan is sending has been programmed to believe that it has been siting in the satellites memory banks from the very moment it first began its journey into orbit. The satellite will believe that this programme is an essential part of its own memory." Betty flicks a finger across her screen opening a new page to a view of data for the young woman to read, "Look, here is the binary code Stan will be sending." The young woman stares at the screen her eyes wide with shock.

"But it's just numbers, 1's and 0's. I don't understand, how can that be a message?"

"I told you, it's binary code, an old computer language. We don't use it anymore, but fortunately Ian and Stan both understand how it works. We need the satellite to believe this is original code remember? We had to use what it would understand. Stan has also programmed a count down within the code he is sending to the satellite that will activate the message to be sent to all computers in our time. On the exact date as programmed the messages will come streaming in, it will be repeated every half an hour ceasing any work actively being used at that time. The message will flag itself as to us as vitally important. Once recognised it will give us in our time, now, the knowledge of how to put things right. You could say that we will have the answers before we need them, we will know exactly how to fix the sun."

"But you said that the solar flare will stop all of this vital information reaching the satellite at the correct time?" She doesn't wait for an answer but asks immediately. "So why not just send the information now, what is there to guess about. The satellite you want is already in space and can receive the information now? You said it was there waiting, you picked it because it was already there." Her voice was hysterical, her face reddening with emotion. Stan steps towards her, his own slab features open and honest.

"We have to choose the correct moment because we will be travelling back in time ourselves. If the code is released too early the satellite will try to release the code it holds almost immediately, thinking it has passed the time to start its send time." The camera operator shakes her head in confusion.

"But it is programmed not to do that." Stan attempts a smile but instead shrugs slowly,

"As I have said. Because the message in the satellite that will be sent to us here on earth will start sending the moment the satellite believes it reaches the required date. If we send it too late and the satellite thinks that now is the required date then it will start sending the message. This would be too late for us, we would miss the required information. We are here effectively forcing a message to travel from the future to the past to begin transmitting in its new future, this is an untested and unproven science. Our calculations show that there is an optimum time to send the message and an optimum date to send it too, but much is unknown. I trust our figures, I trust the maths, it is all we have, anything beyond this will be." He pauses, "Nothing but guesswork." Stan breathes deeply before offering the girl a shallow smile "I do not like guesswork." He finishes, before turning away from her, returning to his work station. I can see the girl struggling with the concept and take my last remaining piece of coffee bar from my pocket offering it to her.

"Please. I do not want to appear rude." I feel a sadness for this young woman, she is after all an innocent bystander caught up in a situation she has absolutely no control over. "We have to concentrate, we have to try to work this through." I call Stan to my side and whisper quietly into my oldest friends ear. "Stan, we have absolutely no chance of trying to calculate a new time line nor of understanding the concept of missing the mark." I place a hand on his shoulder feeling the muscles bunch beneath his lab coat, "I am afraid my friend that I have only one possible suggestion." I take a breath, "Do what you have feared the most and... Guess." I see the look of fear in Stan's eyes, I understand his thought process. Slowly his head nods forward, more surrender than acceptance.

"Yes Ian, I shall do this." He steps away from me but halts suddenly "We shall not know the result of my... Guess. We will not know the affect on the code if it is not received at what we know is the correct time. I will never know if I am successful, but I shall in these moments carry the weight of the fact that if my guess is incorrect, I and I alone will be responsible for the death of my truest friend." I do not hide the tears that flow freely from my eyes as Stan does not hide his.

"We are ten minutes from impact of the flare." Betty is standing with her arm around the camera operator studying the timer. "It is all yours Stan." I watch as Stan bends over his work station and counts slowly on his fingers, even now he is desperately trying to do the math, seeking out the equations. I join Betty and the young woman wrapping my arms around both of them, for my own comfort or for theirs I am not sure. I lean close to Betty and whisper softly into her ear breathing deeply her scent as I do so,

"I hope we meet again in the past Betty, it's been," I cannot help myself "Nice." She turns her face towards me and kisses me deeply.

"It certainly has Professor, it certainly has." Across the workbench Stan raises his head and faces us, holding our gaze.

"I guess it is about now my friends." He raises a finger dramatically and places it gently on the keyboard pressing the command button, 'send'. I close my eyes and try not to think of the space shuttle so far ahead of us hurtling towards oblivion in the sun.

A balloon pops! Or is it a cork escaping the neck of a bottle? The celebration from the office next to ours is in full swing now. Whatever it was, the popping sound, neither myself nor Stan could draw ourselves away from the chart in front of us. Can this be true. Could this really be about to happen?" Stan stares at me, the corner of his mouth giving that tell tale twitch, a nervous thing.

"Surely to God this must be wrong. We must check again!" I shake my head, abject fear causing beads of sweat to line my top lip even in the coolness of the air-conditioned room. We both know there is no mistake Our calculations are correct. Every digit and symbol checked and checked again. Nothing has been left to chance. Everything has been verified. The results are one hundred percent accurate, proven. We stare silently at each other across the metal topped work bench seeing our own terror mirrored in the face opposite. Two colleagues, friends alone with their thoughts and yet joined together as no two people have ever been joined before. At some point approximately mid day two weeks from now, the sun is going to explode and in doing so bring to an end all life for ever.

Beer, Chips and Conversation

Kev sat on the beach bar stool and gulped at his cold beer greedily. This was it, this is what he loved about his yearly trip to Benidorm. Two weeks of cheap, cold alcohol in large glasses, chips that arrived with every meal and the sun on his back which no doubt burned his pasty skin to a blistered red with every passing moment. He didn't care too much about the sunburn, the alcohol would numb that, along with the very frequent and very loud belly flops into the hotel pool before pulling his England football top over his head and taking his seat in the hotel restaurant for his all inclusive meal.

"Would you like another Señor?" This was something else he liked, waiters like Ramos. He didn't have to finish his pint before the young man was by his side offering him a refill.

"Yes mate, don't mind if I do." He watched as Ramos smiled that too bright smile, (the one that all the women in this bar seemed to find so appealing) before moving away with almost dance like steps. If he was honest he would have liked to have been on the sun bed in his hotel now, pint in hand, stretched out with nothing more in mind than when to flick the paddle connected to his arm rest to indicate another all inclusive drink was needed but Evie had wanted them to do something.

"Why don't we go and explore a little bit today?" She had said, "Why not go down to that little beach front market we so love?" Every year it was the same thing, first Thursday of their holiday and he had to walk the 10 minutes to the market to sit by a bar where he had to pay for the food and drinks. He would sit and wait for her knowing that she would be wandering around in an almost hypnotised trance drawn like a magpie to shiny things to the tat that glittered amongst the shaded stalls whilst over friendly vendors would smile their encouraging smiles and nodding in satisfaction as she parted with his hard earned Euros.

"Pero la amo mas que a la vida misma!" The voice of the young man seated at the table next to him rose above the sound of the waves and the call of the gulls. Kev was drawn more to the sound of the voice than the words themselves not surprising as he couldn't understand any of their foreign gibberish, why should he? They all spoke perfect English. He leaned forward and listened catching snatches of the mans words ".. rompe el corazon... no estoy con ella!" The young mans voice was pleading, his face a picture of agony. The young man finished speaking and the guttural sound of his older companion broke in, drowning the sounds around him.

"Eso es.... es el amor... mi amigo... suelo próstata..." As he spoke he threw back his head and laughed the sound harsh and uncaring. The young man grabbed his older companion by the arm and stared urgently into his eyes uncaring of anyone including Kev who sat open mouthed watching this open air performance before him. Again the words came to Kev's ears broken and staccato against the sound of the crashing waves, the call of the gulls and the screams of holidaymakers who filled the sand in rows of cooking flesh and exuberant, beer fuelled enjoyment.

"Pero que si ella me....no siente lo mismo?" The laughing friend suddenly became sterner in his response, his thick brow furrowing with concentration.

"Amiga mia... no seas el burro... solo por miedo... compañera verdadera." As he finished talking the gruff man pushed hard at the first mans shoulder rocking him hard in his seat "Ve ahora..." As he finished speaking he thrust his chin sharply forward in a sign of dismissal "Ve ahora!" Without waiting for what was obviously further rebuke, the young man rushed from his seat and ran from the bar stumbling along the sand calling loudly.

"amo, amo!" Kev sat back on his stool and whistled, a dull nasally sound before draining the last of his pint.

"What a spectacle!" He wiped his hand over his short cropped hair and wiped the sweat on his naked belly

"Here we are Señor." The waiter placed a small paper beer mat on the table and sat the cool glass of liquid on top of it. "Can I fetch you anything else?" Again he flashed the too bright smile and wiped a delicate hand through the sheen of his jet black hair. Kev pulled his bucket hat from the pocket of his shorts and placed it on his head, he was it seemed, here for the long haul. No sign of Evie yet.

"No thanks Ramos, I'm good." The waiter turned to leave signalling to a second waiter that the table nearest him needed to be cleared of empty plates as a group of aged, leather skinned women hobbled from the taverner on high heeled shoes better suited to dance halls than a beach front bar. "I tell you what though mate." Kev's words halted Ramos who twisted towards him in one easy movement.

"Señor?" His face was a picture of attentiveness, ever eager to show complete dedication to any guest who was surely prepared to spend as many Euros as this customer was.

"You Spaniards certainly don't give a toss where you have a row do you?" The waiter shrugged with only a momentary frown crossing his face.

"Señor?" Kev pointed towards the older of the two men who sat alone now slowly finishing the glass of wine he held lightly in his large hand.

"The fella there." He jerked his head towards the lone figure, "He certainly seemed to put that youngster in his place, proper row they were having. Surprised you let them get away with it. Not a great advert for a welcoming atmosphere is it?" Kev reached for the glass that was already slick with a sheen of condensation and slurped noisily wiping his mouth on the back of his hand. "That sort of noise is enough to put anyone off." As they watched, the elder man placed his now empty wine glass on the table and silently rose to leave dropping some money onto the table as he sauntered away. "Look at him as cool as you like. Talk about ice cold." The young waiter smiled easily and leaned lightly against the table.

"Ahh Señor. It appears you do not understand what it is you have just witnessed." He pointed quickly along the beach in the direction the younger man had taken, "Our young friend was expressing his love for a young lady he obviously had his heart set upon. He spoke of his love for her being more than life itself. He told his friend that his heart breaks when he is not with her. His friend, who I say is his example, his… his… how do you say, his go on?" He shook his head "No his go to, his friend who is his go to, told him to throw himself on the floor before her, to lay prostrate and tell her of his love for her. The young man showed fear and asked 'what if she does not feel the same?' His go to friend replied that she, the girl he loved was his own sister and that he knew of her feelings well and that she did love him the young man." Kev shook his head.

"But he grabbed him, the older man grabbed him." Ramos smiled

"Yes Señor, he did grab him. He told him to not be the donkey who wanders lonely for fear of calling to its one true mate. He sent him on his way telling him to show her his love." Kev whistled again a sound of amazement.

"But the man ran off calling something that sounded as though it were a call for help. The older fella was so gruff." Again the waiter smiled,

"Ah Señor you forget. We are Spaniards, we are a truly passionate people, we speak with our hearts. Where love is concerned and true love at that, we feel the blood pump through our veins. We are brave in our quest of true love and will fight for the gift love bestows upon us. The young man needed his guidance, he needed to be spurred into action, his friend showed him the way and in the heat of passion he ran to his love across the sand, not in a call of fear but with the call of 'I love her! On his lips." Ramos finished speaking and smiled wistfully into the distance "Ah it was the same when first I met my own dear Valentina." He focused again on Kev who sat silent, his mouth open as though to catch the slightest moisture in the air. "I say Señor, you English men could learn much in the study of love if only you followed our lead. Let your hearts not your heads rule your love. Allow your words to caress the woman you love, allow your every breath towards her be a word spoken in that love, and then and only then, shall you truly know how to conquer her heart." With a flick of his hips Ramos moved quickly aside heading to the table of three young women who sighed in unison as he smiled down on them, holding each of them in his gaze as though his smile was for them and them alone.

"Kev. Look what I got. Bargain!" Evie had arrived at his side clutching a string of brightly coloured beads and some garishly patterned material, "Honestly that market just gets better and they are all so friendly." Kev swallowed the last of his beer and placed the glass carefully back on the table. With a sideways glance towards Ramos, who just for the briefest of moments looked up from his salacious encounter with the girls at the table and gave a small nod in Kev's direction. As though reaching for his pool cue Kev took Evie by the hand. He wasn't sure why, but in that moment he suddenly felt the flow of romance surging through him. Was this feeling spurred on by the sun, the sound of the sea or the words of Ramos words which seemed to wrap themselves tightly around him in a comforting embrace? He wasn't sure. What he did know was that he had to seize this moment for all it was worth.

"Christ that bikini looks great on you Evie'. He smiled brightly, "You look proper bangable." Dropping a large tip on the table and a wink towards the smiling Ramos, Kev strutted along the beach Evie chattering happily beside him. Pulling the bucket hat low over his eyes Kev wiped the sweat from under his armpits and smiled.

"Who says the Brits don't understand romance?" He mumbled taking Evie by the hand.

The Potting Shed

"You've had another good year Charlie. What was it in the end, 3 firsts and 2 seconds?" Charlie stared through the open doorway of the potting shed, absently watching the rain that fell in a steady stream, soaking the rich soil of his allotment.

"4 firsts and 3 second places." There was no boast in his voice he didn't boast, wasn't his way. With a shrug he sighed deeply, resigned. He took a long gulp from the glass tankard nestled in his large work-worn hand savouring the taste.

"That's right I was forgetting the onions." Beside him Maurice settled back into the worn fabric of the deck chair and took a gulp of his own beer, falling silent, lost deep in thought. Both men remained motionless side by side for many minutes, comfortable with the silence that had descended in the close confines of the potting shed, both content with the company they kept. Conscious of the rain, comforted by the sound.

"Disappointing crop of runners this year." Charlie's voice was deep and slow, resonating in time with the beat of the rain. As though acknowledging the beat Maurice nodded slowly

"Mmm. Black fly did for mine." He agreed without haste "Well that and the rain when I first set them out. Poor buggers didn't have a chance.'

"No." Agreed Charlie "Not a chance."

"Shame really. I've always done well with runners." With the groan of age, Maurice reached beneath the deck chair and retrieved a single bottle. Pushing two fingers into the watch pocket of the old waist coat he always wore he plucked the worn bottle opener manoeuvring it deftly into place and clicked the cap free, tossing it into the small metal bin that stood acceptingly at arms length from where he sat. Without looking, he passed Charlie the bottle and accompanied by the same guttural grunt and the patter of rain duplicated the same routine. In what could, if observed by a casual passer by have been called synchronised movements, each man filled his tankard and placed the empty bottle at their feet joining an earlier victim of their initial thirst silently. Satisfied that the dark liquid was settling correctly both men nestled themselves comfortably back in their seats continuing the silence that bound them together.

"3 beers on a Wednesday." Charlie tilted his tankard slightly towards his friend, a salute.

"Yes. Seems right though."

"Yes seems right." Both men took a swallow of the ale making the obligatory "Ahh." The sound of satisfaction, before resting their tankards comfortably back to their starting positions. Outside the rain momentarily eased before taking up its now familiar patter. The two men sat staring through the open doorway hardened to the cold wind that sought them out, held their silence oblivious to anything except their own deep thoughts.

"You manuring next week?" Maurice made the usual 'Ahh' the noise of consideration

"Thinking of it." He answered eventually "Depends on this rain really." He nodded towards the doorway as though needing to point out to his friend the conditions they could both hear "Forecast says cold spell on the way. If this rain eases I shall get it dug in and let the frost do its work. After that, in a month or so, I will give it another good turn over and let it rest for the winter. It seems to work." It was a long speech by their standard and deserved another slug of ale. As Maurice drank, Charlie placed his tankard on the floor before reaching into the ancient suit jacket that now served as his gardening coat and pulled out the black leather bound notebook no larger than a cigarette packet. Methodically he turned the dog eared pages of the book, moistening his finger with his tongue on each turn of the page. Slowly he ran his finger down a list of pencil written notations before closing the book and placing it in his pocket securing it in place with an absent minded pat of the pocket. Retrieving his tankard he settled back and sipped thoughtfully at the liquid, his pause before breaking the silence.

"May be as well to think about adding ash to the soil if you're thinking of parsnips." Maurice frowned and turned his face towards the roof of the shed as though seeking guidance for his response from the creosote etched planks.

"May be a bit late for that don't you think?" His response, slow, uncertainty in every word. Charlie scratched the bald pate of his head beneath the faded flat cap,

"No." It was a long drawn out sound. Not the sound of impatience or condescension but the sound of a man who was still considering the science behind his statement. He nodded, the movement almost imperceivable, the nod of someone who although certain was assuring himself of the facts. In truth he knew the answer. Years of experience had confirmed his process, honed his skills. "Autumn is best, of course it is." He spoke as though to himself, reasoning out his thoughts. "But this has been a bad year for rain. There has been no chance of putting it down dry. Soils too wet for that. In my opinion a drop of ash around root vegetables is never wasted." With his thoughts spoken he fell silent, expanded no further, no need for that. Beside him Maurice took a gulp of beer before placing his dulled pewter tankard on the floor to his side. Reaching beneath the dust coat he wore over his waistcoat he pulled out his own small notebook. Unlike Charlie's book, this was thinner and covered in old brown sellotape that had brittled and yellowed with age. The pages seemed more material than paper, dirty fingerprints smudged the pencil marks which had become almost unreadable with age. With great care he pulled the pencil from where it sat tucked between the spine and the cover and wrote solidly in the next available space, small marks, code-like. He wedged the book back into the waistcoat and regained his beer, settling back with a contented sigh. The men sat for many minutes sipping their beer in tandem both listening to the rain that bounced from the roof of the wooden potting shed. They were again lost in thought. As the rain fell Charlie drained the last of his beer and adjusted his large frame in the deck chair. Thrusting his arm out straight as though an involuntary action he bent it at the elbow and glanced at his watch now uncovered from its hiding place beneath his sleeve, gold case, gold elasticated strap engraving barely legible on the back 'Charles 60 years valuable service'

"Its that time Mo'. Constance will be waiting." Maurice swirled the last of his beer around the bottom of his tankard before tipping his head back and swallowing the contents.

"Yes. I suppose it is." Both men pulled themselves to their feet with a grunt, placed their tankards on the potting table and folded their deck chairs closed. Charlie placed his chair onto the hooks screwed to the wall of the potting shed gave a cursory glance around checking as always that nothing was out of place, nothing left behind and pulled on the waterproof coat which had been hanging on a wooden hook by the side of the open door. Stopping only to retrieve his tankard he zipped the coat and squared his shoulders. With the shuffling tread of a condemned man he stepped through the door and stood in the rain turning to watch Maurice emerge clutching his own tankard and deck chair. Once outside Maurice stood to one side allowing his friend to close the small wooden door, securing it with an oversized padlock. Checking the lock was securely fastened Charlie briefly studied the key in the palm of his hand before dropping it nonchalantly into the large button down pocket of his waterproof coat.

"Well Maurice."

"Well Charlie." The two men stood by the potting shed, shoulders hunched against the rain, unwilling to seek shelter.

"Devon's a long way Charlie."

"Yes Maurice it is." The rain fell heavier punctuating the silence

"It will be good for you and Constance I suppose, closer to Heather and the girls."

"Yes that's true. It will be good for Constance. Closer to the girls" The two men moved as one thrusting a hand towards the other, each gripping the soaked hand offered to him in a firm, meaningful grip. With no more than the slightest of nods as a signal they released the grip and took a half step away, the first step of a great distance.

"Charlie." The hesitation in his voice barely allowing the words to make themselves heard. "You know I can't drive well not anymore, not since…" He shrugged.

"I know Maurice. I know." With a measured movement Charlie stepped towards his friend of so many years and with an awkward gesture offered Maurice the glass tankard he held in his hand, "Why don't you look after this for me?" Maurice accepted the tankard, weighing it in his hand, liking the fit. With a small smile he held his own pewter tankard towards Charlie,

"And perhaps you could look after this for me, eh?" The two men faced each other a look of stoic acceptance passing between them, nothing to add, all that needed to be said was spoken. Charlie watched as Maurice turned away, hunched shouldered against the rain, deck chair clasped beneath his arm, tankard held carefully at his side. He waited as Maurice reached his own potting shed, saw him pull open the door and without a backwards glance disappear inside. With a squeak of wellington boot on grass path Charlie moved to the small gate of his own allotment closing it carefully behind himself. Head down the shambling figure clutching a pewter tankard thanked God for the heavy rain that washed over his weather beaten face. He thanked God that it disguised the tears that now fell so freely.

A C STOCK

The Passing

1 The Middle.

Death sat on the bench and watches the girl as she chases the ball skilfully around the park. Her dark hair is laying flat to her scalp slick with sweat, her face is contorted in a frown of concentration. The reflective stripes of her football top flash dangerously in the sunlight as she skilfully traps the rolling ball beneath her foot turning, quickly shifting her weight ready to move again in one fluid movement.
"That's it Marcie, take a touch then pass it off. Good girl." The man standing some distance away claps encouragingly, his face a picture of pride. "Pass and move." He calls "That's it, never stay still. Work those defenders hard." Death watches as Marcia almost casually flicks the ball to her other foot in a move he is sure would fool the greatest of defenders. Marcia drops her shoulder and in the same movement moves the ball back to her other foot and without breaking stride sends it soaring towards the clapping man. "Brilliant Marcia." He cheers, as the ball falls directly at his feet, perfectly placed. Checking his own stride he taps the ball away from himself before sending a wayward pass back in the direction of his daughter. Death smiles as the girl sprints away, head down determination to catch the ball her only goal. Regaining full control of the ball as though it was part of her own anatomy she flicks it skywards before bringing it under her spell first

on her chest, then her knee until finally it sits beneath her boot totally submissive. The man laughs, swinging the dreadlocks from his face. "Keep this up and I will be watching you from the stands." He puts his hands to his mouth as though he is nestling a megaphone. Imitating the plummy voice of some nasally sports commentator launches into a well practiced routine. "Marcia Deslandes scores another wonder goal. She really is unstoppable. England are lucky to have her."

"Or Jamaica dad." Her voice is high, the giggle of childish excitement obvious

"Yes Marce' or Jamaica." He mimics the megaphone again. "And Jamaica win the world cup for the first time in their entire history, and it's all thanks to." He pauses bowing dramatically "The wonder kid Marcia Deslandes. Youngest player to ever score a hat trick in the finals." His face breaks into a wide toothy grin as he continues "And it's all thanks to her dad who taught her so well at the local park."

"Ahh stop it dad." Death watches as Marcie steps deftly over the ball and back heels it towards the laughing man who, lost in his own mirth is caught by surprise. The ball bounces off his shin and rolls away with gathering speed. Death nods to himself, Marcia certainly has talent this is obvious. Such a shame, really it was. He reaches into the pocket of his cowl and pulls the large leather covered notebook onto his lap. Without looking, he has no need to look, he flicks open to the page and tracks a long yellowed fingernail down the black ink of the list.

"Marcia Deslandes." He mouths "9 years 8 hours and 27 minutes." With a languid move more ethereal than man, Death clutches the watch from his other pocket and stares at the face intently mesmerised as always by the 4 hands on the dial. Each hand spins around the yellowed face beneath the cracked glass in their unrhythmical symmetry. "9 years 8 hours and 10 minutes." Death rolls his shoulders and relaxes, 17 minutes to go. Closing his eyes he listens to the voices of those yet to meet their time, each voice a jumble of sound and yet each one individual. Shutting the book on his lap, Death settles more comfortably on the bench and plans through Marcia's final moments. There is no need to plan really, there never is but it is always best to be prepared. He concentrates, considering every moment. A small pain in the centre of her chest, 'It's nothing Marcia just indigestion. Eaten your cake too quickly.' Ahh the comforting words of a worried parent. Death frowns to himself, he will let her go quickly, time it to perfection. No time for dramatic last words gasped through tears and pain, words that would linger in her fathers mind forever. Spare them both from that, spare them from any more horror than was needed. The fight for breath or the struggle to survive. No, Death will make this as quick and as gentle as possible. A slump to the floor, a last expulsion of air and it will be over, this talented girl will rest peacefully. Sad but necessary. All part of the bigger plan, all as it should be, all preordained. Death sighs softly, resting his eyes as he waits, enjoying this moment of peace in a busy schedule.

"Yeah I'm here nearly overrun but made it now. I shall wait on the bench." Death opens one eye and peers at the young woman sitting at the other end of the bench talking loudly into the mobile phone clasped to her ear. He shrugs with disappointment, silence is so short lived now. "No its fine I'm all over it, yeah, yeah no worries. Ok yeah right see you soon." The young woman presses a button and throws the phone nonchalantly into the canvas backpack held between her knees before placing it on the floor at her feet. Death rolls his shoulders knowing he will be unable to rest now. He straightens his fingers hearing the creak and crack of the joints beneath the grey of his papery skin. He looks towards the sky, appreciating the clouds that drift softly overhead. So many clouds, so many years. Glancing at the watch in his hand he flicks a blue tongue across his thin cracked lips and sits a little straighter. It is time to begin. Looking again at the watch he quickly counts along with the tick of the third hand watching it reach the required mark and slowly raises his finger pointing it directly towards Marcia who flashes past him, cheeks puffed out, sweat beading her forehead, mouth wide open sucking large gulps of air. The ball is only centimetres ahead of her running feet looking as though at any moment it will escape her touch only to be brought back into line with the deftness of touches. Looking along the length of his crooked outstretched finger Death makes a small flicking motion, imperceivable and yet filled with power.

"So it begins." He whispers, his voice full of reverence. As he speaks, so Marcia rubs distractedly at her chest. The lapse in concentration is enough for her to momentarily lose control of the ball which bounces ahead almost gleefully, but the girl is practiced, ready for any eventuality during a game. She grits her teeth and pushes on against the stab of pain tapping the ball quickly to the right changing its path, regaining her composure and focus. Controlling the ball she twists skilfully sending it curling in a perfect arc towards her waiting dad who whistles in appreciation. Death lowers his finger and watches as Marcia's father catches the ball skilfully in one hand before tossing it high into the air.

"Heads Marcia come on, you must be ready for those." Death looks at the smile on the big mans face and shrugs. So sad. Really it was. Always worse for those left behind no hurt or fear would or could ever be felt by them again that matched it. Until? Death nods knowing the answer. No fear would ever be felt like it until it was their time. With a movement that almost surprises himself, Death flicks open the book on his lap and turns a few pages his eyes scanning what is before him quickly "Dennis Deslandes," He whispers ruefully looking towards the man who is now juggling the ball that had been returned to him left foot, right foot, left again.

Death sighs "Will not be seeing you for some time yet Dennis." He follows the flight of the ball as Dennis nudges it into the air from his foot, and with a degree of skill controls it with his knee allowing it to drop once to the ground before sending it skywards for Marcia to control on her chest allowing it to drop to a dead stop in front of her. She rubs her chest where the ball had struck, a casual movement but not unnoticed by Death who slowly bends his finger and allows his hand to fall into his lap.

"You alright Marcia?" She waves her hand in response

"Yes Dad just a bit out of breath." Dennis pulls a long multi coloured ribbon from his jeans pocket and ties it loosely around his hair.

"Ok love lets give it a rest shall we? Been at this an hour now. I don't know about you being out of breath I'm exhausted."

"Ha that's 'cause your old Dad." She picks the ball from the floor studying it trying to hide the smile from her face.

"Hey missy I'm not that old!" He laughs with pretend indignation "Anyway you're the one who's getting old." He laughs again, bending at the waist as though walking with a stick and rubbing his back furiously. "Why old lady." He says mimicking the voice of a man decrepit with age "How old are you today. What?" He says, holding his hand behind his ear as though unable to hear her answer. "Nine you say. Why that's practically ancient." He straightens up giggling joyfully, "Come on we had better be heading home. Your mum has just sent me a text saying that your Aunt and Uncle have arrived for your birthday tea." He points towards the small car park at the far end of the parkland. "Come on Marc' I'll race ya."

"Sure dad, if you are certain you can't beat me in a quick game of one on one?" Marcia picks the ball up and tosses it towards her father "We could always walk back slowly to give you a rest." Dennis Deslandes gave a bark of indignation.

"Why you cheeky…" He passes the ball back to Marcia who recognising the signal claps her hands together excitedly.

"I will take it easy this time honestly I will." She passes the ball between her own feet and pushes a strand of her dark hair away from her cheek where it rests slickly against her skin.

"Ok Marcia, but we will have to be back soon or your mum will skin me alive, honestly she will. I promised to help get everything prepared for your party and I'll never hear the end of it if I don't. The large man makes a 'come on' gesture with his hands signalling for his daughter to begin the game "Seriously though Marce'" he shouts "It will have to be five minutes and no more ok?" As he speaks he alters his stance to one of 'side on' to his daughter and his face becomes a mask of concentration. Death glances at the watch in the palm of his hand and nods, 'five minutes. Yes there would be time for that.' He thinks 'Well, just.' As Marcia moves forward the air is filled with a blast of noise, something between music and cats screeching. The young woman on the bench snatches the bag from the floor where it rests between her legs and begins rummaging untidily through the contents within. The phone secreted inside continues its trilling, more noticeable now as a long jumble of mechanical notes. With an exclamation of success the girl slams the phone to her ear simultaneously using her manicured nail to press the answer button.

"Hello. Yes hello" She calls into the phone whilst casually dropping her bag back to the floor where it comes to a messy rest by her feet. "Yes, yes!" She calls again "Hello, hello. Ahh yes hello!" Death watches her performance a look of confusion shrouding his face. Why was she shouting into the phone. Why did she have to be so noisy? He shakes his head sadly. It seems that people these days have no understanding of the beauty of sitting quietly and relaxing. He always wondered why people of this time felt the need to fill their short lives with so much distraction and artificial noise when the planet had so much beauty and sound to behold. Before he has time to ponder this point the girl barks an over exuberant laugh into the phone.

"No I'm not ignoring you, why would I? No of course not, its just that I couldn't find my phone in the bag, too many pockets and too much clutter, much easier when... What? No of course not, no nothing else on. Yes of course I can wait." She sits for a few seconds listening intently flicking at a leaf with the toe of her brightly coloured boot. The large sole clumps noisily against the floor with each attempt at dislodging a leaf from where it sits, stubbornly lodged between the floor and the leg of the wrought iron bench "Yeah well ok as long as you're sure." She sniffs loudly and scratches at her tight cut, bleach blond hair its slightly longer fringe peaking out from beneath the small woollen hat that sits precariously atop her head. "Ok no probs." She says seriously, straightening the hat with one hand "I will. Yeah. See ya soon." She ends the call and studies the phone as she begins flicking her finger over the screen. Settling herself into the half sit, half lounge posture of the young her brow creases into a frown of concentration. She moves her fingers with practiced ease across the screen and grows silent, lost in thought. Death watches in fascination his own concentration fully engaged as the girl pushes a small delicate hand into the pocket of the oversized woollen coat and snuggles her chin into the large collar. Eventually he sees the girl tire of the phone and smiles as she slips it into the other pocket her hand remaining almost elbow deep in the heavy material, silence at last. The feeling of contentment is only fleeting as Death gasps audibly. The sudden involuntary image of a soldier pushes its way forcefully into his minds eye. The soldier is at rest. The heavy trench coat wrapped tightly about him, chin buried into the high collar, helmet tipped forward covering his eyes. The sleep of the soldier was fitful and filled with the terrors and stench of warfare. The soldier had called out in his sleep,

"Rose!" A name. No more than that but Death knew who Rose was. He knew her time line, would meet her eventually, as he would meet them all. In this unwelcome memory the soldier smiled at last, comfort in his dream. But alas this was a comfort which would be fleeting, momentary for the soldier was unaware that Death was standing by him now, watching his sleeping form, waiting for the moment, the exact moment that the shell would land beside him turning the sleep he craved from earthly to eternal. Death felt the weight of these times, heard the cries and remembered the names. He forever remembered all of the names.

"Great shot Marcia left foot as well." Death jolted back to the present and focuses again on Dennis Deslandes who runs hard to catch the ball that comes to rest within feet of the bench where Death now waits patiently for Marcia. The large man flicks the ball backwards with his left foot and turns to face his daughter, panting hard. "That may be enough now Marce' I'm exhausted with all this running about. Much more and you'll be the death of me." From his gallery seat on the bench Death smiles slowly.

"Not quite Dennis, not quite." With a flick of his wrist Death peers at the watch in his hand and then consults the large book. It was time to begin. Without rising from his seat Death raises his arm towards the running child and points again the skeletal finger carefully towards her. With a whisper of words known only to himself he begins the final call. The child, Marcia Deslandes places a hand in the centre of her chest and looks towards her father.

Dennis Deslandes is unaware of the anguish in his only child's eyes for he has his back to his daughter chasing her last ever great shot, a shot which sent the ball with gathering speed hurtling down the slight incline towards the tennis courts. Death feels the moment, the thin ribbon between life and eternal rest. He focuses holding the girls final moments in the crook of his finger.

"I suppose really that these are the hardest." The girl at the far end of the bench voice breaks into his concentration, threatening to dislodge his thoughts. Damn the girl, could she not take her phone conversation somewhere else, leave him to his work? Bending to his task Death watches as Marcia raises her second tiny hand to her chest and kneads at the material of her football top as though to pull the ache free from where it sits just below the surface. Death sees the confusion and the glimmer of anguish in the small child's eyes just as her father catches the ball and holds it aloft triumphantly. Poor Dennis, how soon his triumph would turn to horror.

"I said… These must be the hardest." Death growls with frustration. This moment was to be handled with care, given his every concentration and somehow this young woman's loud, insistent chattering on her phone was intruding. Death focuses again on the child who in his momentary lapse has forced a deep breath noisily into her lungs and is staring around wildly as though she were silently calling for help, pleading for rescue.

This was not how it should be. He has promised himself from the start that this would be quick. Has he not promised this to Marcia albeit without her knowledge? With a sigh to focus his thoughts Death begins again the long practiced words that would conclude Marcia's short journey in this life and catapult her into what was to come. The young woman on the bench coughs once a small polite sound, a sound of nervousness. Death chances a quick glance towards her his growing annoyance etched in his already darkening features. He stops. No longer was the young woman talking on her phone nor was she sitting hunched in her great coat as though she had not a care in the world. Somehow without his realisation she had moved closer towards him, almost but not quite within touching distance. As Death recognises the young woman's closeness, a feeling of discomfort chills him to a stop. Frowning deeply, he watches carefully as she raises her delicate hand and scratches just once beneath the woolen hat slowly taking time to carefully tug it back into place. Obviously satisfied that it was now firmly where it should be the annoying young woman raises her chin towards him and smiles. A feeling unlike any that he has ever felt before shivers through him. Everything he should be doing leaves his thoughts and instead his mind runs through the possibilities. Perhaps she was not in fact looking at him, perhaps she could sense him or had caught a shadow in the corner of her eye? Fully forgetting the purpose of his time here in the park he steals a quick look over his left shoulder, yes, perhaps she had been looking at the someone she had been waiting for. Yes that was it, the person whom she had been speaking to on her annoying phone had come up behind them and was even now going to speak. The young woman would raise herself, walk around the bench and greet loudly the object of her smile. But no. Death could see instantly that this was not the case. There was no-one behind them. He faces the young woman, unsure of the next moment, uncertain of how to proceed. And then the young woman speaks again.

"Is it? Is it the hardest, I mean?" Death sits transfixed. There is no doubt about it she is, this young woman is talking to him. For the first time in his existence Death sits motionless, unsure of how to react. It was not that he was unused to being seen or should he say acknowledged? Yes, acknowledged was how it was. Many before had sensed his presence, recognised him for who he was but this was only those in their own final moments not a girl on a park bench who had years before her. Yes, countless individuals had spoken of him and to him in their final moments not as observers but as participants in their own end. These souls who were about to begin their journey saw through different eyes. They listened to different sounds, returning to their natural state and not that of learned behaviour. In their ending they returned to the state of birth, innocent and open to that which in life they called mystical. These souls would call to him by name, speak to him, welcome him as host. Any who heard their loved ones speak in such a way before their end passed it off with little interest reasoned it as the babbling of delirium. Some called it a visitation from God himself. Others offered that the dying were in fact in some way possessed. Many a watcher of dying would hurriedly cross themselves and offer a prayer begging for the comfort of those that were to depart. Begging that they would rest in peace. Those who spoke to Death knew the truth for they all had but one thing in common. Their end was certain. In their certainty was the fact that Death had come for them. Not the imaginary death of story books and wives tales but the physical presence one who's sole task was to take them from their earthly realm to a place unknown. It was in this certainty that they were gifted what the living were not. They could look death in the eye and make their peace in this knowledge. Death frantically searched his reasoning for why this young woman could see him and yet could find no answer. She was not known to him. Her name was nothing to him. Death scrabbled for the large book in his pocket, perhaps she was to become known to him soon, perhaps he had missed her name, perhaps her time was coming and he had missed the call?

"I'm sorry I've disturbed you haven't I?" Her bright blue eyes widen as she shrugs apologetically "I sort of can't help myself. You know how it is?" She reaches for her phone and scans it quickly before dropping it back into her pocket "No silly question ." She says more to herself in a mocking rebuke "How could you?" She laughs, a sound that twitters birdlike on the breeze. "After all its not like you can mix with that many people, well, not on a conversational platform is it?" She waves her hands as though wiping away the previous comment and continues, her voice low almost conspiratorially "I mean not that you don't have someone to talk to. I'm not saying that." She holds her hand to her mouth in mock embarrassment "I'm sure you have plenty of." Her pause stretches for moments as she searches for the correct wording "People?" She shrugs again obviously settling on the word "People. To talk to I mean." She laughs again brightly "Anyway." She sighs "It's just that I saw you sitting here and I'm well, I'm fascinated by this sort of thing and me being me, well I just had to ask that's all." She finishes her garbled sentence and blows out her cheeks in a large expulsion of air. "Wow just listen to me going on. I get like that when I'm nervous and to be honest I really am proper nervous now, well why wouldn't I be? What with you being who you are and all." Death sits rooted to the spot unable to think clearly. Her words were crashing over him in a jumble of noise that scraped and gashed at his skin as though he were no more than driftwood being battered against the rocks by waves of enormous strength. Each word causes him to wince inwardly as it grinds through his brain and reaches deep into his consciousness. Death fights through the fog that was threatening to overpower him. Although her words were unclear they had true meaning, they were precise. This young woman could see him. She begins to fidget as though the silence has highlighted that in some way perhaps she has broken an unspoken agreement or unwritten rule. Death takes this moment in time to calm his thoughts and searches for his voice.

"You can?" Although as a being he has always been fully certain of himself, confident in his own strength. Not for the first time in these many seconds his courage fails him and he comes to a halt.

"See you? Yes I can." She smiles casually picking up on his half finished sentence seemingly unconcerned by the roughness of his voice "Oh don't worry I'm sure no one else can see you." She says pointing aimlessly around the park "Its just that I have." She pauses as though again searching for the right word "Shall we say, an ability?" She nods to herself as though this were just the right word and the most normal thing for any mortal person to be saying to the figure of Death. "Yes the ability." She repeats, her smile wide and inviting pulling a lightness into her eyes, eyes that Death realises for the first time he was unable to tear his own gaze from. "Well is it. The hardest I mean?" The young woman blurts the words as though the unanswered question has been burning in her mind since it was first spoken. Death saw that she was almost bouncing on the hard planks of the bench beneath her such was her excitement, but takes his time to consider the correct response. The very fact that he was considering a response to her somewhat bemused him. Why did he feel the necessity to communicate at all with this annoying woman? Her bouncing becomes more pronounced as the silence grows, so much so that Death fears the planks would crack under the movement. With sudden decisiveness but for no real reason other than perhaps his own interest had been piqued he decides that now perhaps a reply would be warranted. In truth he knew that he did not wish to have a conversation with the young woman. He wanted no more than to end what had started here in the park with Marcia Deslandes and move to the next name on his list. Something inside him however needed to have some answers. He needed to understand how he was being seen at all. He hesitated briefly wondering at his own decision. Had he really thought through all the implications. What would happen if he did in fact respond, could there be repercussions? As though reading his thoughts the young woman leans towards him whispering softly

"It's ok. I won't tell anyone we spoke. Honestly I won't." She makes a crossing sign over her chest "Cross my heart and hope to …" She giggles more childlike than adult "That was a silly thing to say especially to you, eh? Crossing her fingers and holding them in front of Death she scowls dramatically "Let's just say, I promise I won't say anything." Death takes a moment ordering his thoughts, gathering his wits running through every possibility. With a small nod of the head acknowledging that this strange turn of events were in themselves intriguing enough to allow him to follow through. He takes a calming breath.

"Before we continue to....chat." He emphasises the word chat as though it were a word that held strong significance which in a way he supposed it did. "Please excuse me. I have an event to attend to." Rising to his feet Death turns his attention away from the young woman and back towards Marcia. The girl has fallen to her knees and is gasping for breath. Her mouth, wide, a dark dry circle of death. She falls forward one hand holding her weight the other clutching at her throat kneading her windpipe as though the action would in some way free air to her screaming lungs. Immune to the struggle of Marcia, although saddened he has been unable to offer the painless end she deserved, Death again raises his hand and the mournful hum of the incantation begins to fill the air; slowly, methodically, precise and determined each word finds its mark.

"Heads up Marcia!" The football comes soaring into the air rising high above the struggling child. The orb hangs for a moment before gravity takes hold pulling it ferociously arcing towards her a missile from space. The ball has been kicked hard by her Father his foot making a satisfying thunk. Due to the topography of the ground he is unable to see his gasping daughter who kneels helplessly dying some meters away at the top of the slope. Death waits for the precise moment studying the watch he has withdrawn from his pocket. All thoughts of the young woman behind him on the bench forgotten as he moves comfortably back into his own, private, practiced, respectful routine. The third of the four hands on the watch stop precisely where it was destined to end, the mark outside all interference, predetermined. Now there is just one to go. Death waits, serenaded by the slow rumble of words that fall from his lips. With a slow, creeping stealth the fourth hand moves to follow the track set by its brothers where in but a few short moments all four would be one atop the other the barbs pointing ominously at twelve on the face. Death speaks again tightening the pressure on the girl. The hand ticks again moving relentlessly forward, the destination what mankind would percieve as twelve on their timepieces would soon be reached. For Marcia Deslandes the clock will have stopped. Death counts the seconds his mind hypnotised by the movement, his finger ready to sign off her life with a flick of his wrist. The ache of excitement grows in his chest at the usual pressure of this, his responsibility thumps in his head. He counts the seconds. Five. He spreads his arms in a gesture of welcome. Four. He steadies himself aware of the weight he would carry. Three. He calms himself against the tingle that runs the length of his body. A life was to end and he was in place to guide their journey. The hand ticks once more and; stops. Death stares at the watch a puzzled look on his face. The hand has stopped. He looks again, his eyes disbelieving what he was seeing. With a panicked move he shakes the watch gently at first and then with greater conviction. Staring at the face he fiddles with the small round button set at the top framed by the loop of chain hoop. He twists the button violently and mutters under his breath before shaking the watch again.

"Is everything ok. Has something happened?" Only half hearing the voice of the young woman, Death gasps audibly as before him Marcia is frozen to the spot the ball kicked by her father hanging unmoving above her head. Death becomes aware that the ball and Marcia were not the only things that were not moving. Nothing around him moved, no birds flew, trees had stopped their swaying, clouds sat motionless held in place, surreal in their softness. Death wipes a hand across the slick sweat soaked skin of his face hearing the bristle beneath his touch rasp against the roughness of his palm. He stares around himself struggling to comprehend, fights to keep the bile that rises from the pit of his his stomach firmly in place. He is witnessing the tableau of a girl in the throws of dying an artwork created for his torment.

"My time piece has, stopped!" The words come slowly staccato sounds, each word punctuated with a gasp of breath. "I do not understand!" Death slowly turns and faces the young woman behind him. She too remains still her face a picture of excitement, her hands laying still and unmoving on her lap. The silence surrounds Death growing in its fury, beating hard against him, hammer on anvil. He was for the first time in his existence totally alone, submerged in silence and despair. This was a feeling like no other, a feeling that he had never before experienced. He knew that this was completely outside his understanding of events. This was something outside of his control. The stillness and the silence envelope him, squeeze him, trap him. He was being thrust into something he feared more than anything else, the loss of control. Without any warning a movement, fleeting in the corner of his eye forces him to take an involuntary step backwards. Throwing his hands over his face to keep him from the terror he was now witnessing he barely manages to control the grinding groan that escapes his lips. He, Death, master of all ends feels the sting of fear prick painfully at his soul. The slap of emotion which catches him in its grip spreads throughout his very being painfully driving home the realisation that in this moment he, Death, feels all of the years he has encompassed. Where once these years had been knowledge and power now they press heavily upon him. The sensation grows stronger as from the bench, the young woman winks.

2 The End

"Who are you?" Death feels his voice

crack, not from lack of use but from a fear that tightens his vocal cords and chokes the words making them small and insignificant. Still smiling and yet ignoring his feeble voice the young woman leans close to him as though totally unaware that she is in the presence of death. He watches in fascination as the young woman begins fiddling with her hat, first straightening it, then moving it to the side before placing it where it had first sat perched brightly on her white bleached crown before starting the process again. In a quick movement she suddenly plucks the hat from her head and with a flurry of action she reaches for the canvas backpack which sits desolately on the floor by her feet and slams it onto the bench beside herself. Ripping open the drawstring she stuffs the small hat unceremoniously inside all the time mumbling to herself as though berating the hat for some unseen failure in purpose. Clutching the drawstring roughly she yanks it tightly as though she fears that at any moment the hat would jump from its canvas prison and bolt for safety. Breathing more evenly the young woman pats the backpack before placing it gently to the floor where it nestles close to her heavy booted foot as though a small dog awaiting its loving mistresses full attention. Finally managing to swallow the dread that up until now had held him vicelike in its grip where he stood, Death begins to speak but stops as quickly as he starts realising the young woman was still mumbled beneath her breath. The words although not powerful enough to carry to his ears pricked at him. The indecipherable sentence she spoke held a melody that forced him to silence. As he listens on helplessly the tune forms a disturbing rhythm, dark and foreboding in its simplicity. There is in the phrasing, a power that chills him to his core. He wants to listen no more. He needs somehow to break this spell, for that is how he thinks of it, a spell that holds him transfixed, lost and alone. Summoning his strength, Death calls on all he knows of himself, his great knowledge, all of his power and his purpose. Gathering these thoughts together he uses them to fight against the fears that have overcome him. She has not answered him. This young woman has ignored him. With a building anger Death speaks harshly his voice deep and booming, filled with menace and danger.

"Who are you?" He roars "Speak to me I say!" The young woman remains seated, eyes closed, hands resting easily in her lap. She has heard his words he can see that, her eyes flick quickly beneath the closed lids but still she sits unmoving. Her mouth, her only outward sign of movement speaks silently issuing words he is still unable to hear. A dark anger surges through him raising him unbidden to his full height, all sense of fear leaving him. His anger leaves no space for hesitation and self doubt now only the sense of who he is fully controls him. As the anger grows so he feels the power in his heart and feels the destruction in his hands. Is he not the almighty force which holds the demise of mankind in his grip? Does not all living beings fear his form as he makes himself known to them? Certainty grows within him. He fears no creature for he holds the power over them. Whatever magic and spells this young woman holds are no match for him. Death knows that he would do her no harm this day for her time has not yet been written for him to collect. No, she was safe from his touch for now, but this was knowledge of his and his alone. Stalking towards the young woman Death spreads his arms wide and calls forth his scythe brandishing it before the relaxing woman as though about to strike her mortality from the register.

"Answer me!" He roars bringing the blade within inches of her exposed neck "Speak of who you are and how it comes to be that you see me." He lowers his voice threateningly "Before your name is struck from the register of life." Moving the blade to within the thickness of hair from her pale skin he breaths heavily "For I shall add your name to the book of the dead with no regrets." The young woman opens her eyes and ceases her mumbling. Slowly she lifts her arm from her lap and gently placing a finger tip on the blade of his scythe pushes the weapon away as though it were no more than a mirror in which to reflect her humour.

"Please put that away." she says her words soft, placating "Now, rest yourself, come." She pats the bench next to her "Sit with me. Let us talk." For a moment Death maintains his stance hoping the imagery he displays will throw this young woman off balance. Such is his confusion he no longer wants answers he simply wants her to leave, he hopes his stance will force her to return to her own simple existence, content in this brief meeting until they meet once again sometime in her own demise, her pre-written future. His hopes falter as her smile grows wider stretching the juicy plumpness of her lips into a soft pink that highlights the brightness of her even, white teeth. With her gaze never leaving him she again pats the wooden bench. "Come." She repeats "Sit." His new found anger and courage pull dangerously at him threatening to tip his now unsteady hand. He could almost imagine the blade nick at her throat, its keen edge slicing deeply, the blood pumping thickly and vividly red against her alabaster white skin. The realisation of his thoughts shock him, appal him even. His free hand falls to his side feeling the bulk of the leather bound book in his pocket seeking the comfort in its familiarity. He can recall all of the names, see all the faces captured within its faded pages. If he so wanted he could turn the pages forward and see those yet to come to him as he had for the soon to be distraught Dennis Deslandes. This young woman was as of yet unknown to him. Her name would be in the book but? Death sighs a sound between a blowing gale and a thunder clap. Her name is unknown. He could no more find a name that is as of yet unknown to him than alter the course of what should be. The anger inside him barks with the viciousness of a rabid dog begging him to end her, to strike her head from her neck, and yet. His shoulders slump driving the image from his mind. He could do no such thing, her neck was safe. He understands that his choices are limited. He could not hurt her. Instead he will have to proceed with these strange circumstances. He will have to allow them to play out to their fullness. Somehow this young woman has affected all as it should be, but how? He shakes his head. Of this he was not certain. Whatever this strange young woman planned or what part she played in his purpose here was unclear. Had Marcia Deslandes some futile guardian angel, was there to be some last minute misguided attempt of a reprieve? Was this young woman here simply to plead her case? He hoped that this was not indeed the cause of this interruption for that would be futile. Seeking a reprieve was as though she were asking ice to survive a furnace. He considered the facts working through each conclusion but where there should now have been clarity only his confusion remained. Whichever of these proved to be true he would have to see it to the end, he could change nothing. He will allow this young woman her moment of time, for in truth Death pitied this young, brightly toothed woman. Her appearance here was of no use to dear sweet Marcia, her fate was written long ago, long before the surface of the world had cooled. He wonders now what this intriguing woman had heard had of him. Was her perception of his persona taken from no more than old wives tales in which she believed too strongly? Surely she did not hope that humans could simply earn their way to a longer life? Inwardly he smiled. These humans were so caught up in avoiding death they often forgot to live. How many times had he heard someone talk of how they cheated death. He steals a quick glance at his timepiece, twisting the small knob at the top. Still the hands remain motionless. He drops it into his pocket and stares at the young woman who sits silently on the bench her lips moving as though practicing her next sentence. No. No-one cheats death he thinks sadly. They may have had an awful event that in the rational of later, seemed as though they had been close to dying but this was not the case. If the event was close to death, he would have been standing waiting and once he was in attendance your end was certain. If he was not at that event then that moment was not your end, you had not survived a near death experience. As though spurred on by his own thoughts and with an invigorated sense of purpose, Death slowly releases the scythe allowing it to fly from his hand to its place in the realm of other worlds. Aware that he is now fully in control and assured in his purpose Death moves with a studied step towards the bench. Turning carefully he lowers his mass onto the seat and places a hand on each of his knees, a man in repose. Taking a moment to study carefully the unmoving scene before him and allowing his presence next to the young woman to reach the full effect, he turns his head purposefully and faces her noting the flicker of concern that darkens her eyes casting shadows on her cheeks. Looking back towards the frozen form of Marcia Deslandes, ball hanging heavily above her head, her very own sword of Damocles, Death breathes a single sentence.

"You have; my attention!" The young woman moves a hand to her head quickly, an automatic reflex checking for the hat that no longer sat in place. Realising her mistake she smiles guiltily.

"Oops. Silly me." Her smile turns into that giggle she uses so frequently, quick and light which she masks with her hand as though embarrassed to be caught. "Sorry. I didn't mean to." Her words tail off as she looks away falling silent. Death saw her frown as her focus moves to the stillness around them as if realising for the first time the absurdity of what confronts her. The silence stretches on between them for some moments, an unwelcome guest at the party awkwardly standing close to her. Death could have if he so wished waited in perpetuity, he is used to silence, he is practiced at waiting but the tapping of her large booted foot against the hard earth of the floor irks him. The way her lips half part as though to speak before they close into a thin smile more secretive than inclusive pull at his patience.

"And so?" He begins "You know who I am. Perhaps you should introduce yourself." Finding that his words elicit no response Death speaks again this time gruff and demanding "So who are you?" He relaxes, conscious of the effect of his words the power of his voice. The young woman's features pull in on themselves as though she has suddenly tasted the bitterest of foods. Her mouth moves thickly chewing over the words she is choosing to speak. Her foot clump, clump, clumps against the earth. Her hands flick and twist at each other wringing out her bravery until slowly she turns her face towards him.

"That is much better." She nods encouragingly "Perhaps now at least we can talk properly, eh?" Death splays his hands more in resignation than acceptance, he realises that he is in fact perplexed that his words seemed to have elicited no real fear in her, failed in his attempt to wrong foot this annoying woman. He sighs resigned to the fact that at least to allow her to continue will bring an end to this he is after all anxious to move on with his work. "So where to begin?" The young woman pulls at her bottom lip pondering her starting point. "Well." She begins "My name is." She pauses for a moment frowning as though uncertainty had crossed her mind. "Erm." She continues looking towards him earnestly "Before I tell you my name. I need you to promise me something." She frowns looking intently at Death her face pleads for an answer. With a sigh he waves his hand nonchalantly towards her

"I suppose as with all things, it will depend on what I am asked to promise."

"Oh yes. I suppose it is. I hadn't thought of that. How silly of me." The young woman blushes slightly. A colour he realises which highlights the youthfulness of her face.

"I promise that it is nothing serious, just, well." She pauses for the smallest of times before whispering breathily leaning close to him "Just something I would like to." Again she pauses, this time he is certain for no other reason than to add gravitas to her words. "Be certain of something to ease my mind." She finally continues sitting back lightly against the bench her foot begins again the heavy thump, thump on the compacted soil. Death sighs loudly, his own turn at adding dramatic effect.

"I suppose I must agree." He says with as much implied disinterest as he can summon "Or this conversation it seems will never end." Before the words fully left his mouth the young woman sits straight, excitement filling her every move

"Yes! You are sure now. No doubling back?" Death is not sure what she means by doubling back but he nods once, a slow deep movement

"Yes of course no... doubling back." With a fast precise movement the young woman reaches for his arm and grips it tightly. For a moment he hears nothing, can make no sense of what is being said such is the shock of feeling that possesses his body. The warmth that flows around him merely from the touch of this mortal burns at him, searing his senses. It is he, Death that touches mortals first, never they that touch him. It is only once he has laid his hand upon them, the dying, that they will reach for him. Sometimes their touch was in fear, sometimes for comfort but theirs was never a touch such as this. No, theirs was the touch of a cold clamminess. A touch of futility and of finality.

"So you understand that I wouldn't want that would I?" The young woman waits, her grip firm upon his arm her face passive and yet expectant "Well is that ok or not?" Death squirms and snatches his arm from her grip releasing himself from the feeling of the warmth that has come from her hand. Rubbing at his flesh as though it has been burned by the hot coals of hell, he breathes deeply trying to wipe away this new sensation.

"You talk too loudly." He growls pulling the sleeve over his arm still sensing the hotness, "Please spare me your minor details and tell me simply what it is you wish." The young woman giggles

"I'm sorry I do become quite loud when I'm nervous." She fixes Death with a serious stare and sniffs loudly. "As I was saying, all I want is that when I tell you my name you don't start looking it up in that book of yours." Death feels himself on the verge of laughter, a reaction he has never partaken in. This woman is concerned that if she tells him her name he would look it up in the ledger and do what? He considers her fears and realises she has reasonable concerns that he may do one of two things. Firstly he could taunt her with the day and time of demise or secondly he assumes that she may be concerned that he may be able to bring her name forward and end her time now. He shakes his head, the first was possible but something he had only ever done once before and that was in extreme circumstances and a long time ago. The situation now he was certain was not extreme by any measure. The second option was an impossibility. He had no say on when the end of a person would come, he simply followed the ledger and the timepiece. The date and time were not of his choosing he was simply the vehicle to bring those pieces of information together. Slowly as though giving her request vast amounts of consideration he nodded sagely. The young woman yelped with gratitude.

"Thank you, oh thank you for that." She twists towards him bringing one leg under the other as though making a cushion to sit on more comfortably. "My name is Deborah." She waits as though expecting something disastrous to befall her immediately. When nothing materialises she physically relaxes "My name is Deborah." She repeats "I'm so happy to meet you." Death cocks his head to one side

"Deborah. You say that name as though it should be of some meaning to me." The young woman, Deborah shakes her head.

"No. Not really, not unless you've seen it in your book I suppose." She shrugs dismissing her own words quickly before thrusting her chin in an awkward sideways nodding action "I thought it may be him you know." Death shrugs confused

"Him?"

"Yes him." She points "The dad, the one that's kicked the ball." Deborah points towards

Dennis Deslandes, "But it's not. It's the girl isn't it?" She looks to where Marcia kneels a living statue in the throws of her demise. Death nods slowly, a frown creeping across his face.

"But surely you knew that?" He glances towards Marcia before staring intently at the young woman he now knew as Deborah "You must have known it was her. Is that not why you are here?"

"What?" Deborah gives a small laugh "For the girl? No. I told you, I saw you here. I was curious." Death jumps to his feet angry with himself, furious that he has been distracted so easily. This had gone on long enough. If this young woman, this Deborah had not been responsible for this freeze in time. If she had been merely interested and if she had only by chance been engaging with him as this mysterious event took place then he needed to end it now. He steps from the bench wrenching his timepiece from his pocket and begins furiously twisting the winder and shaking it as though it were a sticky substance holding stubbornly onto his fingers. As he twists the winder he begins his words again their meaning known only to him. With a practiced flourish of his hand he aims the final words at the frozen Marcia and growls in frustration as the image before him remains the same. Chancing a look over his shoulder towards Deborah he notices the slight smile of amusement on her lips. Was she silently mocking him? Was she happy to see him allowing his pent up rage to take control? Protectively he hunched his shoulders as though guiltily shielding the view of his actions from her. Quickly he forces a long yellowed and twisted fingernail beneath the glass of his timepiece. Its hinge solid with age fought against the interference. With more care than large fingers should be able to posses he began rotating the hands on the face manually with little success. Each time he aligned the four hands towards twelve he watched them spring back to their original positions. He tried holding them in place and speaking the words associated with the twelfth hour, but as truly as though it had a life of its own each time he released it, the fourth hand moved back to where it had began. Death angered by his failure looked towards the sky as though amazed suddenly by the clouds above.

"What madness is this that I am unaware of?" He called, baring his teeth in anguish "Tell me what is it you require of me!" Aware that no answer was forthcoming he stuffs the watch deep into his pocket hearing the material stiff with age rip beneath his anger. "I shall put an end to this!" He bellows angrily striding determinedly towards Marcia rolling back the sleeves on his habit. "Stand aside from my work!" He calls as he strides closer to the girl "I shall complete my task and you shall hinder me no more!" Death glances angrily around the silent stillness that has befallen everything he sees. Pushing aside the fear that fills him, he reaches the side of her and kneels close. Laying his hand gently upon her small head he notices the frozen bead of sweat halted in its tracks cresting the arc of her brow, reflecting his own silhouette in its glassiness. "Be at peace Marcia Deslandes child of the earth. Be at peace." with the final words spoken he gently brushes a hand down her face closing her eyes beneath his palm. With a sense of relief that at last this end was in place and that the girl would have to suffer no more he slowly removes his hand ready to lay the body that was now soulless to the floor. Gently he takes her small form by the shoulders tipping her softly to her side. He leans over her and places her own hand beneath her cheek. The other hand he leaves resting lightly on her side. He moves a small strand of hair away from her forehead and tucks it neatly against her scalp. Moving deftly he removes the bead of sweat and flicks it casually away where it hangs in the air having left his finger, a raindrop ready to fall. Content with his handiwork Death rises from the ground and steps away pleased he has left a scene to be discovered that will bring no terror, nothing that reflects a struggle to survive. Dennis Deslandes will discover his daughter peacefully at rest. Stopping suddenly he turns quickly, a small smile on his face. Reaching up he plucks the ball from where it hangs above the fallen girl. He places it under her arm as though she cuddles a toy in her sleep. At last fully satisfied, he turns away heading towards the bench, ready to send this Deborah on her way. He is convinced now that her intrusion has somehow unsettled the balance of what should be and has caused what was. As he approaches her something in her look unsettles him, causes him to slow. He wants to speak, demand to know why she stares at him as she does, but his words and not for the first time fail him.

'It won't make any difference you know." Death halts completely his mouth opening and closing wordlessly. The young woman Deborah raises an arm and points to a place just behind him. Although every part of him wants to turn and look in the direction she points fear freezes him.

"Just how would you know what would make such a difference?" His words are brave, strong although he feels no such bravery. She does not answer merely tilts her head to one side and draws her eyebrows together knotted in what?

Pity? Death snorts. An act of disbelief. "I asked. How you would know. How could you?" He stops speaking, the feeling of his own weakness washing over him, drowning him. There was something in the way Deborah looked at him just a nuance of knowing. He tries to look away from her gaze, tries to summon his earlier bravado. He needs to be in control but there is something in the gentle smile, the smile that now turns the corners of her mouth and tells him what her face displays. From the very start Deborah had known! With a sense of dread Death slowly turns his large frame from her and studies with horror the sight before him. Marcia is now back on her knees her face etched in anguish. The same bead of sweat placed again on its original course and the ball that he had placed with such care is no longer lovingly nestled in her arm but hangs ominously above her, a planet on its own course of lasting destruction. Death groans, a low guttural sound. Waves of emotion wash over him. Emotions he had no understanding or words for wrack his body painfully. With trepidation he faces Deborah and takes a halting step towards her. His hands splayed his fingers punctuating his next whispered words flicking at each syllable. "Who are you Deborah? I ask again, who are you?" Now he needs answers, no longer the need for her to leave. He had to know, "I believe you have never truly answered my question. Who are you?" He knows he sounds feeble, weak as though he were but a child of the human race not the angel of death, not Thanatos nor Mot or Namtar or any of the other names humankind refers to him as in whispered voices. He is at a loss, floundering and adrift. Deborah calls to him again her voice breaking through the screams in his head. He looks up and stares again into the eyes of the smiling young woman. She speaks again her voice somewhere between forceful and pleading.

"Please sit with me." She repeats her words from earlier "We need to speak, urgently." Heavily, Death moves towards her, his face set, his eyes blank as though walking in a dream. With a sigh of resignation he falls awkwardly onto the bench which creaks with his new found heaviness.

"I have wondered how it is so that I

should be able to meet with you, to look upon your face." She begins before being distracted by a tune that punctuates the silence that fully surrounded them in this moment. Reaching for her bag Deborah pulls the phone from deep inside and looks at the screen nodding to herself as though the message were spoken aloud. He wants to grab the phone with every part of his being. He wants to snatch it from her grip and fling it with all his might sending it end over end to the furthest point of the park and beyond. It seems to him now that even in this the most serious of moments she was like the rest of mankind, unable to tear her eyes from this mobile device. She was as much a slave to this devil as any soul lost in a sea of despair. Tossing the phone back into the rucksack she lays it on the bench to her right before smiling seriously towards him.

"I have never met someone quite like you before." She begins "Someone so...." She searches for the word. "I want to say awful." She giggles nervously "Not awful more awe-full. Someone who fills me with awe. Does that make sense?" She laughs again almost reaching out to touch him but stopping just short. "You do understand my meaning don't you? I hope you are not offended, not angry at my bad choice of words." Her voice rises in pitch and the words come in a rush almost tripping over themselves to be heard. "Its just that you being, well, you, fill me with so many mixed emotions." Her voice tails off and she shrugs. A tiny movement that seems to say 'you know what I mean.' He understands her meaning very well for has he not heard the sentiment spoken many times before? He considers her reaction and relaxes his shoulders, allows his feet to rest easily upon the floor. This Deborah was expressing the facts as universally known. Never has his name truly been spoken of lightly. Never has he been dismissed glibly. His was and is a presence that created fear and yes, awe. His was a name that demanded respect. Suddenly he saw the chink of light in what was befalling him. This Deborah was not in control. True, she may have interfered and altered what was to be, but. He allows himself a small smile. This effect was not of her making it was simply the result of her being. His thoughts came clearly. Of course she was different to other mortals after all had she not seen him? Was she not speaking to him now? A lightness comes over him. Deborah was in awe of him. She was as fearful as he had been moments before. And why should this not be the case? Here she sat alongside death itself realising the magnitude of what she was witnessing, of what she was involved in. She was afraid that now was to be her moment, now she too would reach her own mortal end. Feeling the power flood back into his every fibre Death smiled widely.

"Such as?" The words are a sneer, thin and sharp, coated with venom "What emotions?" Deborah shrugs again, a habit that is beginning to irk his temper.

"Well." She reaches for the rucksack and fiddles with the strap working it through her fingers "I suppose if I had to name them." She counts them off on her fingers as she speaks "There would be fear and nervousness, obviously. There would be elation, admiration, sadness, pity, regret, fascination…"

"Wait." He raises his hand bringing her words to silence. "You say regret. Regret for what?" Deborah drops her hand from counting, a look of confusion on her face. Before she can infuriate him by shrugging again he continues. "Regret for meeting me, regret for the tasks I undertake?" Deborah bounces on the bench words rushing from her

"No, no of course not. I am so glad to have met you. I admire you greatly and having the chance to sit here speaking as we are is amazing." She grabs at his arm again this time the touch soft and gentle bringing with it none of the sensations it brought before. "I understand fully the heavy task you have to undertake. I see the pain etched on your face." Her voice becomes more somber, her grip slightly heavier. "Your task is a heavy burden but a burden that must be achieved. Without you no living thing would reach its end. Without you, well let's just say the natural circle would never close. No, I do not regret either meeting you or the role that you play." She removes her grip from his arm and sits back. To any casual observer she was a woman at ease, a woman at rest. Death leans forward bringing his face close to hers. Hears her breath coming soft and calm, notices her eyes flicking beneath her closed eyelids as though blindly searching the horizon.

"Then what is it you regret in our meeting Deborah and please no more word play. Speak to me honestly. What is it you regret and tell me who you are." Deborah opens her eyes the blueness meeting his gaze calmly. Looking at him as though she were seeing everything and nothing.

"Well. If I can be honest." Now it is his turn to grab her. Quickly he lays his hands on her shoulders stopping the shrug he is certain that is to appear

"Please Deborah. If nothing else be honest for patience runs thin and I have much to do." Deborah reaches for his hands and gently removes them before continuing

"Well in that case." She begins "I suppose you could say that my meeting you here today was not an accident." She waits allowing the words to settle before speaking again.   "Not an accident." She says at last more to herself than to him. "No, it was perhaps ordained?" She rolls her tongue around her mouth as though tasting the flavour of the word. "Yes ordained." She nods up at him seemingly satisfied with the word she has chosen. He sits quietly for some moments looking past Deborah across the park towards the entrance gate the very gateway he had passed through to begin his work. It seemed so far off and so long ago, the gateway, further than he could remembered. Suddenly he longed to be away from here. He wanted nothing more than to reverse his journey through that very gateway and onto his next order of business,

Mary McConnell, retired nurse, ninety nine years three hundred and sixty four days old. The details came to him easily. Poor Mary McConnell to end her life nineteen hours before her hundredth year. It was his turn to shrug now. The details were not of his choosing. He focused again on Deborah her blue eyes staring at him intently, expectantly. Death smiled weakly. He would have to continue to play her game.

"Ordained you say?" Deborah nods, pleasure filling her face.

"Yes ordained." She thrusts her hands into the pockets of her great coat before pulling them quickly out holding them tightly in her own lap, a sure sign of nervousness. He speaks casually feigning disinterest despite the curiosity that fills him.

"That is a very interesting word Deborah. Ordained. Are you sure it is not too big a word? Perhaps fortuitous or strangely significant would have been more apt." The smile on his face aches as it pulls against muscles so rarely used. The young woman shakes her head furiously.

"No, no, no! Oh Death I thought you understood. I thought perhaps this would have shown you." She points quickly to the frozen scene in the park "I had hoped that this would have informed you well enough." She puffs her cheeks and blows air noisily "Ordained is the very word, the exact word. I did not chance upon you. I have not entered this park blindly and seen you about your work as happenstance. No dear Death. I was sent here to meet with you. It is my position to meet you here, at this time, in this place and on this very bench. It is on our meeting that I am to deliver a message to you a message that is for your ears alone and for no others." She stops speaking, her cheeks flushed pink against the effort. So it was to plead for Marcia's life, he thinks. Perhaps it was more than to plead, perhaps for the first time a reprieve had been given and this young woman was to be the implement used to convey the message. He is tempted to reach for his book, to study the words, read again the name, spot the alteration to the time line. He stills his hand before it moves towards his own pocket. No, let Deborah speak. Allow her to deliver the message she had been chosen for. He motions towards her signalling her to speak. He tries to remain impassive but in truth his heart flutters as it had never done so before. This is a monumental occasion, the girl is to be saved, spared as no other before. Deborah nods quickly acknowledging his gesture. She again reaches for her rucksack and pulls the phone from it checking its screen. Death laughs to himself. Of course, the phone. It all made sense now. This Deborah had been summoned through a higher power to deliver the message. The phone was the conduit that carried the details, assured the tasks completion. The phone was a tool not just a distraction. Deborah tosses the rucksack to the floor and pushes the phone deep into her pocket setting her face to pure concentration.

"Death." She begins " I have been sent here to deliver a message of great importance."

Her words are stunted as though remembering lines written by a playwright. "You have been served to act in your duty to bring about the end of the child Marcia Deslandes." She rubs at her scalp where the small hat once sat "I must ask you to desist from this task. I request you heed this as the message I carry brings about a greater urgency." Death waited impressed with her manner, she had been chosen well. "I have been asked to deliver you and you alone this message personally, as a sign of the respect you truly command." She continues solemnly her face set a picture of respect "I ask you to listen closely to what follows as it is of the greatest urgency." Death holds himself still respecting the seriousness marked on her face. "Death it is my duty to inform you that I have been sent here this day to say that for you." Her voice lowers "This is to be the moment of your end." Again she lays a gentle hand upon his arm "I am to be the vehicle that is to release your soul. I am tasked with allowing your spirit to enter the realm of restful eternity." He feels her fingers grip lightly at his arm this time a grip of comfort, the touch of regret. He sits stone still allowing the words to come to rest, feeling their effect on him, understanding the banality of this young woman's delusion. Releasing the breath that he held pent in his lungs he sneered widely no longer able to contain his fury.

"Stupid girl! Foolish mortal child of the earth. Have you no understanding of whom it is you speak to so brazenly? How dare you carry such illusions of power that you threaten me with your idiocy. I know not how it came to pass you were able to see my image nor how you garnered such bravery as though it were a shield carried before you. Hear me now. You speak to me as though I were naught but a mere mortal such as yourself. I tell you this, I am far from that image you have of me. Tread with care Deborah for your foolishness shall lead you to fear me for the rest of your time here on earth. I cannot decree your demise, nor can I hasten it." He is shouting now such is his anger, the veins stand against his pale skin pushing hard to break the surface. "You have made yourself known to me, you are in my mind. You shall come to regret this interruption to my schedule as you have never regretted anything before. I have promised you that I would not seek your name in the ledger and to this I shall remain true." He lowers his voice hearing the anger he knew he was now displaying, "Be aware. Although I do not fully know your name as I do not know the date of your demise. I do know your presence. This knowledge of you that I now hold shall enable me to visit you." He moves his face close to hers his words brushing lightly against her skin. "Deborah. I shall visit your every sleeping moment. I shall curse your rest with nightmares such as you have never before experienced. In times of loneliness or silence I shall be there behind your shoulder. A chill along your spine. A shadow past your eyes. Believe me foolish child that with every shiver you make, you shall curse the day you threatened death." He leans away from her and rises quickly feeling his chest heave with an anger that refuses to leave him, threatening to encompass him entirely. How dare she speak to him so. How dare she! Bringing his breathing under control he turns his back to her dismissively studying the stillness that still surrounds them both. "Be gone girl. Allow your leaving to return the balance to how it should be. Spare Marcia Deslandes the agony of a protracted end. Go and allow me to continue with my work." He waits for some movement behind him, waits for some recognition of his power and threats. Where there should have been movement or pleas for forgiveness comes nothing but silence. Turning slowly he faces Deborah again fury surging through him. A fury that freezes itself to stillness, a fury that refuses to reach its conclusion. Where there should have been a terror obvious to see Deborah sits studying her phone silently mouthing again the words that pass beneath her gaze. Vexed beyond even his own understanding he stoops at the waist bringing his face to within inches above her head "Stupid girl. Do you not hear me. Do you not understand my words?" To emphasise his words he now lays his own bony hand, claw like upon her shoulder squeezing with enough strength to leave small red weals upon her skin. At last she stops staring at her phone using her free hand to remove his own grip from her shoulder. She nods, quickly rubbing at where he had touched her, a small tear in her eye. Slowly she reaches for the rucksack and pulls the small knitted hat from inside placing it carefully upon her head. Testing that the hat is properly in place she pulls the drawstring of the rucksack tightly closed and places the phone in her pocket. With a small grunt she rises from the bench and straightens her great coat picking absently at a small silver cobweb that has attached itself to her in flight. Finally she raises her face towards him frowning deeply, opening her mouth and closing it again as though unable to find the words to speak. She lowers her gaze briefly and hoists the rucksack onto one shoulder testing the weight with a small shrug. Eventually she focuses again on his face, a sorrowful look clouding her usually clear blue eyes. Breaking the silence Deborah takes a large breath and speaks calmly.

"Oh I understand very well what it is you have said." The words are flat, expressionless. "But I fear it is you who does not understand my meaning." Instead of the expected backwards step she moves closer towards him crowding his space, invading his certainty. "I have said that I was sent to serve you the courtesy you deserve. I speak to you kindly, I allow you the honour of preparing yourself adequately for your own demise." Her features cloud matching her eyes "I expected your shock and confusion that much is true but I am alas, disappointed with your reaction to such knowledge. I misjudged your understanding and your." She shakes her head sadly "Your venom. Especially towards me." A look of forced patience washes over her as though she were a parent with an errant child . "After all, am I not here to guide you and to be with you. Am I not here to facilitate your end?"

"Why do you persist?" Although shocked at the young woman's conviction he needs to make her understand, needs her to recognise her error. "You are misguided. I am not who can be subjected to death. I do not answer to the rules set for mankind. I am Death. I am the taker of life and the facilitator of the journey to come. I am the one who has been and always will be. I am a messenger. I am forever!" His anger returns quickly, unchecked, pulling at his ribs, tearing at his throat wracking him to coughing. "See how the anger attacks me now. Hear how your insolence forces my blood to rise? Still you persist. Your words peck at me as hungry birds peck at the rotting flesh. Let this madness of yours end. You must see for yourself now that I cannot be ruled by someone such as you, someone, who has nothing but the ability to see those that exist on the other plain such as me."

"And can stop time?" The words are quietly spoken but able to halt him in his sentence.

"You forced this?" Now it is his turn to speak quietly. His words full of disbelief. Deborah smiles thinly

"Yes. This is my doing." He glares hard at her hoping to dislodge her confidence but she returns the look unblinking. "Surely this was the result of you entering a world that should be entered by no mortal. You cause this stillness by falling upon a moment shared by that of the dying and the carrier? This is a private moment that must be interrupted by no other. You broke what should be by nothing but intrusion. It is that and that alone which causes how it is now." He realises that his words are spoken in a high pitch, rolling over each other in a torrent of sound. He sounds fearful even to his own ears. The girl Deborah turns from him and sits lightly back on the bench rubbing a hand over her weariness.

"You are correct. My being here has altered how you truly believe things should be. And yet?" She shrugs, a movement that this time does not anger him instead adds to his new found fear. "It was not my presence that froze the world as it is now. I had to stop you in your task, for you are not destined to end the life of this young girl. I needed to speak with you, at this time to explain what must be. The only way for me to achieve this goal was to freeze the time in which all existed to hold time as it is. She smiles sadly seemingly noticing the questions that he knew truly formed on his face.

"But this makes no sense. The girls name is in my ledger. My time piece is set for her end I have to…."

"Yes, yes it is and yes, you did." Deborah interrupts him the strength in her voice overpowering his own. "My heart is heavy, a feeling I now recognise as one you carry as one carries a great weight, but still I must say that your time, and by your time I mean your own time not that of this world." He sees the sadness he knows so well, mark her face "It fills me with dread to say that your time Death, is destined to end before that of young Marcia Deslandes." Deborah points towards the frozen figure of Marcia. "Her end is not to be your responsibility but that of another." Again she searches for the right words "Oh Marcia Deslandes will reach her end that is certain for it is so written. But my dear, faithful, friend what is also certain is that her guide will be at that time someone other than you." He stands rotted as though a tree of the earth solid in its place and watches as again she pulls her phone from her pocket and runs her finger over the screen concentrating hard as though held in some hypnotic trance. He glares at her unable to speak, his breath coming in short rancid blasts, the sound of his own pulse beating strongly in his ears.

"But?" The word fails him as he scans the park, seeking the answers, searching for the words "But I am Death. I cannot die!" Deborah looks up at him sadness in her every movement.

"No. You were Death. And like all things you can die!" She moves as though to reach out to him but something stills her hand and she sits back, hands held still on her lap. When she speaks again it is as though the words are heavy to release from her lips and the effort seems to drain the colour from her cheeks. "I am sorry Death that this has to be. It is just that for you now. Your time has come." Her tone although heavy remains even, measured, a placating mother "Please have no fear. Relax." She pats the bench by her side and smiles as he sinks quickly onto the bench by her side as though his legs have lost their strength. "You have nothing to fear. You have been a good servant. Please enjoy your last moments and let us celebrate all that you have been and all that you were. Let us end your time here together as friends."

"Friends. What do you mean friends? I do not know you. You certainly do not know me."

"But I do. I do know you." She replies quickly "In fact is it not so, that I now know more of you than you know of yourself?" Her head leans slightly to one side inquisitively "Is this not true? You must accept this for am I not the only one who knows the time of your end?" Again she smiles at him a smile that says 'my how the weather has changed' or 'we should walk together and take the air' not the smile of one who has told him of his own demise. "Please." She continues "Fight me no more. Accept what is said and prepare in these last and oh so brief passing moments for your own end." She falls silent allowing her words to sink in, giving him he knows the space to think more carefully. He wants to show her his fight, he needs her to understand the implications of what she has just said and of what it is she believes. He cannot die. He is death, he is the journeyman, he is necessary. Summoning his remaining courage he brings a power to his voice, a power he feared only moments ago had left him for good.

"How dare you threaten me with the end of my time. You have no authority to."

"But I do! I do have authority. I have been. …" Now it is his turn to halt her words. He forces a snarl into his voice crushing her to silence.

"You say authority is yours. You say that this is the end of my time. How can I believe this. I ask, why should I believe this?" Deborah moves closer to him and places her small hand on his knee eliciting this time no feeling of shock or pain.

"You ask me this even though it is that I have frozen time?" He laughs at her sincerity, relief coming into him that her answer was so weak, so fragile.

"A cheap trick. A clever trick I grant you but one that can be performed by any minor spirit for some small amusement." Much had began to make sense to him now. This Deborah had revealed more of herself than she had perhaps intended. She of course would have to be of some ethereal form. There would be no mortal who could choose to see him nor could they speak freely in his presence unless he alone decreed it. It was a fact that no mortal would be able to achieve the freezing of time. No mortal would have the skills to halt the ticking of his timepiece. He tried to suppress his excitement. A spirit or some ethereal being she may be but this did not amount to the claims she made. This young woman the one who called herself by the name of Deborah was only half of what she claimed. Her ego was driving the limited power she possessed. She was less than half of who he really was. He studies her carefully as she sits by his side, the sides of her eyes lined with thought. With great care he speaks again enunciating the words carefully so as to be certain they were understood. "I feel now that I have the mark of you, Deborah. I am now aware that you present no more than a persona to me." He claps his hands noisily as though applauding the thought that had just come to him. This is why you asked me not to look in the ledger to spot your name. You are not there. Your name is not to be found there. You will have no existence within the ledger for you are not who you profess to be." He smiles as a new thought comes to him gleefully "Are you in fact sent from Momus?" Deborah looks up from her phone.

"Momus?" Her brow furrows "The God of humour?" She laughs shrilly "No it is not from Momus I come." Her voice becomes lower more reverent in its sound "But you are correct in your thinking. I am not truly what I present here. How could I be?" Her question is rhetorical "I have been sent to you but it is not from Momus for Momus would dare not set himself against one such as you. Momus understands that although his power is great his use of humour would fall greatly short of passing beneath the power that holds you so. No, not Momus." Deborah sets her face solidly "I have been sent. As I have said, to you directly because of the respect in which you are held." She stops speaking her eyes staring to the distance as someone who had fallen into a dream may look. "I have been sent." She continues her words torturing his very core in their breathy softness "By a greater power." She wraps her arms about her own shoulders comforting her body against the enormity of whom she spoke.

Death watches her as her attention turns once again to the phone screen she has pulled from her pocket. He notices again her lips moving silently as they read what was beneath her gaze. He wants to snatch the phone from her, read the words for himself, see what holds her attention more than his presence before her. As the thought comes to him she speaks snatching the thought from him. "I fear that you are now entering your final moments, moments that I understand will be precious to you. Please!" Again her voice takes on a pleading yet gentle tone "Do not waste these moments in futile argument with me. Now is the time to accept with good grace what is to befall you. Let us make peace. Let us share this time together gently. Let us." In a blur of movement that would catch any mortal unaware Death roars with rage and snatches for the phone she holds lightly in her hand. His roar turns to a cry of anguish as his own hand comes away empty from the movement nothing for his efforts save the surge of blood that now thumps heavily in his ears. For her part the young woman, Deborah, holds the phone aloft almost wearily. A look in her eyes reflecting the pity and disappointment her features showed.

"I am afraid this is not for your sight." She lowers her hand and glances again quickly at the phone "It is no more for your eyes than your book is for mine. Please can you now accept that this is how it is meant to be? I am here for you and will support you as you have supported all of those you have taken when their time is done. She rests back onto the bench signalling that he should do the same. As though her signal was an instruction he could no longer disobey he feels himself lean back beside her. The ache he had been unaware of until he allowed himself to lean against the solidness of the bench burned at his very being joining the weariness that pulled at his aching body. Turning stiffly he faced Deborah feeling more than seeing her slide closer to him.

"I have began the incantations for your end." She smiles sadly. He was not certain but the blink of her eye removed a small tear that moments before glistened in the light. "My incantations cannot be stopped. You know this." She nods as though confirming what she had spoken was indeed fact, "Your name appears on the list, the incantations are spoken, it is your time." Her last words came slowly, reverently, and yet were words which seemed to fire into him causing his head to spin and turning his thoughts into a jumble. "My friend, and I mean those words, my friend! I see that already your body grows weary, your breath grows shallow and your vision grows soft. Listen to your body, how it speaks to you. Again I implore you think of what you know, of those that have gone before you. You will see that all I have spoken is the truth." As though her own energy had drained from her with these final words Deborah closes her eyes and rests her head against the bench silently; body motionless, breathing even, shallow, face serene and yet although in repose so alive with energy. He can take no more. Fear has stalked him down, captured his heart and holds it vicelike between its teeth, a wolf with its prey. He, Death, master of all ends, tries to stand, wants to leave this place to find safety, to wait skulking in the shadows for this horror to end. He pushes against the bench for support but finds to his horror that his legs have betrayed him, refuse to give him purchase. An ache somewhere deep within the hollow of his stomach pulls and knots as he moves, squashing the air in his body forcing his breathing to come in short shallow sucks. Flopping back to rest wearily against the bench the truth of the situation washes over him bringing with it a despair such as he has never before experienced. The words of Deborah come to him in their truthfulness. He is exhausted and his body feels the rip and tear of age. He was, he realised, all of his years. Gone now the sense of immortality. Fleeting the time he had served. No more the stretch of future. No more a beginning just an end. And yet this could not be so!

"Surely this cannot be the end?" His words sound tired even to himself. His voice echos with fear. "Have I not served well? What more could I do than what has been asked of me? Surely in all of this I deserve to be served a better meal than that fed to mere mortals? I am a being of power, sent here to perform the most onerous of tasks. I have performed these tasks well and unquestioningly. What more could I have done?" His voice is pleading. Where argument should have been now only hollow words remain. "Deborah I beseech you. If I have offended or failed in some way then perhaps there can be a chance to make amends. Perhaps I can put right any failings I have made. If this is but a test, it is a test of the most vile kind. Allow me to put right my wrongdoings. Show me what changes I need to make. If my tasks have been treated with nonchalance or casually on my part and this has led to errors please I beg of you, let me atone for these errors. I shall do whatever is required of me. I shall do anything, but please, not this, no, not this." He reaches for her ready to persuade, ready to convince

"Hush. Please hush." With the simplest of movements Deborah takes his hand in her own two hands clutching it to her chest cradling it as a mother cradles a child. "Hush." She says again soothing him with her tenderness. "This is not a failing on your part. How could it be? You have always served well in everything you do. The love for all of those souls you have carried forward onto their end has been nothing but genuine. Believe me when I say that all you have have done is recognised. I plead with you to understand that you are held in the greatest of esteem and shall be forever remembered. This is not a punishment as it is not a disgrace. You have served well, done nothing wrong. It is simply that." She grips his hand urgently imploring him to understand "It is simply that this..." She pauses briefly staring hard into his face, "It is your... time." Her look is caring and yet resolute, she needs him to fully understand her words "You are tired, your years have been long. For you there has been no rest, no peace. All things tire and weary it is the way." She raises his hand and kisses it gently. "It is time for you to be at rest." Although he understands her words, feels their sincerity terror drives him on.

"But if I am to leave who would be best suited to carry on in my stead. As you yourself have said I have dedicated all of myself to this work and have served with no one to follow on. Surely I am best placed to continue? It would be in the best interests of all beings for me to carry this task forward." Slowly Deborah releases his hand and sighs deeply the sound soft and gentle.

"Death I understand your plea for it is well spoken and yet." Her gaze meets his solidly "Is this not the very plea you have heard so many times before?" She concentrates as though remembering some long ago learned fact. "Have these very words not been spoken to you by Queen and pauper alike? Was it not Galileo himself who quoted those exact words to you?" Death blanches at her words, shocked at her knowledge

"Yes, but Galileo was aged for his time when he left this earth." Deborah nods again.

"And what did you respond when he protested this fact. Death lowers his head remembering.

" I assured him that others would follow and expand his work using his knowledge to complete the journey."

"And did he succumb peacefully?" Death takes a moment before answering realising the mistake he has made in using this line of argument. It is his turn now to nod his head feeling heavy for the task.

"Yes he did." As he speaks a new line of thought flashes to him, a lifeline perhaps. "But I have not yet finished my work. Look there." With great effort he raises his arm and points to the frozen form of Marcia Deslandes who remains as she has a forgotten figure for so long now "I still have work to complete and….'

"Mozart!" Deborah strokes soothingly at Death's hand as she speaks "Are they not the words used by Mozart as he lay dying. Did he not have unfinished works in the very room in which he passed from?" The futility of this argument crashes around Death each shard of broken hope piercing his heart. "And how did Mozart greet his end?" Death sighs, a sound full of sorrow and tears.

"He accepted that his work was done here on Earth asked no more than to be allowed to conduct the choirs of heaven." Deborah prompts him on with a look of encouragement

"And?" She says eventually. Death speaks quietly fearing his own answer

"Mozart accepted his end with a courage that seemed larger than the form itself could contain."

"Yes that is so. His courage carried him forward…"

"But I am still strong. I have the will to continue." Death pulls his hand from her, pain racking his every joint and yet he fought to keep the hurt from his eyes "I am keen to explore more. I would like to serve in a greater way, seek new paths to follow."

"Scott, Earheart, Alexander." She lists the names on her hand as she speaks "And there have been so many more. Death you are the one who has been at the side of all those who have ventured and adventured. You have carried those that have and those that have tried or simply many who could only dream of trying. Each of them have spoken words similar to those you have spoken and yet still they have had to accept your presence." Tears fall along his cheeks as Deborah speaks moistening skin that has remained barren for many centuries

"But I am different." He pleads finally "You talk of mortal souls who age and weary, who tire and succumb. This is their way. They have to accept their end but this is not the way for me. I am, I am." His voice breaks with emotion imploring her to understand "I am immortal." The tears that forge their hindered journey across his skin are soon joined by others "I just cannot cease to exist." Deborah rises from the bench and arches her back, rubs her legs and rotates her shoulders.

"Death." She begins, "Immortal is only a word given to beings such as ourselves by what we call mortals here on earth. I tell you now, all things pass from being what they are into something they do not comprehend or truly understand. Does not even the very oxygen the mortals here breath for survival cease to be what it is at some stage. Is it not taken from what it is to become something else? Perhaps in this journey it does alter, reform to what it was but is it the same or is it in some small way different?" Death tries to move, to join her but the heaviness he feels holds him where he rests his face wracked with a pain such as he has never known. Slowly befitting his addled mind he forms the words of a newly thought idea.

"But Deborah should it be here on a simple bench? The very concept is ignominious. Can I not at least choose a more noble end, an end that shall be remembered and spoken of for millennia to come? Have I not earned that right? Have I not at least earned that much?" Deborah silences him with a look.

"My heart understands your wish and yet I say to you now. The way of death is not the glory." She pauses allowing his breathing to return to normal, seeing how the efforts of his words have drained him. "The heroic death you talk of is the chance to leave this realm having made the difference to so many lives before you. I have seen this of you and have also witnessed the words spoken of you. The end you so crave has already been assured." Death finds a surge of energy from deep within himself pulling himself straight from the slump he had reclined into.

"But a heroic death, a chance to die making a difference in that moment, that is what I wish for. So many times I have seen that. Witnessed this as part of the final act."

"You have witnessed it?" It was a

question. Death paused panting hard

"Yes of course for I am at all deaths."

"Then have you never understood the role you have played?" Death begins to raise his arms despondently finding the action impossible instead he nods slowly.

"Yes of course I have but…" He sighs sadly and Deborah takes his pause to continue.

"Then you have witnessed death through the final act. You and you alone have understood what occurs after the final closing of the eyes and the stilling of the heart. It is you who fully appreciates what is after the shutting down of the brain and the moment the soul leaves the form. Understand now, that it is the very act of dying itself that is the heroic moment. Not that which leads to it. For any being to accept their own physical end that is what will forever be known as being courageous." With nothing but the hollow sound of his breath coming in short ragged gasps Deborah leans towards Death and speaks softly "My friend. Your protestations are well founded and are as natural as the moment you came into being but they serve you no better than those that have gone before you." She reaches for her phone and looks again at the screen. Silently she begins again the incantation raising her hand firmly towards the figure of Death.

"Wait!" His words come to her from a place as close to the end as was possible. Slowly he raises his head, his eyes boring into her, fear etched onto his face. "I am afraid! Never have

I know such terror. Please do not let me face this alone. Please stay with me." Deborah kneels down gently by his side and mouths the last of the incantation known now only to her. As she finishes she wrapped her arms around him pulling his head to her shoulder, whispering gently. As she rocks him in her arms her fingers gently stroke the clamminess of his neck as her words calm his soul.

"You are not alone dear friend. For I am with you and it shall be my honour to guide your soul and bring you to your rest." As she strokes his neck she hears one last time the softly breathed words of one who is at peace.

"I am ready."As the words end she lays the figure that once was Death softly to the ground and steps carefully away.

3 The Beginning

Deborah moves from the bench with no backward glance. She does not see the light that shines brightly around the fallen figure she had no need, her task here has ended. He has passed and his way is assured. Moving gracefully to the side of the frozen child Marcia Deslandes, she kneels, running her hands gently over the pool of black hair. Even in its frozen state the hair feels soft, young and vibrant and she takes a moment to relish its youth. Taking a moment to study the young girl's features wracked with pain she sighs with a finality. Moving swiftly now but with the tenderness of a mother she gently pulls the girl onto her side and lays her peacefully on the grass. She takes a moment to wipe the frozen horror from her face instead leaving features resting at peace. She leans close and whispers gentle words into the child's ears and feels birdlike fluttering of calmness fill the tiny heart. Regaining her feet Deborah takes the phone from her pocket and frowns at the list on the screen, she has been summoned to another place. A virus is to take many today. Every name on the list would need her care. Flicking her finger across the screen of the phone the face of a clock appears, four hands sweeping electronically towards the twelve. She will need to hurry for there is much to do. Pressing the button on the side of the phone she hears the ball thud to the floor by the prone figure of the child and the movement of the park begin. Dennis Deslandes moves to the top of the slope, calling proudly.

"Hey Marcia did you catch it? Not bad that. Left foot as well. Your old man still has it in him you know. Marcia. Marcia?… Marcia! God somebody help please! somebody help!"

Dabria the angel of Death walks towards her next task. She places the phone into the rucksack where it sits next to the small knitted hat. She pulls the drawstring tightly closed and with a flick of her wrist allows the bag to fly from her hand to be seen no more. Now as is correct she has at last cast off the remnants of her assumed persona. Deborah was no more, only Dabria remains. She straightens her back feeling the weight of the cassock she now wears pulling at her frame. The heavy responsibility she was mistress of weighs heavily upon her shoulders. It is now she and she alone who will carry so many to their end. Reaching into the large pocket she pulls the ledger that is now hers open, feeling the sadness leak from every entry. Quickly she flicks at the pages finding the place easily. Reading the words she allows herself a small smile, this will be she thinks the last smile she will ever know. It is there beneath her finger that a name appears, a name she knows so well 'Marcia Deslandes.' A problem with her heart halts her hopes of football success. Spurred on by the skills of the surgeon who brought her to health a change of direction ensued. Dabria studies the words. Marcia Deslandes, Surgeon, Wife, Mother, Grandmother. She closes the ledger with a deep thud dropping it heavily into her pocket. Gracefully and silently the figure of Death continues her tread towards the gateway of the park calling silently to a time that is and a time that is yet to come.

"Thank you young Marcia Deslandes. Death has not come for you this day. For you young Marcia there is still life ahead. So until we meet again, live your life to the full and celebrate your being." Unseen by all but those who were listed, Death passes by.

The Dress

She tucks the rain mack firmly beneath her legs as she settles onto the roughness of the once soft, now stiffened with grime bench seat at the back of the bus. She is not alone, she like others is a regular traveller on the city busses. She is used to the jolting, the cigarette fume filled interiors and the dull routine. Without realising she has become oblivious or at least numb to the claustrophobic environment. She ignores as always the intrusive touch of unknown fellow passengers, who, avoid direct eye contact as they themselves are roughly jostled together. Confined in the tight interior they sway in a seemingly choreographed dance that allows bodies without introduction or request to rub together. They waltzed in time to the tune of grinding gear and squealing brakes. She, like them concentrates on no more than the journeys end and the dark evening to come.

Although in essence her journey is familiar, filled with the mundane, littered with a banality that quashes any sense of hope, tonight her journey is different, tonight is special, for tonight is the night that she finally, wears the dress. Pushing again at the heavy fabric of her rain mack she folds the beige material under her legs ensuring it would protect the silk of the dress from contact with the seat. Turning her face to stare out into the blackness of the evening through the fog of the window, a small smile curves the edge of her mouth and she sees her reflection imitate the action. She looks 'pretty'. Her reflection gives a wide eyed reaction, shocked by the thought, amazed at her own revelation. She has never been referred to as pretty, never turned a head or elicited a whistle from lads either in half jest or half hope. Lads whose muck stained hands cling to scaffolding as they silhouette above the gloomy rain filled skyline, scurrying on builders planks, rebuilding the city that is scarred by bombs, ravaged by fire. Lads whose eyes are turned by a stockinged calf or a fur trimmed collar, lads who cat call the pretty but ignore the plain. No never for her the two fingers in mouth, glass cracking trill, the momentary pause, the halt of her step. No never the workman's whistle, the 'Cor' or "Up ere darlin'!' Not for her the mating call of the crude. Why should they? For she is Mary, plain Mary. Mary the good girl who 'elps her ole' mum, Mary who studies hard and has practised her shorthand. Mary the one you can ask, the one you can call on at a minutes notice to baby sit whilst you meet the girls for your well deserved break at the bingo. Mary the one who will run an errand or cook dinner for her dad. Mary the dependable one. 'Good old Mary', always with an ear open to listen and a hand to help. Mary who is never quite 'one of the girls.'

"Come on, you know it's not the same without you." Mary who is willing to hold the handbags and save the table, as her friends are whisked away to the dance floor by acne faced and Brylcreamed boys. Boys who have not seen or known the true horror, boys whose hands move with frightening speed towards buttocks and breasts whilst their faces maintain the Rigor mortis of concentration, and the deeply furrowed brows of inexperience. Yes, she is Mary, plain Mary. Mary who walks tipsy girls home, and is prepared to hold their hair. Happy to guide and protect, to steer them home. Mary who watches them wave a bleary goodbye and close their doors against the cold and the damp their virtue barely intact. Mary who returns to her room and stares silently into the mirror as she wipes away the makeup that failed to hide the ugliness. Mary who hugs the pillow to muffle the sound as she mourns again her own crushing despair.

She pushes again at the rain mac forcing it beneath her thighs, relishing the feel of the silk beneath the mac as it brushes against her skin, bare against the stocking top. She stares out into the darkness and allows herself to picture again the shop. It is tucked in the gloom of an unknown alley, seen by a quirk of fate. She recalls the workman pointing the way, heading her away from her normality and without realising towards what could be.

"Sorry Miss road closed along 'ere, demolishing a house, clearing a bomb site." He pointed along the narrow alleyway "Diversion through there." She had nodded, understanding, she accepted the detour ignoring the minutes it would add to her journey, accepting the inconvenience with a smile. She had followed the diversion without breaking her stride, switching her satchel from left to right, prepared for the small inconvenience, oblivious almost of the 'miss' not 'love', thrown so casually towards her, accepting perhaps, oblivious? No. The shop when she noticed it was the only establishment open along the winding alleyway. It's bow fronted window gloomily lit, bereft of any finesse and yet as she passed she was drawn to the centrepiece as a moth is drawn to a flame. The dress hung limply on a mannequin that barely completed its task, the gloom of the alleyway tried to sufficiently suffocate any chance she had of studying the display with any accuracy and the groans of passing pedestrians halted in their own time consuming detour as she stood solidly in the centre of the pavement almost succeeded in evaporating the magic. The overall sense of desolation nearly broke the spell and yet the pull was too strong, hypnotic. It was silk, the dress, pure silk, a commodity that was in the shortest of supplies. It's cut was wide on the shoulders, pleats diving away towards the breast revealing she imagined more flesh than should be seen at the local bath house. The waist was forced tightly into a solid band that would encircle the torso, holding it firmly in its grip just as the hands of a long imagined lover would lift her from the balcony on which she stood. The band was secured in its place with a buckle that seemed larger than required, heightened in the effect by the rich black hue of the metal. The length would end at her calf allowing an acceptable view of leg. The hem, not straight but gently curving accentuated every half an inch with a piece of shaped glass that twinkled as diamonds a feat she believed should have been impossible such was the gloom of the alleyway. She had stood transfixed, almost leaning against the shop window as though a child held in awe at the jars of brightly coloured sweets that tempted with every roam of her eye. For the first time in her life she cared not for the price ticket, she almost ignored the expense, which when if calculated properly would be the sum of just over a weeks wage. She shrugged aside the feelings of selfishness that reared against her and pricked at her conscience. This would be a purchase made for herself, a purchase with nothing or with no-one in mind save herself. Without a second thought, she pushed open the glass panelled wooden door and accompanied by the tinkle of the small bell entered the interior of the shop to arrange a fitting and if successful a downpayment on the dress.

The bus comes to a halt and the occupants ripple in time, steadying themselves before parting slightly to allow her through. Stepping to the kerb she takes a moment reassuring herself of her direction, pulls her patterned headscarf tightly about herself to protect her newly curled and set hair. She nods once in affirmation before stepping out and heading towards Leicester Square. The club entrance is set in a dark doorway off a side street but she does not hesitate, merely nodding at the heavyset doorman who holds the door open with a large square hand.

"Good evening Miss." His accent is rough and yet fills her with a confidence, his voice is somehow soothing. She is too excited or is it nervous to answer, her smile will have to do. Making her way down the narrow flight of stairs she can feel before she hears, the music, the heavy thump of a double bass, the high sharp blast of a trumpet and the rhythmic, tuneful crescendo of the piano. She has never been to a jazz club before, never been to any club without the girls who call themselves friends only to leave her stranded for most of the evening. Parting the bead curtain she enters the small cave like room full of music, laughter, sweat and friendship and instantly feels welcome, feels as though she belongs. A tall man dressed in a dinner jacket arrives at her side and gently takes her elbow, leaning close to her ear against the noise.

"Welcome Madam, please follow me to the coat check. My name is Thomas I am the manager here, if you need anything just signal." With an air of professionalism he steers her to the small cloakroom where a pretty girl in a plain black dress smiles warmly before passing her a small metal disc.

"Lovely to see you. My name is Jackie. That disc is your coat number just pass it back when you are ready to leave." She smiles sweetly holding out a hand to receive the rain mac. Mary smiles back timidly her nervousness too long a firm friend holds tightly to her spirit. With a deep breath she shrugs herself free of the mac and with wide eyed fascination turns and studies the crush of bodies in the small room. The smiles of the dancers and the heat of friendships surround her, hold her close, draws her in. She catches the eye of the tall man Thomas who smiles towards her his teeth bright against the darkness of his skin. Slowly with the smallest of movements he inclines his head as though offering her the freedom of the room. Mary looks again at the scene around her and knows she has found her place. She takes a breath to banish the last moment of nerves and steps from the shadows out into the muted, cigarette smoke filled light of the dance floor and heads towards the small bar at the end of the room. Dancers smile as she pass accepting her for who she is and she smiles back happy to be seen, happy to be recognised. Reaching the bar Mary smiles at the barman and straightens the silk dress that fits her so well, the silk dress that is as yellow as the sun itself.

Groundhog Day?

The mechanical drone of the digital bedside clock roused the sleeping figure to a slow, thick wakefulness. Reaching out a skeletal arm that he barely recognised, he grunted with effort groping to silence the intrusive alarm. Finding the large flat button he stabbed a bony finger hard against the coldness, feeling the ache he knew would be there run along his knuckle forcing its way deep into his wrist. Squeezing his eyes shut against the pain he breathed deeply.

"6.27!" The words wheezed from his cracked lips loud against the silence. "It's always 6.27" he said forcing open his eyelids. His hand which rested lazily on the clock slipped almost automatically to the top of the cabinet finding the glasses laying next to the clock where he knew they would be. There the dirty pink plaster wrapped around the bridge. Here the large scratch scarring the left lens as though cutting his vision in two and there the chip on the tip of the arm just as it always was. Gripping the glasses, he fought to control the shaking that seemed to accompany his hands making every task a trial. Forcing the arms of the glasses over his ears he focused on the neon red numbers displayed on the clock

6.27. His groan of disappointment broke into a cough, a wet slippery sound that wracked his body and tore at his throat pulling at his ribs as though to break them in two. Clutching his arms tightly around himself, feeling the boniness of his own body he slowly gained his composure, his breathing returning to something that resembled normality and his tired heart beating less violently. He wiped the tears that filled his eyes behind the thick lenses noticing as he fought for breath the thick cloud of hot air that left his lips. The breath rose majestically into the cold of the room hanging above his prone figure as though it were the cloud on which God himself perched as he reached out lovingly towards, who? Someone. The name came to him through a fog, Adam it was Adam. God was reaching out towards Adam in the painting by? He shook his head, the name escaping him slipping away as quickly as the breath had disappeared from view. With a feeling of dread he ran his hands over the length of this thin body that lay prone, entombed beneath the weight of the heavy grey blanket. His hands began their exploration but already they knew what would be found, "Pyjamas, flannel, striped, blue?" There was a weariness to his voice, he knew the answer to his searching hands, after all was he not always wearing these pyjamas? This realisation was followed quickly by the smell, it was always followed by the smell; Damp and fetid. The heavy aroma assailed his nostrils; thick, cloying, the smell of mould, the perfume of age, the stench of death. He grimaced, there was no surprise in the scent that radiated around him was there? After all was it not that same stench that greeted him every time he opened his eyes, every time he awoke?

Laying for a few moments he gathered his thoughts. They came slowly, fighting through a denseness that pulled and sucked, holding each thread threatening to swallow them whole. It was like this as he woke, always the same. The certainty of what he knew dragged away into the swamp of confusion, his reality replaced with this never ending loop. Baring his teeth in a primal grimace, he rolled onto his side grunting as pain wracked his joints. Slowly straightening his legs beneath the blanket, he slid them out towards the cold of the room and pushed himself into a sitting position. Thin legs protruded from the bottom of the rumpled pyjamas meeting the veined feet that hung limply as though not quite alive. The blueness of the veins stark against the pallid flesh caused a momentary surge of fear in him but he calmed himself. "There is nothing new." He whispered "Nothing new." He waited for the fear to leave his stomach which pulled and lurched around him alarmingly. It was another nights sleep, another of those mornings, of waking of finding himself here again. How long had it been now? He had lost count, couldn't remember. The alarm, the waking, same pyjamas, same sense of confusion, same legs, same feet, the same yellowed nails twisted and claw like. Shuffling forward on the bed aware of the cold now his feet found the slippers. He didn't need to look he knew they would be there they were always there. On the second attempt he managed to find his way to standing using the worn padded headboard to steady himself. Straightening himself by degrees he shuffled into a forward movement heading across the small bedroom, his slippers catching the threadbare carpet, his eyes scanning the bareness of the room. The familiarity of this, his surroundings although uninvited calmed his mood, at least it was no worse, things had remained the same. He came to the small chair placed at an angle in the corner.

"A nursing chair." The words came uninvited. He did not need to look at the bundle that lay folded neatly on the seat they would be the same as every morning. He listed the items touching each piece of fabric carefully; Jumper, blue, sleeveless a hole just below the neckline. A pair of old grey suit trousers, the fabric worn to a shine. Jacket, another suit from another time, pockets loose with use, collar frayed. Under the chair sat a once smart pair of dress shoes the folded leather and worn heels signs that their long ago grander existence had fully passed. "No underwear, no socks." Never any underwear he would have to seek some out, he needed to make this change. With studied care he began removing the items from the chair and pulled them onto himself over his pyjamas. "Until I am warmed through." he thought. Pushing his feet into the shoes knowing there would be no laces he began the shuffling walk towards the door out into what he knew would be a landing. Without pausing to open the two doors that sat blankly either side of the landing he continued his journey to the far end where a door stood open revealing a scarred toilet bowl cracked and surrounded by sheets of yellowed newspaper and a small sink. Suddenly aware of his burning need to urinate he lurched forward the toilet his focus, his leaking bladder his driving force. Struggling with the trousers and pyjamas he sighed with relief as a halting dribble of urine found the water of the bowl. Straightening his clothing he felt the dampness of the crotch, he had not been quick enough. Embarrassment burned in him but quickly left as he saw the newspaper he stood on glistening wetly. He searched the small bathroom looking for something to place over the dampness beneath his feet. A white enamal bath stood just to the side of the toilet, heaped inside was not the remnants of long hot soaks but piles of discarded newspaper. Automatically he reached for one and removed some loose pages. Laying them on top of the now damp pages he pushed them into place with his foot he would come later to clean them away. Leaning heavily on the sink he prepared himself for what was to come next. Reaching out he pulled the cord of a small light that hung connected to a lamp over a mottled and cracked mirror. The bulb whimpered into brightness, its yellow glow barely able to light the room but it was enough. The face in the mirror that confronted him shocked him, it always did. The questions formed themselves in his throat. 'Who are you?' And 'Why?' But he would not ask them for they would not be answered he had tried before, hadn't he? Pulling at the cord he extinguished the reflection of the old wrinkled man and headed for the steep, dark stairway.

At the foot of the stairs everything was familiar. Nothing had changed, nothing ever did. He knew that yet again today would be the same as every other day on his waking. He breathed heavily feeling the sweat bead on his brow from his exertions, yes everything would be as it always was unless he somehow changed something, altered how things could be, stop this continual loop. He entered the long galley kitchen and reached for the saucepan that sat where it always sat, on top of the fridge. Filling it with water he placed two eggs from where they lay waiting in the double egg cup an egg cup that displayed some cartoon version of a fireman with the words 'Begin the fireman way' written in bold yellow writing. Only half hearing the click, click, click of the spark trying to ignite the gas of the cooker he breathed a sigh as at last the flame caught and burned with a blue intenseness. Placing the saucepan on the flame he shuffled back to the hallway turning right through another doorway which led to the living room. The room was dark, everything within looked tired and worn and yet unlike any of the other rooms an overpowering aroma of sickly sweet furniture polish filled the air. Heavy curtains although obviously old and faded continued to do their job blocking out early morning light. Without thinking he walked to the wooden cased television set and pressed the round power button and waited for the screen to brighten. Pressing the play button on the old VHS video player an image appeared on the screen. Jane Fonda dressed in a bright blue workout suit and leggings jumped up and down encouraging him to join in and feel those muscles burning. He was never going to take part but he admired her determination and enthusiasm. No, there would never be a chance for him to join in because in 2 minutes and 11 seconds exactly, the picture would become fuzzy and turn itself off. It always did. He watched for a while as the jumps became higher and Jane Fonda's smile became wider. As the timer clicked to 2 minutes and 10 seconds the picture began to wobble and twist. At two minutes and 11 seconds the picture stopped completely and the high pitched whine of rewinding tape began. He turned from the screen and left the living room calling a hollow,

"Thank you Jane!" He hoped he would not have to see her tomorrow, he hoped things would have changed. But in his heart he knew he would miss her if this really was the last time he saw her. Removing the pan from the oven he spooned the eggs back into the egg cup and cracked open the top with the flat of a knife and began spooning the contents into his mouth.

"Perfect." He mumbled 2 minutes and 11 seconds plus a little walking distance, the perfect egg cooking time. "Good old Jane." He finished the eggs a little disappointed that there was no bread, there never was. Every morning there they sat two eggs in the egg cup, the saucepan on the fridge but no bread. Just once he would love to have bread. He would make soldiers covering them thickly in butter and force them deep into the egg watching the yolk run thick and yellow onto the china plate before mopping it up greedily.

"Naughty! That is naughty." He shrugged away the words and rinsed the egg cup, spoon and knife under the running water before placing the saucepan back on the fridge. Taking the empty egg shells he placed them on the floor by the overflowing peddle bin deciding that later he would begin a long overdue cleaning session. Perhaps that could be the change. And then it struck him, it was him, he was the change. He had to do something different, break the spell. Moving as quickly as this aged body would allow him he came to the foot of the stairs and reached for the oversized overcoat that hung from the bannister. Shrugging it on he reached into the pocket and removed the old flat cap knowing it would be there. Placing the cap firmly on his head he became aware of an odour new but familiar. Was it vanilla?

"Yes just a small cone for now. Your supper will soon be ready." Vanilla with sprinkles, hundreds, no thousands of them brightly coloured. He shook his head clearing the thought and reached for the door. Twisting the latch he pulled at the resistance and as the door creaked open felt the blast of cold air hit his face. With a deep breath he took a step into this outside world shivering from what, the cold or just from pure excitement?Pushing his hands deep into the pockets he stepped away from the house and out into the street beyond

Keeping his head down he moved along the path following a route he knew well. No-one passed him the street was empty. A few cars passed by in either direction but the occupants showed him no interest, the business of their days blinding them to everything but their journeys end. He was happy that no one saw him or wanted to speak to him. How could he explain to them that he was not supposed to be here. How could he tell them that their lives were repeating the same as his? Two cats ran from an alley hissing and screeching at each other before changing direction in the blink of an eye and disappearing between two parked cars. Was this new? Had this happened before? He stopped his journey leaning against a fence, placing his hand on his heart feeling it thumping heavily beneath the overcoat. The cars. The two parked cars. He did not remember these. He was certain he hadn't seen them before. What was that noise? A high screaming noise, a siren? He had not heard that before he was certain of it. He groaned loudly confused by his surroundings, confused by all this change. If this was changing then why hadn't he, why was he still here like this? Finally settling his heart he moved stutteringly forward following the path ignoring the changes trying to make sense of what had just happened. The sign in the corner shop window flashed repeatedly advertising 'Newspapers, Booze and Fo d!' The second 'o' had stopped working making food, fo d. His breathing calmed more now, that hadn't changed that was the same. He stood silently outside the shop entrance knowing what would happen a man, a man? 'Hello call me Arshad.' Yes Arshad, A man called Arshad would talk to him. He would be friendly. A bell? Yes a bell would ring and there would be a bag. He looked at his own hands, they were empty. Where would the bag come from? The thoughts and questions jumbled around his head each one fighting for its own clarity, each one confusing him making him uncertain. The bell tinkled brightly forcing him to look up from his hands which remained splayed out in front of him.

"Hello Mr Evans. Are you not cold standing outside. Why do you not accompany me inside? It is much warmer there." Without waiting, the small man took him gently by the arm and led him into the shop the bell tinkling as they passed. He looked at the small man, he was he wearing trousers and a long dress? The shop smelled strangely a thick spicy smell, a warm smell inviting, he liked it. The man in the trousers and dress smiled at him before speaking in an almost sing song voice.

"Now don't you worry Mr Evans I am Arshad I will look after you just as I always do my friend." So this was Arshad. Before he continued his friend Arshad disappeared behind the counter and came out holding a blue and white striped plastic bag. "Here we are Mr Evans everything as you like it." Arshad held the bag towards him smiling warmly.

"Its....."

"Blue and white like your pyjamas. Yes." The man Arshad motioned him to take the bag the smile never leaving his face. "Take it Mr Evans it as always, Yes? I have never know a man who loves his eggs such as you do." The man Arshad pushed the bag gently towards him the weight causing it to swing in a slow lazy arc. Reaching out as though it were the most natural thing for him to do he took it. Surprised by the weight and at the same time wondering how the man Arshad knew of his pyjamas a question forced its way into his mind. "Was he, the smiling shop man a part of this, was he watching him, did he watch him all the time?" So lost in his own thoughts he realised that the man Arshad had been speaking.

"You look confused Mr Evans. Are you feeling unwell?"

"Unwell?" He shook his head struggling

to understand this exchange. This man before him acted as though he knew him well. He knew of his pyjamas and eggs, he had spoken of eggs. It was happening as it always did he was sure of that and yet; he could not recall it. The man smiled up at him a small crease of concern marking his brow.

"Mr Evans?" He needed to answer, he knew that but what to say, how could he break this spell?

"Yes." He said eventually his voice sounding strange to his own ears "Yes. But." The man Arshad smiled again almost clapping in relief seemingly relieved that he had answered.

"I know Mr Evans, yes I know. You have no money to pay me." The small man laughed warmly spreading his arms as though to embrace him "Mr Evans we have known each other for many years now. What friend would I be if I took money from you hmm? No my friend take it and go with my blessings as always." As though to emphasise the point the man Arshad nodded encouragingly signalling towards the door. "Go my friend. I shall watch your return along the street until you are safely home." It was then that the man Arshad did something that rocked him to the core. Taking his arm with surprising speed he pulled him close and whispered gently in his ear the warm breath scented strongly with tobacco tickled his skin.

"Stay safe my friend, stay safe. Remember your way here. I will care for you whatever you may need." As though he had become suddenly embarrassed by this exchange the man Arshad sprang backwards laughing brightly calling as though to a child. "Come, come, shoo now Mr Evans. I am sure you have much cleaning to do." He laughed again and winked as though sharing a private joke. "Come my friend. I shall watch." He pulled at the door and again the little bell tinkled a bright cheerfull sound, 'Tinkerbell' who was Tinkerbell? before he could find an answer he found himself outside the shop blue and white bag heavy in his hand. He wanted to drop the bag, wanted to toss it at the smiling man, scream that this was not his and to run. He wanted to run, he wanted to run, run on the young legs he knew were his, run as he had done, run a race,

"you have won, you are the winner!" He felt the bag bump against his leg and looked at it swinging slowly, he wanted to run but run to where? Slowly he turned and shuffled along the street, head down, concentrating hard, the bag bumping painfully against his leg. He stopped for a moment checking his surroundings, yes he needed to go this way. He nodded to himself. 'Yes.' This was the way he wanted to go. He was tired, why was he so tired? As though borne along on a breeze he soon entered a small garden that he knew. Familiar concrete path, small wooden fence overgrown with a thick bush that impeded his journey along the path to the scarred wooden door, a door that stood open and inviting. Once inside the dark of the hallway he breathed hungrily at the familiar, safe scent of damp. Leaning against the door feeling it shut reassuringly behind his bony back he felt safe, secure. Wiping the sweat from his brow he walked dreamlike towards the living room placing the bag unceremoniously on the floor where it fell to its side spilling some unrecognised contents skittle like over the frayed flower patterned rug. Sinking to the chair he pulled the coat tightly around himself and shivering against the cold fell into an exhausted sleep.

The sound of a distant car horn dragged him violently awake. His hand flung to the side seeking out what? He looked at the outstretched arm bemused by his own action. What had he been reaching for? He moved slowly trying to release the stiffness in his body. The alarm clock! He had been reaching for the alarm clock, 'Hickory dickory doc, the mouse ran up the clock!' Had there been a mouse? What mouse? Mickey, Mickey mouse? He shivered yawning widely. No a dream just a dream, or a memory?

Gazing around the room he stretched feeling every sinew creak and crack. Everything was as it should be of course it was, everything was always as it should be; and then he saw it. A bag, a blue and white carrying bag.

"Carrier bag." He corrected himself leaning forward in the chair. "Now where have you come from." He said softly, frowning at the bag whilst gently slipping his foot into the shoe that had somehow fallen from him and lay on its side like an abandoned rowing boat, 'the owl and the pussycat'. He wiped a hand across his tired face and rose unsteadily to his feet and scuffed his way to the abandoned bag looking around his surroundings as though at any moment someone would make themselves known to him as the tormentor who kept him trapped here like this. He kicked the bag with his toe and saw a bottle of water flop from the opening. With great care he leaned forward and reached for the bottle placing it on the largest of a nest of tables. Repeating the movement he took up a loaf of white sliced bread and a newspaper. Each of these he placed on the table with the water before reaching one more time and taking up the bag which crinkled delightfully in his hands. For a few moments he scrunched the top of the bag forgetting his nervousness in finding it. Carrying the bag back to the armchair he sat as comfortably as his back would allow and peered inside. Closing the bag quickly he stole another glance around the room certain now that this must be a test. When nothing happened he peeked again at the remaining contents; A carton of eggs, garlic bread and a foil tray wrapped in cardboard professing to be lasagne. He shuddered noisily, he hated garlic bread, why would anyone leave garlic bread for him.

"My friend stay safe." Stay safe? The vision of a little man swam into focus.

"Of course, the man!" He puckered his lips his face a drawn picture of concentration. "I am, I am, I am.." He said each phrase becoming hoarse with frustration as he tried to again recall the name. He could see the smile, almost hear the voice, just out of reach, just in the distance. "I am." He said again before spotting the bread "I am.... hungry." Clutching the bag, he crossed the room stopping at the little table to gather up the water, bread and newspaper. He walked into the kitchen pulling the cord of the light switch. The dim bulb fought a brave battle against the gloom of the small room but eventually settled on a draw. Walking to the formica worktop he unloaded the bag and studied the contents. Greedily he ripped open the paper and plastic of the lasagne, grabbed the small tea spoon that lay on the draining board and spooned the solid mess into his mouth one chunk at a time. Wiping his mouth on the sleeve of the overcoat he twisted the top of the water bottle which slipped unyielding between his fingers. With a roar of frustration he reached for the half glass back door behind him and pulled it open its hinges squealing in complaint. With what little strength he could muster he threw the plastic bottle out into the growing gloom where it bounced once on the broken concrete of the small weed ridden patio area and disappeared into the long grass. He stood panting at the exertion the need for water burning at his throat. He turned back into the kitchen and twisted the tap open to full and dipped his head beneath the flowing stream sucking with little care of the noise at the water which splashed back at his face from the yellowed porcelain sink. Feeling refreshed he felt the chill from the open doorway. Staring out, a condemned man looking for freedom he wiped the excess water from his face with the sleeve of his coat,

'Come on in. It's raining, you will catch a chill'.

'Yes, I will. I will be in soon'. The breeze cooled his face and he pulled the cap further onto his head relishing the little warmth it brought to him. Why was he standing here, what could have held his attention for so long? The back garden was small room for a patio, a scrub of overgrown grass, a shed in disrepair and a high wooden gate set into a crumbling brick wall. Birds. Yes he was here to feed the birds. Reaching for the loaf of bread he quickly tore open the wrapper and sent slice after slice spinning into the air landing with soft flops onto grass and concrete alike. Next he reached for the garlic bread and tossed it end over end to join the water bottle now lost somewhere amongst the high grass. Finally satisfied that all was as it should be he wrestled the swollen door closed and turned his attention to the eggs. Taking two from the box he placed them carefully in a double egg cup that someone had left prominently on the kitchen top. The cartoon fireman waved brightly at him the smile undeterred by the lacquering of dried egg yolk that darkened on the china. Now aware of the remaining eggs he closed the cardboard lid of the box uncaring of the cracking sound that accompanied the action. Shuffling to the fridge he pulled open the door and looked without understanding at the sight before him. Dozens of battered and torn egg boxes crammed violently together spilled their hidden contents pungently inside the silent fridge. He wrinkled his nose at the smell before nodding slowly. When, no, if tomorrow he awoke still trapped in this hell, a hell that held him in this vicelike grip, he would make this his first job.

To clean out this fridge may break the cycle it may begin his journey to freedom but for now he was too overcome with tiredness to make a start. Looking down at the egg box in his hand, he thrust it heavily into the blackness of the fridge crushing it alongside those that had gone before. Slamming the door with a determination that rocked the fridge on the uneven floor, he wiped the stickiness from his hands onto his trousers whistling tunelessly. His stomach rumbled, a good feeling he was sure. He had eaten, he felt as though although tired he now had more energy. Rolling up the newspaper he thrust it deep into his coat pocket. He needed to do something, time was quickly slipping away from him.

"Idle hands are the Devils workshop!" Yes, yes. He must not be idle, he must do something. Wandering into the living room he noticed a can that must have rolled from the bag and nestling against the leg of his chair. Reaching down he took up the can and read the label.

"Beeswax Buffer, furniture polish."

"You have much cleaning to do." The grinning man's voice echoed in his mind.

"Cleaning to do." Yes that was it he had to clean. Opening the lid of the polish with a pop he sprayed the room liberally wiping off any that landed on the table, chair or television with his sleeve. Seeing that everything was now clean and tidy he placed the can on the small nest of tables and sat in his chair surveying what he came to realise was his kingdom. But wait! Should a kingdom not be clean? He walked to the nest of tables and picked up a half used can of furniture polish. Tutting to himself he sprayed the can liberally and wiped off any excess that fell on the table, chair or television with his sleeve. Happy that his work was done he shook the can close to his ear. The can was empty. Tutting loudly he tossed the can to the far end of the room where it clanged loudly against other empty cans that lay silent in their unheard admonishment. Collapsing into his chair with a swoosh of expelled air and dust particles that circled the dim overhead bulb the tiredness which caught him so easily off guard finally took over and pulling his cap low over his eyes drifted gently off to sleep.

The nagging in his stomach grew worse pulling him to slow wakefulness. He needed to pee and quickly. Rousing himself from the chair he stumbled exhaustedly to the stairway hesitating only to switch off the naked bulb of the room. He finally shrugged himself from the overcoat and hung it haphazardly on the newel post whilst stuffing the cap from his head into the pocket. As he rammed the cap inside the voluminous space he closed his hand around the rolled up newspaper which had suffered from his sleep. Now crumpled at the edges the ink smudged and worn, it sat in his hand sullenly disappointed and disapproving, headlines unread, stories untold. Without pausing any further, he climbed uncomfortably, each tread of the stairs a mountain, each step a chore. Clutching the creased newspaper tightly he grimaced, his forehead beaded with a sheen of perspiration. The pain in his stomach was growing stronger and as it grew his strength failed. With only seconds to spare he reached the small bathroom and made use of the toilet thankful that at least the trousers and pyjama bottoms were loose enough to shrug over his slender hips. Washing his hands under the cold running water of the small sink ignoring the chill the water brought to his skin his attention was drawn to the newspaper now laying abandoned on the cistern. He wiped his hands on his trousers and carefully unrolled it. Headlines that made no sense danced before his eyes. Names that meant nothing to him passed under his gaze. It was always like this, sent to mystify him. Carelessly he tossed the paper to one side where it spread its pages as though a wounded bird heroically fighting to stay airborne. He watched as it finally lost control and crashed amongst the forest of other discarded newspapers in the abandoned bath. Before the newspaper had fully come to rest he was shuffling along the hallway to the place he knew so well, exhaustion blurring his vision. In the bedroom he stopped by the chair trying hard to remember. With great care he removed the jacket and folded it neatly patting it gently as he placed it down smoothing the soft collar as though it were a sleeping kitten. Next he pulled the blue sleeveless jumper over his head aware of how the striped pyjama top raised itself revealing his yellowed torso. Folding this he resolved to patch the large hole that seemed to have appeared just below the collar before placing it on top of the now restful jacket. He allowed the trousers to fall from his hips with little ceremony to lay rumpled around his ankles. As he stepped from the trousers he stepped free of the shoes that lay covered by the crumpled material. Using the chair to brace himself he bent at the waist to retrieve the trousers and folded them carefully.

"Crease to crease, keep them straight you horrible little man. Move it, move it. Attention!" He added the trousers to the pile and placed the battered shoes under the seat of the chair toes just visible. Shuffling towards the bed he coughed wetly before reaching for the alarm clock. He stabbed a bent bony finger at the large button causing large red letters to shine their message. 'Alarm set 6.27. Climbing slowly onto the damp unmade bed he clutched one arm around his stomach and pulled the heavy blanket over his shivering form. His Breath came in small shallow breaths as he waited for the pain that seemed to grip him anew to subside. Once he was certain that for now all was calm he removed his glasses and placed them gently by the clock nestling his head wearily on the pillow, waiting for sleep to take him, as it always did.

"Perhaps tomorrow will be different." He mumbled dreamily "Perhaps tomorrow I will not wake up in this place." He yawned loudly, his dentures clacking freely as his breathing deepened. "Night night, sleep tight." From above the bed the picture of the young woman smiled down at the sleeping form her eyes alive with love.

"Mind the bedbugs don't bite."

Letters

Sunday 31st March 1912

1 Hope Cottages
Middlesthorpe
Southampton

Dear Sir

It is with a heavy heart and a sense of remorse such as I have never before experienced that I feel obliged to write to you, this, a letter that bares for me such overwhelming regret.

Over the past 12 years you have nurtured and above all encouraged me to succeed where others certainly would have overlooked me for the ruffian who first presented himself to your door all those years before. Such has been your kindness and wisdom that I am no longer said ruffian but, in word and deed one who would be considered now, a gentleman, albeit of the simplest kind.

Your trust in me, your wise words and instruction have blessed me not only to succeed in my skills as a draughtsman but in the journey I take in life. It is your moulding of me which has led in no small part to my success. I shall forever more be indebted to you. This shall be not a debt that makes us estranged with regret or sense of ownership but a debt which sees me hold you as close to my heart as any Father I may have had. I speak not lightly when I repeat here what I have spoken aloud to any who will listen. It is you Sir who allowed me to grow to become the man others see today. You have created a man who found such confidence that he was first able to woo, then court and finally have a proposal of marriage accepted by my darling Eliza. My dearest Eliza who dares to kiss your cheek and hug your arm as though you were the father in law she deserved. Eliza the very girl who brings the smile to my face and the spring in my step, for she is the woman who guides me now as surely as your hand steered me before. And now alas it is with mention of my darling girl that I must bring my first statements to your attention, to the very heart of what forces my hand to pen such a letter to yourself. I wish not to write these words but write them I must, so as you have taught me and without further preamble or procrastination I lay before you my innermost thoughts.

    You are aware Sir that in recent months my angel, my heart, my Eliza brought to me the finest of gifts, the revered of all treasures, my son Arthur. Arthur who bares my name as is a fathers right but carries with pride your name as his middle, the name of the man who his father acknowledges as the strength that flows through his soul. This is a small token but one honestly given. Now alas, and how my heart breaks as the ink dries on what I write, I fear the needs of my small but much cherished family have shown themselves to be greater than I can in truth accommodate with any success, working as I do and so far away.

Sir I beg of you forgiveness as I finally allow my pen to write words such as these. The boy who you nurtured has now become the man who will turn from you in favour of his own dear family and beg to be released from his contract of work. If dear Sir you find it in your heart to allow what must be this seemingly ungrateful cad the freedom to start if at all possible his own small business it would give him freedom to finally accumulate a small wage whilst wrapped in the bosom of his family. I shall if released from your kindness serve my family from nearby and not be called to far flung corners of this great country spending weeks away from those I love the most. In short Sir, forgive me for such a request, but please I hope, find it in your heart to do this callow youth one last kindness whilst knowing that if ever you call I shall be at your side to assist.

    With the kindest of regards
        Arthur Sedgwick

A C STOCK

Wednesday 3rd April 1912

The Old Vicarage
Hope Street
Liverpool

Dear Sir

I call you Sir in only formality as in private I think of you as Son. It was with the greatest of regrets and yet the most overpowering sensation of pride that I read your recent letter to myself. Never has a man felt his heart swell in such a way. To hear of another's success in business but moreover in life, brings the greatest of satisfactions known to man especially to such a man as myself who has little in the way of dependants of his own. Although your words touch me I fear that you offer me more praise than is becoming of one who did no more than allow a young boy to grow into who he was always destined to be. I carry pride of successes thrust upon me uncomfortably and wish not to sully our relationship with thoughts of any manipulation or moulding. Let us if we can, consider any interaction between us as a joint venture, a meeting of minds and kindred spirits. Allow me this small kindness and I shall smile contentedly into my dotage.

You speak of Eliza and dearest Arthur so lovingly and again my heart thumps with a rhythm it has forgotten in the mists of time. My own darling Rebecca left this earth too early and too young, a pain I have borne for these past 5 and 30 years eased only by the kiss on my cheek and the hug of my arm so recently and kindly given by your own darling Eliza.

My boy. You speak of leaving what we do here so as to cast out your own net on seas anew. You talk of your own small family as though they are in some way a hindrance to what we have achieved here together. You separate me from them and in turn them from me. Now be warned for I shall speak harshly over this matter, I shall speak as a father if you can so forgive me the impudence of the remark, but still I shall speak as a father to a son. I will honour the role you yourself bestowed upon me.

To beg freedom from a contract such as I offer you, marks a fool easily parted from his money. If as you say you have grown into a man who is no longer the ruffian or urchin who stood before me, then use these new found ways and see what is really before you. I beg of you stand silently as you have learned and think of the issue not as a problem but a challenge to overcome. I smile as my own ink dries on the harshness I have metered out to you in this past sentence. I see your face before me, brow furrowed and eyes slits to the anger that burns within. Again I say use this, use my words and consider what is on offer, think what it is that solves the issue before us. Perhaps I have misjudged, perhaps you are still that young boy who although with obvious talents for copying work laid before you needs those prompts to explore and discover for yourself? Here I jest with you, I make sport of you as a kindly father does his beloved son, and yet? Still I see you with pencil in hand as a boy marking the paper as though you copied holy script itself not allowing yourself the freedom to design as you knew you could. Do you recall these days, do you still feel the excitement that shone from you as all at once you realised the alteration that could be made, the difference that could be newly created with a simple stroke of your pencil? See now how I dally with my own writing as you procrastinated before.

Let me now speak clearly. I shall not free you from your contract with me as I can offer better than any thought of separation between us. My Son and here my words are true, I cannot separate you from what is rightfully yours, I cannot set you free from what you have always been destined to own upon my demise. My business (or should I hope) that this day, 'our' business, shall thrive as best we see fit. You shall work there in Southampton I shall remain here in Liverpool. You will seek out new business but not alone, not in fear of risk or destitution and not as a fatherless man who ploughs a furrow lonely and unsupported. You as of this day have been named as my partner and my heir apparent. When next we shall meet together my solicitor will have the papers about him ready for nothing more than your signature.

My Son. I now beg your forgiveness. I fear I have twisted your arm from your general thinking. I must insist that you speak this through with our darling, again I take a liberty, our darling Eliza. Contact me at your soonest to confirm or rebuff my humble offer, but I pray as a lonely old man for the former.

I end this now so as to catch the evening post for fear of missing you by moments in a venture of your own making.

In anticipation and respect

Sir Douglas Follington

Saturday 6th April 1912
1 Hope Cottages
Middlesthorpe
Southampton

Dear Father

Forgive my impudence but I feel the need to respond as my heart decrees. Father in more than just hope, Father in deed. I shall if I may, forgo a dithering response such is my excitement at what is to come. You offer me more than I could ever imagine, more than any young boy who shared rooms with nothing but beatings and rats for company dare allow himself to dream in the darkest of nights. I shall of course be honoured to take on the position you have offered as I shall with all humility and thankfulness become I hope as much a son as you are a Father to me. Our Eliza, for that is how she now wishes you to think of her thanks you as she has never before thanked anyone in her life and in this I include her own departed Father who like your own darling Rebecca passed too soon.

And so to the business with which we are now together so embroiled. Dare I say this again for fear of the truth I have been offered becoming no more than a jest? The business we are entwined in as partners has already taken my imagination by force. I have found a small property close to the docks which will serve me well as an office until such time as I need more to work with me as the business grows. Yes as you see I have plans already for growth in your name. Perhaps you have in a moment of recklessness unleashed Pandora from her box? I now jest at your expense, my eagerness is from thankfulness, my thirst for growth is from gratitude, my need for haste is borne out of the need to please you as a son pleases his Father.

I as promised shall keep this my acceptance brief until we meet again in a few weeks and I can shake your hand warmly and bestow my gratitude upon you fully. So until such time I bid you the fondest of farewells and have you know that I am always at your call.

>With devotion
>Arthur Sedgwick

Post script
>In my haste to be about the business you intended for me to grow, I omitted to inform you that it was only 3 days since that I saw the results of our past labours glide into view. She is as magnificent as Mr Andrews predicted she would be. I thank the lord that we were fortunate enough to be employed in his charge

to work alongside him. Oh how we will all go down in history thanks to such a remarkable man.

                        Monday 8th April 1912
                            The Old Vicarage
                                 Hope Street
                                     Liverpool

My Son

   I send this letter via the speediest courier such is the haste of the content. I fear this matter is to be considered of the highest importance and is a request I make of the gravest nature. I apologise in advance that I have to bestow upon you such a task. Such is the urgency of this message that I must forego pleasantries but instead act in haste hence the brevity of this short letter. Mr Andrews has requested that he has someone travel with him on the forthcoming journey as there are to be slight modifications needed to some of the internal fittings in preparation for further journeys. He of course, Mr Andrews, is a highly skilled draughtsman but fears he may be taken up with publicity duties on the outward journey. Mr Andrews has specifically requested our finest of draughtsman who is to accompany him for the purpose of translating his scribbles into detailed drawings. it is with much trepidation, especially with your wish to be closer to your wonderful family, that I suggested yourself, especially as you are so well situated being already in Southampton. To allay your fears for darling Eliza and little Arthur I shall have a carriage sent for them and they shall reside with me until your return.

I do regret having to ask this of you my boy but our good name needs to be upheld however immediate the rush may be.

Forgive me my son
Your father

Telegram

To Sir Douglas Follington. Stop. 10th April. Stop. Am aboard Titanic. Stop. Andrews sends thanks. Stop. She is a creature of beauty a truly magnificent ship. Stop. See you on my return. Stop. Love to all. Stop. Arthur Sedgwick. Stop.

Take Away

"Are you sure you will remember?" Barry sighed with exaggerated expansiveness.

"Yes of course. 3 cod and chips, 1 with extra salt, 1 large battered sausage and chips, 1 kebab meat and chips no chilli sauce and two children's cod and chips." He studied the snapped lace he had successfully managed to knot together wishing he had remembered to pick up a new pair with the shopping. "I will take a quick walk to the chip shop and be back in 20 minutes."

"You are walking?" A look of horror creased Julia's face, it was look he knew well, he would have to be careful.

"Yes I thought I would." He kept his voice light and breezy, no need to panic yet.

"Right!" Now it was time to panic, this was the response Barry feared. This was the word that carried so much danger. How did she do that, make the word 'right' carry such weight? He knew what it meant, understood the tone. She was not pleased. He would have to act quickly, he would need to justify his choice. He must find a reasonable excuse, one that could not be pushed aside like the weakest of children.

"I thought the exercise would do me

good." He felt more than saw her stiffen by his side but he must forge on, show no weakness. "You know how difficult it is to park by the chip shop and just think, all those cars with their engines running polluting the environment. Consider this my little effort to help save the planet." He stopped talking and waited patiently, this was the moment, zero hour. Julia would either be forced to accept his answer for the brilliance it was or go into a full nuclear meltdown. He waited patiently hoping the thump of his heart did not betray him, he needed to remain calm. As though finding it hard to speak, Julia made a long slow sucking noise, her tongue firmly against her teeth. This was the sign, he had defeated her, she had nothing to add, nothing to throw at him as a comeback. He had won. He tried to hide the smile that crossed his face, tried to keep it under wraps, God he was good. He had given her three reasons in one go and for once she had absolutely no tetchy retort to offer.

"You forgot to go to the petrol station didn't you? Her voice was low, each syllable spoken as though it was a word of its own. Damn her, how did she do that? How did she get right to the heart of the lie in under a second? He was on the back foot again, there was no getting past her psychic abilities. He needed a lie that would sail somewhere close to the truth, a lie that would make this a score draw.

"Well yes," He began "Well, sort of." He finished tying his other shoe lace and straightened to face her from his seated position. "You see…" He wasn't quite sure where he was going with this but his next words had to be good, "In essence you may have a glimmer of what went on when in fact, I didn't forget to go. I went, I really did but the queues were massively long. I decided that I would leave it for a while, come home and just go back later when the queues were gone." He smiled his winning smile and reached towards her gently stroking the back of her hand "I suppose you could say in essence that I did not forget to go, I simply forgot to go back." Perfect. This was an absolute winner, 'The defence as they say, rests M' Lud."

"Mmm." Julia looked down at him with the withering look she usually kept for rude people on the underground, for smelly pets who thought that jumping up to be petted was ok and for bawling children who did not understand that their snotty noses and bright red tear infused cheeks offered little in the way of cherub style beauty.

"So in essence…" He hated it when she used his own words against him. "In essence you just forgot." Flicking his hand from hers Julia turned to leave, "I had better write that order down for you. You are bound to forget it."

He had to do something, had to make amends and show her for once just how reliable he could really be.

"No!" The word came out with more force than he would ever usually dare use. Julia stopped in her tracks her fingers bending and flexing, the sign of agitation. "No, honestly no." He had to recover this quickly escalating situation, laughter was the best defence weapon. "Honestly Julia." He laughed softly waving away the whole sentence as though it were an annoying spiders web. "Honestly. I've got this." He tapped the side of his head signalling just how deeply routed the list was in his brain. " It's not hard to remember is it not even for a numbskull like me." Clever, a little self deprecation goes a long way. "After all there are only six things to remember." He smiled broadly, game set and match.

"Seven," The word hung in the air between them.

"What?"

"There are seven things to remember Barry." She turned and faced him her features somehow flat against her face, "There are seven things to remember." Oh sweet Jesus this was getting worse,

"Well yes, of course there are seven things." He began frantically trying to recall the list, "But two of them are the same." Before she could respond he jumped from his seat and reached for his jacket turning his back on her as he fastened it, the zipper sticking halfway along its travels as it always did. Ignoring his struggle with the zip Julia graced him with the 'Mmm' sound that she made so well, drawing it out, stretching it beyond even his greatest fear.

"Ok, I suppose so but please be quick because Sally, Colin, the boys and Angelica will be here in 20 minutes." He heard himself before being able to stop the words leaving his mouth.

"As though I could forget." He quickly pushed aside the fear that crushed his spine and knocked the wind from his lungs, "How could I forget? I've been looking forward to this for days." The lie felt good, felt as though it had covered his slip although it did not cover the feeling of pure frustration he felt. The sense of dislike and annoyance that slammed into his stomach just at the very thought of his oh so perfect sister-in-law and her self righteous knob of a husband threatened to spill over into a physical gagging motion that would have been far from ideal. He was still unable to put aside the shock of hearing that they, Sally and Colin, along with their two identikit twin boys, who no doubt would be dressed as the angels they were always identified as and their stroppy 10 year old daughter Angelica had invited themselves down for the weekend. The thought of another weekend in the company of 10 year old Angelica who's temper tantrums put her as far removed from angelic as Cliff Richard was from heavy metal burned in the pit of his stomach. He tried to focus on some of the positives. What were the positives? He sighed heavily deciding that perhaps if having fish and chips was the only positive then life really had got as bad as it possibly could have especially when he had already made plans for the weekend. He closed his eyes and thought about these now defunct plans, simple, enjoyable plans. He could picture himself, sitting on the sofa surrounded by beer cans and empty crisp packets, football blaring away on the television, his lap-top open to view the racing results and then a quick trip into their small back garden (weather permitting) and if he was really lucky he would cop an eyeful of the new woman next door hanging out the washing wearing those skimpy red shorts and that very tight, white vest top that revealed just how chilly the air was.

"Yes can't wait to see them again. He said, shaking away the vision he carried with him daily, hoping that Julia would not notice that he was definately not, talking about the family. She wouldn't, would she? He decided that to stand clear of her eye-line was probably best, just in case. "Still best get going, don't want to keep them waiting." He called pulling open the front door and instantly regretted not going to the garage for petrol as a fine rain blew into his face. "I won't be long." He shouted over his shoulder tugging at his jacket zip which still stubbornly refused to move any further than half way along its supposed destination, "See you soon." He ignored her call of…

"They will be here in twenty minutes," Which whip cracked towards him from a quickly moving Julia who headed up the stairs, no doubt to put on something more fitting than the already perfect skirt and blouse combination she was wearing. Pulling his collar around his neck he allowed himself the dignity of sauntering at his usual lumbering pace away from the house towards the high street. Why was everything so urgent for Julia? Why did everything have to be done at a rush? No, he would not rush, he would take his time. So what if he was late back? With a determination befitting the hunter gatherer he set his jaw, pulled back his shoulders, tugged at the stubborn zip, nodded at his powerful decision making and assured himself that if he was late back and Julia was unhappy he could always blame the queue.

Walking along he kicked at a discarded empty soft drinks can enjoying the sound it made as it clattered away noisily and high fiving an invisible sports fan as they celebrated with him the fact that he had managed with great skill to leave it defying the laws of gravity hanging half on the path, half over the kerb.

"Oy, you, pick that up!" A car pulled up silently alongside him, the driver buzzing down the passenger window. "Bloody litter lout. Man of your age should know better."

"But it's not mine. I only…"

"Don't give me that crap. I saw you. Its on my dash cam. Pick it up or I report you to the Village Council." The driver pointed at the front of his car as though Barry was interested in his bloody dash cam, well he wasn't going to stand for this.

"Listen, mate." The word 'mate' sounded impressive, made him sound tough, the sort of thing that bald bloke of the tele says in that show Julia loves so much. Yes the word 'mate' made him sound very London, very gangster. He wondered if the new woman next door would have been impressed?

"Don't 'mate' me. Pick your can up or I will come out and make you pick it up." Barry snorted in derision, bending over and wordlessly picking up the can and shoving it into his pocket, hearing the lining rip in protest. "I've got you on dash cam remember. Don't let me find any more litter round here or I will report you." Without waiting or indeed having the manners to witness the two fingered salute Barry offered him from the inside of his pocket the car driver pulled silently away. Barry hated electric cars he hated anything that allowed old men the chance to sneak up on people who were just trying to have a bit of fun. He allowed his fingers to explore the large rip in the lining of his jacket pocket and cursed silently. There really were too many people who were more like the fun police than human beings these days. Ignoring the lumpy can in his pocket he began his trek to the chip shop running the list through his mind, just to be on the safe side.

"3 cod and chips, 1 with extra salt, he paused thinking hard, 1 large battered sausage and chips, 1 kebab meat and chips no chilli sauce and 2 children's portions of cod and chips," 7 items in total, simple. Sometimes he didn't really understand why Julia never trusted him with the most simple of tasks, why she treated him so much like a child? He pulled the can from his pocket and leaped high into the air tossing it like a pro basketball player towards an open dustbin and wheeling away in celebration as it landed with a satisfying thud dead centre.

"Yes, get in there. 3 points for Barry the Shark." Barry the Shark, he liked that, good nickname. Perhaps when he got his courage up he may have that as his first tattoo, 'Barry the Shark' in red and blue. Julia would hate it of course, she hated tattoos unless they were on that big fella in the films Dwayne 'The Rock' Johnson, oh yes she liked them then. Barry wondered if Dwayne's wife moaned about him getting tattoos or having fun, no of course she didn't. Barry was certain that Dwayne would forget things, he bet he forgot all sorts of things but his wife wouldn't care she would say,

"Oh Dwayne never mind, we all forget things. Now why don't you go and get yourself another tattoo whilst I hang out the washing wearing nothing but these skimpy red shorts and see-through white top." Barry shook his head, sometimes Julia was far too harsh on him. Ok he forgot to go to the garage and now only had enough petrol to get him as far as the garage on Monday before he went to work, and yes he did forget to buy the wrapping paper she had asked him to get for their 'sweet' goddaughters birthday present but what child didn't love pretty pictures drawn on a carrier bag? Stuffing his hands deep into his pockets he trudged along cursing the weather and the rubbish weekend they were about to have but at least the fish and chips would make up for it... or should he have pie and chips? The thought of a beef and onion pie began to form in his mouth and he swallowed noisily, yes beef and onion pie and chips lovely. He made a mental note,

"Change that for 2 cod and chips, 1

pie and chips, 1 large battered sausage and chips 1 kebab meat and chips no chilli sauce and 2 children's cod and chips." Yes that sounded good, pie and chips. He looked down as something flapped around his foot, the broken shoelace had come undone, perhaps he should have bought some new ones when Julia suggested it. Bending over ignoring the wet seeping into the knee of his jeans as it made contact with the pavement he began the task of retying the broken lace.

"Conrad, Sylvester. No! He heard the voice before he felt the impact. At first he wondered if he was being attacked by two oversized rats but soon it became apparent that two small brown dogs had decided that his rear end was fair game for an over exuberant humping session.

"What the f…."

"I'm so sorry. Get down you naughty boys, leave the man alone, Sylvester no. I'm so sorry, they haven't been done you see. It's just instinct. Conrad no!"

"Get your dogs off me. Stop doing that you little shit."

"Oh I'm so sorry. It's just they saw you there and well they are that age you see. You know what boys are like?" Barry flicked his leg trying to remove the thrusting dog but found the second dog joining his brother

"Boys I understand, but these are bloody rats on a lead. No, get of you little shits!"He stepped away from the leaping dogs who made choking noises as the leads tightened around their necks although the pain did not seem to diminish their ardour as they pulled more frantically desperate to hump his leg. "Christ keep them away from me." He said rubbing at his trousers to make sure there was no unwanted stains. "I mean for Christ sake look at the state of my jeans. Keep those bloody mutts under control will you." The woman holding the two frantic dogs finally managed to draw them in, their extendable leads grinding in protest.

"I will have you know they are not mutts." She exclaimed furiously "They are Dachshund dogs Miniature Dachshund's or to an ignorant individual such as yourself they are two highly intelligent sausage dogs."

"I don't care what they are. You need to keep the bloody things under control. The rate they were grinding at me if my jeans hadn't been thick I would have been bloody pregnant. If I was you I would get their knackers chopped off, that will stop them jumping everything that moves." As though suddenly understanding what had just been said both dogs cowered tightly behind their mistress looking at him from between her legs.

"How dare you! How bloody dare you!"

The woman reached down and scooped the two dogs quickly into her arms hugging them tightly to herself. "Don't you listen to him my lovelies. Don't listen to the nasty man, you were only doing what was natural. How would he like it do you think if some evil person cut his knackers off. Oh you vile man, you cruel, horridly vile man. What a terrible thing to subject animals to." She kissed each dog on the head clucking soothingly, "Don't you worry my lovelies we will report this horrible person to that lovely community support officer Sophia Henderson, she will understand, she will keep an eye out for this nasty man, this animal beater." Offering Barry no chance to answer, the woman turned bustled away carrying the two dogs as though they were babes in arms. Barry watched her cross the road and disappear down the close opposite whilst all the time the 2 sausage dogs stared back at him over her shoulders with what he was sure was a small smile on their faces.

"Bloody hell." Barry cursed reaching down to rub at a stain on his jeans that didn't have the consistency of water. Who would ever believe he had been molested by a sausage dog, no forget that molested by 2 sausage dogs, this really was a shit day. Wiping his hand quickly through a bush to wash away the residue of the…. He didn't want to think about what it was so decided just to think of it as thick rain. He wiped his now wet hand on his jacket to dry it but in truth the jacket was already as wet as his hand. Moving away suddenly aware of the time slipping by and Julia's voice ringing in his ears,

"They will be here in 20 minutes." He turned the corner onto the high street and stopped in amazement. Where there should have been a communal recycling bin and a placard announcing 'Sturton-under-Lyme Village in Bloom Winner 2021.' Which in truth was not the greatest advertisement of achievement, as since that metronomic rise to fame they as a village had been disqualified and banned for the next three years from entering any village horticultural event due to the discovery of artificial flowers being added to the displays in place of real plants, now stood a very damp and lonely gazebo. The gazebo contained the form of two men and a banner that read S.A.L.T (sad and lonely trio). He looked at the men one of whom banged unenthusiastically on a single drum and a cymbal whilst the other crashed awkwardly on a tambourine. Normally Barry would have passed by, having little interest in the daily lives and activities of firstly anything to do within the village and secondly anyone who advertised themselves as sad and lonely but he noticed on a small stool by the man with the cymbal lay a towel perfect for him to wipe dry his sticky hand.

"Hi there." He kept himself bright trying not to make it too obvious that he was eyeing up the towel.

"Ow do?" The 2 men stopped playing and looked at him, their faces matching the faded crimson of their well worn waistcoats.

"You from up north?" The man on the drum sighed his breath as weary as his features.

"Yep. Bolton." Barry nodded, opening and closing his hand feeling the palm sticking with each movement.

"Right."

"Right."

"Long way to come."

"Yes. Yes it is."

"Especially in this weather." Barry gestured to the rain which was now dripping through the flimsy material of the gazebo. "Can't be much fun?" His question was he realised was superfluous, as the hang dog expressions they both wore with conviction was proof enough.

"No not really." The man with the drum, beat a couple of heavy slaps on the damp skin but seemed to lose heart as quickly as he began, "No fun at all really." Barry nodded as though this were answer enough.

"So, What is it you are doing here?" It was again a wasted question as quite clearly the two men were both standing in the rain under a leaking gazebo banging listlessly on sodden instruments better suited to a very poor school percussion group. The obvious answer was 'standing in the rain playing instruments' but the man on the drum graced him with a shrug.

"Playing for your Easter fete." Barry nodded

"Right."

"Right." The two men looked at each other, both men of the world fully understanding the mysteries of life. Eventually more to break the hypnotic trance that had fallen over them than the need to clear his throat Barry coughed.

"Erm. You know the Easter festival is next month don't you? The man with a sincerity Barry admired immensely shrugged and nodded a slow, almost wise nod.

"Yes we do. Well, at least we do now." Barry offered his own nod hoping it matched the elder statesman sincerity of the drum player.

"Right." The drum player responded with another shrug which again only added to the look of grandeur he seemed able to posses whilst sitting behind the sodden drum and cymbal set.

"Yes bit of a mishap with the booking I'm afraid. Seems I misread the flyer and

I booked us in for a prime spot on the first Saturday of March." Again Barry nodded sharing the news of a sad fellow traveler who forges a lonely furrow along the rocky road of misunderstanding.

"You know the fete is on the first Sunday and not erm, a Saturday? Again the drummer nodded.

"Yes. Not my finest effort I'm afraid." Before either of them could continue the heavy debate the voice of the so far silent tambourine player scythed through the comradeship so newly formed.

"Not your finest effort, not your finest effort? Wrong month, wrong day, wrong date, wrong weather, wrong bloody everything. No, not your finest effort at all. This whole thing has been a total bloody cock up, that is what this is, no more no less just an unmitigated bloody cock up. To emphasise his point he crashed his thin hand onto the tambourine catching his knuckles on the wooden rim.

"Shit on this!" He bellowed throwing the tambourine to the floor and kicking it violently away towards the back of the gazebo where it hit the stone wall of the adjoining garden and came to a stop with a shotgun crack! "Now just look what's happened. Shit on all this." He marched to where the broken instrument lay and bent to pick it up only to snatch his hand away in one swift exaggerated movement, "Oh for Christ sake, dog shit." He began wiping his hand on a bush just as Barry had only moments before. Pulling his hand from the bush he sniffed at his fingers and made a harsh gagging sound at the back of his throat. Without hesitating he thrust his hand back into the bush cursing loudly as he ripped a hole in his rain sodden shirt. "Oh for the love of God when will this end?" He sniffed again at his fingers and reached up to the roof of the sagging gazebo thrusting his hand into the large puddle of rainwater that had gathered in the corner. Barry supposed his idea had been a good one, in fact one that he himself would have thought of but saw the error of the idea as a large newly freed cascade of water fell in a deluge over the side of the gazebo and slid gleefully between the gap of his collar and his neck. "Jesus Christ holy mother of God! That's it I'm going to the car to change my clothes. You can pack all of this shit away Roger." The wiry man turned forcefully towards the man seated passively behind the drum "No in fact leave it here, leave it all here. Let's hope that some other fool feels the urge to stand on the street corner in the pissing rain playing to idiot passers by who have as much interest as the woman who let her dogs shit on the floor."

"Ahh sausage dogs." Barry offered helpfully glad at last that he could offer something useful to help ease the man's pain.

"Piss off." The tambourine man stalked away kicking the remnants of his instrument along the road seeming to take great pleasure when it skidded from his foot bounced once into the road and was instantly crushed beneath the wheels of a Range Rover pulling a caravan. "Take that you evil piece of shit." He called shaking his clench fist in a gesture of pure hatred.

"Sorry about that." The drummer, Roger, placed his drumsticks into a blue plastic box which hung on the side of the drum. "Keith has not been too happy about this gig since we got here." He pulled a handkerchief from his pocket and blew his nose noisily, inspecting the contents of the tartan handkerchief before pushing it sullenly into his pocket, "He feels it's a waste of his talent, a misuse of his ambition, well that and the fact we are we are one month and one day early." Barry watched as the furious figure of Keith the disgruntled tambourine player stormed along the high street snarling at anyone who dare look at him.

"That's ok." Barry shrugged "I know how he feels, cock ups seem to be my thing at the moment." The drummer raised an eyebrow in way of a question, "Two cocks actually." Keith continued, subconsciously rubbing at the patch on his jeans, "It was probably the same 2 sausage dogs who left your mate Keith the shit to put his hand in as mounted me like a couple of stud bulls just now." If he was at all mystified or surprised by the statement Roger kept the same bland look on his face as he began unscrewing the cymbal from its stand.

"Right." The word hung between them as though it were the perfect response to what he had just heard. Holding the symbol between his legs he reached for the battered leather case and placed the symbol carefully inside. "Don't worry Keith gets like this. It's nothing a long hot bath, a glass of his favourite Pinot Grigio, a romantic movie on the tele and a long cuddle on the sofa when we are both in our pyjamas wont sort out." Barry nodded stuffing his hands back into his pockets

"Right."

"Right."

"Sorry about the cock ups quip."

"No worries."

"No offence."

"None taken." Roger reached up and began untying the sign folding it neatly into a perfect square.

"Erm, Roger." Barry opened his hands in a flat, friendly manner, "I hope it's ok to call you Roger?" Roger held the sign to his chest the water dripping onto his already damp shirt,

"Yes of course." Barry smiled holding out

his hand ready to accept a firm handshake, gentleman to gentleman.

"Great. I'm Barry by the way."

"Good to meet you Barry, by the way." Barry laughed, he quite liked this Roger, seemed like a good bloke, had a good sense of humour.

"Barry Porter."

"What?" Roger inclined his head a look of confusion on his face.

"My name. My name is Barry, Barry Porter." The drummer Roger, nodded his frown growing deeper.

"Yes I'm sure it is." Barry dropped his hand to his side, things had changed, the look on this Roger's face had altered, this Roger bloke suddenly looked pissed at him.

"Yes it is. I'm Barry Porter." Roger grimaced and exhaled a long not overly patient breath towards him.

"Yes, you said." The two men stood looking at each other, the sound of the rain hitting the roof of the gazebo growing louder by the second.

"I'm sorry have I offended you?" Barry used his winning smile, the one that sometimes worked on Julia. Roger shook his head patiently.

"No it's just that I need you to step off the handle of the bag." He gave a quick flick of his chin in Barry's direction motioning towards a canvas bag by his legs, the cord handle trapped beneath the heel of his shoe. "I need you to step off the bag so I can put this bloody sign away, it's heavy and wet." Barry jumped back as though pushed by the words.

"Hey I'm sorry, I didn't realise." He reached down and grabbed the bag holding it open to accept the soggy contents. Roger tied the rope straps around the bag sealing the sign inside.

"Thanks." Barry shrugged.

"No problem. You should have asked sooner instead of standing there struggling." Roger straightened rubbing at his back with exaggerated movements.

"I started to but you cut me off and started the whole bloody re-introduction thing again." Now it was Barry who looked confused Sorry I don't understand?"

"You introduced yourself as Barry."

"That's right."

"And I said Barry. By the way could you step off the bag so I can grab it, but you cut me off before I could finish what I was saying." Barry slapped a hand to his forehead laughing.

"Oh right, God yes. I understand it now. I thought you were saying, good to meet you Barry by the way, not good to meet you Barry 'and' by the way." Both men laughed at what would have been an only mildly amusing exchange if written into some second rate comedy sketch. "Wow what an idiot I am."

"No honestly, my fault. It's been a very long and wetly disappointing day." Roger looked down sadly at the canvas bag as though it were a coffin waiting to be lowered into the wet soil. "Yes very wet and very disappointing." Barry nodded and gave the bag a poke with the toe of his shoe.

"I was going to ask about the sign. It says 'S.A.L.T.' Sad and lonely trio." Roger sniffed loudly and pulled the handkerchief from his pocket blowing loudly the contents of both nostrils into the already damp material.

"Mmm yes it does doesn't it?"

"Well there are only two of you. Couldn't the other one make it or did he bugger off early?" Roger laughed without any real humour and stuffed the handkerchief into his pocket.

"No. Well, yes sort of. He did bugger off early but that was about six months early. We started our little group as a trio a threesome, 3 sad and lonely men. Me and Keith were and if truth be told still are a sad and lonely couple. Colin our other erstwhile member was a sad and lonely individual. We soon discovered that we had a love of music and the idea of forming a band was born. Myself and Keith would be on percussion, Colin on keyboards and singing. It soon became apparent that of the three of us not only did Colin have the only talent, but he was not quite so sad and lonely as he believed. It was only a few months into our musical adventure that he met the blessed Sebastian at one of our very few gigs. It was a lovely moment, quite romantic, so much so that in approximately...." He looked at his watch, "40 minutes they are about to become a married couple." Barry stepped forward a look of disbelief on his face.

"What? Wait a moment he's getting married and you are not invited?" Roger kicked gently at the canvas bag with the toe of his wet brown brogue

"No. It seems that myself and Keith somehow did not fall into the friend category. I told you, we really are sad and lonely." He sniffed once more and began disassembling his drum from its stand now either uncaring of or bravely able to ignore the large drips that seeped through the roof of the flimsy gazebo and fell heavily onto his balding head. "We did offer to play at the wedding you know."

"Did you?"

"Yes. Offered to play for free, for old times sake and as our little wedding gift to him and the sainted Sebastian." Barry shrugged understanding the disappointment.

"Don't tell me. Your mate Colin went all modern and had some pre-recorded mix compilation played through a sound bar. Bloody Scrooge." Roger zipped the large black case around the drum patting it sadly before answering.

"No, he hired a professional drag act called 'Feltum Long' as compare, comedian and singer. Cost him a bloody fortune but said he would sooner pay the earth than have two dead beats on percussion playing 'Here comes the Groom' as the man he loved walked down the aisle." He laughed sarcastically "Mind you, probably best eh? Otherwise it would have clashed with this little gig."

"Ah."

"Yes, quite so." Roger kicked the canvas bag once more only this time with more conviction. "It seems that it was chips for S.A.L.T." Barry nodded sadly.

"Yes indeed. S.A.L.T was now no longer required." He lay a comforting hand on the soaking wet man's shoulder and dropped his voice to no more than a low whisper, "If you ask me this Colin did not know when he was on to a good thing, bloody 'Feltum Long', sounds like a right tosser if you ask me." Roger smiled wistfully.

"Oh if only that were true. 'Feltum Long' is a very close friend of mine and a fantastic drag act, worth every penny." Barry slowly removed the hand that now seemed to rest a little uncomfortably on Roger's shoulder.

"Right, yes, I'm sure he is, brilliant that

is, anyway." Pulling his collar up against the rain he knew he must now fully enter he smiled brightly. "Well best be off, I'm on the way to the chip shop. Great to meet you Roger. All the best. Hope the bath works out for you and Keith." Barry wasn't sure if Rodger deemed to answer as the rain had grown in intensity and made a thrumming noise as it beat down mercilessly on his head.

"Christ that was awkward."

"Sorry. What?" The small woman who stood before him, hair plastered to her scalp with rain glared up at him. "I should say that perhaps if you watched where you were going young man it may not have been quite so awkward for you." She shoved past him her small body more compact than her blue rain mac gave her credit for. Barry tried to stop her, to explain that firstly he wasn't talking to her and secondly he didn't really believe she did have to say anything but his words were lost in the speed of her departure.

"Bloody hell, what a day." He checked quickly about him afraid that in his use of expletives he may upset some other passing pedestrian, not that there seemed to be many around such was the persistence of the rain. He looked at his watch, "Shit!" He had already been out half an hour, Julia would be going mad. He would ring her, use his panting voice, tell her he had witnessed an accident and the police had stopped him, asked him for a statement. No. He shook his head, she would never buy that as a story and anyway it was too easily shot down as an excuse the whole village would know if there had been an accident. He stood still concentrating, he needed something good, something powerful and yet not something that anyone would witness, a fight, a fire, an alien invasion? He shook his head, stupid, but cool, just imagine if aliens did in fact land here in this very high street. "Stop that!" He berated himself angrily, now was not the time to think about aliens. He needed to concentrate. "Mind you aliens are cool." Deciding to remember the alien thing for a later date he thrust his hands into his pockets balling them into tight fists, "Think Barry, think." He needed something that would send a chill through Julia's body, something that would send a shiver running the length of her body, something that would make her quiver as though she were suffering the effects of the most relentless of flu like bugs, not that Julia ever suffered from flu like bugs. Barry had never seen Julia ill, not one day in their married life, she was far too resilient for that. Barry was certain Julia had bypassed all illnesses even as a child… A child! That was it.

"Lost child!" The words sprang from his mouth before he could control the thought.

Scouring the empty pavements he sighed in relief, still no-one in sight. "That's it, that's it." Repeating the words for clarification he reached for his mobile phone, Julia would be so proud of him rescuing a lost child. She would take him in her arms and kiss him fondly on the mouth. He would feel her breath hot on his lips, feel her hand slide from his neck and trace its way lazily down his chest coming to rest with just enough firmness against his...

"Bollocks!" Where was his phone? He patted frantically at his jacket, the comforting bulge of his brand new mobile was not there. Ramming his hand deep into the pocket his fingers poked the newly torn hole in the material. The can had torn a millimetre perfect, mobile phone sized hole and he in blissful unawareness had supplied the very phone to fall through the said hole,

"Shit, bugger, bollocks and fu.."

"Enough of that sir." He spun around quickly to see a traffic warden scowling hard towards him, "We don't need any language like that, now do we? There may be children around."

"Children? For the love of God man, have you not seen the weather out here? What idiot would bring their children out on a day like this eh in fact what idiot would be out here at all in weather like this?" The traffic warden stood looking at him, hands placed behind his back, rocking in rhythmical movements from heel to toe, toe to heel.

"Well sir, as I have to be out here as part of my duty I would say that the only real idiot who is standing in the rain cursing to himself for no apparent reason is…" He paused, "You." Although Barry wished it wasn't true he had to agree with this pretentious little man.

"Well, yes, technically I am an idiot but not because I am standing out here for no reason. I have to be out here." He quickly continued forcing the point, "I am on my way to the chip shop, Julia sent me, although she doesn't believe that I will remember the order, has absolutely no faith in me."

"I see." Said the traffic warden although the look on his face showed anything but understanding, "Hence the quite crude swearing moment I presume. Forgot the order, proved the good woman right?"

"No! No, nothing like that." Barry pointed to the pocket of his jacket and pulled the lining inside out to demonstrate the hole. "My pocket has a hole in it and I've just discovered that my phone has fallen out. That is why I was swearing."

"I see." Said the traffic warden again, nodding slowly, "A mobile phone." Something in his voice caused Barry to stop the useless inspection of his torn jacket pocket in the scant hope that he had missed the phone on his first and subsequent searches.

"Do you know something about my phone?" The traffic warden rocked slowly backwards and forwards as though he were considering his response, "Well, do you?"

"Mobile phone, yes, well, perhaps." Barry removed his hand from the ripped pocket and took a half step towards this annoying man.

"Well do you, is that a yes or a no?" The traffic warden smiled encouragingly.

"Yes."

"Yes what. Yes that's a yes or yes that's a no?" The traffic warden smiled again making him look to Barry as though he were a pudgy puppy who was desperate to please.

"Oh yes, that's a yes. I found it." He said brightly

"You did? That's fantastic, that is the best news I have had all day. Thank you, thank you so much." Barry held his hand out as though he were a child meeting Father Christmas and stood waiting for his gift "Thank you." He said again pulling a wider than normal smile. The Traffic warden laughed along enthusiastically.

"Oh I don't have it."

"What do you mean you don't have it. I thought you said you found it?"

"I did, I did. I found it around the corner

saw it under a bush. Well I didn't see it if I'm honest, more heard it than saw it. It was ringing. He said in way of explanation, "Playing the music from 'Star Wars' I think it was."

"Darth Vader's theme." Barry remembered how much he had laughed at the annoyance on Julia's face when he first downloaded the ring tune and allocated it to her number when she rang him, "It is Darth Vader's theme."

"Ahh yes, of course. Thought I recognised it."

"Great, glad you recognised it but that doesn't answer the question does it? Where is my phone now?" The traffic warden straightened his peaked cap as though he were a soldier about to deliver the bad news that they would have to 'go over the top' he straightened his shoulders.

"Well. By the time I had managed to pull it from where it lay, it had stopped ringing and locked itself so I was unable to phone whomever had just rung me…"

"Me, they had rung me."

"What?"

"You said they had rung you, they had not rung you they had rung me, and it was Julia."

"Julia?"

"My wife. Julia."

"Her of the chip shop list?"

"Yes her of the… No wait a moment, it doesn't matter whom, no not whom, who, who it was, where is my phone?" The traffic warden nodded as though suddenly remembering what it was he had been asked.

"Oh yes, your phone. Well as I say I had just found the phone and two young lads were walking towards me. I suppose they must have seen me retrieve the phone from under the bush. 'What you got there? The first one asked me. 'Looks like a phone' the second one said, 'My phone?' The first one asked, 'Looks like it' the second one said, 'Brilliant' the first one said, so I said…" Barry groaned stopping the little man in his flow.

"You gave it to them didn't you?" For the first time the traffic warden appeared anxious.

"Erm, yes."

"Bloody hell, you gave them my phone. Why did you do that?" The traffic warden laughed nervously.

Well, they said it was theirs." He shrugged apologetically. "I'm so sorry I thought I was doing a good thing but it appears now that the two boys were actually being a couple of scamps, pulled the wool right over my eyes."

"A couple of scamps, a couple of scamps?" Barry was hot with rage, he couldn't stomach standing there any longer. Without a backward glance he stormed away from the traffic warden cursing loudly.

"Shit, bollocks, piss and …"

"Please I know you are upset but mind your language!" The words sparked his fury all the more and he turned around and gave a long slow two fingered salute to the traffic warden who blushed with a fury of his own. Before he could retort Barry marched away, head down desperate to get to the chip shop and out of the rain.

The chip shop was for a Saturday afternoon relatively empty of customers and he leaned against the warmth of the counter watching the water fall from his hair onto the fake marble effect surface as he waited for the mother and her three children to be served. This really had been a disaster of a walk especially when it should have been so quick and easy. Julia would be hopping mad when he returned especially if Sally, Colin and their tribe had arrived. He wiped his hand over his face and recalled what could only have been called a horror of a journey. Julia would never believe him, whatever he said. True, he had wanted her to feel an extra chill as he explained his missing child theory but now there seemed little point in fabricating anything especially when the truth was more far fetched than anything he could concoct. He could picture her face as he tried to explain the circumstances of his late arrival back from his simple task.

"Honestly Julia," He would begin, "There were two randy sausage dogs, a sodden trio who were now only a duo and who basically had, had their chips in the music industry called S.A.L.T. two children described as scamps by the traffic warden who were basically just devious little shits and to top it all he had lost his phone. Christ she would never believe him.

"Yes. Can I help?" The girl behind the counter gave him a bored smile, "Watcha want?" Barry smiled back, taking only a moment to think,

"Erm yes. Can I have 2 sausage and chips, 1 cod and chips no salt, kebab meat with extra chilli sauce, 2 children's scampi and chips and erm, and erm." A cold sweat ran through him, 6, there was only 6. Julia had stressed there were 7 items. He quickly ran through the list again, what was he missing? "Pie! pie and chips." He had wanted pie. Barry watched the girl start the gathering and wrapping process, he may be late back but at least he had achieved the task just as he said he would. He listened to the satisfying beep of the card machine and felt the weight of the bag in his hand.

"Nailed it." He said aloud striding out towards home through the rain drench streets. Yes he had nailed it. And yet as he marched triumphantly towards his final destination he could not shake the feeling in the pit of his stomach, that something felt very wrong indeed.

Whispers

It began, with a whispered one sided conversation.

"I heard!" Just that no more. Two words, casual in
appearance but cautiously spoken. The weight of the words hung between them for no more than a second. A second that would have been insignificant, if they had not been punctuated by the look in her eyes.

The response to this conversation came, three days later, not in a verbal exchange, not with two bodies in close proximity their heads together as though lovers sharing a secret, but in the written form. A note, tucked into the pages of a book, her book. Her book which had lain for barely a moment, unguarded, on the large wooden table, a table scarred with use and enriched with age. The note lay, precisely placed between the front cover and the first yellowed page, obvious with its luminous glow, stark against gloom of the leather bound tome. The only darkness to this note was the foreboding black scar of ink which formed her name in precisely written script. The secret creator of this penmanship had a steady hand, flowing, cursive, practised. She extinguished the light she feared lit her features closing with a heavy thud the book who's heavy leather binding extinguished the beacon that was hidden silent beneath its pages. The fire of the note warmed her hands as it lay trapped in its paper tomb beneath her grip. Such was her terror of discovery she slapped her hand against the book pressing harder to extinguish the note hoping she would not be discovered in her secrecy, praying that she would not yet be discovered by the light of the note which surely lit the very corner in which she sat, illuminating her to all. To hide the sound of her sudden action fearing the noise to be that of a thunderclap amongst the sleeping, she nudged the heavy wooden bench opposite with her foot. Feeling the bench send its reverberating scrape on the heavy stone slabbed floor she allowed herself to slide the book to her lap, placing her pale shaking hands over the soft, familiar leather, taking comfort in its familiarity. She calmed her breathing so as to steady the beating of her heart, a sound which was certain to expose her subterfuge. Maintaining an outward appearance of calmness that jarred against her inner turmoil she dared no more than a cursory glance hoping that all would seem as it should be to any casual observer. A mask to those who may be watching her with malice and unnatural interest. Casually, keeping the action hidden below the safety of the table top she slipped the note from where it lay and tucked it securely into the confines of her expansive pocket where it would remain burning hotly against her thigh, untouched and unread until she was safely alone later that evening.

Perched birdlike on the edge of her bed her nervous hands pick at the thin material of the cheap cotton nightgown which offers little protection. She breathes with short shallow breaths daring herself to wait before opening the note which lays ominously beside her. She is alone, here in her room, she knows that and yet... Somehow even here she is unable to shake the feeling that she is being watched, eyes are searching her out, watching her every move and boring deep into the very fabric of her being. The shiver that runs the length of her body confirms her feelings, heightens her sense of foreboding and she pulls a thin blanket about her shoulders to what? Ward off the cold that seeps through the aged stonework, to protect her from those unseen eyes or to cocoon her, hold her in the bosom of warmth she so craves. She stills her hand from again clutching at the nightgown and instead reaches nervously to the note who's presence screams loudly in the dark silence. Now it is finally in her grasp she works with small deft movements flattening the page on her lap, never allowing her eyes to lose their view of her door, taking solace in the silent words her mouth speaks, finding strength in the act of secrecy, fighting down the terror of discovery with each movement. The paper fights against the flattening, screeching with every press of her hand, more rusty gate than single page. She winces at the sound, holds her breath at the echo which retorts around her small room with the anger of bullet on brickwork. She pauses her actions breathless with anticipation, eyes wide with terror, heart hammering the beat of warning she feels for all to hear. She will be discovered, they will come, the knock on the door, the lift of the latch, the discovery, but, no. Minutes tick by and all is still, all is as it has been. Slowly she releases the breath she has been holding too long, hearing the blood pumping in her ears, the small dots of light flickering in the corner of her vision, for now she is safe, undiscovered. Slowly she allows herself a small nod, her only gesture of affirmation for now the feared knock would not materialise. Wiping quickly cooling sweat that has glistened her brow she allows herself a moment to glance down towards the note which still remains fully open and exposed on her lap. With the self preservation of prey avoiding the sight of a predator, she turns her back to the door and in one quick movement falls to her knees by the side of her bed clasping her hands in the safety of enactment the posture of prayer whilst cradling the note smooth between her spread elbows. The guilt of her actions bites hard at the pit of her stomach and yet she cannot stop, there will be no change of heart, she must continue at all costs. Finally focusing her courage she allows herself to read the note, holding her breath against each syllable.

"Thank you." Two words, no more than that. It is the same dark black ink that scribed her name so clearly on the front, each letter formed with skill, each mark precisely where intended. There are only the two words but each somehow able to display their true meaning to her, these two words scream thanks, a heartfelt thanks and more than this, they shout relief. She moves her face closer to the page, so close that her eyes ache with the pain of focusing, but she does not pull away so intent is her desire to study every facet of every word in the note. Forgetting her need to remain inconspicuous against prying eyes, the eyes she is certain watches her every move she allows her finger to trace the words on the note slowly following every stroke of the pen, every line, every curve, drinking in the shapes as though they were the finest of wines. Her knees grow sore against the cold and the hardness of the floor and yet she cannot draw away, cannot remove herself as she knows she should do. The words she reads become more powerful with each passing moment, larger, each taking on a life of their own. She feels the words twisting, turning moulding themselves to her, filling her, living deep within her very consciousness as though they are and have always been part of herself. Drawing finally from this trancelike state she is aware of the movement of time, not by the ticking of a clock nor the calling of each hour but with the thickening of the blackness that pushes hard against the candlelight that forms the only light within her room. Her only source of brightness to read the note. Her only beacon of hope against the thick suffocating terror that creeps towards her. With a slow ache that cracks at her knees and stiffens her back she pushes hard against the solid bed and rises to her feet knowing what must be done. Moving to the small enamel sink set against the wall she touches her small candle flame to the note and watches through the mist of tears as it burns brightly for the briefest of moments before the paper folds in on itself moving from first black then to an ashen grey which lays stark against the cracked enamel. She reaches towards the thin tendril of smoke that rises to freedom, a pillar of hope, daring to believe that she will be able to catch hold of the words contained within for one last moment, to hold them to her, but alas they are gone. The water slips towards the ash washing it away blood like towards an escape she can only wish for, leaving no more than the memory and the slightest scent of burning. Her heart gives a momentary flutter of fear against the scent, but she is calm, practiced now in deception, ready to react to any eventuality. With a last look towards the scene of her crime she returns to her small bed, her coffin in all but name and climbs beneath the cover, worn thin with age and extinguishes the candle light with a practiced flick of her fingers, "the heavy scent of burning? Why no more than her candle perhaps." Beneath the shroud that covers her in the dark of the room she grips herself foetus like in the constriction of the darkness and waits for sleep to take her.

It comes eventually as it always does but this is not a heavy sleep, the sleep of the dead for that is too much to hope for. No, her sleep is no more than a slumber of restlessness, a waiting. As her breathing deepens into the blackness, as she passes from all knowledge to that which she can only recall in heavy fragments of the early morning light she realises that for her, this night, there is a change. Her inner self has a companion, a companion that has until now remained hidden from her sight, 'Thank you!' As her eyes finally close in heavy lidded exhaustion, as her breathing consumes the darkness, she allows herself a small involuntary smile. There will still be the dreams, memories of stillness punctuated by violence but now, this night, she has made a beginning, a hope that all can be well. She places a hand against her own mouth, not to gag, not to silence but to hide the smile, a smile that has for too long remained chained behind words, suffocated by threat, drowned by submission. If there are watchers in the dark would they see her change, would they notice in her the slight difference this night? Her sleep would be fitful, wracked with fear, she knew that still, but would they, the watchers see into her heart where at last the light had began to shine? Tonight her sleeping form would not be alone, she had started an event, a conversation and she had companionship, she had understanding.

The conversation between them continued a week later. She had wanted to speak sooner, needed to continue what had been started, but care was required, stealth was needed. Now the chance had arisen, a moment only, the briefest of interactions, a whisper as between them they passed the plates.

"I understand." It was no more than that, two more words to add to their total, a total that had risen to only six, "I know." Then "Thank you." And now "I understand."

Six small words and yet so many. Some would say that these six words were no more than an utterance, a whisper on the breeze and yet what could they know? The understanding in those words was more, so much more than the sum of their parts, they were; a sonnet, a play, an encyclopaedia, a life's work, they were everything. These words had proven to her that they were the same, women, friends, sisters. They were connected by events and struggles, joined together as one. A power that was greater than theirs. A violence more vengeful and more destructive than death itself, moulded, contained and totally controlled them. Kept them as they were, trapped. This power used its strength to maintain its hold over them, it locked itself deep within them making itself, until the first moment she had uttered her words, unspeakable. It was only now with a courage greater than she would ever have believed was truly possible within herself had she found a way to tear down the barrier of evilness. In this moment they had in some small way shared their burden, acknowledged their pain, made it real. Together they had lifted their gaze from the floor knowing that this was just the beginning, they saw the hardships that would follow but they had together started the journey that would allow them to speak of the horror that stalked them mercilessly.

Over weeks, more words were whispered, always close, no more than a breath of air, a gentle sigh. Notes were passed from hand to hand, slipped between them still warm from the others touch. Messages were shared hidden between willing, expectant pages, secreted amongst the well thumbed leaves. From book to book they passed, each note a paper hawk hovering between them with the power to swoop down in a rush of plumage calling loudly 'here I am, here I am, see what I say!' Birds of prey that could destroy them without warning. To fly from their hands to land on the shoulders of those who waited and whispered in their ears. They would drip the poisonous words towards them trapping them with a venom that could destroy all that they now dared to hold as light before themselves. She knew. They both understood the need for care. The danger of carelessness filled them with dread, nothing must be taken for granted, every precaution must be paramount. It would be as ghosts they would move carrying their greyness amongst the shadows and use its blandness as camouflage. They made themselves as one with their surroundings, trees hiding amongst the oaks of the forrest. And so she hoped, dared to believe it would remain, prayed that it would be.

But now. Now sat on the hardness of her bed, alone again in the sanctuary of her room she stared at the latest words with horror as the crows of death sharpened their claws with intent. The whiteness of the moon cascaded foreboding light through her narrow window lighting her face ghostlike in the glass. Words, no longer solidly written but scrawled in hasty hand punctured her heart, pierced her flesh, the arrows loosed towards St Sebastian taking flight.

"I fear tonight!" The note lay in her lap heavy in its intent. No more had she the energy to turn from the door. No more the desire to hide from the eyes she still feared who sought her out malevolent in their watchfulness. Shock had replaced the care she had for so many weeks practiced. A numbness held her, strongly renewed with a vigour that tore tears from her eyes deflated her and knocked the breath from her lungs. Terror again filled her as it stalked mercilessly the corridors of its lair unrepentant in its evilness. These new words on the note began to smudge at the edges as her tears fell, droplets of despair dampening the the ink. With no recollection of her actions, she curls her form on the bed unable to gather the strength to cover herself. Alone with nothing but the ever present starkness of the moons sallow light to illuminate the scene, she waits for what will be. When it begins she can do no more than place a hand lovingly on the wall and allow the tears that freely soak her pillow, her witness to the remorse she can no longer hold bottled within herself. The dread they had feared, the evil they fought to control had returned. The Devil himself had entered just a brick width away and brought with it the clicks and the creaks of its lust, a lust that was violently accompanied by the mewling of an animal in pain.

Days passed, slowly. Minutes ticked as hours, hours as years. Empty passages of time passed by, broken only by moments of necessity, fractions of normality. Her life lived now in nothing but silence and the ability to remain hidden in the shadows. Cloaked by routine and self discipline she dare not think freely, could not allow sudden unconscious thought to catch her unaware. Nothing must cause her to act in some small way which to others would seem normal, but to the observers, the fear bringers, would became a beacon of light. This light would shine upon her illuminate her as un-protected, alone. She would stand before them, lit by her inability to remain hidden, bereft of the armour she had thrown around herself. She would stand a ghost of herself, hollowed from within, un-protected, vulnerable, a gleam in the eyes of those that sniffed at her scent. Loneliness encompassed her being as fear weighed her tread. Her one flicker of hope was silent, her one touch of warmth was mute. No notes appeared, although she checked the pages of her book. No whispered message came to brush softly against her ear, tickling the skin with the breath of hope. No comfort came to her from heavy lidded glance or brush of hand on arm. Coldness was her companion, dread her bedfellow.

Night regained its terror. Where once there had been hope now sat only fear. The warmth of dreams had been torn from her, replaced with the salt of tears. Her source of strength had been forced from her side although still only a brick width apart. Darkness was her torturer filling her nights with terrors unbounded, forcing her eyes to search the darkest corners, and keeping the sleep from her soul. In the darkness of her room she knew she would find no rest. She would turn in terror as meat turns on the spit. There would be no sleep for sleep cannot find a resting place with her here, for there is no room for rest when terror occupies the largest space. It was during such a night, a night when her mouth formed itself into the 'O' of a silent scream from the nightmare which scratched at her inners and tore at her soul that a note came into her being. Its scrape along the flagstone floor sprang her to action, her senses already alert for any gentle sound, cloth on stone, scrape of leather on flag, hand on door. With shaking fingers she touched match to wick, squinting against yellowed light, breathing softly for fear of gasp. The note lay silent a broken nailed,hook fingered beckon towards her, pulling her close as the sirens pulled at the ears and heart of Odysseus. With measured tread she moves from her bed, leaving behind the sweat soaked sheet. Ignoring the stench of fear she gives herself no time to ponder her actions such is her need. Instinct driving her on, want and need guiding her movements she unfolds the note with the ravenous intent of the starving, the desperation of the condemned.

"I. AM. SORRY!" Three words scream at her, the hurt in each letter breaking through the gloom of the candle, I. AM. SORRY! Gone the neat print of a sane mind. Each letter is now an individual, a block capital followed by a full stop. The pain of the author screeches with a sound that would surely fill her room and spill out into the ears of those that watch her, those that wish her harm. She sinks to the floor reading again the note, her fingers tracing the thickly drawn letters, the marks of pain, each gouge of pen on paper, the rent of nail upon skin. The words roared their anguish, yelled of their fear and wept in their finality. She knew in her broken heart that there would be no others. This would be the last. This would be their final conversation. Without realisation she pulls herself to the bed and lays curled against the cold of mortality, these final words offered no resolve or resolution, they offered no hope. Closing her eyes she began as was her way to offer prayer, screwing the note close to her breast, uncaring of discovery the need for comfort overcoming the fear of wrath. The words to her prayers would not come to her aid. The divine she offered them to as distant as the rising sun.

The morning came with a chill as familiar as her fear itself. The icy fingers that accompanied her every moment raked their nails deep through the soft tissue of her soul. During the night she had heard the noises. She had sensed the commotion from behind the fragile safety of her keyless wooden door. The whispered voices although spoken with calmness and care had carried admonishment, had hissed disgust. Standing alone in the dark of her room, hands flat against the roughness of the door, ear pressed close she had understood the sounds, she had understood the finality. She found the words of prayer that offered little comfort, were of little use. The prayer was not for her. It was not for her ears nor was it for the ears of her God. The prayer was whispered into the darkness with little hope, with little faith. The prayer was offered as hope for another. That it would find its way through the blackness of the night and the darkness of the evil. That it would break through all that had enacted itself with desperate finality breaking the heart of the other, the one separated by the wall, the author of the note. Prayer completed she had listened to the rustling and bumps from beyond her room and moved numbly back to her bed laying beneath the cover feeling the change that now held her, surrounded her. The author of the note was gone. She had not simply packed her belongings, she had not departed as one departs for a holiday. She had not faded into the distance. The author, her author, had departed and was no more of this place, no more of this realm. She looked now towards the small, dull window of her room. The heavy frost of the outside air had scratched and etched its hate on the glass rending the surface with scars that mirrored the tiredness in her own eyes. Even now in the horror of those frosty fingers that lay sparkling in the early morning light there was a beauty, a beauty that turned her gaze from where she lay and focused her mind from this place pulling her thoughts heavenward. She could not curse her author for the pain she now felt herself. There would be no fist shaken with hate, nor oath spat with venom. She recognised that in the author leaving, she who was her fellow whisperer had taken back control. Achingly she pulled herself to sitting and took a moment to gather her thoughts, to study with fine detail the frost that formed not only scars but crystals of beauty. Here, here was the final note she had been left, not the screwed and damp paper she still clutched to her chest. The author was gone. This was true. She had stolen herself away and could continue the conversation no more, and yet... She run her own finger over the small pain of glass her nail tracing the pattern of frost, feeling the coldness burn at her finger tip. The author had become free, she had taken what she, what they desired, she had taken control for herself, she was as one with all that is and all that would be. She moved from her bed to the sink and sets a match to the last physical note she would receive, watching the blackness spiral away and manages with muscles unused to pull her lips to a smile. The author was free. She had escaped all that was, the author was free from terror, she was free from hurt, she would have peace, only peace.

Alone in her room heavy with exhaustion she is thankful that her friend, her whispered conversationalist, the author of nothing that remains is at peace although she herself is now alone she understands. Her own journey will return now to that which it was before. Her only confidant is gone. There shall be no other heart that knows her plight, all remnants of truth and belief are hers and hers alone. Where for the briefest of moments there had been a companion, however silent, now she would continue her journey as one. Hers would be a trek that she would take as a solitary figure, a disfigured saint back from the Holy Lands. There would be no summers for her now, no steps taken through bright, sunny days, instead only harsh winters and cold winds greeted her every step. Brightness had been stolen from her, extinguished from this place, night had stolen her away.

She moves alone, feeling the creep of hours, measuring every passing moment. She maintains her invisibility, continues her days as one who is seen and yet unseen. Sometimes she feels as though she sees the author, always out of direct line of sight always at the corner of her eye. Time moves as it always has, slow passing of every minute, turgid movement of every hour. And then there is the night. The darkening of the room, the heightening of every shadow. Night heightens it grip over her smiling at her with teeth that drip with excitement, barely able to keep itself from tearing her, gnashing at her flesh as though it is a delicacy to be enjoyed without care of hurt or harm. She uses the cover of darkness to allow her thoughts to solidify themselves into solid bricks of consciousness, using each brick as something to build her plans for survival. Her efforts remain futile as each plan begins to raise from the solid footings created in her mind so the waves of despair wash away her foundations leaving no more than ruined castles of decay as evidence of her failures. As the light returns so her truth, the only truth is left floating away, drifting further to sea from the safety of the shore. No one is left to help her to capture this truth and to steer it safely towards the crowds who she hopes one day will see her plight, understand her needs. Her truth is watched by slack faced observers who stand silent and remain unaware or uncaring that the vessel they see is listing to the crash of waves. Her truth will become lost beneath the sea of lies and deceit. This ocean, this body of water will if unchecked swallow other vessels, vessels much like hers who would travel serenely forward only to be torn apart by the same jagged rocks.

When it comes, it comes with a whisper

as she knows it must. Not the heavy beat of shoes hard against the flagstones, not the hard rap of knuckle on wood nor the cough of just interruption or good manners. She is laying beneath the same thin blanket, the blanket that has mopped so many of her dreams and will soak up so many more. Staring through the window, the glass her only witness, she is taunted by the moon who displays its freedom without care of her feelings. It cares not for the abhorrence to be nor for the heaviness of her plight. Her heart falls in time with the soft steps that carry pain towards her, each step although light in touch hold her with weight unconquerable where she lays, frozen, stiff and alone. She squeezes her eyes shut against the click of the latch, willing it to be no more than the wind itself, knocking cruelly against her protection, teasing her to panic. This is not the truth, the panting of the animal itself betrays this hope. She cannot move, she dare not make a noise. To play dead is her only escape. To view this as one views the sad demise of a loved one, from the far side of the room, from somewhere deep in the recess of the shadows, this is how she will survive. Deep now within the darkness she has pulled about herself she remembers the notes, the warmth of their understanding, the strength in their knowledge shared. She does not feel the roughness of the cotton betraying her dignity. She does not hear the squeal of the mattress announcing evil intent. She does not feel the acrid breath of Satans servant hot against her ear laying claim to what is not his.

"Sister Evangeline, it is good for you to serve God in such a way. Truly you are blessed." Sister Evangeline opens her eyes and focuses hard upon the moon, a moon which stares back unblinking.

Nothing moves in the darkness of the corridors, although no-one rests behind the rows of wooden doors. The figures curled tight against their nightmares, cross their hearts and cover their ears against the familiar sound of the animal who, trapped and snared, mewls in the night.

A C STOCK

Panel of Inclusivity

"The year is 2257. This is choice board, system 1. I am choice board executive panel member RB 71357. The panel today consists of AD 3614, MM 44174 and also local member CR 978713. The panel is being recorded as per protocol 7 of the species alliance under sub section D. Todays Newbies who stand before us ready to make their choice are 1 born with now inward genitalia and 2 born with now outward genitalia all of whom are of the required 13 years and 1 month age limit. They were taken from the birthing pods after their 9 months with no complications. As the Newbies before us will have no given prefix initials and numbers until they have chosen and been assigned they shall for the matter of the choosing be as usual designated with temporary identification. The one who stands before us with the inward genitalia will be referred to as is standard as FG 1 and the two who present with outward genitalia will be referred to as MG 1 and MG 2 respectively. We will now start the choosing process with FG 1."

"FG 1 do you understand why you are here?" The girl before them nodded. "For the sake of audio as well as visual please answer verbally FG 1. In the interests of the panel being fully aware of all answers I will ask the question again. Do you understand why you are here? Again the girl nodded,

Yes I understand." RB 71357 smiled broadly

"That is excellent. Now I wonder if you could explain for the panel what your understanding is as to why you are before us today?" The girl took a moment as though considering the question deeply, a small frown line creasing with perfect symmetry from her forehead to the bridge of her nose

"Well." She said eventually, "I am here to pick who it is I want to be." She looked up towards the four panel members as though expecting a sharp rebuke but was instead greeted by the encouraging nod from who RB 71357 who waved her to continue.

"And what else?" The girl shuffled nervously as though at first unable to recall some relevant fact or nervous to speak again. As the silence grew to a length that seemed as though it would have to be broken the girl spoke quickly, the words a rush of energy.

"I have to choose who I want to be and to decide of what group I shall belong. I do this in the name of equality and also in recognition of my true self." Before her RB 71357 nodded again an action that was mirrored in perfect unison by the other panel members.

"Congratulations FG 1 that was word perfect. I can see you shall be a credit to whomever it is you decide to become and whichever group you shall join." RB 71357 tapped at the screen on the desk and read quickly the information displayed. "It seems that in your growing you have shown great aptitude for lifting and carrying. You have been exuberant in sports and have an ability to work in a team and as an individual. I also see that when seated your leg placement is described as splayed and that you have the tendency to be fired into over exuberant displays of argumentativeness that have leaned you towards altercations and in two cases language that could be called earthen. Your tutors describe you as quick witted and often humorous with a nature that leads to offer apologies and forgiveness with unhindered honesty. Your assessors describe you as solidly built with little interest in appearance with a keen interest in mechanics and construction." RB 71357 quickly consulted with the other board members, their voices low no more than a hum of sound which finally fell to silence. "It seems FG 1 that we the panel are in complete agreement. The report we have before us leads us to believe that you would suit very well all of the four main groups. This is not unusual and in some ways makes your choice all the easier. We the panel believe that as we are in need of such skills they should be nurtured. With this reasoning we strongly suggest that you choose gender reassignment classification 4B to become a transgender male." Nodding as though the decision was made RB 71357 made deft strokes on the screen frowning as the words flowed to the overhead screen. "Congratulations FG 1 in supporting this choice. I have marked you down for your new gender reassignment early tomorrow morning. Your life can now truly begin FG 1. You will, by the early hours of tomorrow evening be safely ensconced in the TRAN-MALE conclave." RB 71357 sat back steepling long fingers beneath the whiteness of the finely sculptured chin.

"No I don't want that." The girl spoke quietly and yet her voice was filled with a firmness that caused RB 71357 to halt. "I do not wish to be a transsexual man." As the girl spoke AD 6314 sat slightly straighter on the chair.

"If I may RB 71357?" With a nod of acceptance RB 71357 relaxed back into the chair allowing AD 6314 to hold the full attention of the room and the watching recorders.

"Do I take it FG 1 that you have decided against gender reassignment to male? The girl nodded. "For the audio please FG 1 speak for the audio." The girl blanched at this new verbal rebuke and spoke quickly.

"Yes I have decided against that. I want to …"

"That is good, yes very good indeed." AD 6314 leaned forward and faced the girl a small smile registering the pleasure, "I felt the moment you entered the room that you were better suited for non-binary augmentation. There is an air about you that shows a naturalised way of being. You carry yourself with a demeanour that fits all around you. It is as though you have no wish to be either, or, you shall be neither or in fact either." AD 6314 scanned the notes that filled the screen. "I can see that you mix well with all chosen configurations. Your assessments show that you are as I perceived welcomed by all. You are at ease with any." AD 6314 nodded as the notes on the screen flicked past. "I suggest that the facts speak for themselves. For you non-binary is the best and most worthy of reassignment." Quickly pressing at the hidden keypad AD 6314 watched as large lettering floated above them on the screen, "I have made the necessary arrangements for you to have the altering procedures and in all but the briefest of moments you shall join the NON's conclave. You shall be …"

"No!" The girl raised her hands in protest, her voice raised in rebuttal "I do not want to join the NON's I do not wish to be non-binary." To strengthen her argument she wanted to step forward and to plead her case close to the panel, but the circle in which she stood flashed the colours of the rainbow holding her where she stood. "Please, I do not want to be non-binary." she repeated more slowly standing where she was, "It is just that...."

"Then in fact it is androgynous modification you call for?" MM 44174 silenced the girl with a voice that oozed silky pleasure. "It is a choice that more are taking, a choice that of course I am happy to see raising in popularity." MM 44174 smiled warmly, "Yes indeed I am happy with your choice. Unlike my respected colleagues on the panel I have held the opinion that your notes prove a different theory." MM 44174 glanced at the large screen before continuing. "You do not just act in a way that makes you accessible to all but your whole demeanour is one that attracts itself to being a simple being. It is not that you do not care about your appearance, quite the opposite. You have chosen outfits and clothing that represents nothing. You have made this choice quite simply and almost without thought or planning. Anyone of any other conclave could and again with the greatest of respect to the other panel members have mis-represented. I say that you have chosen these styles for the love of who you truly are." MM 44174 flicked again at the unseen keypad. "The choice you have made seems in its simplicity to be the easier path but I fear needs the most work to accomplish. I, we the conclave, shall assist you in all you need. The first step is to have your brain reconfigured to complete your feelings. Once this is achieved we shall ensure that your body is altered to complete the required look." Again MM 44174 smiled down at the girl content that the work would be completed to perfection. "Once all is as it should be myself and the other androgens shall welcome you to the ANDRO enclave.

"No! Please no." With desperation guiding her the girl stepped forward with no consideration for the consequences. Without warning a shock ripped through her body tearing the breath from her lungs. Falling to the floor she fought hard to remove the rainbow lights that wrapped themselves around her although she soon realised the futility of the fight and fell still. Once she lay silent gasping for the breath that seemed to have left her body the rainbow lights unwrapped her from its all encompassing grip and allowed her to crawl back to the circle that was designated for this choosing.

"Please do not attempt that again FG 1." RB 71357 leaned forward and faced the girl. "The rainbow wave is there not just as a warning but to protect you as much as it is to protect us. Please I ask of you to remember your teachings and to respect the rainbow and all it stands for. Now it appears that you have chosen against the three main conclaves, all of which offer you a safe haven as deciphered through the reports received about you." RB 71357 waved a hand almost dismissively before speaking again "As you seem to have dismissed what we see for you, may I enquire which other conclave it is you deem to choose?" Before the girl could give an answer the last and so far most silent member of the panel sat forward.

"I fear that perhaps we have overlooked something in our haste and kind natures to help FG 1." CR 978713 spoke with words that were clipped and precise. Unlike the other panel members this was a voice that spoke in a gruff, no nonsense way. " I am the newest member of the panel, voted to my place only two years ago. My role as described by the great book of certainties indicates that although I myself am of the INTERSEX enclave, I shall offer no public favouritism nor bias to any given enclave. My role shall be one of adviser in cases where there is indecision or misunderstanding." The three other panel members nodded acceptance.

"You are correct CR 978713 we look to you now to fulfil your duties." RB 71357 waved a hand over the screen and saw the writing blank out ready to dictate the words of CR 978713 who would guide the panel and FG 1 to the correct decision. CR 978713 took a long deep breath and spoke more gently perhaps than they were used to. "Before I speak, I would ask only that FG 1 must regain their feet and to face us straight on as the rules of engagement dictate." CR 978713 waited for FG 1 who pulled themself to the recognised stance before the panel, standing shoulders back and head held high, the stance of full respect. Satisfied that FG 1 was as they should be, CR 978713 spoke. "I believe we may have found someone who wishes to join a conclave so often ignored that they fall almost into the obscurity they crave." CR 978713 leaned heavily across the desk and whispered the words in a way that brought terror to those that heard. "FG 1. Are you wishing to enter the HOMO conclave?

"Surely not CR 978713. There has been no one who wishes to be singly homosexual for at least four years now." MM 44174 spat the words around the room such was the venom of disbelief in the statement. "How can you suggest such a thing. To just love one of the same sex is a dying and if I may add outdated request of a choice. The HOMO conclave is a failing conclave, antiquated and in the opinion of this panel and those before us. A waste of potential for any who choose this as an option."

"I agree MM 44174." RB71357 tapped at the screen with hard punctuating fingers, "To suggest this, enters us into a backward step. I understand that you must consider all of the possible eventualities CR 978713 but this is an avenue that I wish not to venture down." CR 978713 shrugged sadly.

"Panel members I of course agree and this is hard for me to mention but..." CR 978713 paused briefly meeting the gaze of the other panel members before continuing, "but I ask you to think on this. We are here to facilitate in what is right and correct are we not?" Without waiting for an answer knowing the truth in the statement CR 978713 continued, "I must in my position consider this as a decision possibly made by the chooser. I do not say I agree nor do I say I welcome the choice but it may be a choice all the same." Pausing for no more than the beat of a heart CR 978713 spoke again. "I fear that you in your position as Choice Board Executive must ask this Newbie if this is in fact the true destination of their decision." Sitting back CR 978713 gestured to RB 71357 to continue. RB 71357 stared hard at FG 1 uncaring of the seconds that ticked by, using them to allow FG 1 the girl time to consider the answer fully. Finally once FG 1 made no effort to end the silence that had befallen the proceedings RB

71357 spoke.

"If you are to make this answer your final choice know that it fills us with dread. I ask that you think carefully FG1. To enter a conclave such as you appear to be choosing ends in an outdated lonely and often ignored life. Homosexuality as it was called in the distant days left a Cis man loving a Cis man and a Cis woman loving a Cis woman only." RB 71357 looked towards the floating lens and breathed deeply, "I apologise to all observers for the use of my language in this moment, to have spoken in such a way shows no acceptance on my part for these old genders and I hope never to be forced to use such prounouns of man and woman in the singular usage again." RB 71357 turned the small rainbow ring which had been placed onto their thumb during their own time of choosing with quick jerky movements, "Unfortunately in such a case as this it is important to make FG 1 aware of the limits of the choice that is being made here. It hurts my lips as it hurts my soul to make mention of old genders as though they are still deemed acceptable words to be used in a public space. I hope all who listen or view can expunge those words from their minds and forget the feelings of non inclusivity they evoke. Now FG 1, do you accept that your thoughts of being purely homosexual to use the old vernacular is a belief system that breeds a way that is not inclusive. Do you accept that it is outdated, full of old dangerous and extreme views and something we moved from as soon as true identities and sexual orientations were recognised as the only true way." FG 1, still shaking from the effects of the rainbow circle nodded dumbly using the action to clear the stinging sensation.

"You have been asked repeatedly FG 1, please for the sake of audio speak aloud." FG 1 remembering the years of training spoke aloud pronouncing each word clearly.

"Yes I understand all that you say."

"And you do not wish to join the unwashed of the HOMO enclave?" As the words were spoken the panel nodded in unison at the humorous barb befitting the very thought of the failing enclave.

"I think we can agree FG 1 is under an inordinate amount of pressure and perhaps needs to take a moment to think through the choices?" AD 6314 looked along the panel for confirmation before continuing, "Why, I remember at my panel when I almost chose poly gender when I actually meant non-binary and all for the pressure I felt. If my first answer had been accepted without the exacting questions of the panel I could have been assigned....."

"No!" With a fury not witnessed before, FG 1 stamped hard on the floor causing the metal tiles to ring with a bell like reverberation. "I do not want that! I do not want that." The voice reverberated off the domed walls echoing back to the listening panel causing them to sit back on their chairs identical looks of surprise etched across their sculptured features.

"Please can't you understand? I do not want any of that." With the smooth ease of command RB 71357 raised a hand and a silence fell instantly across the room.

"Please control your temper FG 1. Explain to us for I do not understand. What is it you do not want. More time?"

"No, not more time." FG 1 raised her head and looked up at the floating camera eyes ablaze with a passion that sent a shudder of fear throughout the panel and watching audience alike. With straight back and shoulders squared FG l faced the camera as though it were the nation itself and spoke with a voice full of clarity and bravery. "I do not wish to join any of the enclaves. I do not want your choices. I do not wish for any of this. What I wish for is that from this time forward and for ever more my name shall be Evie, I wish to be known as Evie!" Before the panel could react FG 1 stepped to the limit of the circle close to the humming of the rainbow and raised her arms towards the panel and the floating camera which had moved close to capture the scene in full digital detail. "I shall be known as Evie. I shall remain as I am, a woman. I am proud to have the body I have, I am proud to be who I am and wish nothing more than to share who I am with others."

"FG 1 Remember where you are. Remember the rules as you have been taught. Consider those around you." Before RB 71357 could continue FG 1 silenced them with a shout

"No! It is you who should remember who it is before you. I am Evie and I shall meet a man who I shall fall in love with. A man who will love me for who I am as I love him for who he is. In our lives together he will care for me as I care for him. We shall live the old life. I shall become a mother. I shall be who I want to be, who I choose to be and not what is chosen for me. Panel I have made my choice. I choose to be heterosexual.

Findings of Rainbow Court, case 9456-345. The anomaly known for these proceedings as FG 1 has been sentenced to immediate and non reversible banishment to the penal colony known as Hebrides 1. Hebrides 1 is the internment camp used for gender refusers and non conformists. In their summation of the case the High Advocate has decreed that.

"The court has found no substance to the case that brings mitigation to the subject know as FG 1. The arguments that the sexuality and gender they request and strenuously argued for are those that were originally and legally recognised. Although sadly this was accepted as an argument in the world as once it bares no resemblance to the inclusivity we recognise today. We are in a place now that recognises and encourages all sexual preferences as well as genders. We will however not accept that one persons misguided beliefs are acceptable to us especially when that belief encourages the concept of turning from full inclusivity. In the eyes of the court any gender which segregates itself by choice from inclusivity is not to become the norm. The penal colony will be the only fitting place for a deviant to remain. Here separated from our all inclusive and accepting societies they will be unable to practice outdated and hedonistic ways on innocent life forms. I pity the soul of FG 1 as they are now subjected to remain amongst other such deviants for the remainder of their lives." In a footnote to the ruling the High Advocate assured all watchers and listeners that full therapy sessions had been offered to the esteemed members of the panel to aid their recovery after such a painful and traumatic event.

On what she was informed was Hebrides 1 penal colony, a small boy took her by the hand,

"Hello you must be Evie? We were sent a message that we were to expect you. My Mum and Dad asked me to make sure you got from the hover boat to us safely. Mum said you haven't got a Mum and Dad but that's ok because you can stay with us. You will have the spare room it's next to mine. Where are your mum and dad? No I shouldn't ask that. Dad said I should not ask you lots of questions because you might be tired. Are you tired? You will like it here, everyone likes it here. My Mum and Dad have lived here for years and years, but I have only lived here for 8 years that was when I was born. I am very excited. My Mum says that I talk a lot when I'm excited. Am I talking too much? I like your name it pretty. My name is Adnam and I think we will be friends." As they walked from the jetty Adnam clutched her hand chattering loudly. As they walked he took great delight in pointing out various points of interest and guiding her towards the groups of small huts in the distance. Evie felt the fine patter of rain wash over her and looked away into the distance at the bright rainbow which had formed over the far end of the island and smiled.

Brighton

"I just fancied something different. I told you that Mike."Casey pulls the straighteners through her hair concentrating furiously as she works. "The break will do us good." She smiles into the mirror seeing her husband of ten years shrug in response, an action she knows so well, an action she had noticed for the first time when he had been the new boy in class. Both of them, thirteen years old, she, settled into her new school for the past six months, him, newly joined having only just moved into the area.

"Casey Edwards, this is Mike Streeter. He's a new boy. Needs someone to look after him. Why don't you show him round the school?" She could picture it so well. Mr Brough, Head of English and her form tutor. A man who struck fear into the students with his broad Welsh accent, a man who suffered no fool gladly, and made this point well known. "I think that perhaps you should sort of take him under your wing eh?" He had nodded towards the gangly boy by his side as though suddenly aware of his presence. "Keep him with you for a few days until I can sort out which classes he will be best suited to." He broke off to bark loudly towards two boys who ambled past, lost in the depth of some schoolboy conversation. "Simpkin, Edwards, get to your lessons, now!

If that is gum you are chewing Edwards, it had better be gone by the time you reach the classroom. Am I clear?" He had turned his back on the scurrying of feet and the hasty

"Yes Sir." And focused again on Casey,

"Yes keep him with you. Give him a fighting chance in this hell hole of delinquency we lovingly call New Uxbury Comprehensive eh?" Without waiting for a response he limped away all responsibility for the new boy passed on sufficiently. Casey had smiled at the new boy, aware that he had not taken his eyes off her since he was thrust towards her.

"Hi Mike. I'm Casey, stay with me and you will be ok." It was then that Mike had shrugged the first of what she realised would become his trademark shrugs, an action which caused his loose fitting shirt to untuck from his trousers.

"Its Slater." He shrugged again "My names Slater, not Streeter."

"Oh right. Mike Slater it is then. Erm, you had better follow me." Casey had looked at the ground her own tell tale response and felt herself already shrinking from this sudden responsibility foisted upon her. She had wondered why Mr Brough had chosen her but if truth were told was too much in fear of Mr Brough's disapproving look and if she were honest too much in awe of the boy who stood before her to ask. It had not been the most romantic of first meetings but one that would be recalled between them numerous times, for him when pressed as a passing anecdote, one of those funny almost inconsequential events.

"It was just a teacher getting rid of the thick kid as fast as he could." For her it was and always would be fondly recalled, a memory to be cherished, an understanding that it was her who had captured his heart instantly and forever.

She smiles at the memory and pulls again at the straighteners guiding them more harshly than was probably good for her hair over the stubborn bounce that refused to be tamed.

"Seriously Mike. It will be great." She places the hot straighteners on the protective heat pad she'd lay on the makeup table in preparation and turns to him swivelling on the small leather stool. "It's a lovely hotel and we have a great room. The view is to die for." Mike shrugs again and places his camera on the bed next to him. He leans slowly back against the padded headboard and nods towards the window,

"But Casey, this is Brighton, not Bermuda. It's pouring with rain and the forecast says it's set for the whole weekend." As if to emphasise the point he pulls the complementary white cotton bath robe around his now powerful shoulders and shivers dramatically. After all their time together she still admires the change to his physique, the hours of training moulding him into the figure he has become. She wipes a hand over her face as though to waken herself from sleep, an action that hides her blush. He was certainly no longer the gangly boy with the start of the burning acne that had earned him the name 'crater face' for so many years.

"I know love but…" She smiles again, a genuine warmth filling her face, "Treat it as a long weekend away. Treat it as a chance to relax. Just think, we won't be tripping over the girls all the time, catering for their every need." She gives a slight giggle thinking of how quickly the girls had called 'bye Mummy, bye Daddy,' before skipping down her mothers hallway to the promise of a thick slice of homemade coconut cake. "Yes we get to try something new, something just for us, and they spend the whole time being spoiled rotten by my Mum and Dad." From the bed Mike sighs and picks up his camera studying it as though it were a work of art, something precious to be admired. She smiles softly, "Who knows, perhaps you can get some good photos, atmospheric, wild and romantic." She turns back on her stool and picks up a small tube unscrewing the cap slowly. "Please love, try and enjoy yourself, let's make the most of it eh?" In the mirror she sees him try to resist but eventually shrugs again causing the gown to gape open around his chest

"I will Casey, of course I will but I mean….." He looks out of the large window barely able to see the small Juliet balcony beyond such is the force of the rain hitting the glass. "I mean, of all places, Brighton?" Casey shushes him with a click of her tongue and a smile.

"Yes love, Brighton." She hears the rain force itself harder if that was at all possible onto the glass and hopes that the hotel has a good heating system and the indoor pool is as warm as advertised. Undeterred she continues brightly "You said I could go where I liked for a break, and after much in depth research, I chose here." She kept her voice light but needed him to understand her reasoning for this, her need to be here, the two of them together, no distractions, just them reconnecting. She nods to herself happy with the choice of word, 'reconnect,' that's what they needed, just to reconnect. She squeezes a small amount of cream into her hand and begins smoothing it gently into her skin. The scent wafts over her and she relaxes enjoying the silkiness beneath her fingers and the calming sensation in her concentration. She had good skin, been told it many times before.

"Hey girl, I wish I had skin like yours."

"Casey I would just die to have the glow about me that you carry so easily on you. I don't mind saying you have skin that is just pure perfection." She smiles at the thoughts and rubs her fingertips into her cheekbones. If only they knew that so called perfection takes work.

"Do they dress for dinner here?" The reflection in the mirror rises from the bed and stretches loudly before walking to stare out of the window. "God this weather is awful." Casey smiles to herself, seeing the rows of white teeth flash against the brightness of the table lamp.

"Yes the weather is awful Mike, and no I don't think they do dress for dinner, I think it's just come as you are." She sees Mike shrug and listens as he blows out a long slow breath.

"Mmm ok." He was thinking, she could tell. She continues rubbing at herself, her neck, the top of her chest allowing the silence to fill the room, allow Mike the space to think. He had always needed time, always needed to think carefully about what it was he wanted to say. She supposed this was one of the things she loved about him, his considered approach to any situation. Her mind wanders back to a distant time, a crowded bus, windows steamed with the condensation of many breaths and damp clothing.

"Oy, you! You'll have to move." She

remembers now how she had looked up from her book the title still strong in her memory, 'The Art of Diplomatic Discussion.' She had looked from the pages which intrigued her so profusely and had stared into the face of a large bulldog of a man. He had leaned over her with a look of snarling disrespect carved into his face. She had tried to remain calm, tried to maintain a look of stoic composure.

"Excuse me?" Her smile had been forced, tight with an apprehension that hid the fact that she wished she could have been anywhere but where she was. As she stared up into the man's dark eyes she had cursed the fact that her cheaply bought second hand car had chosen this morning of all the mornings to finally commit itself to the great scrap yard in the sky.

"I said you'll have to move." His voice had taken on a gruffer edge, more growl than speech. "Me and my mate are going to sit here. You…" The word 'you' somehow managed to feel as though it were a slight, a word of disrespect, "You, are taking up our seat." Without realising she was doing so she had glanced around the bus seeing multiple double seats taken by single travellers, all of whom seemed to find something much more interesting to look at as long as it was not in her direction.

"I am sorry, but I'm a little bit confused."

She wished she hadn't spoken, hadn't engaged with them, but this was not her way, not who she was "There does seem to be an awful lot of available seats for you and your friend, I just wondered why mine is so special?" She wished that she was further through her book which sat uncomfortably mocking her from her lap. Chapter one was interesting, it really was, but at that moment she believed that no matter which chapter she was on the only real use for this book would be to beat the thug around his head with it.

"What did you say?" The bulldog man leaned in closer assailing her with the mustiness of cigarette smoke and the sweetness of age old sweat, "Now don't you get above your place bitch, just move!" It wasn't an invitation and the reason for her being chosen was obvious, her sex and her skin had made her the prime candidate for this unwarranted attention.

"I'm getting off in five stops…" Her voice was now barely audible, hushed by fear and the hiss of the bus door as it opened to allow passengers to exit and enter from the latest scheduled stop. She had wanted nothing more than to leave with the departing passengers, to stand in the cold at the bus stop until another came along to offer her the final few stops home, but she had to respond, her dignity would allow no other course of action. "I will be getting off soon and then you and your friend can sit together. Please just allow me to finish my chapter in peace." The thug had rocked back on his feet as though shocked by a sudden noise or noxious smell. Folding his arms around his barrel chest he had glowered down at her, the caricature of every heavyweight bully.

"Move your fuckin' arse or I will move it for ya." She had hesitated for only a second before he was reaching for her, no doubt to drag her from where she sat, "Come on bitch, you ain't no modern day Rosa Parks." Although frightened for her life in that moment she was somehow impressed that this thug even knew who Rosa Parks was. If it had not been for the terror that engulfed her she may well have inadvertently congratulated him no doubt making the situation worse.

"Honestly, I really am getting off in a moment..." The thug gave her no chance to finish, instead stepping close and making to grab the front of her raincoat. She had half closed her eyes waiting for the tug, the thrust, but the expected grab never came for it was then that fate stepped in.

"Leave the lady alone." His voice was as recognisable to her soul as music was to her ears. Mike had appeared smoothly behind her from the rear entrance and was now standing square on to the thug, hardly swaying as the bus continued its journey. She had looked up at the six foot three slab of granite that was now Mike and smiled.

"Hi Mike."

"Hi yourself Casey." His eyes never left her aggressor who seemed to physically shrink the harder Mike stared at him. "You got problems here?" Casey had smiled, all feelings of fear leaving her the moment she took in his presence.

"No, no problem, thanks Mike." Mike had ignored her comment and took a step towards the oaf who had moments before exuded so much power.

"Wasn't talking to you Casey, was talking to this…" He stretched the word out "Gentleman." He took another step forward, keeping his head ducked to avoid hitting the roof, "Well?" The thug waved a hand in a 'I'm sorry you must have misunderstood what was happening here' sort of a gesture and mumbled something over his shoulder to the forever silent friend, who quickly about turned and knocked on the drivers plastic panel indicating that he wanted to exit at the next stop. Mike had stood by her seat waiting to make certain that the men both left the bus and then he had scrunched with little finesse into the seat next to her almost squashing her against the window.

"Thanks Mike." He had nodded as though almost unsure of what she was thanking him for and stared vacantly past her profile seemingly ignoring the two men who ran alongside the slowly moving bus flipping two fingered gestures through the window. "Not seen you around for a couple of months. How are you?" She had known it was coming but inwardly smiled as his large shoulders shrugged in response.

"Yeah good, been busy working at the new photographic studio, learning loads."

"Thats great. You still love it. The photography?" She had watched as he gathered his thoughts, considered before answering.

"Yeah, I love it." He had shrugged again, fallen silent, staring ahead biting his bottom lip, he was thinking. "How are you. How's college?"

"Yeah good, going really well. I've just been really busy. Don't know where the time goes?" He'd nodded then shrugged understanding.

"So," he'd said eventually, "This Rosa Parks woman, friend of yours from college is she?" Casey had laughed softly hugging his arm tightly,

"Oh Mike." She'd rested her head against the warmth of his jacketed arm smiling into the solid muscle beneath the padded material.

"I have missed you." They had travelled in silence for the rest of the journey, comfortable in each others presence, happy just to simply be together with no interruptions, no distractions, no need for anything but each others company. The bus had made slow progress in the heavy traffic and the weather had worsened by the time she came to her stop. Mike had insisted on walking her home, 'just to be safe.' They held hands as they walked, talked little, fell into step.

Now, she watched as he turned to face her from where he stood by the window, he was biting his bottom lip. She began to apply her makeup, taking extra care with the lipstick although managing to keep good sight of his reflected image, waiting for him to speak.

"Casey. Are we ok?" His face was a cross between hurt schoolboy and worried parent. It was a look that pulled at her heart strings, melted her. Quickly she placed the lipstick into her makeup bag and rose to her feet crossing the room to him in only a few hasty strides. Throwing her arms around his neck she stood on tip toes to reach and smiled up at his large square face with genuine sincerity.

"Of course we are. We really are." She spoke with care emphasising her words with a gentle stroke to his cheek "Why wouldn't we be?" She looked up at him studying the shrug when it came, remembering all of the good times.

"Well. It's just, all this." He nodded a glance around the room, "I mean, why this?" Casey laughed and moved towards the bed and sat neatly across the corner folding one leg under her other leg as though riding side saddle.

"Mike I thought I explained?" He nodded quickly

"You did but…" His mouth worked the words free, "Well its just a little bit, well I'm not sure what's really going on, I keep thinking that…" He stopped speaking and leaned back against the wall his brow furrowing in confusion. Casey felt her breath tighten but fought through the constriction, calmed her breathing and nodded, she must speak carefully, she had to word this correctly. Taking the silence between them to choose her words carefully she patted the bed for him to sit next to her. As the bed sagged under his weight she clasped his hand in hers and spoke softly.

"I love you very much indeed." A good beginning but she didn't wait for an answer, "We are really good together, always have been. We have a great life together, us and the girls." This was all true, she absolutely believed in them as a couple, as a family. Squeezing his hand she continued, "Its just that with the girls, with your new photography studio and the contract with the B.B.C. for the wildlife show and my new contract in London with TATE Modern, things have moved fast, exceeded all of our expectations." She hurried on, "We really are doing fantastically well, great home, great lives, great everything, but…" She paused seeing Mike's eyes widen in what, shock, surprise, fear? She had to get this right find the right words, "Mike we are busy. We are busy people, with busy lives." Now it was her turn to feel anxious she was doubting herself certain that she was not making herself clear. "Honey, I explained to you how Bev and Keith and Stephanie and Marco have recently split after years of marriage." She thought of her friends Bev and Stephanie, how they were struggling to come to terms with what they had lost. How could that be possible, she wondered? It only seemed like yesterday that they were young, full of life, the new 'Charlie's Angels.' They were the closest of friends, had been her bridesmaids at each others weddings. Sitting beside her Mike nodded,

"I know. Sad that." As always he was the master of understatement. She continued quickly not wanting to lose the thread of her thought process

"It was the conversations with both of them that made me think, made me consider things, made me think of us." A slow look of sadness spread across Mike's face,

"So there is something wrong, with us?"

"No, definitely not, and that is how I want it to stay." Casey shook her head quickly desperate now to make him understand. The threat of nervous laughter forced itself hard behind her lips but she swallowed it down. The way she was trying to explain this she wasn't sure she would really be able to understand what it was she was trying to say. She took a large breath and laid a hand gently on his knee before speaking again. "I have spoken to Bev and Steph many times about the breakup of their marriages, you know that?" Mike nodded not quite able to meet her gaze "I told you that ultimately they both blamed the same thing on the breakdown of their marriages." In truth there had been many reasons for the sudden separations, affairs, arguments, alcoholism and in Steph's case an attack on Marco's Aston Martin with the leg of an antique table, but ultimately it had been down to one factor. "Mike they both stated the same reason for their marriages dissolving. They both had.." She paused, "They both had, too much, yes too much. Somehow they became lost as couples, they drifted apart in a river of excess stuff." She counted out on her fingers as though counting items on a conveyor belt. "Too much wealth, too many gadgets, money that became a constant fight to keep, friends that were good time Charlies praise heaped on them that proved to be true until the moment their gaze was turned away, fast cars, posh holidays, fine clothes and the love of expensive restaurants." She stopped speaking panting with effort, "But do you know what they had lost whilst gathering all of this, this, this… stuff?" She spat the word out. "Each other, that's what they lost, the sense of each other and who they were." She gripped his hand again wanting him to understand "And that, that is what frightened me." She shook her head hardly believing herself what she was saying, "It seems as though my friends, our friends had failed in their marriages because of their success." She smiled thinly into the face of her adoring husband, her soul mate, "It was because of too much they failed, too much success, too many possessions, too many worries and concerns, just too much of everything." She lowered her voice and spoke almost reverently "I could hardly believe it myself. How can too much have such a detrimental effect? Well Mike that's when I started to investigate, to look things up, read more. No don't laugh, please don't laugh." She dropped her gaze from Mike's face embarrassed now by her own passion. Perhaps he would see her anew and not like what he had discovered in her. Perhaps he would now turn what she saw as his concentrating frown and bottom lip bite of thought into his winning boyish grin, the one that lit his dark eyes so dangerously and use it to mock her but she dare not stop now. She had started this journey, believed in its course she had to trust herself and to continue trusting him as she always had done. "I listened to a fantastic pod cast." She managed a quick upward glance noticing that Mike had remained motionless, concentrating fully. "I told you about it, the Australian lady who talks about relationships and of being at one with all that surrounds us. How that to really connect with each other we need to let go of all things foreign to us as human beings. She speaks with such authority, wants us to concentrate on just what is important to us, and only what is important to us." She realised now that she was close to tears but she had to remain calm stay focused. "It's you Mike, the thing that's so important to me, is you, it always has been. I know that and I know you know it but…" She was suddenly lost for words. Without thinking she grasps Mike's hand and lays it flat against her chest, "You feel my heart beating Mike, you feel how it thuds against my chest, against your hand? Well that is what is so important to me. Of course the girls are, and my parents and your mother and what we do for a living, but none of that can be as important as this." She drops his hand and points at her chest, "Its not as important as the flutter my heart makes when I see you, it's not as important, as the history we have together, it is not as important as the boy you were when we first met and the girl I was who fell in love with that boy the very moment I saw him." Her sentence was long and growing in passion, she knew that, but she needed him to understand. "This is why I chose this hotel, why I decided on this simple rain sodden adventure. It is not because we were are in danger of breaking up, not because I do not love you, nothing could be further from the truth. I chose this hotel in Brighton because it is basic and in its own simple way allows us to get back to the very basics of each other. It allows us to be just us, to reconnect with nothing blocking, nothing to hide behind no bells and whistles, nothing what-so-ever to distract us." She stopped speaking and stared hard into his eyes imploring him to understand, "You do see this don't you. You do understand what I am trying to say. I organised this because we are ok and I want us to keep on realising we are ok, I want us to always be able to remember what we mean to each other despite of what we have or in fact should we lose it all what we had." She stopped talking, suddenly aware that she was gabbling and had given Mike no chance to speak, no chance to respond in any way. With bated breath she waited, her heart thumping ten to the dozen. And then it came, that slow, almost casual movement, Mike shrugged.

"Casey, I do understand I really do, but…" She felt the lump hit her throat as an unwelcome fear forced its way up from her chest, "But…" He continued, "All of this really is so unnecessary," He waved his arm vaguely around the small room "I could never stop loving you, I could never put anything before you, or the girls." He added almost shyly, "You are and always have been the girl for me," He reached across and gently stroked her cheek "Casey I have adored you from the first time we met. From the first smile you gave me. From the very first moment you linked your arm through mine and led me through the corridor of the school unashamed to be seen with a gawky boy covered in acne." He reached forward and slipped an arm around her waist pulling her towards him, "Casey, I know I do not tell you often enough just how much I love you." He stared hard into her eyes as though willing her to understand what he was trying to say, " I never tell you this because I never seem to know the right words, never have the language to tell you, because deep down I am still that skinny kid from Uxbury Comprehensive. I am the boy introduced as Streeter not Slater, the boy who knew from the start that you were too good for him, the boy who was happy just to walk by your side until you realised what a loser he was. Casey…" She heard a small catch in his throat, "I could never write you a love poem or compose a piano piece, I just haven't got the brains for it, I'm just not clever like that." She wanted to stop him, interrupt his words, tell him this was not true but he gave her no chance, simply continued, his voice rich and deep. "Casey I suppose…" He held her away from himself and looked directly into her eyes, boring deep into her soul, "I suppose that all I could ever do is be there for you in whatever you wanted, to support you in anything you needed. Whilst I did this I knew that all I could really do would be to love you as furiously as I could and hope Casey, that you never came to the sudden and obvious realisation that I was just in fact Mike Slater the lonely, skinny kid with acne." Casey wanted to speak, wanted to crush his head to her breast, to stroke his hair and tell him that she knew who he was, had always known who he was and had loved him then as now, but the words would not come, could not force their way through the tears that washed small rivers of colour down her cheeks from her eyeliner. She brushed at them with the heel of her hand smearing the oh so perfect forgery of a picture she had created only those few moments before. She knew her actions revealed the naturalness she had worked so hard to disguise she displayed the 'self' she had dared only to reveal in the darkest of rooms in the most private of settings. As though hearing her own silent, internal revelations Mike held her face between his two powerful hands and gently leaned forward kissing her mouth softly, a tenderness that belayed his natural strength. As though to complete a holy trinity he moved his touch from her mouth and reverently placed his lips to gently caress each of her eyes ignoring the dampness of the tears.

"You are the most beautiful person Casey, both inside and out." He said hugging her to him, forcing the words through tears of his own, "There are no distractions to me where you are concerned, you are my everything." As though suddenly becoming aware of something he held her away from his body, keeping her at arms length whilst wiping the tears from his eyes with a sleeve from the robe. "Casey." Her name seemed to be no longer her name but the meerest of whispers as though he were afraid to speak it out loud. She dare not break the moment, could see the way in which his lip pulsed beneath the bite of his own teeth and the colour flushing his cheeks. She saw close the vein pulsing at his temple and the sweat that beaded his brow, the nervousness that creased the edge of his eyes as he cleared his throat deciding to continue. She waited seemingly sapped of all strength in this moment. It was a strength she had moulded to herself, learned to control. It was the strength that although learned had only managed to hold her loosely together all these years. It was a strength that came born from her own frailties and fears, she realised that now and only now she was seen as she truly was. Tears blurred her vision again as she looked into the face of the man she had deep in her heart always feared would see through her disguise and leave her. She had always known that in his new found discovery of her, disappointment would rule what had before been his acceptance. She saw it then, just a twitch, a flick, a rend to her heart. Mike's eyes looked from hers, looked to a place beyond her, looked past and did not return. The disappointment had found him. The rain crashed heavily on the glass, the wind blew furiously and the waves crashed with anger on the beach beyond their room. Casey knew now that the elements themselves were telling her what he could not. It was over.

"Casey." His voice pulled her gaze towards him, blocked the storm that raged outside from entering her fully. Mike cupped her cheeks tenderly, looked to her and held her gaze with an intensity that bound her to him and him to her, both physically and emotionally. When at last he spoke, his words were soft and gentle they were an echoed psalm through an empty Cathedral. "Casey." He whispered her name again as though it to were the start of a prayer, a reverence spoken in adoration,

"What longing in tears for you. You. My Life. My all. Oh, go on loving me, never doubt the faithfullest heart, of your beloved. Ever thine, ever mine, ever ours."

As Mike finished speaking the walls of the room span towards her. The elements crashed and thudded against the glass of the balcony doors but now as a celebration set in time to the beating of the blood in her ears and the deep hammering of her heart in her chest. In this one moment the realisation came that for all of these years she had doubted herself as much as he had doubted himself. Her fears were his fears. His shrug was her makeup. His lip biting, was her downward glance. She feared herself as much unworthy as he considered himself truly undeserving. They were the same, they were a match. In this moment of realisation came at once another truth, another understanding an understanding that had been hidden from them both. They were as one and nothing could come between them separating them with their promises of gluttony and excess. Her fear of barriers between them were her fears of self depreciation, and past prejudices forced upon her and believed wholeheartedly without question. His fears of worthlessness were schoolboy taunts and teachers jibes of 'thick' and dumb'. They were the adult versions of themselves as children, frightened that they would always fall short, they would always fail to be as good or as accepted as those around them. They would be found out, revealed for the frauds they obviously were. Here in this room in a stormy, blustery, basic but beautiful Brighton these two lost children who had always hoped for acceptance, found that they were already accepted for just who they were.

Laying wrapped in his arms with nothing but the applause of the elements for company Casey smiled into his chest, feeling the hairs rub softly against her cheek and sighed contentedly.

"Hey, you awake?" Mike kissed the top of her head and mumbled warmly,

"I won't be if we don't make a move soon." She nodded

"Mmm, I know what you mean." She lay for a few more moments listening to the waves, considering her next question carefully, "Mike."

"Yeah." His voice was sleepy, he really was relaxing.

"What you said to me."

"Mmm?"

"That thing you said to me, the 'ever thine' thing."

"Yeah?" He drew the word out, more alert now.

"It was beautiful."

"Yes you said."

"Was it your own?" His laugh rumbled deep in his chest tickling her ear. He ran a finger slowly along her spine, as he spoke.

God no Case' I told you I'm no good at that sort of thing." He paused but continued moving his hand along her spine, "No I learned it years ago."

"Really?" She pushed herself up onto one elbow so that she could see his face.

"Yeah."

"When?" Mike chuckled and looked down at her, smiling.

"When we was in Mr Brough's class for English. We had been learning about famous diary writers or something like that. Well old Broughie started talking about Beethoven and how he had left a letter to someone that they didn't know who it was. He showed us the letter and read it out."

"And you learned it from that?" Mike shook his head slowly,

"Not at first no. It was a few weeks later

that we were learning about public speaking and he said we all had to find something to share with the class that we had learned by heart. I chose the end of that letter, it was about as much as I could learn in a week, you know how I am with reading." She nodded understanding everything about him. "Well that was what I learned, just that piece. I think I misquoted it earlier by the way, not sure I got it all right." He laughed again, "Still nothing unusual in that." She slapped him playfully on the chest.

"Stop that." She said "I think it was beautiful."

"Yes you said." He laughed again, it was good to hear him laugh, it was always good to hear him laugh.

"Mike?" she said eventually breaking the silence that had drifted over them.

"Mmm?"

"I don't remember you ever speaking anything out in class." She felt Mike shake his head slowly,

"No I didn't do it in the end, couldn't." Casey ran her fingers through his chest hair and kissed him gently on his shoulder.

"Too much for you?" She asked kindly. Mike's chest rose as he drew in a large breath.

"No, not that." He said expelling the air.

"Why then?" She asked, "It was….."

"Beautiful, yes you have said." Mike's hand ceased the stroking movement along her back and he fell silent. She could picture him now biting at his bottom lip, thinking. "I couldn't do it Case'" He said eventually "I couldn't do it because the person I had learned it for wasn't in school that day. She had broken her finger playing hockey and was at the hospital getting it straightened." His hand began the long languid movement along her spine, "It wasn't for anyone else, only her." Casey subconsciously rubbed the permanently swollen knuckle of her right hand and allowed the single tear that had formed to run smoothly down her cheek and fall gently onto his chest.

"Oh Mike." Her words were whispers, mere breaths against his skin, "Ever thine, ever mine, ever ours. That is us Mike, that is us." Twisting his body to face her, Mike tilted her chin towards him and gazed into her eyes with an intensity that burned into her soul and caught her breath.

"Yes Casey. God yes. Always." He leaned down and kissed her gently, "You are and always have been, my immortal beloved." Casey lay in his arms unwilling to break the spell simply content to savour the moment. As though aware of her thoughts Mike hugged her towards him, and as his breathing shallowed in sleep he shrugged.

In Emergency…

I wake with a jolt, my heart thumping noisily in my chest. My eyes begin scanning the room even before my eyelids have fully lifted. I have no recollection of where I am. These, my surroundings stark and unfamiliar to me. I close my eyes against the harsh white light, a light that leaves bright circles hovering sickeningly beneath my closed lids and I try to think clearly. Perhaps it had been the large industrial bulbs bursting into life that had caused me to wake, or had there been a noise. Perhaps the noise was from an unseen other occupant in the room? I listen hard but there is no tell-tale clue, all is quiet. Fear grips me as I force myself to look again and realise I can remember nothing of where I am. Slowly at first I pull myself into a sitting position expecting at any moment a stab of pain from some unnoticed wound. When there is none I release the breath I had been unaware of holding and roll my shoulders and carefully flex my arms to be sure. Nothing hurts there are no mystery aches or pains. Everything seems to be working. I take a few deep breaths to help me focus. What do I know? I am aware that I am not on a bed it is more like a trolley that would be found in a hospital emergency room. The rubber mattress creaks with somewhat of a familiarity and in its way confirms my thoughts. So, I must be in hospital? Tentatively I swing my legs over the side of the trolley and sit silently waiting. For what? I am unsure. I shiver slightly and look for a sheet to wrap around my shoulders, there is nothing available which takes on a more significant meaning as I realise for the first time since waking that I am totally naked. I cover my embarrassment with my hands and stare out at my surroundings drinking in every detail. I am in a room that is like no other I have been in before. The walls, ceiling and floor are constructed of what I can only describe as a glass like substance. This substance is shiny, reflective more mirror than glass I suppose. I study my duplicate image opposite me. I look well cared for. Nothing out of place, no hidden marks or wires, no monitors. My hair is short, black, shaped close to my skull. My jaw is strong and square, no stubble of note. My reflected self strokes his chin as I stroke mine. Lack of stubble shows that I have been here for no more than two days unless those who care for me, whoever they may be shave people as they sleep. I frown as I concentrate on what I do know. Hi, my name is Bobbi, Bobbi with an 'I' not a 'Y' how do you do? Be careful I am highly skilled and I can defend myself. Do not hit the glass! I leap to my feet ignoring the shortness of breath that washes over me in a wave of apprehension,

Abbi! The name crashes into my consciousness. Where was Abbi? I am certain we were together before… I concentrate as the almost grasped but just out of reach memories slip from the fingers of my mind before I can grab them. I am sure we were together before I ended up here. What has happened to Abbi? Have we been in some sort of an accident? Is she safe? I must find her, I must protect Abbi. I stride from the trolley uncaring now of my nudity and search the glass walls for a doorway. My mind races. I can see nothing obvious, no tell-tale handles or levers, not so much as a key pad system. Inwardly I roar with frustration, what sort of a place is this? It was as if I were trapped in an upturned goldfish bowl with no hope of escape and no way of finding Abbi. I must, I must protect Abbi. After minutes of walking the room running my hands over every surface frantically, I come to a stop I am unsure of what to do next. My rage is building, Abbi must be protected. I want to hammer my fists hard against the walls but somehow know this would be the wrong thing to do. I must think logically. I lean heavily on the trolley and close my eyes. I must have been brought in here no one would have constructed the room around me so there must be an entrance however simple it may be. Although I could not locate it this does not mean it is not here. Why had they, whoever they are made it so difficult to find, were they imprisoning me, was I a risk or was I indeed the one at risk? I had wasted time and seemed to have more questions than answers now.

My next few hours pass in moments of high activity searching the walls and floor, through long moments of quiet contemplation and rising anger. As time passes I have some moments of clarity, half returned memories, completed tasks. A book, Abbi, a conversation, 'Be calm, we must...' I shake my head each memory a small piece of the jigsaw. I can hear them rattling in their box they can complete the picture and yet the box stays firmly shut and out of reach. It is in these moments that the walls of my cell, for that is how I think of it now, seem to shudder and compress towards me bringing sickening waves of claustrophobia. I must act. I spend many minutes moving the hospital trolley around the extremities of the wall, climbing onto it to better explore an escape route higher up. It is a futile gesture I am sure, but one worth attempting. As I search and without warning from somewhere over my left shoulder a soft hiss breaks the silence. I whip around without care searching for the cause of the noise and the trolley moves under me causing me to crash heavily to the floor. I ignore the electric shock that runs the length of my arm to my shoulder and spin myself left towards the sound. A black leather bound book skids to the centre of the room and stops, spine facing me. I flick a glance to the right following the direction the book came from in time to see a small hatchway at floor level whisper shut forming again the solid wall of glass. I spring to my feet and half dive, half skid to reach the spot where the hatch had been. Nothing is visible, not a mark, line or shadow. It was as though the glass had moulded itself into a oneness again. I roar with frustration, a sound I was unaware I could make something between an animal in pain and the mechanical grinding of gears. I like how the roar tastes in my mouth and roar again until my throat burns dry. I push my back hard against the glass but stop myself the moment I begin. I must not attack the glass, never attack the glass. Breathing heavily, I compose my thoughts whilst staring at the invader in the room, for that is how it feels this foreign object. It taunts me as it lays there, so small, so normal, so ordinary and yet taking up so much room. It somehow sucks the energy from me with its presence. Finally, the book wins the battle of wills and I know I can no longer resist its call. I move wearily towards it and reach out to close my hand around its form. I am certain before my fingers touch the book that it will not be the hardness of board or the silkiness of velvet, every part of me believes that when my palm presses against this silent object it shall be greeted by the feel of a soft, worn, leather. I am as sure of this as I am that it will be soft, smooth to the touch, warm, with a rip on the front cover that will split in two the faded silver italic writing. This writing will say. 'Rules and Thoughts'. I am not sure how I know this, but I do. Words fill my mind, 'Write in the book, do not hit the glass, do not damage yourself, you must protect Abbi.' Instructions clear and precise, but from where? The book rests on my lap now sneering at me from the rip in the cover, 'Coward!' it's torn mouth screams, 'You have to complete the tasks.' I sigh my acceptance of the inevitable and open the book to the first page, avoiding the grinning rip. I need not have looked for I somehow already knew; clear blue pen, neat precise handwriting. Mine! A list, my list? It must be my list and yet I do not remember writing such a thing. The words lay boldly on the stark white page 1. Protect Abbi 2. Do not damage yourself 3. Do not hit the glass. On and on they went, rule after rule each one as familiar to me as my name. I scan through the book hardly needing to read. I notice that slowly the handwriting changes, it is still mine but now each word is heavily pressed. Each note is a deep score of thick blue pen. Underlined words repeat on the page; Caged, angry, alone, frustrated. A circle of ink traps a thought surrounding it as though a stockade... ABBI IS MISSING! Two lines are drawn from the statement connecting corresponding words WHY! And WHO! I flick the pages forward and a small pen drops to my lap and lays there silently. I study the pen it is clear plastic, a dark ink entombed inside. For the briefest of moments the ink reminds me of me. I hold the pen in my fingers and it feels... familiar. Moving my hand over the page words begin to flow as the plastic releases the captured liquid. I look at the words written almost subconsciously. 'Confused, yelling, LONELY'. I stare at the last word again it is written in capital letters. I study it hard before underlining it three times each line slightly heavier than the last. With a sudden burst of pure energy, I slam the book shut trapping the pen between the pages. I jump to my feet anger and loneliness coursing through me, I want to hurl the book at the glass, 'Do not hit the glass!' I hold the book in two hands and bend it backwards and then forwards feeling the cover tear more beneath my grip. It feels good. "Where is Abbi? I must see Abbi!" I yell into the space. I scream at the glass watching my reflected self yell silently back his wild eyes willing me on. I take large lungfuls of air and bellow to whoever or whatever is lurking menacingly behind the crystallised darkness hoping for an answer and yet already knowing there will be nothing but silence returned. Moving around the room I hold my face close to the glass, peering into the darkness hoping to catch sight of something, anything.

"Where is she? What have you done with Abbi?" The anger feels good and my burning desire for companionship and to protect Abbi begins to take control. "Where is she, where is Abbi?" I must protect Abbi.

"WAIT!" This single word crashes into my space, it echoes around my glass cage and in my head. This intrusive voice crushes my brain and knocks the wind from my chest. I fall to one knee and look wildly around the room. It is a shock that a word has been spoken to me but relief that I have been correct. I am being watched and there is someone out there. I want to communicate but am now unsure of how to proceed. Have they taken Abbi, is she safe? Before I can formulate the correct response to this new event the lights of my glass cell, extinguish. I kneel for many moments in total darkness. There is no sound save the rasp of my breath which comes in short shallow bursts. Something has changed in me now. No longer am I the trapped creature of moments before but, here in the darkness I am now a cornered animal with muscles tensed. I am ready to spring forward and attack whatever comes to me be it man or beast. I must protect Abbi! Without warning one wall of my cell burns with a whiteness that has the intensity of a searchlight. I shield my eyes as they adjust to this intrusion. As I become accustomed to the light I see that one wall of my glass cell is now fully transparent and I can see beyond my own confinement. Slowly I raise myself to standing transfixed by what I see. There before me in full view is Abbi. Naked and alone standing in a room that mirrors mine. She is staring at a book she holds in her hands soft leather I am sure. As I watch, Abbi tosses the book onto her hospital trolley and moves to the wall furthest from me and begins studying it with her eyes and her hands. I realise that she is unaware that I am there, she cannot see me. Just what kind of sick game is this? Without realising I have done so I move closer to the wall and rest my hands flat against this strangely warm surface. I am calling her name.

"Abbi, Abbi!" She does not hear me. She has stopped moving around the room and fallen in a slump to the floor, her dark hair covering her face.

"Abbi." It is a whisper at first but soon grows in intensity as I study her still figure, "Abbi." As though I am watching and hearing myself from some other place. I hear how pitiful I sound and my anger grows again.

"Abbi." I call again, gently tapping my hand on the glass. Do not hit the glass. "Abbi, Abbi!" My voice is loud now my frustration grows to a fury, I must protect Abbi! My hand makes a slap on the glass. 'Do not hit the glass!' I feel a warmth on my skin as the slap grows stronger. 'Do not damage yourself!' I call and slap, slap and call, "Abbi, Abbi, Abbi!" Slap, slap, slap. Bang, bang, my fists hammer on the glass. 'Do not damage yourself, do not hit the glass, do not hit the glass, do not damage yourself… hit the glass, damage yourself, hit the glass, protect Abbi. I pound the glass my hands no longer feeling the pain, I rush the glass with my shoulder, I must protect Abbi. The glass bounces under my attack, it is futile I must do more. 'Hit the glass, protect Abbi, damage yourself, protect Abbi.' I grab for the hospital trolley, it is the only thing in the cell. Wheeling it to the furthest wall from Abbi I stand behind and take a moment planning my movements, steadying myself and pick the exact spot. I will ram through this glass wall. Whatever happens to me, I will protect Abbi.

They watch in silence as his body slumps to the floor heavily. He slides down the wall, a wall he has only moments before been bracing himself against full of power and action. His body folds over on itself and lays prone behind the trolley which now without any force or direction rolls in a lazy arc coming to a gentle stop centimetres from the glass behind which they sit.

"Well I think we have seen enough." He removes his gloved finger from the shutdown button and pushes away from the control panel with a sigh. The second figure nods slowly.

"Yes, I believe we have, but to be honest we have so little time it really has to be now or never." The two figures hold each other's gaze for a few moments in silent recognition of what they have achieved.

"I shall let the Capital know that we are ready. I of course will include these latest recordings of his inner thought processes but in all honesty the time for study is over." He sighs wearily before continuing with a heavy sadness in his voice, "I shall stress the urgency of their need to act and to act now. They must set the final date!" He places his hand on his colleagues' shoulder as though using her as a support for his tiredness.

"Thank you, Madeline. Your skills have created for us the perfect humanoid robot. It free thinks, disobeys those long ago programmed direct orders for the good of its other selves. It risks danger to itself for the good of the mission. Your loyal dedication has probably given us the greatest chance for mankinds survival." Beneath the respirator mask, Madeline allows herself a weary smile.

"I hope so Dr Randell. I really hope so." As though he is moving in slow motion the small man heads wearily towards the exit of the pod dragging his oxygen bottle heavily behind himself, the wheels leaving narrow lines in the dust. His voice crackles in her headset.

"Copy the programmes from Bob 1 to the other Bobs. Tell the impregnation team they can now load the human embryos into the female Abbesses. Be certain now, two embryos one male and one female for each." We must believe that the Abb 1 programme is now complete. All we have to do is fire them into the far reaches of space and hope to God one of the pairs finds a place of safety to restart humankind."

"Do you believe in God, Dr Randell?" He stops with his finger on the keypad of the door frozen for a moment by the question, before giving a small laugh.

"With the end of the world in sight my dear, I suppose I will believe in anything that may bring us to safety." He jabs his finger on the pad and the pod door slides open bringing with it a blast of hot, putrid air.

Madeline watches as the scientist shuffles away until the door slides shut with a hiss behind him, a hiss that leaves her with nothing but total silence.

The Eulogy

Trevor sat and stared at the blank sheet of paper placed on his leather topped writing desk in front of him. The regular A4, lined page glared back defiantly. It had been like this for nearly an hour now, neither man nor page able to release their gaze, neither willing to be the first to cede.

"God! This is crazy!" Trevor threw back his head with a frustrated roar, hearing the words thud heavily against the walls of his small home study, softened by the cork boards that were festooned with story plans and post it notes, post it notes that taunted him with their yellowing curled edges and faded pen marks. He stared again at the blank page in front of him and rubbed a weary hand over his tired eyes. He was writing a eulogy, a simple eulogy no more than that, so why was it so bloody hard? Again he rubbed at his face perhaps in the vain hope that it may force more blood to his brain and stir up some semblance of an idea, but more than likely the desperate action of a man devoid of any idea or hope. He groaned, a low guttural sound, animal in its origin

"Think will you. Just think." He rapped his knuckles on his head feeling the pain it brought but not caring, "it can't be that difficult, can it?" Standing quickly he grabbed at the beer can on the table but realised it was empty. In a surge of temper he crushed the thin can in one hand and violently tossed it towards the waste bin in the corner. The beer can hit the rim of the waste bin and fell to the floor wobbling to a halt where it lay abandoned next to its recently departed brothers. He strode towards the kitchen feeling the weakness of inaction in his legs, sensing the inactivity of his mind mirrored in his muscles. As he made his way along the hallway towards the kitchen he passed the display cabinets he had once been so proud of but which now contained trophies and certificates that mocked him, ridiculed his ineptitude. Reaching into the refrigerator he pulled another six pack of beer towards himself and cradled the cans in his arm Ripping the next victim from its plastic holder he tugged at the ring pull enjoying the snap and hiss before pushing the can too roughly towards his own mouth and slurping noisily at the contents as though he were a hungry child at its mothers breast. He smiled through the cold liquid at this imagery, why now such imagery and not when he needed it most? He dropped the empty can into the sink and tugged at the ring pull of the next in line, Christ this was torture. Leaning his back against the kitchen work top he took a long gulp of beer aware that in his study, mocking him without mercy lay the single sheet of paper glowing with a white danger under the stark white light of his desk lamp. He could hear it, as it called to him, its voice thin and harsh scratching at his soul like fingernails down a blackboard.

"Eulogy, write the eulogy!" It taunted, "Just write this simple eulogy. How hard can it be?" He took another sip of beer and pushed himself slowly from where he leaned and reached for the four remaining cans still gathered together in their plastic holder. He walked towards the office trepidation slowing his tread, fear holding him back. What if he could not do this? Reaching his desk he sank heavily into the leather captains chair, an antique bought during happier, better times and began the staring game again.

If he was honest with himself, something he had found easier to be in the last months, he had known the problem from the beginning. It wasn't the writing part, no that was not the problem, that was easy. He had proven this time and time again, was he not after all Trevor Collins, the world renowned and celebrated author. Had novels and plays not flown from his pen as though he were really just copying from another source, a source that was only open to him? Trevor was lauded, a master of the written word, fiction was his life, he was the personification of a modern day Shakespeare. He could make sinners into saints, and saints into sinners. His fiction could engage, enrage and emote. He could create, destroy and he could resurrect. Most of all, he could imagine, and this Trevor knew made him a figure fit to be called a raconteur, a guardian of the written word, a keeper of the modern day language, a hero. He placed his palms flat on his desk and stared harder at the blank page.

"Hero." The word cracked in his throat. Trevor shook his head sadly "I am no hero."

A eulogy was to celebrate and to educate those listening. To tell of the wonderful things, the good deeds, the kind acts, the fun times and the fond memories of the recently departed. A Eulogy should be honest, sincere and heartfelt. It should be something to cherish and to carry away from the graveside. A Eulogy should bring a sense of meaning as its truthful words wash gently over the hearts of the bereaved. Yes, Trevor knew the problem. A Eulogy was supposed to be truthful and in this case he could think of nothing good to say. It did not matter how he tried to dress it up when the word that fitted best was despicable. There really was no wriggle room despicable suited, it fit perfectly. He picked up his mountain pen slowly unscrewing the lid for the umpteenth time and held the nib centimetres from the page, sometimes the truth really could hurt. He dropped the pen onto the desk and reached instead for the beer shaking the can to reveal scant liquid held inside. In one smooth movement he tossed the can towards the waste bin seeing an ark of brown liquid escape the can and mark the wall in defiance, he shrugged, wounded not dead. Without concern he opened another can and drank noisily,

"A list, if in doubt, write a list." The words crashed into him, a voice from the grave, Mr Stephenson, his senior school English teacher, a good man, a man to be proud of, stoic, solid dependable, one arm, never dared ask how?

"Trevor Collins, you have a talent, son, use it." "Collins, don't sit with a blank page write a list." And so taking his long dead teacher and mentors advice, Trevor took up his pen and began to mark the obstinate page with a list.

'partner, friend, workaholic, fun, happy, obsessive, sad, narcissistic, rude, obnoxious, despicable…..' He read the list back to himself and began crossing out parts that did not fit, the words that were unwarranted or simply untrue. Once the scratch of his pen had ceased he read aloud from what remained.

"Workaholic, obsessive, narcissistic…." He stopped. No need to go on, nothing good, absolutely nothing.

"Look to the good in life Trevor, there's a

good boy." It was an evening for ghosts,

"Hello mother.' A fine woman, strong, loving, proud. "Give your old mum a kiss, eh, Trevor. Just be the best you can be."

"Yes Mum." Trevor looked at the page, it didn't seem quite as smug anymore with heavily scored marks and slightly crumpled edges tarnishing its once pristine condition, he needed another beer. As he drank he re-read the list, peering through the score marks,

"Partner, friend?" Well yes, he supposed there had been that. He thought of Simon, pictured him, tall, elegant, loyal, loving. What was it partner first and then friend or friend first? He closed his eyes feeling the room spin slightly, why couldn't he remember? He should remember but then he supposed it didn't really matter. Simon had been a good man, a caring man, tender, respectable. It had ended badly, of course it had. The truth hurts sometimes doesn't it? Without understanding how they had formed he found he needed to wipe tears from his eyes. He reached up and wiped his cheeks dry, God where had they come from? This eulogy writing was hard, harder than it should be. Picking up the page with no other thought than to screw it into a ball, the tightest of balls, a ball that crushed the life from it chocking it until it flew across the room and into the bin his hand was stayed as he noticed the word 'Fun' Why had he written fun, he searched his memories but nothing sprang to mind.

"Come on jump the waves, higher, higher than that." 'Mary', of course she would be here tonight, could no one leave him alone?

"Hello, Sis."

"Everyone has fun Trev' everyone can be happy. Come on we are all going to the beach." Yes, yes the beach oh he had forgotten that. They had all been there. Mary had been there.Lovely Mary. Beautiful in heart and body. Everyone loved her, gone too soon, God how he missed his sister.

"Don't leave a job half done son."

"What you too Dad?" He reached for the last can. All of these what, memories, visitations? were beginning to hurt, but he got the message. Dad would have sat with the eulogy until it was done, no messing about with him, if a job needed doing it needed doing well.

"It's easy for you Dad you don't have to write this crap. I mean honestly, what can I say thats good eh?" Dad of course did not answer, he didn't expect him to, wasn't his way. Dad would ask the questions and leave you to find it out on your own, trusting you to figure it all out, and never berating you for failing. Trevor wiped the tears that now seemed to flow so easily from his eyes with the back of his hand.

How he missed him, how he missed them all. His head was spinning and his eyes felt as though they were full of fine pieces of grit, the beer had really taken effect his head had the thickness of alcohol and he felt as though he were somewhere between awake and asleep but somehow, somehow he now knew what to write. With a reverence he did not believe he was capable of he slid a new piece of paper from the drawer and placed it alongside its original sister, a sister that was quickly scrunched and tossed with a direct hit into the waste bin. Reaching again for his fountain pen Trevor leaned to his work, relishing in the sound of the gold nib making the marks he could be proud of, the marks of his trade. When finally he finished, he lay the pen next to the paper, reading it one more time to be certain. Satisfied that at last he was finished Trevor Collins pulled the white bottle from his trouser pocket and staggered from the room without a backwards glance.

The paper lay on the desk haloed by the bright light of the lamp, if it could, it would have cried, but then its tears would have smeared the words so carefully written.

To whoever finds me,

I have managed to ruin most things in my life, so not much to celebrate.

I wanted to leave something more than just words, but hey, I guess that's what it is, that's life.

As I wrote this I searched for what I am really most proud of and realised that my pride is not in my work, the countless words nor the many pages that sit unread on peoples bookshelves waiting to be gifted, unread to charity shops and sold for a pound. No, I want to be remembered for the love I received without condition from those I truly cared about. It is important to me that when you think of me you do not dwell on who or what 'I' was but instead remember those who loved me and knew me for just 'being me'.

To the public or should I say those called my 'adoring fans' I am a hero, an idol who deserves worship but this is not so. I can say now that I carried the title of 'genius' badly and that of one who is 'renowned' all the worse. Sometimes adoration from the masses is too hard to take, especially when I know how much I have failed them all. I hope they can forgive me for not being the man they needed me to be but can allow me to live on as one who is forgiven and simply known as the author who made them think.

To my family I end now by saying what I should have said many times before and with as much conviction as I could gather when I had the chance. I thank you all for being there (even now.) The love you gave me was and is unconditional and for that I hold you for ever close. When I failed you or fell short of the Son or brother I should have been you never turned against me but loved me all the more.

To Simon my one true love (how I mourn the fact that this was not said before and so often), I say simply, I am on my way to you now. Please find it in your heart to forgive me one last time and to welcome me as you always did. My love for you shall act as the guiding light that carries me now to your side.

A eulogy it seems can lay bare a mans soul and point out his faults but it does not diminish the man he was. I leave you now with not my finest writing but the writing I wish to be known for. For in truth this simple piece is the most honest of all my works and shall be known as 'The Eulogy of Trevor Collins'.

A Modern Fairy Tale

Spending an hour randomly browsing through shoes on numerous displays in countless shops, I realised as always when it comes to buying myself any item of clothing, my heart simply was not in it. I think the matter is made worse when I know that I am being forced into making a random decision on what will look good for someones wedding. In all truthfulness, I am more of a jeans and t shirt sort of a guy who likes nothing better than propping up a bar and talking to some other identikit loner who happens to land next to me. I look at the left shoe I am holding in my hand and hear myself sigh loudly enough for the old lady next to me to break away from angrily stuffing her own foot into a shoe with the aid of a long handled shoe horn and smile at me.

"Can't decide?" She sits back on the low level padded bench and smiles again. "I know how you feel. Do I go for the extra wide black or the extra wide brown? I don't know why I care. At my age no-one is looking at my feet, not exactly my best feature are they?" She makes a theatrical stab at me with the shoe horn as though wielding a sword. "Pick the ones you like, throw yourself a party, enjoy life." She winks a lop sided, conspiratorial wink "I bet it doesn't matter what you wear, that young woman of yours will love you all the same. Good looking bloke like you." She viciously rams the shoe horn into the back of the shoe and pushes firmly, grunting loudly. "Get in there you bugger." She sits back and admires her handiwork. "After all that I think I prefer the black." She looks around, her attention diverted from me. "Miss, over here, Miss." She waves a hand in the direction of a frustrated sales assistant who seems to be assisting numerous customers in their quest to fit their feet into the correct sized shoes. I place the shoe I am holding back onto the rack and stare absently out of the large plate glass display window. Opposite the shoe shop is the small independently run coffee shop, the one we used to love so much. I try not to think of it but memories of happier times flood in fast. A flat white for me, oat milk latte Brazilian santos for Nicola, an egg custard tart, my favourite and a chocolate brownie (Oh I shall never eat all of this) for her. I catch myself smiling sadly, (she always did, eat it, the brownie.) I haven't been back in that coffee shop, not since our (It's for the best, we both know its for the best) separation. Strangely despite her assurances, I still haven't realised it's for the best. What I have realised is that standing here now, I don't care what shoes I wear to this wedding. I hate being the odd number at every event and most importantly I will not be throwing my hat in the ring for any woman again. I am from now on a dedicated bachelor. I shall lock myself away in a refuge of my own making and emerge only when I want to. I shall avoid the crowds and become that reclusive figure people talk of in hushed and reverent tones. The man who lives deep in the castle unseen by anyone. I shall remain a mystery, distant and enigmatic.

"Can I help you sir?" The young sales assistant has without my noticing materialised by my side, her hair coming loose from the clip and her collar slightly askew. Although obviously frazzled her smile remains bright and refreshing.

"Erm yes, I would like these in a size 9." I hear myself say as I pluck the shoe I had recently replaced onto the rack. The girl smiles at me and speaks quickly into a small radio ordering the shoes from some unseen colleague. "If you wait just one moment I will bring them for you to try on. I shake my head.

"No that's ok. I will just take them, they will be fine." She looks at me a small frown crossing her face but just as quickly as it appears it is gone and the smile returns.

"Certainly Sir. They will be behind the counter when you are ready." She moves away and is quickly mobbed by a woman whose face frowns towards her as the four unruly children pull random shoes from displays and begin throwing them at each other. I walk away and stand patiently in line at the long counter. My turn soon comes and I purchase my shoes with as little fuss as possible from yet another assistant who looks as though he would sooner be anywhere else apart from here. I swipe my card and raise my eyebrows indicating to my bored assistant that I too would rather be anywhere else but here. He chooses to ignore me and instead smiles brightly towards a teenage girl who pops a bubble from the gum she is noisily chewing before leaning chest forward onto the counter. My stomach I realise is rumbling with hunger and I suddenly crave an egg custard tart. Clutching my purchase to my chest as though I carried the crown jewels, I push my way through the throng of moving bodies trying desperately to make my way to the exit.

"Bought yourself some then?" It was the old woman still clutching the shoe horn. I nod politely trying to move through a group of teenagers who seemed to be growing in number in front of my eyes. "That's good. Your young lady will love you in them I bet." I must have given her a weary smile because she stops in front of me her head cocked to one side. "What's the matter, have I said something out of turn?" I shrug I just want to be away from here, out of the crowd.

"There is no young lady, no lady at all. She…" I pause unsure why I need to share this information in the middle of a shoe shop "Left me." I finish sounding sadder than I had intended. The old woman nods slowly before taking my arm and pulling me into a stoop towards her shorter figure. I see the shoe horn wave towards me circling above my head barely missing me, narrowly avoiding doing me some very serious damage.

"Do not worry young man. I believe there is someone for everyone. I believe that you will find your perfect person." She releases her grip and smiles up at me a sly wink closing her right eye. She pats my arm and says almost as an afterthought "You must keep believing, for anything is possible if you truly believe hard enough." She bustles away from me calling a cheery 'Goodbye' over her shoulder and disappears from my view, masked by the crush of bodies circling around the sales rack marked 'back to school bargains.' I stand for a moment bemused by the strange interaction that had just occurred but soon find myself brought back to reality by a grumpy.

"Are you looking for something or what?" The voice is that of a scowling man who stands behind me. He is pointing at the bargain shoe rack, his identical looking son scowls at a small screen clutched in his hands and I see a fiery dragon breathing destruction on a small figure on horseback whose armour is turning red. Suddenly the words, 'your knight has perished. Game over' flash noisily in gold lettering and the boy lets out a curse better suited to a workman. I move on heading towards the exit hoping to escape this madness and yet still perturbed by the words of the old woman, 'you must keep believing.' I realise then that no matter how much I tell myself that I have given up, no matter how often I say that I am happier alone, this simply is not the case. Head down, I make my way towards the exit and yes dammit! I would have an egg custard tart in the small coffee shop opposite. It was then that two things happen almost simultaneously. The first is an annoyance. Two young mothers with pushchairs, turn into the shop at the same time, neither willing to give way. The first pushchair swerves to the left catching me mid way up my shin scraping the skin viciously beneath my trousers. I spin half in pain, half in fury to remonstrate with the woman who had surged into the shop seemingly without a care. Then to my amazement the second happening, happens. I see her. It is just a glimpse, there on the other side of the shop. She is almost out of view but not quite, partially hidden behind the display of high heel shoes. As I look a large man steps into my line of sight momentarily blocking my view. As he moves away following a young child who calls

"Quickly daddy, I want the blue ones, I really do." She had gone. I scan the area frantically, searching above the heads of the crowd in the shop, my breath seeming to stick in my throat. I cannot see her. Suddenly a flash of gold seems to fill my eyes as just to the left of the display I see her in half profile. She tosses her hair and ducks back out of sight. I cannot quite explain the feelings I have other than to say that for the first time ever my heart quite honestly misses a beat. I want to chastise myself, to laugh at my overreaction. I have never been the sort of man who believed in love at first sight. I have never been the man who secretly reads love stories hidden beneath fly sheets of other books and cried as Mr Right meets his Miss Perfect. No this simply does not happen at least not to me. Not to Mr dumped on Valentines day. The thought of those long ago purchased presents wrapped in gold and silver heart paper. Those presents hidden just out of sight behind the over sized potted plant next to the table in the most expensive non chain restaurant I could afford send a shiver running through me. I shrug the memory aside and concentrate. The very idea that I could meet the perfect woman and fall in love knowing that we would settle down to happily ever after was until that moment quite simply not possible. But now my beliefs have been turned on their head. In just a few seconds and only feet away is the Princess I am destined to marry. I lean against the doorway watching the high heel display area. She has not emerged back into my eye line but I know she is there I can feel her presence. My throat is dry, not in a thirsty you need a drink sort of a way but in an excited, your breath has been stolen and it is hard to swallow sort of a way. My mind is working fast, faster than it has for months. I do not know her and she, this vision, certainly does not know me but somehow I would have to engineer a meeting. I quickly think through what would be the right approach. I consider every eventuality. I don't want to come across too desperate and definitely not creepy. No. I had to play this right, had to play it cool. Who was I kidding? I had never been cool, never had that swagger, the one possessed by all of those heroes in cinematic history. Recognising my lack of a solid plan and the certainty of the need for haste I quickly grab the first shoe to hand from the nearest rack and ignoring the pain from my now screaming shin I wander with a casual air towards the seats near to the high heel display. My plan, if you could call it that was to play the bemused man uncertain of his choice. I will sit on the seat near her inspecting the shoe in my hand and ask her opinion. God no! Creepy, too creepy by half, probably too direct. I slow my pace slightly reforming my idea. I will sit on the seat, stare at the shoe and, and? I can feel my panic growing, and what, what would I do? I will sigh, yes that was it, I will inspect the shoe and sigh loudly. This will gain her attention, she will smile at me and I will respond with a bright smile and a small shrug. Then almost as though I am embarrassed I will strike up a conversation asking her for an opinion, nothing heavy just something like, "oh what do you think, brown or black in these with a blue suit?" She will find me charming and smile sweetly knowing instantly that there was a spark between us. She will play it cool perhaps give a laugh that tinkles like a crystal chandelier and say

"Why black would be perfect." As she speaks she will run her fingers through her hair and her voice will sing in the air. We will laugh heartily together and then move to the coffee shop where we will share a heart shaped croissant. Later there will be a meal by candle light, healthy walks in the woods, horse riding across the hills. We will have a simple wedding nothing too elaborate. We will have two children a boy and a girl, both will be fit and healthy, they will grow....

"Can I 'elp?" I am shocked from my day

dream by an acne faced sales assistant. His bloated face bobs next to mine as he stands solidly in front of me. I take an involuntary step backwards fascinated by his vividly coloured and gelled hair, the spikes glowing red at the tips. The large hole in his ear which sports a solid black ring wobbles as he speaks. "What size do you want them in?" He points to the shoe I am holding as though this action was far beneath him but one he was forced into making. I look at the shoe for the first time noticing that it was in fact a waterproof overshoe, I can already feel my plan slipping away.

"Erm a size 9 please." I didn't care I just want him away from me. I need to find the woman of my dreams.

"Do you mean you are a size 9 or you want these to go over a size 9 shoe?" The hole in his ear wobbles fiercely.

"What?" I look around him trying to spot her.

"These are overshoes." He says it as though I understand his meaning but my frown must give my confusion away. "They are overshoes." He begins again the sneer obvious in his voice "If they are going over the shoe you are wearing they need to be half a size bigger, so if you are a size 9 you will need a size 9.5 if you are a…." I give a yelp of surprise which cuts him off mid smirk. The group of youths have passed in front of the high heel display and I can see that the area is empty. I have lost her, she has gone. I spring into action spurred on in my panic. I push past the pointy haired golem and rush to where she had been standing. Frantically I look around as though she may be hiding in some dark corner unseen but my urgency is to no avail, she has simply disappeared. I want to curse like the dragon fighting child. In the moments taken up distracted by the toad-like figure of the shop assistant I have lost her. I rush towards the back of the store glancing down every isle I pass, she must be here. Finally in desperation I spring onto a bench seat and look around the store taking full advantage of my added height. Just as I felt ready to scream in desperation I see her. There she was, my vision of perfection standing at the counter paying for her purchase. Again my breath is torn from me as I see the reflection of light from the overhead strip lights encircle the gold of her head and reveal the whiteness of her figure hugging dress which clings to her elven form. I stand open mouthed as I marvel at the perfection of her alabaster skin which is heightened by the redness of the silk scarf she wears casually thrown around her shoulders. At last I fully understand how someone like me can so easily fall in love at first sight.

"Will you get down? Those are not for

standing on." I simply ignore the spiky haired shop assistant but jump down because I choose to. I sail elegantly through the air and using my natural agility nimbly avoid the small child who has been staring up at me. I have to get to her, I have to make myself known. Stopping only to pick up the shoes I have knocked off a display as I landed my gymnastic dismount from the bench seat I join the rear of the queue at a run. There are only two people between me and my Princess, two people between me and my destiny. I pick up a pack of foam insoles clutching them as though they are a prize of the highest value, these shall be my excuse for joining the queue, my subterfuge. I fidget as I wait so much so that the woman in front of me turns and glares as though I have been performing some ritualistic warrior dance behind her. I smile widely and look at the foam insoles and begin measuring them against the soul of my shoe. The woman tuts loudly and steps closer to the man in front of her as though seeking safety in his presence. I look to the front of the queue and see the checkout girl smile down at my angel.

"Would you like the box with these shoes madam?" I watch as again the blond hair shimmers in the light as she shakes her head in response.

"No, just bung them in my bag." I almost

speak aloud with adoration, her voice was like the silken scarf she wears around her neck. I watch the poetry of her movements, I notice again the delicacy of features, the smoothness of her skin and breath deeply hoping to catch the scent of her perfume. I see her look at the gold watch she wears around her slender wrist and note the look of horror that masks her perfect features, "My God, look at the time! It's nearly midday I must go. I have to go. I promised I would be back at 12." She snatches her bag from the assistant and dashes from the shop. I have to follow I dare not waste a moment in indecision. Dropping the insoles to the floor I swerved around a heavily pregnant woman who is struggling to reach the bottom shelf of a display. I push aside my normal gallantry which would have forced me to assist the poor woman in her task but now such is my focus on maintaining sight of my angel I ignore my duty and continued in my pursuit. I spring from the store narrowly avoiding a tartan shopping trolley being dragged noisily behind a small woman who screams loudly into a mobile phone which she has clasped tightly to her ear.

"No Henry." She yells "No Henry!" She bellows again, her voice is so loud that I am certain poor old Henry would have heard her without the use of a phone. "I said no Henry they didn't have your haemorrhoids cream. No

I know. I suppose you will just have to carry on using the baby lotion." She grabs with a speed I would have thought impossible for a woman of her age the shopping trolley handle that slips from her grasp as I land noisily beside her. Obviously shocked she halts her conversation with Henry to yell in my direction, "Watch where you're going you oaf! Who do you think you are, royalty?" I notice the rude one finger gesture she makes in my direction before she again thrusts the phone to her ear and continues shouting at poor unfortunate Henry whose afternoon it seems would contain nothing more exciting to look forward to than a hag of a wife and a pot of baby lotion. I leave the yelling woman trailing behind me and focus my attention on finding my Princess. I am frantic, blood is rushing in my ears as fear grips me. Somehow I have lost her again amongst the crowd. I stand lonely amongst the throng of shoppers and feel the weight of despair threatening to overtake me completely. As if by some miracle I see her, ahead of me, rushing towards the exit by the fast food outlet. I allow myself a momentary shudder of revulsion, this was the very fast food outlet that had recently suffered the misfortune of being overrun by rats. Shaking away the memory I charge head down towards the exit in time to see her disappear through the doorway. I know that exit well I can picture her every move. Once through the doorway she would be heading down the large stairway to the street level where she would disappear from my sight hidden amongst the crowds. Again despair is upon me, I may have lost her. As I hurtle towards the doorway my exit is blocked by a group of laughing teenagers all of whom are talking loudly and checking their phones.

"Did you see her; silly bitch nearly went arse over tit?"

"Stupid cow, caught her bag on the handrail and missed at least three steps, her stuff went everywhere."

"Yeah. It was well funny. Got a great video of it though, I'm downloading it now." I push through the crowd ignoring the words 'tosser,' and 'prick' that are hurled in my direction. Surging through the large glass swing doors I emerge out into the daylight skidding to a halt at the top of the large sweeping stairway that leads down to the open pedestrian area below. Crowds of weekend shoppers, tired mothers pushing oversized pushchairs and skateboarders using every available bench, bin and wall as an obstacle to be jumped or skidded over cause a melee that resembles rats scurrying over discarded rubbish bags. I stand panting, scouring every face and form below me but I have to admit to myself that I have again lost her. I have forever lost my Princess.

"Oh Miss! Excuse me Miss. You dropped this." To my left stands an elderly gentleman wearing a smart linen suit neatly topped with a silk cravat. He raises his hand and calls again. "Miss. Your shoe. You dropped your shoe." I spring to his side catching his upraised hand in my own and pull the shoe from his grasp. I see the shoe in my hand and I gasp with relief. This is not just any shoe, not a shoe of insignificance, it was 'THE' shoe, her shoe, the one she so recently purchased from the store. I want to scream into the old mans shocked face, grab him by the lapels and shower him with the spittle of my urgency.

"Where is she? Tell me now. Quickly man!" Instead I take a breath and calm myself whilst trying to paint a very calm picture of reverence on my face but I know I am unsuccessful . With my pulse calming I manage a question which takes the form more of a pleading inquiry than a question with any authority, "Please my good man. Where is the owner of this shoe?" I realise my attempt at civility has failed as the old man steps away from me a look of fear etched on his face. I try again imploring him to grant me an answer. "It is of the most importance that I find her. Please show me where she is and you shall be greatly rewarded." Slowly he raises his arm level to his shoulder and points away into the distance. I can barely discern the direction he is pointing and fail at first to hear his words which reach my ears in tones that at first seem at odds with his dress.

"She's over there." I follow again the direction of his pointing finger but alas still cannot spot her. He must see my confusion as he speaks again, wagging his outstretched hand, "Over there by the taxi rank, she's just getting into that van." And then I see her. With a last flick of her blond hair she has stepped up into the cab of a van which pulls away from the taxi rank in a cloud of thick black exhaust smoke. I move slowly along my vantage point tracking the route of the van. It is easy to spot even amongst the heavy traffic as the picture of the large orange pumpkin and the words 'MARY TODD & BROTHERS, fruit and veg.' distinguished it from all of the other vehicles. Perhaps my luck holds, for the traffic lights are at red. If I am quick I am certain that I could sprint down the steps and across the open space perhaps cutting the van off before it makes its escape from my pursuit. As though playing my life as if it was a game of cards, the Gods of despair work their magic upon me and before I have moved the traffic lights change from red to green. I watch on in despair as with a sharp manoeuvre that confounds belief the van finds a gap which seems narrower than the vehicle itself. Although the gap is small the van but manages to turn sharply across the path of oncoming traffic. With a blast of horns and the high pitched sound of skidding tyres it disappears away along a side street as surely as if it had been covered in the cloak of invisibility itself. I am forlorn and sink to the floor. I care not that the fake marble step is cold beneath my seat. I have lost her and surely this time for good. She is gone and I have no idea where to find her. I look up as a shadow crosses my sunken form and realise that the old man has stepped towards me a look of concern on his face.

"Are you ok squire?" I can only groan a response, my heart is too heavy to contemplate a more succinct answer. Slowly and with great effort the old man kneels by my side his knees cracking in accompaniment.

"Hovel Row." I stare blankly at him, his words making no sense.

"What?" His shrug is barely perceivable

"Hovel Row it's on the far side of town. Hovel Row." He says again as though the repeated words will somehow make themselves clearer in their repetitiveness. He places a hand on my shoulder and aids himself to standing with a grunt and a second retort of clicking knees. "The woman you seek seems to come from Hovel Row." I spring to my feet anger surging through me.

"How can you know this, how can you possibly have this information!" My anger was clear for everyone in close proximity to witness and I realise that I was now being studied with a silence that bordered on reverence or was that the awe inspired silence of fear? I become aware that I am holding the shoe as though it were a sword before me. I had emphasised my every word as though I intended to beat the man to death with its heel. Slowly I lower the shoe and regain my composure hoping that I can salvage this situation, I need this man to be on my side not turned against me.

"I am sorry for my outburst my dear man, but as you can clearly see, I am desperate for information." I move towards him half a step only to see him shrink back from my approach. "Please kind sir, if you have any information that can help me in my search I will be for ever grateful." I take a large step away before continuing, "I have lost the woman I love. We met but for only a short moment in time and yet I know that this is the love of my life, the woman who will change my very existence for ever." Embarrassed by my honesty I stare at the floor aware of the hubbub of noise from the crowd who grow bored of the scene playing out in front of them and return to their own pursuits.

"I think she lives at Hovel Row, number 57." He spoke clearly his voice although rough had soft, gentleness about it that I had not noticed before.

"You know her. You actually know her?" Excitement filled me, I hear the birds singing in the trees and see the low clouds part slightly revealing a soft shard of light away in the distance pointing no doubt to where my Princess lives, guiding me to her side.

"No!" I stopped short in my hopes and face the old man before me looking deep into his eyes.

"No what?"

"No I don't know her, never seen her before in my life." The thought of now beating this annoying old man to within an inch of his life with the shoe now seemed to appeal all the more but I remained aloof to this feeling.

"If you do not know her how can you even guess where she lives. Are you in fact leading me into an expedition that takes me far from my goal. Are you here to sabotage my love?" The old man sighs dismissing my enquiry as though it were no more than a request for water.

"I don't know her, but that's what it says here on this envelope." He thrusts his hand towards me proffering me the contents within. Taking the offered bundle a quizzical look upon my face I shuffle through the contents, a large crumpled envelope ripped open roughly at the top, a small card the size of a credit card and a lipstick. "These fell out of her bag when she caught it on the handrail. She was in such a rush I don't think she noticed the bag split." He was about to continue but I cut him off desperate to find my answer.

"Thank you for your assistance in my quest. You have aided a man lost to the power of love, a love such as I have never felt before." I see him smile, a smile that brings a twinkle to his eyes, eyes of the brightest blue.

"Ahh yes. Love." He now steps towards me all fear wiped from his demeanour, "It is a feeling of such power that once found should be cherished for ever. It is this feeling that binds me to my wife for so many years. It is a love that keeps us still together now. Ahh." He says looking over my shoulder "And so as I speak of her so she appears." He smiles broadly and nods towards the unseen person approaching behind me. I turn and now smile myself. I am somehow unsurprised by the figure which approaches. The old lady from the shoe shop moves heavily towards us the long handled shoe horn still clutched in her hand parting the crowds as a shepherd parts sheep.

"The charming young man from the shop." She coos as she arrives at her husbands side her words showing no real surprise. "It seems as though we were destined to meet again."

"He is in search of his one true love." Her husband quickly responds pointing to the items I clasped in my one hand whilst holding the shoe in the other. The old woman nods and grips her husbands arm.

"Then I suggest we allow him to continue his search with haste." Again she moves the shoe horn towards me narrowly missing my head "Seek what it is you desire and let your heart lead the way." Before I can speak she clicks her heels loudly twice "Always believe young man, always believe." She says before pointing down towards her shoes speaking quickly. "These new shoes need breaking in husband of mine. Why don't you take me to that lovely coffee shop? The walk will help the process." Without waiting for an answer or a backwards glance they turn as one leaving me alone where I stand.

Feeling a lightness of mind I study the contents in my hand. The envelope although badly smeared still shows the wording, neatly typed in bold, thick letters '57 HOVEL ROW.' I had her address! The small plastic card was in fact a security swipe card that displayed her name, the name of my one true love emblazoned on the front, the name of my Princess is, 'Linda Teller.' I slap my hand on my thigh and thank my lucky stars that now at last good fortune had finally smiled upon me.

Moving at pace I jump the steps two at a time uncaring of the potential physical danger to myself. I am on a quest, I am fully prepared to search the whole of this, Kingston if I have to. I am on the trail of true love and I will not be stopped. I did in fact have to stop almost immediately as it was only now that I truly realised had no idea where Hovel Row was and I had no means of transport as my car was in for a service. Quickly I rush to the taxi rank and climb inside the first sweet smelling cab that was available. "57 Hovel Row my man and do not spare the horses." I say, as the taxi pulls away from the kerb and enters the steady flow of traffic. I rest my head onto the seat back and allow myself a small satisfied smile. I shall place my faith in the hands of the 'Trusty Steed' Taxi service and it shall carry me to places anew and adventures unknown.

    I sit restlessly in the back of the taxi and watch the strange surroundings alter with every passing moment. Soon gone from view are the opulent five bedroom and palatial homes of the executive. Left behind the smaller family homes occupied by the hard working, factory workers, the postal workers and the shopkeepers. All too soon we were in an area of hastily built and poorly maintained rows of cluster homes lacking in design, funding or maintenance.

"Hovel Row Sir." The driver pulls up to the curb and waits patiently as I count the money into his hand and smiles as I give him a small tip for his trouble. The taxi pulls away smoothly from the kerb but I notice it halt its movement as quickly as it had begun. The brightness of the reverse lights heralds its return as it comes to a stop directly beside me. The window squeals down and the driver leans himself prone across the passenger seat to call to me from his position across the seats.

"This is not a good area Sir. I would keep my wits about me if I were you. Not the sort of place for people like your good self." Message delivered he nods sagely towards me and clicks the indicator which ticks comfortingly "Yes, keep your witts about you sir. Not a good area, not a good area at all." Slowly the taxi pulls away leaving me standing alone and feeling more vulnerable than I had when first I saw the area in which we had come to rest. Despite these feelings I gird my loins and make haste as I decide to continue. Shaking off the chill which wrapped itself about me I set off along the street counting the numbers on the doors as I moved. Number 57 is in a small row of houses all identical in blandness and disrepair, all with the same sense of dark foreboding. I stand and face number 57 and am amazed that although every house at first glance seemed to be identical this house managed still to stand out from those that accompany it. I am not sure at first if the reason for this house to appear more exceptional than the rest was due to the front of the house being festooned with thick, dark overgrowing ivy or the two large conifer trees which must have kept at bay all natural light that would otherwise have entered the house. After a few moments of contemplation I decided that in fact the thing which made number 57 so unique was probably the very large woman sitting in what can only be called in polite circles as semi repose in the shrub of land called I suppose the front garden. As though she has not a care in the world she engulfs the creaking striped deck chair, wearing no more than a pair of shorts and a rather ill fitting bra which fought in vain to maintain her large breasts which threatened to spill out at any moment. I stand in trepidation as she sits with the round shouldered demeanour of an ogre guarding the open front door. Her face is slack with sleep and yet still she offers the warning to any who dare to try and enter what was clearly her property. The snores that emanate from her open mouth have me in mind of a lion warning those who approach of the certain retribution that would be sure to follow. I swallow hard and screw my courage firmly to my solid but metaphorical mast and push at the iron gate which squeals alarmingly as though it were a sea port klaxon. The noise from the gate wakes the sleeping terror and slowly she raises her head to face me. Reaching between her legs she pulls a gold can of what I can only assume is the most potent of ales and takes a long slow swallow. Burping loudly the brute crunches the can viciously in the middle before throwing it without looking over the boundary of the property adjoining her domain. The ruined can clanks against other long since drained receptacle as the ogre focuses on me and screws her eyes in the most fearsome of glares.

"Want somefin?" At first I am not certain if she was in fact asking me or sharing some information. I think that good manners would decree that I make an enquiry over this point but with the look of evilness that seems to be permanently etched on her face I decide that caution is the better part of valour. "Well?" Her second attempt at conversation makes it clear to me that she was indeed asking me a question and I am now glad that I refrained from engaging her in pointless conversation. I stand mute my heart breaking. If this was truly my Princess Linda's mother I had truly arrived just in time to rescue her from a life of untold unhappiness. Again the strength of my quest proves itself to be vital. I stand squarely in the overgrown density of the garden and refuse to be cowed. I will confront this creature head on if needed. I will without thought of my own safety push myself through the thickness of the branches and bushes to reach my darling girl, I will do whatever it takes. Raising myself to my full height I speak calmly for I wish to make myself truly known.

"Madam," I begin although in the truest sense of the word madam felt a stretch of the imagination "I have come to speak to Linda." At first she does not speak, only pausing to pluck another can from beneath her chair and to rip the small tab free causing the can to hiss its protest. Without waiting for the ale to stop its foaming action she takes three long swallows before crushing it to destruction and sending it to what must now be the graveyard of golden cans on the other side of the boundary. Wiping her mouth with the back of her hand she allows her eyes to fully focus on me and draws in a long hard breath.

"There ain't no Linda 'ere." She pulls another can and gulps greedily on the contents ignoring the liquid that freely spills over her chin. Once fully sated she closes her eyes and without so much as bye-your-leave is soon breathing heavily in drunken repose. I am furious at her lack of etiquette and of being treated in such a manner. Honour decrees that I now have to show my indignation, I have to show my metal, I must be ready to strike should the need arise.

"I have travelled from my Kingston afar," I begin, "and madam I will not be dismissed with such…." She opens one blood shot eye and runs a wet tongue over her thick dry lips.

"Piss off!" She closes her eye and almost immediately begins again the heavy snoring that first greeted me. A lesser man would have turned and fled, taken to their heels and without hesitation disappeared in a cloud of dust, but I am not that man. My courage had grown the moment I first set eyes upon Linda. Oh to use her name, to taste the sound on my tongue. Linda, beautiful Linda, girl of my dreams.

"I said piss off!" Without me realising, the ogre has again woken and is at this very moment rising, slowly from the chair. The marks from where the chair has bit deep into her flabby flesh stands red in their grooves. Her voluminous breasts pull against the thin fabric of the bra and the heavy flesh of her arms swing alarmingly as she begins her first lumbering steps in my direction. As quick as lightening I step from her reach and swing the shoe into the gap between us, my shield against her anger.

"I know Linda lives here, I have her shoe." My speech holds the monster in place a look of detest springing across her face causing the veins which line her cheeks to glow hotly. I stand breathing heavily as finally she speaks, struggling to do so as if the words are alien for her to form.

"For Christ's sake!" She shakes her head which wobbles the flabby flesh hanging around her neck in the process. "I'm tellin you charmin, I'm the landlady of this 'ouse, and there is no bloody Linda livin 'ere." Before I can react she places two fingers in her mouth and blows loudly. The screech of a high pitched whistle erupts from her causing the hairs on the back of my neck to stand to attention. "You three, out here now!" She yells, although the word three was pronounced 'free'. Within moments we were joined in the garden by three men all of whom could not have been more different in size and appearance. "These are the only ones who live 'ere and I should no cos I'm the one who charges them rent." She stops speaking and suddenly rounds on the three men with a speed that surprises me and yet elicits no reaction from the men in the garden. "That is unless one of you has been going behind my back and keeping someone else in your room without tellin' me?" She stands before them a figure of raging power and anger. The three men begin their mumblings avoiding her stare, kicking at the ground as though they had each found something more interesting lurking beneath the soil. The ogre casts a withering look towards me over her shoulder before speaking in the gruff mocking tone I am growing to know so well, towards the three men. "It seems as though this 'ere young Prince of a man thinks that we have a woman called Linda living here. Do you know anyfink about any Linda." She looks threateningly at each of them in turn. The largest of the three men shakes his head slowly the tattoo on his face lining his features making him more devil than man. His shoulders are large he is a solid mass of muscle waiting to explode in violence.

"No Linda lives 'ere, but if you wait a minute I will check me 'eadboard see if her names scratched there." His laugh is evil and I want to thrust the stiletto heel of the shoe into his mocking sneer just for the very thought of his showing such disrespect towards my beautiful Princess. The second of the men, a small wiry creature who picks unselfconsciously at an itch that seems to be troubling his groin, grins lasciviously.

"Does she owe me money? Worse still do

I owe her money?" He makes a sucking sound with his teeth "If I owe her money tell her I will pay her with this." He makes a grabbing motion at his groin stirring my anger to fury.

"Is he trying to sell her to us. I don't mind paying for a bit of something posh especially if its going cheap." The third man who was as round as he was wide raises his arms in a hugging motion revealing yellow sweat patches of material in his armpits. It was all I could do to stop myself lunging at them despite the danger to myself. Guarding my true love's honour is now paramount, rescuing her from certain harm is my one true quest and I will not be deterred despite the risk to myself. I want to question them more, I want to believe that they know more, and yet… I sigh deeply, these fools seem genuine in their lack of knowledge. No-one had heard of my sweet Linda.

"But I do not understand." I mumble in confusion, "I have her shoe, she lives here I am certain of it." The ogre steps closer to me enveloping me in the smell of stewed onions which slowly emanates from her skin.

"So you 'ave a shoe, big deal. Who says it comes from ere, does it look like we own shoes like that?" She laughs loudly sounding more dog than human. "Perhaps we should try it on, see if it fits. Yeah that's wot we will do, try it on. Who's going first?"

"I will, I think it will be just my sort of thing." The giant with the face tattoo steps forward holding out his hand for the shoe. "I reckon I will look good in that."

"Yes give it a go Pavel, see if it fits." The ogre laughs again enjoying my discomfort.

"No let me try. If it doesn't fit I can turn that heel into a lovely knife." The wiry man pushes past the giant and makes a grab at the shoe but I am too quick snatching it from his grasp and dancing backwards towards the gate, sometimes retreat is the best form of attack.

"Do you want me to help you up the road or do you think you can manage that yourself pretty boy?" Sweat patch lumbers towards the gate his hands balled into large fists of solid mass. I can wait no longer I see my exit being blocked. In this moment there are as I see it only two options, The first is to turn my tail and reveal my back as a coward and charge for the gateway. The second is to stand my ground and defend my honour with all that I have. Squaring my shoulders I take a breath and face the the four figures who seem to grow larger the more I observe them. Turning quickly I leap the gate and head swiftly away. I had chosen a hasty retreat above a slow lingering death.

"That's it charmin' make yourself scarce." I hear the growl of derision from the ogre and feel the smack of an empty drinks can hit me firmly between my shoulders, "Go on keep moving, coming round 'ere causing trouble. You've ad your fun now piss off and leave us alone." I march away as quickly as is dignified, ignoring the shouts and jeers that hammer towards my back like the thorns on a quickly growing bush.

For many minutes I stumble along blindly following roads I have no understanding of and no clue as to where they go. The shoe in my hand feels heavy, awkward and I want to throw it as far away from me as possible but it is the last link I have to her, the last real evidence that she has even existed. I stop at a crossroads unsure of which direction to take, my mind awhirl with confusion and sadness. I have truly lost her, lost my chance of love, I have failed her. It was as I stood in this fuge of despair that I remember the words of the old woman with the shoe horn, 'you must keep believing, for anything is possible.' I look one more time at the shoe and gently rub the heel hoping against hope that the old woman is correct, after all hope is all I have left. When as I expect nothing happens I decide to turn left at the crossroads for no other reason than it is as good a choice as any. I walk for perhaps 5 minutes and realise that I am becoming more lost than I believed could be possible. My shoulder blades ache where the can viciously struck me so I stop to rub the pain away, it is then that I hear the sound of running footsteps. I cast a quick look over my shoulder and see a man running furiously towards me, his arms pumping like pistons. Every instinct tells me to run to save myself from a bad situation and yet I stand my ground. I am tired of being mocked, angry at my failure in my quest. So I stand legs braced ready to face certain danger. As the figure grows closer I realise the error of my judgement, it is the wiry man from the garden his face was contorted in anger and sweat. No doubt they have decided fuelled by the ogre, that I need to be taught a lesson after all. I can hear them now plotting my downfall, acting together, a killing machine. The wiry man is I presume quicker on his feet than the others, more able to make up the ground so has reached me first. My only chance would be to dispatch this creature before the other two make contact with me, it would be one down two to go. I flip the shoe over in my hand holding the sole tightly making the heel my weapon of choice, my lance against evil. Calming my breathing I wait the brief moment it takes wiry man to reach me and grit my teeth in defiance. As he arrives within touching distance of my stance he stops dead, leaning forward resting his hands on his knees, breathing heavily, panting with exertion.

"You move fast." He says holding up a hand to still my next question as he recovers his breath. "You asked about Linda." The words come in short sharp blasts and he makes a snorting sound in his throat spitting noisily onto the floor "Jesus I don't think I've run like that for years, I'm knackered." He staggers towards a low garden wall and sits heavily causing the brickwork to wobble under the pressure. He reaches for a pack of cigarettes in his pocket and lights one inhaling deeply.

"You know Linda?" I am confused "But you said you did not know her." He nods once before sucking again on the quickly disappearing cigarette

"No, I know. I couldn't say anything in front of the others could I. Much too risky."

"Where is she?" I demand "I must see her, I must speak to her. I have her shoe." My words are weak, rambling but I could be forgiven, I am confused and desperate to see her.

"If you want her to have her shoe back just give it to me, I will make sure she gets it."

"No!" My words come quick now, I am so close, close enough that I would not be defeated at the last. "I must see her and return the shoe myself. I saw her, just the once but I saw her. It was in that moment I fell deeply in love with her. I knew in that moment that she was the only girl for me. Please if you know of her whereabouts tell me, speak now, put me out of this misery." Wiry man sucked again on his cigarette and held the contents for many moments in his throat. Finally with a look of amazement on his face he released his breath and from the cloud of smoke that emerged he said

"Honey, you are looking at her."

The silence lasts for many moments with nothing but the sound of the breeze in the trees and the voices of the children of the local primary school practicing for their harvest festival. Seeing my bewilderment wiry man leans forward and gently takes the shoe from my grasp. Slipping off his heavy work boot and sock he reaches down and places his foot in the shoe tightening the strap around his ankle. The shoe fits perfectly, the whiteness of his skin heightened by the redness of his painted toe nails twitching beneath my gaze.

"I'm sorry to disappoint you lovey but the Linda you have been so desperate to meet is me Linda Teller, drag queen to the stars." He laughs "Well not quite the stars but I did once do an open air performance at the Edinburgh fringe but usually I am performing every Thursday and Saturday at The Palace Bar." He reaches out and takes my hand gently. "I couldn't say anything before, not back there." he nods in the direction he had come from, "God if they found out they would skin me alive. No, as far as they are aware I am Steve who works at the fruit and veg stall in town. Steve who keeps himself to himself and gets angry when people pry too hard into his private life. I am Steve who must have a criminal background because I share nothing of myself with others and choose to live in a dump like Hovel Row. I only live there so I can save money for a place of my own by the way, not because I like it." He takes a last drag on his cigarette before tossing it aside and sitting back down on the wall to remove the shoe and replace it with the work boot. "Yes I am Steve who made the mistake once of telling someone who I really was and who I really wanted to be and suffered the consequences for many years." He laughs mirthlessly "So many years that I had to leave home so that I could be who I really wanted to be and when I wanted to be her." His look changes suddenly from one of defiance to one of sadness. "I don't know why I told you that? Not sure you wanted to hear it really, but.." He pauses again "I suppose its because you came to find me. It seemed sort of, well, sort of like a Fairy Story I suppose." Without waiting for my response Steve or should I say Linda, picks up the stiletto shoe and walks away her feet light across the ground despite the heaviness of the work boots.

I finally found some shoes to match my suit. Black ones, real leather with a small silver buckle, very smart. I must be going through some sort of transformation of my own as not only have I bought new shoes to match my suit, I have also bought new jeans, trainers and a waistcoat, red and gold thread with an oak leaf motif. I decided that sometimes fairy tales are not exactly what you would expect, how can they be? After all they are just fairy tales. So why the new clothes? Well, I have to have something to wear when I meet the love of my life don't I? Yes I am off to meet my very own Princess, the one and only Linda Teller. Now who said Fairy tales do not come true eh?

Rhona

Rhona stood on the stage and looked out towards the sea of faces. Her peers, the people who attended the same school as her, her so called class mates stared back and still she hated every single one of them. The gasp of surprise when her name was called was not the cause for her hatred nor was the frozen, open mouthed shock that displayed itself so freely on the blue uniformed statues that called themselves pupils. No, she hated every clique and set of them, their arrogance and assumptions of worth. The trend-setters were no better than the swats, the artists were as dull as the music the musicians played and the sports people were as forgettable as the socialites who preened themselves on the sidelines as they wetly enticed their prey. Rhona cared for none of them and was content in the fact that not just they, the students, but the staff and support staff shared exactly the same feelings towards her, the one they called disruptive, the one who would amount to naught. Rhona understood exactly why she hated them, was mature enough, perhaps too mature for the average 16 year old, to understand their dislike of her. She was herself, her own force of nature, a being of protection, one who moved with care. She was a tomb of self defence, a chapel of control. She was Rhona and she quite simply did not and would not conform. She would not wear the uniform or take part in the humiliating dressing and undressing in cold P.E. changing rooms for the ritualistic haranguing by over zealous teachers. These were teachers who thought that the meaning of life was to be able to jump higher or throw further than the next weak specimen of human life who would stand next her ready to please, eager to perform. No, she would not take part in this. She was no limp weakling who would willingly give of herself when ordered by those who used words as weapons and had not the fists of evil to force their will. Rhona would stand glassy-eyed and tight lipped as teachers berated and belittled her in spittle filled, close faced tirades before the group of sheep people who it seemed followed the rules and allowed themselves to be herded through life in every situation. She would stand alone, motionless until the winds of verbal discipline calmed and she was sent as punishment to walk alone around the field of so called sport as bodies covered themselves in mud and sweat for the enjoyment of others. Oh if only they realised how she craved the solitude of these walks, longed for the peace and the bird song. Rhona would walk and listen to the grunts and efforts of the sheep people safe in the knowledge that she would never again bare her flesh for teachers to examine. Never again would she have to suffer their side eyed looks as they wished they had not seen what they had seen, before they took aside to a quiet place seeking straight faced lies to their stiff mouthed questions. Their questions spoken with false care would be full of accusations and a readiness to believe their own truths about the bruises or scars that marked her torso, her arms, her legs. Rhona was not ashamed of her scars, why should she be? Each mark although not always of her own making was borne with pride. Each scar told a story of its own, a reminder of her strengths, her ability to survive. Each yellowing bruise caused her no embarrassment as they marked her body, yellow daffodils against the white of her flesh, daffodils that waited patiently for the next Uncle to paint them as red as new bloom roses with a lust that knew no end as they crawled from her mothers drug fuelled bed to find solace anew beneath the posters of lands afar stuck to her walls with tape that peeled at the edges.

Rhona looked out at the ranks of uniforms who waited with smirks slowly spreading across their beautiful faces, faces that were yet to learn the frown of life or feel the slap of reality and felt the pleasure of the shock she had now inflicted amongst them all. Her name had not appeared on the list pinned to the notice board, a call to the interested or able. It had not been seen by the eager to please or the assured of a place. Her name had not been displayed for the week long avid discussion by those who felt the right. It was not there for the outright refusal from those who believed they held the power but had instead been replaced by a name that did not exist or had not been used. It was a fiction, a fraud, a name of the past, the name of home. Rebecca Murphy, Mummy's little angel, Daddy's little princess, once so long ago when Daddy had been content and Mummy had been herself.

Rhona had seen the notice but passed by with her usual disdain, avoided the gannets who's chattering, greedy beaks hardly allowed the flashing bright teeth to snap at the morsels offered by mummy bird,

"Fill your gullets my precious ones. Display yourselves to the world and be celebrated for the brilliance you are. Treat us to your pride and jealousy, conform, conform, conform" Tit bits for the needy, fed by the saintly hand of the principal, 'All plaudits greatly received.' Rhona had ignored the first flush of excitement, extricated herself from the furore determined to remain apart and yet, with the silken movements of a cat learned from a life of the quiet she returned to pick at what remained, the remnants of the feast unable to resist the calling. The notice had cast its shadow with thick black print, guiding her towards it as Sirens called to Odysseus, but her ears were not filled with wax and her body was free from the mast. Darkly she approached and read as she always knew she would.

'End of year recital. Things of which we are proud...' She read no more, no need, her mind set with a flame that burned from within. She would do this, would bare her soul, would allow them to see behind the mask. With the slightest of smiles kept for the small bladed knife that eased her pain. Rhona wrote her once given name.

She steps to the microphone not as that innocent lamb to the slaughter but as the conductor to the orchestra. She closes her eyes to the brightness of the smirks. Closes her ears to the sounds of the tuts that echoed through her life, the symphony of disappointment and disapproval.

"She has no heart. See how she skulks like a devil in black. See my faithful students how she moves amongst us and yet not like us. My children come to my bosom and suckle, take my love as I take yours. She has no love, knows no love. You must mistrust her as I show you how to live. Follow me for I am how things should be." Oh how little they understand of her. How their preconceptions and shortsightedness lead them to holy sentiments that stand them above all others. How she needs to distance herself from those who cast her aside as one who is lost without cause or broken beyond repair. How she treads with care and separates herself from those who's own fear of failure keeps them from a task to support her, a task that would test the strengths of Hercules himself. Rhona knows of love, feels the pain in her heart. Wishes for the love that once was there. Her breath catches. No not the fleeting love of a father who's needs took his own weak love to the bed of another. Nor is it for the sickly screaming love that comes in tear flooded moments as the stupor of chemical concoctions pass and the weak armed embrace of a ravaged mother's sobs clutches her to her chest. No. Rhona knows the ache of true devotion. She has shared in a love, a real love, not the harsh, bitter, beer reeked love of sweat, anger and pain hanging red faced above her but a true, shared sense of devotion that comes with the gentle eyed understanding of forever. Rhona has known true love and mourns its loss.

Her hand reaches for the microphone and she senses the gasp of amusement filled awe,
"Watch her, see her, fool that she is. Turn

away your eyes my children to one who is wasted and wanton. No good can come of this with her lack of humanity. No good can come of this for one who fails herself!" Rhona sees with closed eyed clarity the love of which she speaks, the thing of which she is most proud of. Her throat tightens against the deed but her need pushes her on. She will share with them, lead them to understand their own hate-filled failings, their compassionless acts of neglect. She will speak but once of her humanity, explain her sense of loss. She will remove of her own free will just briefly the armour that keeps her safe and she will share a love that she has lost which will carve them to the core. Rhona opens her mouth to the feelings and speaks of her love and her loss. As she speaks her voice raises higher as though to the spirit that floats above. As she speaks she orates the words that took a lifetime to learn.

"I stand before you now to speak not of my life for I know how little you care and nor should you for I am as much at odds with you as you are with me. I have no understanding of how you live your lives, the decisions you make or what it is that spurs you to act as you do. I do not concern myself with how you live why should I? I say this because after all it is your life to lead, yours to own. Do not be too downhearted in my seemingly harsh disinterest in you. Sometimes and only sometimes in the darkest of nights as I lay with my head covered by the duvet on my bed and the dressing table pulled across the door do I spare a thought for you. Why do I think of you then? It is only to wonder why it is that although you have no real interest in me or my life you choose to bait me so mercilessly. I ask myself this and then I wonder into the darkness i it for sport, for entertainment or is it perhaps for the simple act of deflecting the ridicule or hurt that sometimes snaps at your heels with the ragged teeth of decay? But I say here and now no more of this for this is not for now, this is a topic that will no doubt be thought upon by yourselves somewhere in the future when times are hard or when times are lonely or perhaps when times are at their best. This is a topic not to be shared with me now but perhaps about me when I creep upon your memories, unbidden and caught in surprise you wonder, 'what happened to…?' But let us not think of this now, let us not concern ourselves with this, instead let me introduce myself to you as I am. I am Rhona! I am one of the lost, the forgotten, the unwanted and rejected. I am Rhona who promises not to force you into thoughts of regret or guilt. I do not stand here to make you hear me as I do not ask you to act against all of your preconceived

TALES OF SOMETHING DIFFERENT

ideas and misconceptions and so view me differently. No! I do this here and now for myself, I do this so that I can leave this place knowing that I have heard my own voice echo from the walls. I will leave with my words vibrating in my chest. I will leave knowing that if I am the only person to have listened to what I say then at least I will have been heard. I will have been heard for who I am and not for whom you believe me to be. Again I feel the need to placate, to stroke, to pander to your childlike needs. I feel the need to assure your very selves, to treat you as the children you have remained. So I say this to you all, to those who are without intention listening to me now, I have no intention of opening your minds to places, my places that you simply cannot understand or comprehend. I cannot ask you to enter fully into my world for this would be unfair, cruel even, pit ponies to the darkest of mines. If I am not here to speak of these things, these things that you cannot comprehend then what, what is it I shall speak of? I shall speak to you of the that which I hold so dear, that of which fits the title, that of which I am most proud. I shall speak of love, I shall speak of love. I see your sneers and hear the inhaled breath ready to free itself in torrents of abuse. 'What does she know of love?' 'Who could love her?' How can she speak of love?' Be aware that here I stand before your ridicule armed in my mind with a strength given to me not from books or from imagination sucking elders but from one who gave me their all, gave me their love and in return deserves to be honoured for that that they gave. I shall wax with a passion of one who against all of my odds and my woes remained the truest to me. My words will hold forth one who gave with a love that was unending, was ceaseless and honest of one who was steadfast and brave. Again I see you wonder why I speak like this, of this as yet unnamed being and their love? I shall tell you now that I do this because I have heard the whips of your tongues, felt the lash of the words against my skin, had my soul torn by the wrist flick of your mockery. I hear the words that cut me as they speak without knowledge and detract me as one who in the glare of your eyes cannot be accepted. You see me as one who is as I am because I do not, cannot have love in my life. Well I say no more! And so I shall take a breath and compose my thoughts. I shall allow myself a moment to gather the words about my head so as to speak them clear. Unlike those who are the studious amongst you who worry over every full stop, comma and speech mark I write nothing down, I have no need, for I speak not from a page but from the heart. My words are learned not by repetition but by life itself. And so with my mind fully focused and my thoughts fully ordered I shall reach, much to your relief, the mains of this humble meal I have brought to your table. Now I shall speak of love and of the being who shared that love with me with a willingness which remained unrivalled. It is because of this one, this presence who stayed by my side that I know that a love so pure can exist in the flesh as in the mind. He without question kept me safe at night with no regard for his own rest. He shared his warmth hunkered close to me when storm bashed and hammered at my locked door as fury threatened to force open the only flimsy barrier that kept me safe. He sat with me as my strength failed and my arms wearied. Together we held at bay what promised harm. He gave me a love that waited patiently for my return with never a question and always a greeting that melted the hate of the day away. He stayed beside me an honest presence where I felt I had none. He nestled against me when gentle contact was all I desired. He taught me of love innocent and true with never an agenda, no thought of favours given for return. He taught me to love, unconditionally. His teachings so pure accepted me for who I am. He allowed me to be who I wanted to be and trusted in who I would become." Rhona pauses her speech and looks again upon the faces of the sheep people. She feels no sadness as she encounters the mistiness of their eyes. Her feelings do not turn to warmth for them, how many years has torment been their God? Instead, she steps closer to the microphone and with hand on heart speaks with a resonance that leans them forward, trees to catch the breeze.

"For those of you who have not guessed, for those who think love is to be freely given with blouse opening, tight skirt lifting freedom to any body that feeds your ego and fills your loneliness, I speak not of love shared by sweaty hand and greedy tongue. No! I speak of love given daily by the simplest but truest of beings. I speak of the love of a dog. My dog, my faithful, fun loving friend who shared with me a love that kept me safe. He shared with me a love that made me someone, made me complete. Where others failed me, where others sought to betray me he remained by my side. My dog, yes my dog loved me till the end of his days. I mourn my friend, I cry for his friendship, I look for his presence but still I feel his love. I shall not allow you to know his name for you are not worthy to mention it either in awe or in jest but I shall tell you of his power, his strength. Although he has gone his love fills my heart still. I move around this place ignored or abused, I walk the lonely path you lay for me but I am not damaged by your hatred. For the love he gave me which surrounds my soul has and will protect me still against your ill wills and ridicule. I am Rhona and he was and is my love and I am proud to have known him.

Not a sound is heard from the sheep people as they sit hypnotised by the music of her voice unable to comprehend their regrets to one who needed their help. Not a movement is made by those who lead, as revelation comes to their mind. Standing before them Rhona, Rebecca wrapped inside.

"Look my students, see how she has grown. Did you hear her words, there is love in her heart. Listen my students, let us be proud, let us celebrate our success as very own Rhona our dearest Rhona joins us at last." She the Mummy bird steps across the stage her painted talons claw-like in their redness. Her skirt tight against her skin shimmers as her blouse white as the snow blinds the innocent, reflects the wetness of her lips. "Rhona, well done, well done indeed. Come let me stand beside you and bask in the glory we so rightly deserve." Rhona sees her approach, sees her wide armed gesture ready to gather ready to ensnare, ready to entrap and… Rhona aware still of who she is and all she will become, slowly raises her middle finger and proudly leaves the stage.

A C STOCK

The Last Dog Fight

Light headed and heavy limbed. It is like this just after take off. I take two deep breaths in the oxygen mask, it will pass always does. I can see the ground falling away from me and enjoy the sensation, all feelings of nausea forgotten as the earth drops away from me and the sense of freedom fully takes over. The sun glares through the cockpit and I feel its heat on my face.

"Welcome, Vera." The voice is muffled, distant in my headset. Jakub the Pole, crazy bastard always flying on the edge, pushing hard, a man totally at one with his machine. I smile at the name, 'Vera'. He has always called me this, they all have. The rough accent he uses on the English language, a new language that has been so difficult for him to master causes him to pronounce it Werwa. It was obvious really, Squadron leader Simon Lynn, Vera to his friends. I sense before I see his Spitfire pulling up tight to my left wing. I look towards him, our wings close enough for me to clearly see his round boyish face looking back at me and my headset crackles again.

"I not think you were coming up Werwa, I waiting, why you so long?" The sentence littered with the mistakes I find so amusing, I smile into my mask

"Always good to give room for your bad take off old boy. Don't want to get wiped out whilst still on the floor now do I?" I hear his laugh as he barrel rolls away and I catch a glimpse of his wing tips each painted with a stork standing in a nest. I will have to speak to him again about this, although I know it will do no good it is an order he simply will not obey, he will not fly without them.

"I have my luck with these birds. No-one kills Jakub today!" As he wheels away I decide that for my own sanity I shall choose to ignore the birds, it is easier to ignore his one, or two? misdemeanours than look at his wide blue eyes staring at me earnestly before he breaks into that wide, white toothed smile. It is the smile the local lassies find so irresistible. 'Yes.' I decide, the storks can stay. I fix my attention forward and screw my eyes shut tightly, my head throbs it will not clear. I wonder if perhaps I am sickening for something? I breath long and slow into the mask focusing all of my attention on trying to bring my vision back on track. After a few deep breaths it begins to clear, I feel myself calming. I want to wipe my hand across my eyes but for some reason feel nervous of releasing the controls, these oh so frequent missions bring about so much tension, so much nervous energy. I roll my shoulders and feel the tension begin to ease, I need to relax.

"Hey Squadron Leader, glad to find you. I seemed to lose you in the clouds." The new boy, what was his name. I shake my head to focus, Marshall, Brian Marshall.

"Good to have you along Marshall, saw you all the way." The lie will calm him, help him feel as though he is part of the team, "How you feeling?" My headset vibrates against my ears.

"Great Squadron Leader can't wait to get at them." I love his enthusiasm, they are all like that, at first.

"Calm down boy concentrate. Let's find them first shall we?"

"Yes Sir, let's find them and get at them eh? Give them hell." I smile sadly behind my mask, what is he 18-19? A boy. His talk is good, playing field bravado. I wipe away the vision of him behind the huts when the call went up, bending at the waist hands on his knees spitting away the last of his grease filled breakfast, reality a punch in the guts. I raise my thumb to him through the cockpit and he waves in acknowledgement "Stick close to me," I say, "If we make contact listen for my call, follow my lead, no heroics eh? Keep it simple." He waves again and I am sure I can almost hear the relief in his voice.

Yes Squadron leader, I shall be on you like glue."

"Marshall." I call again

"Yes Squadron Leader."

"Call me Vera, everyone does."

"Yes Squad… Yes, Vera." I signal through the cockpit for Marshall to follow me and with a flick of my wrists the spitfire as though it were part of me responds, and I wheel away in a tight dive. Again I marvel at how at one I am with this noble machine, not just a throbbing engine pulling its cargo through the sky but a living, breathing, feeling cocoon around me. My limbs feel lighter now the oxygen is working its invisible magic. I breath more deeply. This is known as 'the quiet time'. I scan around the vista, light white clouds, visibility good, perfect flying conditions. Above the roar of the powerful Rolls Royce engine I am pulled away from the oneness of me and my aircraft as I hear a sound, a beep. I concentrate hard yes there it is again. I check the control panel nothing unusual. The beep repeats itself, rhythmical in its regularity. It is coming from above my head. Twisting in my seat as best I can I study all within my eye line, I can see nothing.

"Marshall you with me?" My throat tightens as I hear nothing for seconds then,

"Yes Squadron…. sorry, yes Vera."

"How am I looking?"

"Sorry I don't understand."

"How's my craft looking, do you notice

anything shall we say, unusual?" I see him fly a large loop around me, he handles his aircraft well.

"All perfectly normal Vera all as it should be." The beep comes again and I want to ask him to check one more time but I do not want to worry him as his lack of hours and very basic knowledge makes him my least favourable option for advice. I consider calling for Jakub but I stop myself. My nerves seem to have been on edge since take off, I have felt at odds with myself, I am tired, no not tired, exhausted. I decide that the old girl has never let me down before and she will be no different this time, I have complete faith that she will carry me safely just as she always has.

"Tally ho, Tally ho!" A barrage of chatter erupts in my ears dragging me back to more pressing matters, "On your port wing one o'clock Lawrence."

"Evans pull up I have him."

"Taken one in the tail may have to return to base, sorry chaps."

"See you back there Tom."

"Two of them coming in fast Dave."

"One for me Sid."

"Bloody hell that was close Pete, I'm on him here I go."

"Tally ho, Tally ho!" I search the skies around me but can see nothing, I have drifted somewhat starboard the fight is going on behind me.

"Pull away Thomas your crate is damaged."

"Mac. Coming fast to you Mac. Pull up man, pull up Mac, Mac! Oh God. Mac." The voice of Sid Percival otherwise know as Percy falls silent and is lost amongst the radio chatter of pilots hard about their task. I hear myself groan, surely not Mackenzie, no surely not Mackenzie? I crane my neck feeling my headache return as I search the skies around me, if only I could see what was happening

"Mac are you ok? Mac!" I call although fearing the worst "Mack answer me. Are you ok?" I hear no response from my oldest friend and pull at the controls in frustration but the old girl refuses to respond and stays on her course. The blood beats noisily in my ears and I feel a panic I have never experienced crush at my chest. I need to get back in amongst it.

"Marshall are you on me? Marshall!" He does not respond, probably in the first fight of his life, man and machine against man and machine. I suddenly feel alone. I don't want to be alone! I want to be surrounded by those I trust. my I only hope is that they see where I am heading and somehow keep a note of my direction through all of the madness that surrounds them. The thought comes to me suddenly that I may have to bail out. My stomach lurches, I have never had to bail out. Of course I have practiced it. First from towers and platforms and then flown over unnamed airfields and lovingly pushed with a firm boot in my back out into the open skies to fall with bile infused, stomach churning terror until the snap of the harness straps surge me upwards and leave me hanging beneath a bedsheet of silk that seems barely able to take my weight. Yes I have practiced this but never in action, never for real. I always hoped that if my time came it would be quick, not slung to the bottom of a silk shroud that exposed me as target practice for any enemy sharpshooter who would claim the kill with heroic aplomb to his comrades whilst supping on lager and eating sauerkraut. The beep sounds above my head, it is a low sound lost amongst my heavy breathing and the radio chatter, but it is there, a warning sound. I wonder if perhaps I have missed a briefing or the ground crew have failed to mention some new damage warning system. If this is the case heads will roll when I get back. It makes perfect sense to me now, something has affected my steering and the warning beep was confirming the information. My priorities have changed and I realise that I will not be able to join the fray but am now aware that I am up here flying like an injured bird, easy pray to any enemy fighter that sees me. I struggle to release my safety harness in readiness to bail out but am stopped as voices crackle noisily into my ears.

"Bank hard Squirrel, break left."

"Vic has bailed out, seen his shoot!"

"Coming at me, I'm out of ammo!"

"Bloody hell there are loads of them."

"Tally ho, tally ho!" I am panting and feel clammy it is hard to breath. I struggle again to loosen the belts holding me, they feel tight around my chest, constricting me. I blow two or three large breaths and breath deeply. I am panicking, time seems to move slowly, slower than the fear that rises into my throat causing my eyes to leak the moisture usually kept for weddings or funerals. I curse myself for my sudden weakness but understand that it nothing unusual for any pilot to feel like this especially in my predicament but until today this was something I was not used to. I focus on the chatter on my headset and feel a sudden resentment that the lads are engaging without me. I have been there throughout and want to be there now, they need me as much as I need them. As though the sense of failure I feel at being so disengaged from my lads is too much to take I physically slump in my seat a feeling of uselessness washing over me. I am at a loss worse than that I physically have no control, no way back to the fray I am now drifting without hope of altering my course. I tap my oxygen gage it reads low which no doubt accounts for my feeling light headed. I rub my hand lovingly over the panel in front of me, it seems that my old lady is suffering as I am suffering, perhaps our journey together is coming to an end, perhaps this is as it should be.

"I am with you Vera on your tail." Never have I felt such elation, I want to yell with relief.

"Marshall is that you?"

"Yes Squadron Leader, I said I would be there, like glue I said." I relax back into my seat and I begin to feel more calm.

"Thanks lad, thought I was on my own there."

"Why would you be on your own Werwa?" Jakub, so he has seen me as well.

"Good to see you my Polak friend. My crate has a problem, no steering may have to bail out."

"Stay calm old chap lets not be too hasty eh?"

"Thomas, you here too?" My headset cannot hide his mirth.

"Yes old boy. After all is it not a lovely day for flying? Just look at that sun against the clouds, beautiful." He is correct, it really is a breathtaking sight. The large white cumulus cloud ahead of me is tinged pink at the edges reflecting the sun which shines through as though mirroring my memory of the fields bathed in morning mist on my fathers farm. The bright blue sky surrounding the cloud creates a vision that looks as though it could have been painted by Turner himself. I have to focus and shake my head

"Gentlemen although this is a sight to behold, I am still in somewhat of a predicament. I have no means of steering, my oxygen is running low and have only fumes for fuel." I realise what I have just said. "If I have no fuel then neither will you. Return to base now. Take a reading of my location so that when I bail out you will be able to find me." There is an explosion of voices in my ears.

"Sorry Sir."

"No chance Vera."

"I am staying here with you now Werwa." I look to my left and to my right, spitfires, dozens of them each bobbing like ducks on a pond,

"We will not loose you Vera old boy relax we are here for you!" I do relax now sinking back into my seat, again I am at one with my plane. I breath deeply into the oxygen mask at last my head is clearing. I am no longer panicking, that feeling has gone. I am calm, I feel in control. I am able to enjoy my real love, the only love I have ever really had, the magical sensation of soaring high above the clouds, a sense of freedom, just me and the earth below. I smile at the sun feeling its warmth, bask in its beauty which comfortably envelopes me in its embrace. As at last I enter the edge of the largest of the fluffy clouds I feel the warmth of the sun bright against the acrylic of the canopy and hear my headset crackle soothingly.

"Tally ho Vera. Tally ho!"

Nurse Evangeline Simmonds hears the familiar hiss of the oxygen escaping the mask as she removes it from the recently deceased form in the bed. She disconnects the heart monitor which has now stopped its rhythmic beeping and makes a small note of the time on a chart. With great care she places the chart in a manila file and gently rests it on the old mans inactive chest. Reading the name aloud she completes her own little ritual

"Rest well Simon Lynn, I hope you had a good life and have found peace." She rests her hand on his own still, warm hand and wipes away the small tear that without bidding has formed at the corner of her eye. She turns to leave, her duty done, the care given and reaches for the blue disposable curtain to pull around the bed of this lonely figure, to what, offer dignity or to hide away? She is uncertain. Looking back one last time her heart lifts from the melancholy she feels. Where once she had seen an old man in pain now there is the face of a man at peace. Where there was once the face of fear now only the small contented smile of happiness is displayed.

A C STOCK

You Heard?

"You heard?" Terry leans back on the plastic cafe chair and unzips his bomber jacket shrugging it off his shoulders where it lays haphazardly pooled behind his back. Although the weather is cold outside the interior of the 'Corner post cafe' is humid with the heat of the pans spitting noisily as the bubbling grease fries the pungent bacon and the highly spiced sausages to within an inch of their lives. The aroma heightens as bread is added to the pan where it is coated in the luminous gold liquid to transform it from a simple slice of thin anemic bread into a brightly shining triangle of fried bread that would soon be topped with egg and beans to form the contents of their usual 'hearty' breakfast. He takes a gulp from the white enamel mug wincing as the steaming dark brown liquid burns his top lip. "Christ that's hot." He places the mug onto the table top between them and stares through the heavily fogged plate glass window his attention firmly fixed on the outside world as it passes by, misted like ghosts.

"Yeah, of course I've 'eard, but thanks for the heads up." Opposite him Dave removes his own jacket, similar in every detail to Terry's and carefully places it on the back of his own chair before sitting heavily opposite. "I've been trying to get in touch with ya but your phone's been switched off." He leans forward slightly closing the gap between them, "So what we goin' to do?" Terry shrugs, a movement which sees his large shoulders stretch the material of his white t shirt tight around his chest as though it were the skin of a drum.

"I dunno." They are friends since primary school, they have a short hand in conversation built up over 25 years, no need to fill the silences. "I've 'ad me phone switched off, got to keep on the low down." In unison they raise their mugs to their lips and take equal slurps of tea before placing them heavily onto the formica topped table. "I sent a couple of runners to find you, to let you know, but they said they missed you." Dave nods

"Like you mate, I've been keeping out of the way." They both fall silent lost in their own thoughts, two powerful men at odds with their circumstances.

"Bloody hell mate, I can't believe this." Dave wipes a hand across the flatness of a long ago broken nose. It's his tell, a subconscious movement but one that only those close to him recognise, he is nervous. "How'd it happen?" He folds his arms across his stomach the action making the dark tattoos dance over the muscles, "I mean, How?" He stops talking and waits, his eyes boring into Terry's as though daring him to look away, it's not a challenge but recognition that the gaze will be met solidly, they are equal, together as always, in all things they are the perfect team, always have been. Terry shakes his head he is unable to find an answer, unusually, unable to think clearly.

"I don't know Dave, I just don't know." He rubs the short cropped hair on his head, feeling the patch of smoothness pass beneath his palm where the hair has recently began to diminish.

"Won't be long till you won't need clippers for this. I will just ask for a quick wipe over with a flannel." His mind flits back to his sloppy attempt at humour with the new girl. working in his sisters hairdressers. He wished now that he'd taken the chance to speak more to her as she'd shaved it into shape for him. She'd looked alright, his sort, tidy. Yeah perhaps tomorrow... He stops himself mid thought, tomorrow suddenly seems so far away. "Christ mate, this is bad." He says the weight of the words pushing him back into silence, a silence that once so normal now seems fractured with threat.

"Ere we go lads." Without either of them noticing Ali has appeared by their table and places two plates in front of them. "I've given you an extra sausage each. I thought you could do with it, what with…." He breaks off and spreads his hands in way of an explanation "I couldn't believe it, honestly I couldn't." He wipes his hands on the tea towel he always has with him, thrown casually over his shoulder "What ya gonna do?" He plucks the tea towel from where it lays and wipes at a small puddle of tea near Dave's mug before expertly flicking it back over his shoulder as though he is a matador twirling a cape. He leans against the wall close to his friends and shoves his hands into the pocket of the large chefs apron he insists on wearing, just as his dad had before him. "What ya gonna do?" He repeats as though talking more to himself than the two men seated at the table, "I mean, Tony three dogs, of all the people."

"Christ Ali, not so loud, we don't want the whole world knowing our business do we?" Terry looks quickly past Dave's shoulder as though expecting something to happen, something brutal and instant.

"Don't worry lads there's no-one else here. Too late for the market boys not late enough for the truckers." Ali's thin attempt at a smile although genuine feels as unconvincing as the vague promise the local politician is making on the small television set fastened to the counter with a thick chain. "That is unless you count Dolly there." He jerks a thumb over his shoulder to the only other occupant of the cafe, an old woman who sits at the corner table sucking greedily on a thick bacon sandwich with toothless, lip smacking pleasure. She only stops her sucking to feed tit bits from her fingers to a small scraggy dog that pokes its head from the lid of the old tartan shopping trolley she keeps close by her side, "and she won't be tellin' anyone anything, now will she, not old Dolly?" As though suddenly aware that she was now the centre of the whispered conversation she looks up from her task and smiles a wide, gaping mouthed grin that reveals her overly pink gums and the residue of her last masticated mouthful,

"Well, you two's have fucked it up 'aven't you!" She cackles wetly, licking a shiny residue from her fingers "Can't 'elp but get into trouble, silly pair of buggers." She turns her attention to the small dog who gazes greedily at her through a fringe of matted hair "Always been naughty boys 'aven't they Queenie?" She tears another piece of sandwich from her plate and gives it to the dog who snaps the contents regardless of the proximity of her fingers. "Tony three dogs." She mumbles through the latest lump of sandwich she has pushed into her mouth, "You need to make yourselves scarce boys, you really do. Get away from here, no good for you to be round 'ere, not now." She feeds Queenie another morsel which the dog drops in its haste and disappears into the confines of the shopping trolley to hunt it out. "If 'e' finds you you're done for."

"Bloody hell Ali, did you tell her?" Terry glares at Ali, furious that their friend could have be so loose with his chat.

"No Terry, honest. Dolly told me. Didn't you Dolly?" Dolly looks up from her sandwich forcing her watery eyes to focus properly as though needing them to understand what she was about to say.

"Yeah I told 'im', came straight round 'ere as soon as I found out, first fing I did. I told Ali to get in touch wiv ya to let you know soon as." She pointed the remnant of the sandwich crust she held in her hand as though it were a wand "Frank the 'lid' told me this mornin, proper gloating he was, couldn't wait to let 'is fat mouth tell me what 'ad 'appened'. Asked me if 'I'd 'eard, I made out I wasn't interested but 'e' told me anyway, told me Tony three dogs was after you, asked me if I knew where you two were. I played dumb, made out I 'ad no idea where you would be. Soon as he was gone, leavin' nothing but the smell of that scent he uses too much of, I came right round 'ere sharpish and told Ali." She waves her empty mug in Ali's general direction waiting for him to take it from her. "And all I ask in way of payment is a bit of decent service, but it looks like that's fallen on deaf ears." She cackles again as Ali takes the mug from her silently, "That's it love make old Dolly a nice cuppa." She watches him walk away in the direction of the small kitchen behind the counter before turning her attention back to Terry and Dave. "Ali did his bit, sent his lad round to put you in the know, in case you hadn't heard." She dabbed at her lips with a piece of tissue that had appeared in her hand produced from the darkened cuff of the knitted cardigan she always wore. "His boy found you Terry, told you all right didn't 'e'?" Terry nodded, thankful that he had been at his second lock up behind the old library, and not at home when young Ali had found him. Before he could respond Dolly spoke with the harsh urgency that only age and a life on the streets could nurture, "You need to keep your distance now lads, keep away from 'ere, your mate has done you proud so far but you don't want him and his mixed up in all this do ya?" With a flick of her head she signals in the direction of Ali who is walking towards her with another mug of jet black tea.

"'ere we go Dolly, enjoy." He places it in front of her frowning but ignoring the head of Queenie which pops out of the trolly as though a jack in the box primed for the smallest of touches

"I will so long as it's not that rats piss you

served me last time." Dolly peers into the mug, her face a look of disgust. Tutting loudly, she takes a loud dribbling slurp before placing the mug back on the table, "It will do, I suppose." Smiling broadly Ali walks away calling over his shoulder,

"It will have to Dolly, it's not like you're paying for it, is it?" He nods towards Terry the smile replaced with a frown, "If you two need anything let me know." Without waiting he slides behind the counter and disappears through the beaded curtain into the kitchen.

"She's right Dave, we shouldn't 'ang around 'ere too long."

"No, don't want to drop Ali in the shit do we?" Dave pokes a fork into a sausage and chews without interest, "Silly prick will try and 'elp out." He drops the fork back onto the plate and pushes the meal away. "Where we gonna go Terry, where's safe?" Terry looks at the plate of quickly cooling food, the grease already beginning to congeal around the edges of the bacon with a white candle wax consistency and shudders, somehow this seems to represent exactly how he feels.

"I've been thinking of nothing else since I heard Dave, but I've honestly got no idea." He reaches for the jacket now scrunched behind his back, "It shouldn't have ended up like this. Everything should have been ok, but now Tony three dogs is on to us we need to make this right and fast." Dave watches as Terry reaches for his jacket but remains motionless as though frozen to the spot.

"Perhaps we should sit tight for a bit, let the dust settle." Dave wipes a hand through the fog on the glass and peers through the porthole sized space. "Loads of people out and about now. This is the time everyone travels to work the street is heaving. Perhaps we should give it half an hour? In half an hour they will all be where they are supposed to be. If we leave when they are all tucked away there will be less of them to see us, fewer witnesses. Think about it, makes perfect sense, empty street cleaner getaway." He nods to himself as though the decision is made, it's like that with them, always has been, one makes a decision the other agrees, no argument. Terry considers for a moment, its all it takes,

"Right Dave, sounds like a plan. We sit tight for half an hour, use that time to figure out how the fuck Tony found out, and decide who it is we can really trust to help us out." He reaches for his mug and takes a sip hardly tasting the quickly cooling liquid, "but then we are on our toes, no question." Terry raises his mug as though offering a toast at the finest banquet. His friend copies the gesture answering solemnly

"Figure things out then on our toes, no

question." Before he is able to take a last gulp of the now tepid tea the bell over the cafe door tinkles thinly. Both men twist in their seats to the sound, a look of anger and fear crossing their faces simultaneously. Ignoring the yapping bark from Queenie they begin to rise from their seats fists clenched ready to fight but stop their movement as they see the rushed entrance is made by two young teenagers who run towards the counter. The first teen is carrying a skateboard under his arm, his jacket back proclaiming he 'rides for the Devil'. The second boy is shorter in stature, dressed simply in jeans and puffer jacket he is unmistakably young Ali.

"Dad, Dad!" He calls loudly, "The car is on its way!" Young Ali looks around the room and spots Terry and Dave in their usual seats, "Terry, Dave. Get the fuck out of here its two dog Tony, his car has just come round the corner." Before young Ali has finished speaking Terry jumps to his feet sending the chair crashing over behind himself. Stepping from behind the table he faces young Ali pure venom sparking his eyes like flames.

"How far away is he, how many with him?" Young Ali does not hesitate, he is smart, he understands the situation.

"We were outside Joe the Greeks and saw the car turn into the high street. It looks full,

I think he's brought most of them. You need to get out now!" He shouts the last word unable to maintain his composure. Ali steps to his side, calm, reliable as always.

"Quick, both of you go now. Head through the clothes shop opposite, it has a rear entrance out into the alleyway to the park." Terry pulls on his jacket as he moves, calling to Dave who will be only a step behind, always just a step behind.

"Out of the clothes shop Dave, you head right, I head left. Lay low and then we will meet by Frank's bookies make it stroke of midnight tonight. Ready?"

"Not me Terry, not this time." Terry comes to a stop as though suddenly punched in the chest. He stands where he is all effort to move to the door gone, he will not exit out into the street, will not head towards the bookies, no point. Slowly he turns to face his oldest and only friend unaware of the silence that has now descended over the small cafe, the cafe that has been the witness to so much, for so long. Dave is seated just as he had been as the boys rushed in. Slowly he raises his eyes from the screen of his mobile phone placing it on the table in front of himself as it emits an answering ping to the message he has sent. With a calmness that speaks more than any word is able, he stares hard into Terry's eyes, just as he always had.

Terry is used to this, knows it so well, but unlike any other time, he cannot glare back.
"Oh for fucks sake Dave. Why?"

A C STOCK

The Panelled Room of Arkinston Manor

Jeffrey Thomas White always followed the rules. This was a fact no-one could dispute. As a child he would be first in line as the bell rang, not because he ran or hurried along but because this was how he had been taught things were meant to be. The school rules engraved in gold cursive script resplendent on a dark oak board were there for the purpose of following and not for interpretation. One such rule stated 'When the bell rings line up immediately, in the correct place and in tidy order.' may have been overlooked by others but for Jeffrey this simply was not the case. It was true that this may have been rule number seven, placed well below others of greater importance such as, 'Respect for all others is paramount' and, 'Avarice and greed are reprehensible and not to be tolerated', but it was a rule none the less. This is why at the moment of the first peel of the school bell Jeffrey would be standing shoulders back, ram-rod straight, statuesque in appearance waiting to be led to the classroom where his learning could begin taught by teachers who barely managed to care. These same insipid teachers who although devoid of career interest were the same teachers who had the ability to notice. Often in the safety of their cigarette smoke yellowed bomb shelter staffroom would comment over their mug of strength giving coffee as to how Jeffrey Thomas White stood out from his contemporaries in his manner. They would shake their heads and tut sadly sharing knowing looks and nods about the boy who caused them no trouble, gave them no reason for concern and yet somehow always made them wonder. Some would comment on his promptness, others his attention to detail whilst others would pass a small comment on his appearance noting the fineness of his clothing. A magnate to the majority for ridicule, the piranhas who circled their prey, he was bait, a tied fly on an anglers line, he was the same as them all and yet always just slightly different. He did nothing to gain attention, avoided drawing notoriety, was smartly dressed in regulation uniform, blue tie with three white stripes held at a 45 degree angle, fastened with the perfect triangle of a Windsor knot that sat as large as a plate against the thinness of his throat. The starched white cotton shirt ironed flat with creases along the arms which threatened to draw blood from anyone who dared pass too close. His trousers were pressed between a damp tea towel every morning, steam filling the air with a pungent wetness that clung to the material like a rancid perfume. The creases of the trousers matched those of the shirt as the stiff fabric encompassed his stick thin legs guarding him against the outside world as it protected him from physical contact. Regulation square toed shoes gleamed in the light, polished and buffed with the stiff regimentation of a Sergeant Major ready for the parade. Yes Jeffrey Thomas White followed the rules, each and every one of them. He was a good boy, always where he should be, never out of place, never ran when it said walk, looked both ways when he crossed and never spoke out of turn or answered back because that would mean breaking a rule and that was just not his way.

One morning before assembly as Jeffrey stood at the head of the line checking the mental list in his head to ensure he carried the correct equipment for the day, a large round acne filled face flushing crimson with rage filled his vision.

"Oi White I want a word with you!" Jeffrey recoiled at the closeness of the face wondering perhaps if this would be the moment he experienced his first ever kiss. The roughness of the shove that sent him tumbling from the line accompanied by the deranged laughter of children who acted no better than the animals they were, informed him that perhaps this would not be the case. Dragged onto his toes Jeffrey found himself backed into the corner of a small alcove just outside the dark of the assembly hall. The snarling figure of Simon Hyde, bully, tormentor and breaker of rules grabbed him roughly by the tie dislodging the angle of the stripes by quite some distance. Jeffrey avoided Simon everyone did, Simon had a reputation that filled even the bravest teacher with fear. Yes Simon had a reputation that Jeffrey had no desire to become embroiled with. Again moving close enough to Jeffrey with the overpowering stench of body odour and tobacco that filled Jeffries senses Simon Hyde drawled quietly, threateningly.

"You are going to do me a favour,

understand?" Jeffrey did not understand the statement as there seemed to be in its simplicity neither option nor explanation. This fact did not seem to matter however as the brute Simon did not seem to require an answer instead merely continuing in what Jeffrey decided was a threatening tone. "I want you to look after these, right!" He thrust something into Jeffrey's hand and closed his fingers around it crushing Jeffries fingers and the inserted package in the process "They are doing a cigarette search and are bound to search me but they won't look twice at a weasel like you will they? Give me them back at break...all of them mind or I will rip your head off, ok?" As quickly as it had started it finished. Simon Hyde had stalked into assembly for once first in line, the alpha male leading the pack. Head thrust forward aggressively he walked to the first teacher in sight and turned out his own pockets. "See nothing 'ere." He smirked into her face looking around as though daring anyone else to challenge him. No one did as the scowl on his face bore enough menace to scatter all would be contenders before him. Jeffrey prised open his own bruised fingers and looked into his hand noticing the bruising that had already started its work and had began to discolour his knuckles. A crumpled packet of cigarettes, the red lettering bold against the whiteness lay hotly in his palm. He was now the holder of contraband. Slowly, so very slowly he closed his hand around the packet and breathed deeply, Simon Hyde was a rule breaker and Jeffrey

Thomas White did not care for rule breakers. Picking his satchel from the floor where it had fallen Jeffrey placed the strap over his shoulder and straightened his tie promising to check the alignment of the stripes in the bathroom mirror at the first available moment, but first he held the knowledge of a small misdemeanour and it was his duty to do the correct thing. He needed to report this misdemeanour to whichever teacher had the need to know. Yes, Jeffery Thomas White followed all of the rules to the letter. Jeffrey Thomas White had no friends!

Marion Stewart stared at the graph on her screen for the 20th time that morning, it was perfect, had been since she first read it. She ran her fingers through her hair and plumped the curls into place. It did not matter how many times she looked at the graph it worked, it really did. Cleaning her glasses for perhaps the 100th time she silently mouthed the names, checking again that she had forgotten nothing. Every area was accounted for, there were no shortfalls or gaps. Full coverage was guaranteed and she had achieved all of this well within the required deadline. She shuffled the papers that contained her neat, precise hand written notes and ideas complete with the rough pages torn from her notepad marked with her first draught. The first draught pages contained quick alterations and darkly scored corrections, this was the master copy to her now methodically designed graph that illuminated her tired features in the darkening room from the screen of her out dated computer. Marion allowed herself a momentary nod of encouragement, not only had she successfully worked to the tight timeline she had also managed to stick precisely to the costings supplied in their manila envelope earlier this week by Eileen Hounslow. Eileen Hounslow MBE newly appointed head of the board of trustees had entered the room with an aura of vanilla scented perfume and the unquestionable authority she had garnered around herself in her journey through life. With a quick glance around the small room she marched behind the desk accepting without question or embarrassment the offer of the leather Captain's chair that Marion was surely about to make. Once seated she signalled to the hard wooden chair on the wrong side of the desk and waited patiently for Marion to seat herself as comfortably as the hard seat would allow. Thinking back to the moment Marion shivered at the thought of herself sitting before the diminutive but no less powerful woman and accepting the envelope she held towards her. The starkness of the envelope floated threateningly inches above the desk held in a strong manicured hand. The polish on the nails Marion had noticed was perfect, highly polished and matched precisely the colour of the jacket Eileen Hounslow MBE wore. Marion had also observed that the nail polish was only a shade darker than the envelope she held and wondered if Eileen Hounslow bought envelopes to match her polish? Marion would not have been surprised as everything Eileen did was exact, planned and businesslike. Marion had leaned forward to accept the talismanic envelope as though she were a school child accepting the written end of year report to be taken home to mother, 'without reading mind!' She sighed now remembering the moment and placed the original papers alongside her own notes into the envelope and placed it carefully into the draw of her desk. She ran her hands lovingly over the desk top smiling at the description. Desk was a stretch of the imagination as it had clearly been a kitchen farmhouse table. Its scrubbed clean wooden top now scarred with gouges, ink blots and dried coffee stains that had darkened with age. The sight of the ink blots brought a small shudder that ran the length of her spine and almost forced her to slam the draw more violently than she intended. Calming herself she reached for the vase of daffodils that rocked gently but dangerously close to the edge of the desk. Her hands worked absently as she placed the vase carefully towards the centre of the desk and pulled at the flowers arranging them into another mis-formed display. 'Just how did anyone manage to make daffodils look as though they had been placed with care' she wondered? She supposed that was the problem with daffodils, however they were set in a vase they always looked as though they were wilting against the heaviness of their own heads, as though they were simply bowing to gravity. "Better off growing free," She whispered giving the flowers a gentle plump, "best left alone."

Marion pushed the vase to its original position and sat back staring at the computer screen as though willing it to find some fault with what was brightly displayed. The screen returned the look as though mockingly mimicking the words spoken by Eileen Hounslow MBE.

"The board has every confidence that you will be able to reach these targets Marion." Eileen had gripped Marion's hand tightly as she had reached for the proffered envelope her gaze staring with an intensity that held Marion as though she were caught in the force of an hypnotic trance. "It really is time to let go the…" Eileen had stopped talking, momentarily squeezing tighter at Marion's hand. "All I am saying my dear," She continued firmly, "is, it really is time to make cuts, time to let go." The smile that followed this sentence was warm, almost motherly, a trait Marion did not think the woman in the Captain's chair could posses and yet there it was the smile, the soft voice and the grip, actions that were supposed to display care, concern and regret. From any other woman these actions would fill the receiver with hope or safety, perhaps even the warmth of much needed love for were they not in themselves maternal traits? Marion traced with her finger a large jagged scar in the desk top, feeling its once raggedness worn smooth with age and sighed gently. Eileen Hounslow MBE was not the gushing mother, no, every action served a purpose. To any observant bystander they would see the exchange and would perhaps nod lightly recognising the compassion and the care shared between the highly scented, smartly dressed woman and the tidily dressed, sensible woman before her. Marion was left in no doubt from the conversation however one sided it had been, just exactly what was expected of her. Reaching for the mouse which sat patiently waiting she flicked it with practiced dexterity manoeuvring the small black arrow over the required symbol. With a sharp click she pressed print and listened as seconds later the clunk of the ageing printer in the corner of the room fired into life. Marion forced herself to smile pushing aside the self doubt that had crawled uninvited back into her her chest where it sat gnawing at her heart which beat thunderously beneath her cotton blouse.

"If I have got this wrong..." She shook her head fiercely, admonishing herself, she didn't want to consider that, not any more. She had done everything she could. Pushing the gnawing sensation which sat tight in her chest deep into the centre of her stomach where she could manage it as nothing more than hunger she concentrated again on the good points of her plans. Everything was covered, there was no extra expense, all areas were filled and good standards maintained. The plan was perfect. Pushing herself to a standing position she rolled the chair squarely behind the desk and straightened the mouse mat and stepped towards the printer feeling the warmth of the freshly expelled paper in her hands. She slipped the pages between the leaves of a blue envelope folder not daring herself to look again. She had enough copies for everyone who would attend the presentation this afternoon and two spare copies for the relevant folders in her filing cabinet, no excess, no waste. Clutching the folder to her chest she allowed herself a moment to calm her breathing and to reward herself with a silent 'congratulations' at the most difficult phase of this work being completed. Marion pushed the curls of her hair back into shape and took a small step towards the doorway, she was ready, what could possibly go wrong? Opening the folder for one last time just to be certain, she nodded, satisfied, it was then that her eyes were drawn to one name on the list, one name half way down hidden amongst many others and then, the smile froze on her lips.

Jeffrey Thomas White moved through his life at school in a blur of non description. He attended his classes. He worked studiously through the topics and he achieved top marks in all academic subjects. He avoided over strenuous activity such as physical education and graduated with straight 'A's' to little aplomb or celebration. Jeffrey drifted transparently from the school environment to his work life seamlessly. The sense of order and rules he held so dearly in life he found mirrored in the science of mathematics, a subject that suited him as well as he suited it. His first enquiry for a position of employment proved fruitful and he was soon working as the new junior bookkeeper at Mitchell-Anson and Webb an international trading company. For three years Jeffrey applied his skills fastidiously working through time sheets and wage slips as though each number and calculation before him was a small problem which had to be solved. Such was his attention to the fine detail that his calculations showed without question that the ten employees of the company were in fact being paid exactly one and a half pence a day too much. He carefully noted his calculations on company headed notepaper, placed it into a blue envelope carrying the company logo and placed it before Heather Carmichael the secretary of the company chairman Mr Horace Mitchell. Three days later Jeffrey received clear and precise instructions that all workers should now have their pay altered by seven and a half pence per week and that this should be back dated to the day each employee joined the company, suddenly Jeffrey had come to the attention of Mr Horace Mitchell. Moved to an office of his own Jeffrey worked in his office alone, diligently calculating hour after hour and year after year. Jeffrey happily worked his way through ledgers and files and soon progressed from bookkeeper to the respectful position of senior accountant. This was a title that meant little to Jeffrey but offered a role which presented order and rule in every number, decimal point and percentage sign. As ledgers appeared before him piled neatly on his desk he would straighten his tie, level his glasses and bend his head to the page and lose himself in the rows of neatly columned numbers and the musical scratch of his Mont

Blanc pen. This was his only extravagance, a thick black pen filled with the darkest of black inks as he made bold and precise marks. Life for Jeffrey would have continued this way for many more years had it not been for the 'Maneb' account. The inconspicuous looking folder had appeared in his office late on Friday 4th March 2011 in the hands of Rosie Stewart the young bright eyed secretary of Mr Martin Webb, junior partner of Mitchell-Anson and Webb. Tottering towards him in her unsafe high heeled shoes she leaned over his desk and placed the folder upside down in front of him knocking his calculator at an untidy angle in the process. She smiled brightly before standing straight and with alabaster hands flattened her skin tight skirt against her thighs.

"Mr Webb asked if you could just run your eye over this and sign it off for 'im? He needs it urgent for Monday, so be a love do it ASAP." Jeffrey had straightened his calculator, slowly turned the file the correct way around and stared blankly into the round face standing at his desk. Before he could ask for the relevant paperwork including the specific job number for this file, the tottering Rosie Stewart turned on her pin sharp heels and with a walk that proved her skirt was indeed too tight shouted quite unprofessionally over her shoulder

"See ya." Silence descended the office again with nothing but the overpowering scent of perfume and cigarettes as a reminder she had ever been there, nothing that was except the file. Jeffrey studied the addition to his workload as it lay before him, an interloper amongst the invited. He slowly lifted the edge cautiously as though the contents may spring out to attack him at any moment. Noting the three sheets of paper within held together with a paperclip he closed the file as though he were a priest with a prayer book. With a gentleness that would not be out of place with a concert pianist running his hands over the keys he opened the small draw on the right hand side of the desk and without looking pulled a thick hard backed notebook in front of him. Opening to the last page he studied the final number, not that he did not remember what it was, not that he needed reminding but just to be sure, just to follow the procedure. Removing the lid of his fountain pen he wrote neatly the next number in the sequence from the book onto the file he had just been passed. Writing the same number in the book he added the note 'Maneb Account' taking the name from the top sheet contained within the folder. Next to these notes he wrote clearly in his best hand the date and the name of Mr Martin Webb. Closing the book he placed it squarely back in the draw and closed it carefully. Everything was as it should be, the file now had an official number and an original owner. All the rules had been followed to the letter, everything was in order and Jeffrey liked order. Leaning forward he straightened his tie and levelled his glasses. Unlike other employees who would have tutted or at the very least raised an eyebrow at such a late request for accounts to be checked for Jeffrey this was a challenge a numerical problem to be solved. No sooner had he opened the file excited by the prospect of digging through the columns of neatly typed numbers his work was again interrupted as the ancient black phone on his desk rang noisily. Placing the lid on his pen and then the pen gently on its rest Jeffrey closed the file and picked up the bulbous receiver. Before he was able to speak the voice of Mr Martin Webb blasted into his ear.

"Jeff it's Marty glad to catch you, thought I may have missed you. Wondered if perhaps you had sloped off early eh?" A loud bark of laughter echoed down the phone causing Jeffrey to move the receiver away from his ear. "No not your way is it old boy?" Martin Webb continued "Look Jeff the girl, what's her name Rosie, yes that's it sweet Rosie, well she's going to drop something off, a file nothing to serious but needs signing. Be a pal and sign it for me. Just some sheets for an account that needs closing. Don't worry yourself too much with it I've had some lads look it over and everything is in place. Just needs your signature old pal. Sorry to be a pain and all that but really need it for first thing Monday so if you could just sign it and leave it in my in box so I pick it up first thing that would be great. Like I say no need to check, just scribble that signature of yours and everything will be sweet. Anyway old pal must dash I'm off to St Andrews this weekend for a couple of rounds wish me luck. Thanks again Jeff, chin chin". The phone went dead leaving a soft humming noise playing annoyingly against Jeffries ear.

Replacing the receiver he sat silently for many minutes before picking up his pen, removing the lid and turning to the last page of the three pages in the file. Hovering over the space marked 'signature of accountant' he paused, a slight crease in his brow. With a small nod of his head Jeffrey flicked to the front page and reached for his calculator and notepad. He should just check it, after all rules were rules and it was not as if he had anything to rush home for. The 'Maneb' account as it had transpired was indeed flawed in its accountancy. Jeffrey was not sure who had verified the figures for Mr Webb but their skills were clearly, severely lacking. Somehow these men, these nameless incompetents had missed some false entries and ignored some basic mathematical mistakes. They had quite clearly not been thorough enough. Jeffrey was certain now that there had been a deliberate misrepresentation of the accounts, someone had broken the rules. Jeffrey Thomas White did not care for rule breakers, rules were there for a reason. Taking a new piece of headed notepaper Jeffrey began to make clear, detailed notes of his findings. Once his report was finished Jeffrey placed the notepaper into a blue envelope complete with company logo and mailed it to the offices of HMRC who would definitely like to know. It was only a short time later that Messers Mitchell-Anson and Webb were found guilty of tax evasion, fraud and other various felonies and were prosecuted and sentenced accordingly. Jeffrey was thanked profusely in a note signed by a high ranking official for a job well done. Jeffrey placed the note into his brief case as he walked from the doors of Mitchell-Anson and Webb for the last time. Jeffrey Thomas White had no career.

Marion Stewart walked slowly towards the brightly lit kitchen situated at the end of the corridor. There was a step of urgency to her tread as she wanted to be the first to arrive, more than that she wanted to be the first face anyone saw as they entered. Marion gripped the folder under her arm but felt little relief in the stiffness. She wanted to be ready and waiting, fully prepared. The blue envelope folder containing the freshly printed graphs felt heavier with each step or should she say took on the weight of the decisions she had made. Her confidence had somewhat ebbed as she walked from what was called her office, another stretch of the truth. The small room now labelled as 'office' was once no more than a rather large storeroom, thick stone walls which offered little, or in fact no insulation against the cold and the ugly electric heater which had been attached to the wall by a handyman who for some unknown reason thought overlong screws and a gnarled piece of wood were far more use than a proper bracket, barely warmed her hands when she placed them hard against it during the cold winter months. Her office like many things in this ancient building were no longer fit for purpose, in fact that was any purpose, not just what they were originally designed for. She shifted the folder to her other hand and strode a little faster at least the kitchen would be bright and warm inside perhaps that fact alone would make this whole experience more comfortable. Yes, her plan was good on paper. Her plan would work, on paper. Everything was good, on paper but as she well knew, her one stubborn stumbling block was not on paper. The dark, cracked portraits of long dead members of the Arkinston family watched silently as she passed by. The sorrowful shake of their heads almost visible as her low heeled shoes clopped against the grey flagstone floor.

"Why are you so disappointed eh?" Marion asked them "It's not as if your decisions turned out so well is it?" She moved the last few steps quickly half afraid that Sir William Arkinston, Earl and builder of the original manor house, born 1596, died 1666 may actually splutter a rebuke full of courtly annoyance from behind the trimly clipped beard which covered the thin lips and constant sneer. Marion pushed the heavy door closed behind herself as she entered the doorway to the kitchen ready for what came next but unsure if it had been the wind she had heard or the collective, dissapointed sigh of the portraits.

Jeffrey Thomas White had been interviewed by a very fierce looking lady from the job centre. Her name badge made it known that she was 'Rosemary' and that she was the 'Senior agency administrator'.

"Well Mr White you say you are good at numbers." She had said looking over the rim of the silver glasses that were strung around her neck by a multi coloured bead chain that clashed terribly with the floral patterned scarf she wore. The scarf Jeffrey had noticed was secured in place with a black plastic broach etched with the wording 'Jesus saves.' in thick gold lettering. "I am sure that filing systems these days are all number based so this job will suit you very well indeed." She had removed her glasses and let them hang from the beads against her ample bosom. "I can assure you Mr." She paused to look at the paperwork in front of her although Jeffrey could tell perfectly well that she was fully aware of his name as she had not replaced her glasses "Mr, White." She continued drawing out the pause between 'Mr' and 'White' "I can read people very well and I just know that you will be perfect for this sort of work." She nodded as though daring Jeffrey to broach an argument. "My success rate at matching people against jobs is second to none, so you are in very safe hands." She sat back on her chair which squeaked alarmingly. "Now I will be sending you to 'Givens and Sons' you make your way to their warehouse and tell them Rosemary sent you. They know you are coming and already seem very keen. Let us face it, a person who actually wants a job and can count past ten is a bit of a rarity these days isn't it?" She bared her teeth at him in what Jeffrey realised must have been a smile. Jeffrey looked at the piece of paper in his hand and wondered quite what her success rate really was. Who was she competing against and more importantly who compiled the data for this information? Slowly and with great care Jeffrey removed his fountain pen from his suit jacket pocket and scratched through the misspelling of his name and placed some well needed punctuation in the list of directions to the aforementioned 'Givens and Sons' on the paperwork he had just received. Jeffrey believed in accuracy.

The warehouse situation had not progressed well. Within a week Jeffrey was confronted by a large thick set man who's neck seemed to have disappeared beneath his large shoulders.

"Its no good Jeff, you will have to leave." The man spoke in sharp clipped words his accent definitely east of the Thames "I don't care what you thought you were doing or who this so called Pythagoras fella is but you don't change our system". Jeffrey tried to reason with him but the very next morning he was again in front of Rosemary the stern woman at the job centre.

"There is a short term vacancy at the burger bar on the high street." She said looking up eventually from her computer and staring at Jeffrey as though he were an errant schoolboy returned early from an exchange trip abroad. "This is a small family run business and you will be covering the last six weeks of maternity leave." The catlike smile appeared on her face and her voice took a sweet and yet forceful edge "I am sure a man of your," She blatantly scanned Jeffrey, her eyes boring into him, "Yes." She said once her scan was complete "Yes I am sure a man of your age can manage to stay employed in a burger bar for a mere six weeks."

The position in the burger bar lasted three days. Jeffrey was asked to leave by an acne skinned girl who held out her hand for the apron and paper hat he was wearing whilst pulling a string of moist gum from her mouth letting it stretch until it drooped alarmingly before winding it around her tongue and beginning the procedure again.

"It's no good Jeff. You can't keep sending back burgers because they don't look like the pictures on the adverts, and you certainly can't put a note in the window saying 'Be aware! We sell burgers that are far from the image you see on the menu.' I don't care if you were trying to save us from some small claims prosecution or from the trades description people, you just can't do that. We haven't had a customer all day because of your interfering which means my tip money will be zero. Now give me that apron and bugger off."

Jeffrey sat in front of Rosemary and waited as she read silently from the sheets of paper before her.

"I have here." She began "A list of the positions you have both managed to acquire gainful employment in and the reasons you were asked to leave them. Shall I give you just a few examples, hmm?" Jeffrey was given no chance to answer as this definitely was not a response type question. Rosemary took a large breath and began to read, her voice monotone in delivery.

"Dustman. Caused major delays in the street sorting through the rubbish to find any recyclable items. Call centre. Began every conversation with perspectives customers by moving off script and saying, 'good morning this is a nuisance call. Librarian assistant. Asked to leave when he rearranged all of the books in size order and not alphabetically (volume with the most pages in first place where there was a clash of size.)" She looked up grimly "They put that in brackets." Her head bowed towards the list heavily "Dog walker. Forced each dog to wear a nappy during the walk." She slammed her hand loudly onto the desk sending the photo of Bob Marley in a sea shell frame crashing onto its back. "I mean nappies for God's sake!" Rosemary wiped her hand over her face, slightly smearing the red lipstick into clown-like smile. "Jeffrey, Jeffrey, Jeffrey." They were definitely on first name terms now. "This is proving to be very difficult indeed." She unclasped her hands in front of her laying them precisely on the desk "Perhaps you should take some time out to think about what it is you really want to do hmm?" She righted the fallen photo and smiled warmly across the top of Jeffries head. "Ah Mrs Singh isn't it? You are slightly early but that's no problem as Jeffrey is just leaving." Rosemary flicked her hand in a dismissive gesture and watch jubilantly as Mrs Singh took his place on the chair. "That's it Mrs Singh make yourself comfortable you are in safe hands as I have never had a failure."

Jeffrey had no more job centre appointments.

Marion Stewart placed the photocopied graph in front of each chair around the table. She positioned a plastic cup and a pen at the top of the piece of paper checking that each pen was centrally aligned. With great care she positioned a large jug filled with clean fresh water in the centre of the table and a plate holding an equal split of chocolate digestive biscuits and shortbread fingers. Satisfied that all was as it should be she moved to the small cupboard over the enamel Belfast sink and removed one bone china cup and saucer and placed them on the table in front of the third chair from the door as you entered.

"Now." She said softly "We wait."

Jeffrey had left the job centre and walked. For the first time in his life he had no set direction and he had no set plan. The sun was shining and the day seemed to have an endless quality to it. Jeffrey liked that, a sense of all things being as they should be. Striding along the pathway heading towards the bus stop his attention was drawn to a noticeboard with a poster advertising an Elizabethan banquet and jousting tournament. He studied the poster for a few moments looking at the venue as advertised. Arkinston Manor, ancestral home of the Arkinston's for four hundred years. The manor house was a short bus ride away from the city and promised a number of formal gardens and an award winning coffee shop. Jeffrey tore the poster from the noticeboard as it was now three months out of date and placed it in the bin by the bus stop. Boarding the bus he waited staring hard at the youth sitting in the seat which was clearly reserved for older people or people with disabilities until he stood and offered Jeffrey the seat. Jeffrey smiled and nodded with satisfaction as the youth slumped heavily into one of the many other empty seats and then sat himself beside the youth satisfied that now at least the seat which had been recently vacated would be free for someone who needed it. The ten minute journey flashed by and soon Jeffrey was strolling through one of the large formal gardens enjoying the order that assailed him. Flower beds planted to perfection, manicured lawns that glowed green with a lustre that defied words, topiary bushes that were clipped into truly amazing designs that stole his breath away. He wondered at the skills involved to bring unruly bushes to magnificent forms, birds, dragons, dogs and a peacock in full show. Jeffrey was drawn magnetically along the driveway of trees, trees that bathed him in dappled light softening his tread on the well kept shingle pathway, a pathway that revealed at the very last moment the manor house of the Arkinston lineage. Jeffrey stood for a fleeting moment wondering at the stone work of the manor house. Each stone was perfectly aligned, each of the windows was symmetrical with its partner. Each of the four turret were circular, built with a truly magnificent exactness. Jeffrey paid the pricy entrance fee happy to see that his change was given with the minimum of coins and entered the high ceilinged entrance hall. Jeffrey wandered the rooms silently breathing the history that gripped every room, wrapping them in a shroud of silence that in its own way hugged a warmth into his soul. This was a feeling that he had not felt for many years, not in fact since his discovery of mathematics. Celebrating the order of the indisputable history as explained in the coloured brochure he held carefully in his hand he dreamily followed the route advertised as the best way to cover the most ground. With each new room or display case Jeffrey revelled in the artefacts laid out on display, everything was in its place and everything was as it should be. Jeffrey studied every notice he passed, smiling at the 'do not touch' sign. Nodding at the 'private do not enter' notification and grinning widely at the laminated card held securely on a chain across a walkway stating, 'not for public access'. The rules were clear and precise, the rules were there for all to see. He felt a flicker move fleetingly across his chest and rubbed softly at the feeling hearing the starch in his shirt noisy beneath his nails. Yes. Jeffrey Thomas White had found where he wanted to be.

Marion Stewart looked at her watch, 7.45am. At 7.55am precisely, the door would open. It would open 5 minutes early, it would open softly, without fuss or drama and it would close in the same ordered way. The third chair from the door would be pulled back as noiselessly as possible and the figure would sit, straight backed, placing his fountain pen atop his leather battered notebook and wait patiently for the others to arrive. He would wait silently, hardly acknowledging the new entrants to the room as they arrived amid a torrent of chatter and noise. When everyone was seated and at 8am precisely, the meeting would start.

Jeffrey entered this new venture with his usual, thorough dedication and strict eye for detail. He soaked up all of the factual information he had to learn. He scoured the fact filled pages circling relevant information, dates, names and places and committed them to memory. His knowledge was unshakeable, there was nothing he did not know of the history surrounding this stately home. Jeffrey Thomas White was the newest volunteer guide of Arkinston Manor.

At 7.55am exactly the door to the old Victorian kitchen opened. Jeffrey entered quietly and sat in his usual seat. He concentrated on the task in hand and placed his notebook and fountain pen in front of himself. Marion poured the boiling water into the teapot and checked her watch, in 5 minutes' time she would pour the strong brown liquid into the bone china tea cup, she would add a dash of milk and wait for the noise from the others to die down before she began. As she counted down the 5 minutes neither person in the room spoke, the silence only broken by a cough from the seated figure who studied the room with wide eyed fascination as though this time was the first time he had seen it.

Jeffrey soon found himself very much in demand. Such was his enthusiasm for not only the history of the building but the fabric and structure of each room. He was asked for by excited groups of visitors to lead their tour personally. Groups of school children stood in rapt attention as he told of the priest who hid in the secret room behind the grand fire place. They gasped with delight as he revealed the secret doorway activated by a small rose carved delicately into the surround of a large painting depicting the likeness of the third Duke Henry Arkinston. Jeffrey saw women wipe a lone tear hurriedly from their cheek as he spoke with reverence of the Elizabeth the youngest daughter of the second Duke who fell desperately in love despite the anger of her parents with a shepherd from the nearby farm. He saw their tissues mop again at their faces as with a heavy sigh he described the scene as the daughter was thrown from her horse and died alone on a stormy night as she raced to follow her lover who had been banished from the county by her angry father. Jeffrey added the dates and places, he pointed to maps and to charts filling his stories with the facts and nothing but the facts. Everyone who visited the manor house left noisily exclaiming that 'they had never toured anywhere like this before'. The statement that 'there had never been a more informative or accurate guide than Jeffrey' soon filled the busy tea room. Word spread on many of the social media platforms and soon Jeffrey became somewhat of an attraction himself. Guests would ask shyly if he could pose for a photo? Some would thrust the guide book towards him and ask if he could possibly sign his autograph beneath the black and white photo of himself. Jeffrey would frown slightly confused by the attention he seemed to have gathered but would remove his fountain pen from his inside pocket and with practiced aplomb unscrew the lid. With a polished twitch of the wrist they would stand in awe as he signed the neatest of signatures and returned the guide book to the excited guest who hurried away to rejoin their friends.

Jeffrey enjoyed the hustle and bustle of the visitors, he always welcomed the chatter of people who were keen to hear his facts and to add to their understanding of history. He relished the chance to see young eyes bright with enthusiasm sparked by his words into exploring more and seeking out the truth and not the fiction. Jeffrey enjoyed all of these things and was content to perform each tour or discussion every single day and yet? If truth be told, Jeffrey Thomas White wished for nothing more than just one thing. Every Thursday morning at 10.45 precisely Jeffrey hurried to the staff notice board to study the rota for the following week. Keenly he would scan his name and feel the surge of excitement as next to his name in bold letters the words 'Panelled Room' smiled down at him. He would remove his small notebook from his pocket, unscrew his fountain pen and write carefully his positions to cover or his tours to lead. As he wrote the position 'panelled room' he would underline it twice, the scratch of his nib re-enforcing the fact that on this certain day Jeffrey would be stationed alone in what others called the 'boring room' the 'room no-one stayed in' or the 'dark room'. Jeffrey however was different, Jeffrey called this room 'the best room in the house.' Where others dragged their feet to attend or sat motionless, eyes glazed with boredom counting down the hours they had left with nothing but the steady thunk of the grandfather clock to pull their eyes to sleep, Jeffrey would stand happily, content with the silence and the sparseness of the room. The room was indeed almost empty. Nothing remained to catch the visitors eye. There was no large display piece to tempt them in. They would poke their heads through the open doorway, frown deeply, stare at their brochure and with a shrug move quickly to the next room which held the display of childrens toys owned by the many Arkinston children. Jeffrey would stand in the corner silently, aware but disinterested of the small table beneath the window which was a modern reproduction and held nothing but a sign saying 'Please do not use this table.' He acknowledged the painting on the wall which offered nothing but a country scene and was by an artist of limited appeal and if he was honest, which he always was, was of limited skill. He allowed the scene on the painting to drift from his mind. He was able to ignore the table and allow it its solitude. He did welcome however the tick of the grandfather clock which although large and he supposed imposing was not of the correct period. He allowed the clock to remain in his focus and used it as an accompaniment. He was fully aware that it was not original to the house, it was no more than a cheap reproduction bought from a back street auction house some years ago to 'fill a space' but somehow it brought a somber tone that added to the atmosphere of the room. Although the room was of no interest to any of the visitors just as much as it was 'the worst position' for his colleagues, Jeffrey would hurry along the maze of corridors rushing to take his place when the time came. Yes Jeffrey moved quickly to his posting excited as always to be in the panelled room. If any of his colleagues had taken the time to notice the small smile upon his face as he stood ramrod straight and stone still they would have thought perhaps it was a sign of desperation or the silent pleading to be released from his incarceration in the room and yet nothing would have been further from the truth. The gleam in his eyes and the smile on his lips was genuine. What no-one knew was that here in the panelled room, Jeffrey Thomas White, had lost his heart not once but twice.

"Good morning everyone." Marion coughed feeling the tightness in her throat "Thank you all for arriving so promptly." She looked around the small group, five women including herself and Jeffrey, they were all here. Carefully she poured the tea into the bone china cup and added the milk from the small jug judging ensuring the exact amount. Sliding the cup towards Jeffrey she motioned towards the tea pot to the waiting women. "Anyone for tea?" She asked already knowing the answer. A chorus of "No thank you's" confirmed her thoughts. "Help yourself to water and the biscuits are the best chocolate digestives I can buy on a tight budget or shortbread" She said reaching for the jug of water and poring herself a good measure as though it were in fact the large gin she had promised herself later this evening.

"Chocolate digestives and shortbread? This can only be bad news." Marion glanced towards the imposing figure of Laura Brady, her height very obvious despite being seated. "Last time we had a combination of biscuits like this we were told the sad news about Ethel."

"Ahh yes, Ethel. Such a shame, lovely lady. Created some wonderful tapestries ."

"Macrame, and it was bloody awful Alison. Everything looked the same all knots and hanging bits. Couldn't tell if it was a bag or a plant hanger. I spent two weeks trying to get my fern hanging straight only to find out what she had made me was in fact a bag for my wellingtons."

"A macrame wellington boot bag, what good was that?"

"No good at all. Dave put it to better use in his garage."

"For his tools?"

"No, he untied it all and used the string to secure his new ladders to the rafters." Marion smiled at the banter between the two women, good friends and longest serving members of the team lifting the mood in the room.

"Is it bad news Marion?" The new voice broke through the chatter "Are we losing our jobs?" All eyes focused on Samantha her pale face broken with a large gash of red lipstick. "Are we, are we all out on our ear?"

"Don't be such a drama queen Sam. They can't get rid of us. How could they?" Henrietta Bradshaw reached a hand across the gap between them and grasped her partners wrist lovingly. "If you work yourself up into such a lather I will have no other option than to prepare a warm deep lavender bath for you and a soothing camomile tea the moment we are home." She smiled warmly "Or you shall end up with one of your heads." She looked around the room and gave a silent 'what can I do with her' look?' "Sorry Marion we seem to have hijacked this little meeting of yours. Now may I ask what is all this intrigue?" Marion sipped at the water in the cup tasting the chalkiness and wished she had added some lemon slices to the jug. "As you are all aware the board have become very...." She paused searching for the correct word "Active." There was a general mumbling of acceptance "Eileen Hounslow has tasked me with making a few improvements."

"Bitch!"

"Samantha please." Henrietta Bradshaw silenced the outburst with a patient smile, "I suspect a drop of something a little stronger than camomile may be needed for you on our return home. So sorry Marion. Please continue."

Marion held up the graph displaying it for all to see.

"The board have tasked me with improving the service we offer to our visitors and guests. They feel there is some room for improvement in certain areas. They believe that we have to now focus our efforts." She paused, making a pretence of searching for the exact wording, although the words were very definitely burned into her mind. "Ah yes." She said at last reading from her notes, "They say that we have to be more aware of our costings especially during this present economic climate." She looked at the seated figures around the table judging the anger burning in their eyes. "They have also said that there needs to be more attention to detail." She took a quick sip of the water hoping again for the taste of gin.

"What do they mean. Attention to detail?" Laura Brady pointed a shortbread finger in her direction. "What detail exactly?" Marion swallowed thickly

"Well." She said at last "It appears that…" She fanned her face with the sheet of paper "Well no, to be honest, well." She leaned her elbows on the table and clasped her hands tightly together realising that she was indeed struggling to speak in any coherent way. Taking a large breath she raised her head and met the gaze of everyone in the room "There has been an anonymous feedback sheet sent to the board of trustees that states that, during some of the tours our knowledge has been, 'somewhat lacking' and shall we say 'muddled'." Her heart thudded noisily within her chest as the collective gasp emitted from around the table. This had hit them hard, this had taken them aback. In the third seat from the door Jeffrey Thomas White slurped his Earl Grey.

Jeffrey had never understood love. How could he? There seemed to be no rules to it. Love appeared to be nothing but a confusion of thoughts and feelings. No one seemed able to explain how it worked or how it arrived. Love just arrived in any random way it chose. According to the vast amounts of poems and other literature Jeffrey studied in pursuit of an answer love entered many a persons heart without introduction or former knowledge. Love it appeared often stepped forward without invitation. Jeffrey worked with facts, with numbers that added squarely together, with dates that matched events. Jeffrey worked with precision. During his first visit to the panelled room Jeffrey had seen with his own critical eyes all of his values, all of his beliefs manifested in pure craftsmanship. The skill and precision with which the panels had been constructed and placed were without question the most tactile display of every rule that Jeffrey followed. Each board notched neatly against the other, every joint fit precisely in place, wood on wood, joint in joint. The panelled room of Arkinston Manor wrapped itself around Jeffrey and smothered him in a display of everything that he had been searching for. If a romantic poet such as Keats or Shelley had been asked to speak of Jeffrey they would no doubt have said that 'Jeffrey was the panelled room and the panelled room was Jeffrey. They were the same. Created as many parts but come together as one'. The fact that Jeffrey had found such a love in this room would have been ample reward for a life spent with rules and facts as the driving force but this was not to be, this was not the only evidence of love in Jeffries life. For Jeffrey it seemed, was to be gifted that most unique of events. Jeffrey was to discover that love it seemed refused to come singly. Early on one nondescript Thursday morning he stood sentry like in the furthest corner of the panelled room as was his post. Body stiff to attention, shoulders back, arms straight by his side, head back, chin thrust forward, nothing moved, nothing that is except for his eyes, eyes that took in as always, every minute detail of the panelled room. How he worshiped every line, knot and joint. How he adored every warp and twist that made the perfect line. It was as the grandfather clock struck 10am that 'she' had entered the room. At first she was an annoyance, she broke the natural rhythm of the room, blocked his view as the light finally reached the corner nearest the door. Then 'she' became a fascination. Slowly she walked around the room in a steady anti clockwise direction her head tilted gently to one side as though listening intently to what each panel said. Jeffrey watched as she stopped before the grandfather clock and made an almost inaudible tutting sound. The sound warmed

Jeffrey in its very briefness. Her hand reached out and touched the panel by the clock gently. Her fingers ran lightly over the wood, softly tracing the lines, reverently brushing the panel as though it were a religious relic itself. In that moment Jeffries heart swelled as never before. Eventually she continued around the room until finally she stood before him. Her eyes widened as though only just becoming aware of his presence for the first time. A smile broke evenly across her face lighting her eyes revealing a golden brown which matched without question the panels of the room.

"Hello." It seemed to Jeffrey that she sang the word more than spoke it "I just love this room, it's so.…" If it were at all possible her eyes shone more brightly "Peaceful." The word captivated Jeffrey, held him around the chest as though crushing the breath from his body. He could not move, could not speak, dare not break the spell. For perhaps moments she spoke to him, her words washing over him in waves. Her love of the tudors, her need for facts and for knowledge, her studies into the Arkinston family, the love of history and her desire to write the ultimate historical encyclopaedia. Jeffrey watched dumbly as within moments of meeting she bid him a fond farewell and as smoothly as she had entered the panelled room she retreated through the doorway her footsteps ebbing into the distance but her presence still very much alive within the fabric of the room. Jeffrey clutched a hand to his throat forcing the sound that would be a laugh to remain tightly controlled within. At 67 Jeffrey Thomas White was truly in love.

Marion sat back in her chair and expelled a breath. The large kitchen had somehow become stuffy, constricting. She poured more water into her cup and drank carefully, her throat was dry, there had been much to explain.

"I hope I made sense?" She looked around the table. No-one moved "If you have any questions please speak up." She waited in apprehensive silence but no-one caught her eye or opened their mouth with a half formed question or remark. The figures around the table sat as though they were no more than the statues that graced the well manicured lawns in the grounds they knew so well. "I realise that I have asked some of you to double up at certain times and in specific stations and this adds to your workload. I will understand fully if you do not want to do this I really will." She was gabbling she knew that "I have tried to spread the load but if anyone can see a way that betters my plan please let me know. I am sure we can jig it around if we need to." Henrietta Bradshaw coughed once but no question came, instead her well manicured hand reached for the cup in front of her and she took a small sip of the now tepid water. Marion shuffled the papers in front of herself for the umpteenth time before tapping them neatly together and laying them flat on the table. "I am sorry to ask this of you all I really am, but…" She fell silent finally lost for words, instead she placed her pages into the blue cardboard folder listening to the sound of the fridge as it hummed behind the pantry door. "I think this can work." She said more to herself than the other occupants of the room, but still no-one spoke.

The relationship followed no rules that Jeffrey understood. It began with snatched conversations, it allowed lunch time strolls around the grounds, it grew into sprawling historical conversation and fact finding. Without warning the simple relationship grew into a romance. The twice a day meetings turned into evenings out at museums, meals at nearby darkly lit restaurants, visits to the Globe theatre, historical seminars and picnics. Jeffrey was happier than he had ever been or ever thought he could be. Jeffrey understood the way things were supposed to be, understood that after romance came a long engagement, after engagement came marriage. He purchased a ring, a diamond solitaire and prepared his speech. Early one February morning when next she visited the panelled room Jeffrey inched himself to the floor on one knee and proposed with a seriousness that befitted the occasion, there were no witnesses. She had smiled that beguiling smile of hers and pulled him gently to his feet embracing him warmly. She had accepted the ring and sworn herself to him in every way. The genuine tears of happiness smudged her makeup as they reddened her eyes, there was no doubt that they were in love. She kissed him tenderly gazing up into his eyes explaining that they would not marry not in the true sense of the word, why should they? She held his confused face in her hands and spoke gently of how their love needed no ceremony nor did it need pieces of paper to bind them together. She spoke of Princes and Earls from long ago who bound themselves in marriage with no more than a token. She stared at the ring on her finger, breathlessly talking of how she now had the most beautiful of tokens. She implored him to see that she had what she thought she would never have, a Prince, her knight in shining armour and she would never let him go. The rules may not have been followed, and yet still they could live together and share everything that marriage brings. At the age of 70 Jeffrey moved into the home of the 66 year old woman he loved with all his heart.

Life was good for Jeffrey and would have remained like this uninterrupted and in the eyes of many, unremarkable. This would have been true until it came to the day after his 72nd birthday. The day began normally enough. He checked the schedule written solidly in his notebook frowning slightly at the smudged ink. Today he was to lead the tour for the Women's Institute around the house and gardens. He arrived in plenty of time stopping in the reception area to check his notebook for the exact time he was to be available. Sitting in the large kitchen area he concentrated on the newly printed pamphlet displayed for the comments of staff before it was to be released for public use. A quick sharp rap on the door saw Laura Brady enter swiftly pointing at her ever present fob watch.

"Jeffrey the Women's Institute tour are here. They have been waiting 10 minutes!" He walked briskly to the meeting point fiddling with the winder on his watch. It had never let him down before and now here he was 10 minutes late. The watch would have to go to the repair shop first thing in the morning. The tour was going exceptionally well. The rooms were very much enjoyed especially the panelled room which although sparse warranted some of the most generous of praise. Yes everything was as it should have been, everything was following the tried and trusted pattern, everything was perfect. Everything was perfect until Jeffrey stopped talking, he stopped talking and stood quite still frowning in disbelief. Jeffrey Thomas White could not remember the name of the third Duke's daughter.

It had been a year since Jeffrey had forgotten the Duke's daughter's name but he still followed the rules. He carried his fountain pen clipped tightly inside his top pocket. He carried his notebook, often flicking aimlessly through the pages. He arrived at Arkinston manor and drank his Earl Grey in the warmth of the kitchen. He read the leaflets and followed the signs but most of all he continued to love her just as he always did. He would sit in the reception area helping to pass leaflets to guests who purchased them for a small donation and everyone was very kind. Sometimes Jeffrey simply could not remember things but no-one seemed to mind, they would just smile patiently and nudge him in the right direction, watching him until he was out of sight. Yes everyone was very friendly although he was sure that now they would sometimes look at him slightly differently. Jeffrey Thomas White was, confused.

Marion heard the chair scrape away from the table and saw Jeffrey shuffle wordlessly out the kitchen door closing it as silently as possible behind himself an act of muscle memory more than politeness. She watched the closed door for a few seconds before turning her attention to the notebook which lay desolately on the table abandoned by its owner. She hoped that he would miss it soon and begin his roving search only happy when he clutched it to his chest thankful for its return.

"He needs to stay. It helps him. I'm certain it does." She had spoken the words before she was aware they were leaving her mouth. Embarrassed she quickly focused on the women at the table. Samantha was the first to break eye contact picking up her own copy of the graph in front of her. She sniffed loudly and flicked at the piece of paper her nail making a sharp tick sound as it connected.

"Marion." She began, waving the paper like a flag before her "Why the need for all these graphs and things eh? Of course I will double up to help Jeffrey all you had to do was ask." She looked around the room as though daring anyone to speak differently "We all love Jeffrey. Of course he is a bit of a weird fish, but he's our weird fish." She threw the piece of paper onto the table watching it skim along the surface, a flimsy hovercraft, "We will all double up for him, keep him here as long as he needs. Let's face it, he transformed the whole profile of this place when he was in full flow. As guides go he was second to none." She pushed her chair back and stood quickly her face reddening with energy "We will all double up and stuff what the trustees or the board or Eileen bloody Hounslow MBE thinks and that's a fact." She sat as quickly as she had stood, swigging quickly at her water.

"My God, Sam. After that little speech I can assure you that when you sit in that lavender bath tonight you will not be alone." Henrietta smiled lasciviously wiping a hand with stage extravagance across her forehead before facing Marion "My dear do not look so worried, of course we are all behind you, every single one of us. Take your little paper file to the board, tell them its all sorted and if they don't like it well tell them they will lose us all. If Jeffrey goes, we all go." Marion could control the emotion of the day no more and soon her tears flowed freely prompting the others to crowd around her speaking in a bubble of voices.

"He's no trouble Marion."

"Not as if he speaks much now anyway is it, poor soul?"

"You are a saint for how you cope."

"It must be hard caring for him here at work and at home."

"We are all with you."

Jeffrey made his way slowly along the large hallway. He wasn't quite sure where he was but somehow knew he was heading in the right direction. He pushed a door and studied the room he had entered. The walls were covered in wood from floor to ceiling and it quite simply took his breath away. Standing in the centre of the room he wondered why he had not been here before. With great care and somehow understanding the need for silence he walked slowly around the room running his hand over the panelling feeling each line of the grain, every knot and joint. His fingers explored the intricate carving made so long ago and he wished he could remember where he was. A date 1853 entered his mind but as quickly as it arrived he lost it amongst a fog that seemed to sit more heavily with him now. He stepped closer to a wall and felt a lightness touch him as he studied the panelling which ran from floor to ceiling it was beautiful it took his breath away. The memory of a daughter came to him, her name just out of reach was she 3? No not 3 the 3rd. He closed his eyes and concentrated Marion, was her name Marion? He supposed it didn't matter really it was after all only a name. He opened his eyes and studied the room again certain now that somehow this was the most important room he had ever been in. The insistent ticking a large clock drew his concentration away from the panelling and he moved slowly almost dreamlike towards it, each thunk of the hands calling him forward. He watched for a while as slowly the large hand moved across the face counting down or up, he wasn't sure? The sombre thunk entranced him, held him captivated, a prisoner of sound. With a movement that matched the sound of the clock Jeffrey sank to the floor heavily, his knees bruising against the heavy flagstones. Finding a strength he was no longer aware he possessed he gripped the back of the clock at the base and pulled. A heavier genuine antique may have put up a resistance, may have scraped hard against the flagstones resisted his efforts but the reproduction clock had no such fight. Slowly the clock moved, the sound loud in the emptiness of the room. Recognising the gap that now stood between the clock and the wall Jeffrey ceased his efforts and sat staring at the darkness of the rich panelling now revealed. Automatically he reached into his pocket and removed the fountain pen unscrewing the cap with long practiced movement. Rolling forward on his knees he reached with shaky hand into the gap and began hard scratching strokes that clawed at the hidden panel mouthing each letter as he scratched, needing to be clear for this one last moment in time. Breathing heavily and fully satisfied that the task had been completed to the best of his ability Jeffrey tried to replace the cap onto the ruined nib of the fountain pen. Finding the task impossible he dropped the pen and the lid into his pocket where they clanked together softly both together and apart. Using the last of his strength he leaned his back against the clock and pushing with his heels against the floor heard the clock move back into place keeping its secret safe. He shakily regained his feet and stood distracted by the shadows that now filled the room casting patterns on the panelling that he was sure had not been there moments before. Feeling the ache in his knees Jeffrey walked with a shuffle towards the open doorway stopping only briefly to take a last look at the strange, beautiful room a room he would like to visit again.

Marion walked briskly along the corridor her step was more purposeful than anxious, her face more concerned than it was frightened. She knew where Jeffrey would be, he always was. As she rounded the corner into the corridor she saw him leave the panelled room and stand hesitantly his face slack and yet somehow able to express emotion, the face she kissed so often and yet the face she no longer knew. Swallowing the thought she spoke lightly, her words wrapping him in love.

"There you are sweetheart, I have been looking for you. Now why don't you come and have a lovely cup of tea, it's Earl Grey." Gently she took his arm and felt his movement, felt his acceptance to follow her "I don't know." She said patiently "I will have to keep a closer eye on you, can't have you wandering off all alone now can we? No telling what you will get up to." She was stopped in her tracks as with a determination Jeffrey pulled against her grip his focus back towards the panelled room. "Why whatever is the matter Jeffrey, what's wrong?" The man she loved with all her heart stood swaying gently in the corridor, hand pointing to the room that moments before he had stepped from so hesitantly. She could see the look of determination in his eyes. Slowly his jaw moved fighting to find the words that once before had come so easily to him. With great effort his teeth parted and in no more than a whisper of air the words quietly formed. Marion leaned her ear close to his mouth desperate to hear him speak, to once more hear his now all but silent voice. "Tell me my love, What is troubling you." She waited, her heart thudding in her chest as his fingers gripped her arm, eyes wide with effort as his mind, a mind once so sharp fought to form the words. A slow drone no more than a mumble filled her ears a mumbling that sounded as though it were words trying to form, words forced from a long way away. Marion concentrated hard trying to make sense of the mumbles, trying to piece them together. She stared up into his face willing the words to make sense. He gripped her arm frustration etched in every frown and wrinkle, slowly he spoke again and the mumbles made sense.

"Broken the rules." Marion rubbed his arm lovingly smiling through the sheen of tears that now frequently flowed over her cheeks, made puddles on her pillow when the darkness became too much. Taking a breath she pulled him into an embrace which would remain unreturned.

"Who broke the rules my love? You just tell me and I will sort them out for you." Expecting no answer she began to lead him away but again he stopped and stood looking back in the direction from which he had come. As she waited patiently for him to follow her lead quite unexpectedly and from somewhere deep within himself, a place that was lost, he spoke clearly for one last time.

"Jeffrey Thomas White was here." He said.

Strangers

Vic glares at the reflection in the bottle of Glen Ord single malt whiskey which hangs half filled from the optics behind his bar and rubs the now dry glass furiously with the tea towel.

"Bastards"! He mumbles before turning and slamming the glass on the counter enabling him to face the forms of the two men who's reflection mock him with their presence. They were deep in conversation, seemingly oblivious to everything except themselves. He watches as they physically lean closer together, heads mere inches apart, faces etched in a study of concentration as their mouths move, forming whispered shapes. God they make his skin crawl! They may be whispering now but they showed no signs of secrecy when they entered, no attempt to hide their swagger.

"We will sit at the table over there, by the window if that's ok?" The tallest of the two men had a voice that slid over the sticky bar counter as easily as a curling stone across the ice. "If that's ok?" He had repeated smiling the wide crocodile smile of a predator. Vic had smiled back hoping the bead of sweat which ran the length of his spine did not cause him to shudder too obviously.

"Of course gentlemen. Sit yourselves down and I will bring the drinks over." In truth he had wanted to jump the counter and grab the smarmy git by the throat but had much to his own surprise controlled himself admirably "Would you like me to bring you the menu? I'm afraid you are too early for the evening meal but I can still prepare you some sandwiches if you want?" They had shaken their heads in unison, a sign that things were worse than he thought. Just a drink and no food was a perfect tell, a sign that they were not here for the long haul a simple swoop in and pick up. The taller man waved his card in front of the card reader and smiled down at him as the beep registered the transaction.

"Has that gone through?" Thomas had nodded, curtly too incensed with fury to answer such a blatant attempt to catch him out. They were smooth with their pleasantries and crisp suits and the plummy London accent, but not smooth enough to catch him so easily. He had ripped the receipt from the machine and passed it over silently before repeating the action yanking the small curl of paper furiously from where it laid spewed from the machine to hoop back over his hand. He had punched the sale button on his till and trapped the paper under the metal clasp before pushing more firmly than needed on the metal draw closing it with a gentler than wished for 'ting'. Thomas snorted now as he studied the men again. Oh yes, he was far to astute for that, too clever by half than to fall so easily at the first trap set. He wiped again at the glass which he plucked from the bar before placing it onto the glass shelf above his head using the action to steal another furtive glance from under his arm towards them, he was right. Flicking the tea towel over his shoulder he made an over dramatic pretence of straightening the bar mats which ripped noisily as their rubber backs pulled against the stickiness of the surface. He would have to change these, have to get things straight. He looked again at the two men who had fallen silent and were now glancing around the empty room.

"That's it, have a bloody good look around you scum." Vic swallowed the bile that threatened to rise up from his throat, oh they looked harmless enough but he knew better. There was no fooling him he had been in this game far too long to be caught out like this. 'Brewery men.' The very thought choked him. Brewery men, here to what? Catch him out, close him down, serve him a summons? He shook his head slowly, no it couldn't be that, not a summons. There had never been a hint that they were on to him, never. He had always been so careful. He pushed himself away from the bar more in frustration than anger, why couldn't they just leave him alone? He always made them a profit didn't he? Not a vast sum, true, but a profit none the less. So what if he sold the back door case of supermarket wine or two. Who really cared if he held the odd late night lock in and Christ! Surely he was entitled to a little bit of a scrape off from the profits? The books he presented always showed the right amount, always tallied. True there was never a column in the figures that said 'some for me, some for you,' but they always added up and after all everyone made in the end didn't they? Vic picked up another glass and began wiping furiously, what the bloody hell did they want?

John banged the cement dust from his boots loudly as he entered the pub, he was gasping for a pint.

"Come on Phil, get 'em in, I need a slash!" He called over his shoulder to the figure that followed close behind him. Not waiting for a response he half walked, half ran through the door ignoring the muffled grunt of surprise as the door closed on his friend. Why was it that as soon as he thought about having to take a leak that it became all the more desperate? "Evening Vic, Phil's turn to get the first round, back in a mo" he waved towards the bar as he lengthened his step the urge to urinate stronger than ever. Before he reached the toilet door set at the far end of the pub he was pulling at the poppers on his boiler suit the snapping sound making the urgency all the more painful.

"Evening Vic two of the usuals please mate". Phil shrugged himself out of the top half of his own boiler suit and tied the arms around his waist smiling at the sight of John frantically pushing his way through the toilet door. He leaned his wiry frame on the bar and watched as Vic began pulling the two pints of dark black liquid into the the glass tankards silently. "After you've pulled them pints you may need to get a bucket and mop for the toilet, I'm not sure John will have made it in time. Proper desperate he was. Thought he may piss himself in the van." His brow creased in a frown that wrinkled his normally boyish features ageing him past his 51 years. "You alright mate, seem a bit quiet?" He shrugged as Vic placed the two full tankards on the beer mat in front of him silently. "Christ mate," Phil changed his voice to a sinister, whine that mimicked with perfect accuracy 'Heath Ledger' as the Joker, "Why so serious?" He laughed at his own joke and reached for the glass in front of him.

"That will be £8.30 please". Phil placed the glass back on the counter without it reaching his lips as though his hand had been slapped.

"Bloody hell mate what you trying to do, choke me?" Phil smiled at his friends joke and picked up the glass taking a long swallow slapping his lips together noisily. Realising that Vic was still staring at him arms folded across his chest he sighed loudly, "Ok mate, enough with the joking about, it's enough to put a man off his pint." He took another sip of the beer eyeing his friend over the rim of the glass. Seeing no change in Vic's manner he placed the now half full glass back on the bar next to its full friend and shrugged in confusion. "Come on mate seriously, not funny. Look bung it on the tab, it's not the end of the month yet, you know John hasn't paid me yet...." Before he could finish his sentence Vic reached a large hand across the bar and placed his palm firmly on top of the glass

"Sorry sir, you know the rules there are no tabs here. All purchases must be paid for." Before Phil could react Vic slowly moved the glass away speaking in a voice that seemed too loud for the space they shared, "I said you know the rules Sir, no tabs here." The word Sir seemed to reverberate around the room. Phil took an involuntary step away from the bar a look of confusion marking his face.

"Sir. What the bloody hell you talking about, 'Sir'? Who do you think has just walked in, the King? Look mate stop all this pissing about and let me have my pint back. I'm bloody gasping. John's had me working like a dog all day. All I want is a couple of quick ones before I have to go home to help Jane with the kids. You suddenly getting a sense of humour is not really helping me relax. Sir indeed."

"Thanks Phil. God I need this now I've emptied out. Didn't think I was going to make it. Evening Vic sorry mate was a bit desperate there. Lucky your flower bed didn't get a watering on the way in." John arrived by Phil's side and reached for the glass nearest him but stopped mid-reach noticing for the first time his two friends standing in what could only be described as a Mexican stand off. "OK you two. What have I missed, what's going on?" He looked from one man to the other. He had only been gone minutes what on earth could have happened? Phil broke the silence nodding towards Vic.

"It's bloody Vic here acting all weird. Wants the money for the beer up front. Stopped me drinking my pint he did. I don't understand have we managed to piss him off. Have you two been talking football again?" Before John could answer Vic quickly reached across the bar and laid his large hand on John's wrist.

"Sorry Sir you know the rules. You have both been been drinking here long enough." As he spoke he flicked a sideways glance towards the two men seated at the table by the window, "Don't want any…" He paused dramatically

"Trouble do we?" John saw the warning in his friends eyes and stole a careful look towards the window seat. Two men were engaged in what was obviously a heavy conversation and were studying a blue covered notebook which one had only moments before retrieved from a briefcase that sat under the chair on which he sat.

"I don't get it John, what's he taking about, trouble?" John silenced Phil with a scowl that said more than any words could do. With an expansive gesture and a raucous laugh John called towards Vic his voice full of vigour and good humour,

"Come on Vic don't be like that. Phil was only having a laugh, winding you up. God sometimes mate you need to find your funny button. When have we ever done anything that is not by the books?" He reached into his overall pocket and pulled out a wallet stuffed with notes and pulled a twenty pound note free. "Here we go mate, there's twenty, put the change in the charity box." He laughed again loudly, "Bloody hell your face, put it on our tab. Sometimes mate gullible stops being attractive." Without waiting for Vic to answer but seeing the relief in his friends face John turned to Phil, "Come on Phil let's sit over here eh?" Without a pause he strode to a table in the furthest corner and sat with his back to the wall watching the two men in the window seat carefully. Taking a sip from his beer he noticed how his hands trembled and how hard it was for him to swallow the beer. Vic watched John walk away from the bar and blew a small sigh of relief, thank Christ John was on the ball, not like Phil who still loitered by the bar a look of confusion masking his features. Ignoring Phil, Vic dropped the coins noisily into the charity box knowing that this week the charity would get all of the money deposited. As the coins clanked noisily Vic watched the second of the two men in the window seat point at something in the blue notebook and shake his head. Vic gave an involuntary gasp masking as best he could the noise with a stage like yawn. Realisation hit him, it was obvious now. The blue book contained hand written notes, accounts of the pub. "Shit!" The word came out in a fetid rush of cigarette odoured breath. He understood now that he was only moments away from being marched away to the local nick. These two were good, very good. No lap tops for them, nothing that could show just what they were up to, nothing that would give any fool a clue. Well he was no fool, he was on to them.

Seeing that Vic was going to continue ignoring him Phil shrugged and moved from the bar. He walked casually to where John sat slumped over his pint. If anyone was to take a close look at his friend they would see a man who sat nursing his pint as though he had the weight of the world sitting squarely on his shoulders. Pulling a chair from beneath the table he sat opposite his friend taking a sip of his beer.

"I don't get it John, What's up with Vic. What's he talking about, what trouble?"

"Shut up!" The words hissed from between John's teeth, catching Phil by surprise. Before Phil could show any reaction to the harshness of the rebuke John lowered his voice and spoke in low growl "Vic's just done us a favour there." Phil shook his head confused

"What favour? What's he done?" Needing to break the tension he took the last swallow of his beer instantly regretting doing so as though somehow understanding this would be the only drink he would be having today. John raised his chin towards something over Phil's shoulder and spoke through barely parted lips

"Don't make it obvious mate but those two men at the table". As though a comedy sketch, Phil twisted in his seat eliciting a groan from John

"Bloody hell Phil! I said don't make it obvious." Trying to hide the exasperation he felt he tried again, "Behind you in the window seat are two men, yes?" Phil nodded remembering seeing the two men when he entered. "Well those two bastards in Armani, you know who they are don't you?" This time Phil shook his head confused by all this cloak and dagger carry on. "Well those two vermin are none other than investigators from," John paused for no more than a second but a second that seemed to allow ice water to enter Phil's veins, "Those two vermin..." John continued are investigators from the tax office." Phil felt the shiver run from his toes to his head and back again

"Oh shit!"

"Oh yes, shit indeed my friend." John took a large swallow of his own beer wiping his mouth dry with his arm "We my friend are now neck deep in the brown stuff. We are going to have to think carefully and act quickly." Both men reached again for their glasses, John taking a large gulp leaving Phil staring dejectedly at his own empty vessel. "Someone has dropped us in it mate and now these two are here to catch us. We need to be really careful and I mean really careful. John wiped his hand over his mouth and slammed his glass onto the table slopping beer unnoticed onto his hand " Right, this is the plan. I will get the second set of books ready, you phone your misses, tell her that she needs to hide your work gear somewhere, perhaps take it round your brothers so it can't be found.

If these bastards search your house it's gotta be clear. They can't find anything that shows you've been working can they? Not with you still signing on." He finished talking and looked on in amazement as Phil pushed his chair back from the table rocking the beer glasses as he did so. "Just what are you doing?" John sat back looking at his friend who stood like an expectant schoolboy hopping from foot to foot confusion on his face,

"I thought you said we had to get these second books and I had to phone my missus…"

"Sit down you idiot." John pointed at his friends seat "We can't do anything rash, got to play it cool. Sit down, look as though we are just having a friendly chat. If we go rushing out now they might realise that we have been tipped off. No, we sit here for a while and leave all casual like. I will offer you a lift home, say something like. Hey I'm going your way mate, I will give you a lift, be good to see your missus, I haven't seen her for ages. That sort of thing." Slowly Phil sat back opposite him a look of dejection on his face.

"Bloody hell John, this is bad, but what's worrying me is just how in the name of Christ did they find us?"

Cheryl Evans straightened her skirt as she entered the pub. If ever she needed a gin and tonic today was it.

"Evening Vic, the usual please" she called distractedly towards the bar her focus on the mobile phone in her hand. Scrolling down the internet sales site on her phone Cheryl smiled broadly, two items had sold for better than she could of expected. "Oh and a packet of cheese and onion please." Why not? She placed her money on the counter oblivious to the fact that Vic had served her wordlessly but why would she notice? Her account on the sales sight was showing at £147.50 for just this week. It really was going well. "Thanks Vic." She chirped still oblivious to his silence but deftly pocketing her change into her jacket and picking up her drink. She turned from the bar and headed towards her normal seat by the fire. As she moved silently to her place she noticed for the first time the two builders slumped together nursing beer glasses in their hands without drinking. "Oh hi boys didn't notice you there. How are you both? How's the wife John. Has she managed to get over that cold yet? Loads of it going round, still it's the time of year I suppose." She smiled warmly and placed a well manicured hand on John's shoulder. "Anyway glad I've seen you, that job you're doing for me at the nursing home, I think I have now decided on cream walls throughout. No point spending good money on those old farts is it? I mean half of them won't notice and the other half will be dead soon anyway so what's the point"? She gave a shrieking laugh "Anyway Monday still good for you is it"?

"Quotes in the post Cheryl." John looked up at her, a frown of annoyance marking his face.

"What do you mean quotes in the post, I thought you said…"

"I said I would send you the quote Cheryl. Sorry it's taken so long but needed to make sure I had captured everything." Cheryl frowned, 'what was up with John, why was he talking so loud?'

"I'm sorry John, I don't understand?"

"No, I understand that Cheryl but there really is quite a lot of work needs doing. I've sent you the quote it's all been done properly as usual, VAT included, just as we agreed. Isn't that right Phil?" Phil nodded in agreement

"Yeah Cheryl, John was just telling me. Said it was a big job could need two people on it. Sounding me out to see if I needed any work."

"That's right, I was. Luckily for you Cheryl, Phil is out of work and I may be in a position to employ him now. Yours is such a big job that with two of us, once all the paperwork is done mind you, we can get the job done in half the time."

"What on earth are you two oafs talking

about? Quotes? VAT? Look I thought you were coming Monday cash in….."

"Cheryl"! John stood suddenly causing the small table to wobble as he caught it with his knees, "Why don't you wait for the quote eh". As he spoke he nodded towards the two suited figures who were now staring hard at a large manila folder. "Let's keep everything legal shall we?" Cheryl's hand flew to her mouth as she noticed for the first time the two figures in the window seat.

"Oh my God John, oh my God! Are they from…" John cut her off before she could finish the sentence placing a firm hand on her arm

"Yes Cheryl, yes. Look I'm sorry. We can't stay. Got to go. You understand, yes?" Without waiting for an answer the two men brushed past her rushing through the door as though called to some emergency. As the door closed slowly behind them Cheryl slumped into the still warm chair vacated by Phil her back to the men in the window seat. Her heart thumped and her mouth was dry. With a shaking hand she gripped the glass forcing it to her lips and taking a somehow lumpy sip. The warming liquid tasted bitter, hard to swallow. The usually refreshing drink offered no relief instead highlighting her sense of fear and loneliness. Cheryl placed her head in her hands and screwed her fingers into her hair. 'How. How had they found her, she had been so careful? Dave's warning had been timely 'keep things legal' he must have known these two police officers were here for her. Had they asked for her by name? Perhaps they had asked for the lady who ran the local nursing home? She could see it now, casually walking into the bar, flashing their badges showing Vic her photo. She was well known in the village they only had to ask in the right place and she was done for. Cheryl slumped lower in the seat, couldn't rush, it would draw too much attention to herself she would have to play it cool. Slowly she sipped her drink despite now the revulsion it offered, and calmed her breathing. What to do? Picking her phone from the table she opened the page for the sales site and studied the figures. She had just sold another item taking her credit to a fantastic £191 for this week. As though experiencing an out of body moment Cheryl saw her own finger hovering over the words 'cash in now' on the app and she pressed it with a firmness that threatened to crack the screen. She saw the instant result of her action as the words 'transferred to account' appeared in accusing red lettering. Without hesitating she made a few deft swipes on the app and removed the remaining items she had listed for sale from the auction site. So far, so good. The money that had just been sent to her account could easily be explained away but she would need to delete all activity on the site. With a grimace she quickly deleted the account details and held the icon button until it flashed, then with a determination pressed again so that the icon was removed from her device. As she worked on the phone her mind raced furiously just how had she had been discovered? The police would not be looking for missing items, no one had complained, who would? They were all too busy grieving over a dead relative to notice a small item of jewellery or some clothing that was no longer there. She had been really careful, left a false name and details on the sales site. She had set the account to her maiden name, it had been easy no one should have known. She shook her head tears threatening to spill from her eyes. Everything had been so perfect, she was a pillar of the community, respected, valued and now it had all come crashing down around her ears. The shame would be too much to cope with, she would be tarnished. A plan of action began to form in her mind. She would leave her job, move house, perhaps move in with her sister, yes she would move to be closer to her sister after all Australia sounded like quite a nice place. Cheryl ran through the plan confidence growing with each thought. Move to Australia, meet an open shirted, well muscled, sweat sheened man who did what, raise those kangaroo things? She wondered if they even raised kangaroos? She wasn't sure but loved the sound of the hunky man waiting to marry her. Leaving the last of her drink she stood and calmly placed her phone into her jacket pocket, "Australia here I come." she whispered towards the picture of a sailing ship being tossed on the waves. With more grace than she realised she possessed, Cheryl made her way to the door and out into the night and for the last time drove away from the pub. This time next week she would be in Australia.

Vic physically jumped as the chairs scrapped on the stone floor of the pub, the two men were on the move, this was it. His heart pounded as they walked to the bar, each carrying their glass with them. They placed their glass on the counter and in unison straightened their ties, finally making eye contact. The taller of the two men nodded towards Vic with a slow deliberate movement

"Thanks fella." The shorter man echoed the words

"Cheers Buddy." And then without pausing they turned and walked towards the exit leaving nothing but the smell of overly strong aftershave and an emptiness that seemed to crush everything around it. Vic stood motionless watching the door swing slowly closed. As the lights from a moving car shone through the windows Vic rushed from behind the bar and flung the door open just in time to see a Jag pull out of the carpark and onto the lane it's brake lights glaring brightly as it reached the bend out of the village. Without pausing ,Vic pushed against the door, heavy against the automatic closing device. He bolted the door with the solid top and bottom bolts before turning the key in the lock, he was in no mood to stay open, couldn't face another customer and besides, he needed to get things in order,

"Bastards!" He spat the word now. They would be back. He knew how they worked. Slowly he turned to the table nearest the door, reached down and collected the two empty beer glasses and the half drunk vodka, moved behind the bar switched off the lights and disappeared to his rooms at the back. "Bastards." He called as the door closed behind him.

AFTERWORD

I hope you have enjoyed in some small way my offering of short stories in 'Tales of Something Different'. Perhaps you have been moved, inspired or simply enjoyed the chance to pick up a book and discover the lives of other people, places and times from the comfort of your own surroundings. Could it be that perhaps you have simply re-kindled your own love of story telling and want to try more? After all, everyone has the ability to tell a story...

If you have enjoyed this book, please leave a recommendation on Amazon. If you have any other comments to make please contact me on

acstock.tales@outlook.com

Thank you all

ACKNOWLEDGEMENTS

First and foremost I give the greatest amount of credit and thanks to my gorgeous wife Jane. Without your support and patience this book would always have remained my 'book I'm working on'. Thank you for the hours of reading, re-reading and gentle reminders that I should really be sitting down to write.

I would like to thank my two sons Michael and Matthew along with their partners Lizzie and Hector. You are all amazing people who patiently allow me to stretch a story to beyond breaking and laugh patiently at the punchline.

I would also like to offer my thanks to the Bedford Writers Circle. Writing becomes much easier when you are supported by like minded people who offer encouragement and feedback. Thank you all for listening.

How could I not thank someone who was there at the very beginning? To Mum I thank you for sitting me on your lap and teaching me to read. I thank you for opening so many worlds for me and showing me the adventures held within the covers of books.

Sadly not everyone can be with us to see the culmination of the work they put in and to what has ended up as this book. So to Dad I offer this belated 'thank you'. You were and always will be the greatest raconteur I ever had the privilage to know. Your stories inspired the imagination and helped hone the skills that made me who I am today both as a person and a storyteller.

And finally but by no means lastly to all my friends who have listened patiently and encouraged me as I tested chapters or lines from my writing upon them. Thank you all.

ABOUT THE AUTHOR

A C Stock

Andrew had a dream as a young child to write a book that would be read by many. This compilation of short stories for adults is the first of his books to be published and fulfills that early ambition. He lives in Bedfordshire with his wife Jane. They have two adult sons together.

Printed in Great Britain
by Amazon